HYPERSONIC THUNDER

FORGE BOOKS BY WALTER J. BOYNE

Dawn Over Kitty Hawk

Operation Iraqi Freedom

Roaring Thunder

Supersonic Thunder

Today's Best Military Writing (editor)

Hypersonic Thunder

HYPERSONIC THUNDER

A Novel of the Jet Age

WALTER J. BOYNE

A Tom Doherty Associates Book
New York

HYPERSONIC THUNDER

Copyright © 2009 by Walter J. Boyne

A Forge Book
Published by Tom Doherty Associates, LLC
175 Fifth Avenue
New York, NY 10010

www.tor-forge.com

Forge® is a registered trademark of Tom Doherty Associates, LLC.

Library of Congress Cataloging-in-Publication Data

Boyne, Walter J., 1929–
    Hypersonic thunder : a novel of the jet age / Walter J. Boyne.—1st ed.
        p. cm.
    "A Tom Doherty Associates book."
    ISBN-13: 978-0-7653-0845-0
    ISBN-10: 0-7653-0845-2
    1. Aeronautical engineers—Fiction.   2. Jet planes—Fiction.   3. Aeronautics—
Fiction.   4. Astronautics—Fiction.   5. Aircraft industry—Fiction.   I. Title.
    PS3552.O937S87 2009
    813'.54—dc22
                                                                    2008038105

First Edition: April 2009

Printed in the United States of America

0 9 8 7 6 5 4 3 2 1

THIS BOOK IS DEDICATED TO MY BELOVED WIFE, TERRI,

The most helpful, generous, spontaneous, good-natured, good-hearted, sweetest person I've ever known. Instinctively and intuitively kind, intelligent, and intensely pragmatic, she has been and still is a treasure to hundreds of her friends and family. They value her as I do, for she is a unique, blessed person, a superb artist not only in the art world, but even more important, in the world of human relations.

ACKNOWLEDGMENTS

THIS, THE THIRD novel in a trilogy on the history of jet aviation, reflects the interest, concern, and assistance of literally hundreds of people over many decades, many of whom have passed on. The greatest help often came indirectly, with neither person knowing that help to write a novel was being given. A case in point: The late great test pilot Russ Schleeh used to talk to me at length about his experience in selling the Douglas KC-10 tanker to the Air Force. Neither of us ever contemplated that his wisdom would appear in a book written thirty years later, but you'll find it in this novel. In a similar way, conversations over the years with aviation luminaries such as Dr. Hans von Ohain, Sir Frank Whittle, Sam Shannon, Bill McAvoy, James Webb, William Pogue, and literally hundreds of others of aviation's great achievers contributed directly to the information to be found herein.

And, as always, I received great support from the rather small but very tight community of aviation authors. Among them are Clif Berry, Philip Handleman, Dennis Jenkins, Fred Johnsen, Wally Meeks, Mike Machat, Lon Nordeen, Warren Thompson, and many more. Dr. Richard Hallion, a renowned author and historian, gave me insight into the mysterious world of hypersonic flight, and linked me up with Dr. Mark Lewis for further information.

There were many others without whom the book could not have been written, including C. O. Smith, John Helfers, Marty Greenberg, Melissa Frain, Eric Raab, and of course my editor, Robert Gleason.

Sadly, I will have omitted many names in this short list, not from lack of care, but from that familiar problem, lack of memory. I mean no disrespect to those I've overlooked, and am comforted by the fact that most of them will recognize the difficulty that living long confers on memory.

Many thanks go to all whom I've mentioned and many more to any whom I may have forgotten.

AUTHOR'S NOTE

THIS IS THE story of the fantastically swift rise of jet aviation from a military curiosity to a system of civil and military aircraft that has revolutionized the world.

All of the events pertaining to the advance of jet aviation in this trilogy of novels are real with one exception. All of the production decisions, rollouts, cancellations, first flights, records set, crashes—everything are as they happened. The one exception is in this third volume of the trilogy, in which a fictional hypersonic aircraft is created to bring the story into the next era of the jet age.

All of the real accomplishments are properly credited to the people who made them possible, e.g., Sir Frank Whittle and Hans von Ohain for the invention of the jet engine, Kelly Johnson for the creation of the U-2, Bill Allen and Juan Trippe for initiating the Boeing 747, Andrei and Alexei Tupolev for creating the Tu-144 supersonic transport, and so on through the years.

But these giants would be the first to recognize that the projects attributed to them are the work of a vast system of people—engineers, pilots, mechanics, sales personnel, accountants, and so on. It is, of course, impossible to recognize all of the participants in real time in a novel. Instead, a fictional family, the Shannons, and their associates have been created to provide continuity and insight, and to substitute for all of the thousands of important people who cannot be recognized individually.

Thus Vance Shannon, the patriarch of the Shannon family, finds his way around the world of jet aviation, acting as a facilitator, a lubricant, a pressure pump, for telling the story of the momentous rise of jet aviation from the first successful jet airplanes in 1939 to the hypersonic scramjets of the future. The Shannons are on-scene for most of the major events, or create relationships with those who are.

In some instances, real events have been compressed in time and space so that they can be related as fiction in the form of the actions of the Shannon family. In all cases, however, there has been no alteration to the effect of the events on the development of jet aviation.

WALTER J. BOYNE
Ashburn, Virginia
July 17, 2007

HYPERSONIC THUNDER

CHAPTER ONE

THE PASSING PARADE: Supreme Court rules on Roe v. Wade; peace treaty signed January 27, ending war in Vietnam; Salvador Allende overthrown in Chile; Arab/Israeli Yom Kippur War begins; Vice President Spiro Agnew resigns; OPEC raises price of oil; Juan Perón returns to Argentina; Sears Tower in Chicago finished, 1,450 feet tall; Bobby Riggs defeated by Billy Jean King in tennis; Congress passes War Powers Act.

February 12, 1973
The "Hanoi Hilton"

*T*om Shannon watched unbelieving as the first group of 120 American prisoners of war formed up in columns of two. They looked strange in their ill-fitting new clothes—dark blue pants, light blue shirts, windbreakers, and some kind of little black bag. The clothes were the only new thing in the entire prison, with its worn walls, tired paint, and rusting iron fixtures.

According to the ceaseless tap code messages, those vibrating signals of defiance, they were being returned home. The POWs had tried to argue that the most injured and the sickest should go first, but the North Vietnamese had insisted on them going back in the order in which they came.

The tap code.

It was the only thing that kept him alive. Even though he was forbidden from mixing with the rest of the POWs, they knew he was there, and their messages had sustained him. It came in many ways—the traditional tapping, by hand signal, even by bits of string, knotted in a Braille-like code. The tap code told him things had changed in the last year for the others—beatings had stopped, discipline had relaxed, relief packages were not plundered so badly, and food had improved.

But not for him.

His rations had never improved, but his last beating had been four months earlier, when the Rabbit had administered a scientific series of kicks and blows that brought him near death once again. He still ached, especially his ribs, which always seemed to take the longest to heal. One of the most vicious guards, nicknamed the Rabbit for his manner, had an obsessive, inexplicable hatred for Shannon.

The gaunt fighter pilot, former commander of the 6th Fighter Interceptor Wing, watched with envy from his latest cell, perched on the second floor of the main building. They had moved him around at random intervals, apparently determined to prevent him from making any contact with other prisoners. Now, by standing on his toes and clutching the open windowsill, he could peer through a gap in the wooden shutters for a view of the yard where the six buses were parked. Ironically, the Rabbit seemed to be supervising the departure just as he supervised the torture.

Shannon sat down for a moment to gather his strength. It was emotionally draining to see the months-old rumors about the coming freedom suddenly become real—but only for the others.

Painfully he clawed his way up to squint again through the shutters, his vision, once so acute that he could pick out an enemy plane miles distant, now blurred. He knew that Everett Alvarez was probably leading the group. Everett was the longest surviving prisoner, kept here or in other filthy North Vietnamese prisons for eight years. Now Alvarez and the others were being set free, at last. It was incredible.

A wave of trembling fear swept over him. Now he knew why the North Vietnamese had always kept him separate from the rest of the POWs—they never intended to release him.

In his six years of tortured confinement, he had spoken to only one other American, Michael Pavone, his backseater in their F-4 that had been shot down. Pavone had saved his life, nursing him back to precarious health for months. When Shannon had recovered sufficiently to be interrogated, the North Vietnamese promptly beat Pavone to death, as if punishing him for aiding Shannon.

Six years, that surely entitled him to be in the first group—if they were going to let him go at all. He could never understand why they kept him separated, nor could the other prisoners, who came to know him only by the covert tap code that linked them together, day and night. The other prisoners were naturally suspicious of him at first, fearing that he was a North Vietnamese spy using the tap code to gain information. It took weeks before he convinced them that he was truly an American pilot.

The only rational explanation for his isolation was their resentment for his leading the famous Operation Toro, which trapped and shot down a lot of North Vietnamese MiGs. And later when the North Vietnamese had placed him in one of their crude propaganda films, he had outfoxed them. Even as he parroted their stilted phrases, he had blinked a message in Morse Code with his eyes, one that told the world that he was being coerced. Both events had earned him many beatings. The other prisoners had been beaten for similar things, but were not kept isolated for so long.

Now Shannon was blinking away the tears coursing down his face. He hated himself for crying, but the thought of everyone going free, of them seeing their families again, while he stayed here, rotting alive, was impossible to bear. He was wearing the same filthy, black pajamas that he had worn for months. That was the sure sign that he was not going home, not now, not ever.

Shannon looked out at the grubby yard. There was some sort of disturbance—the POWs were refusing to get on the drab blue buses. He could see the Rabbit, his own particular nemesis, railing at someone—it had to be Alvarez or Robby Risner, the men who had been here longest.

The Rabbit turned and left the yard, and Tom slumped down, unwilling to watch anymore.

I've got to get hold of myself. I cannot give in now. They cannot beat me now. Not after all this misery. He had started his mental rosary, the prayers that had kept him sane for so many months.

Fifteen minutes passed before his cell door burst open and the Rabbit came in, furious and bearing an armload of clothing. As always, the Rabbit's hair was closely cut, his uniform pristine, his lean body erect.

"Put these on. Your friends won't leave without you."

Tom reached out for the clothes carefully, certain that the Rabbit was toying with him. He tossed his filthy black pajama top to the side and pulled on a shirt, his bruised and battered fingers having trouble with the buttons. What a magnificent group of men his fellow prisoners were, renouncing their own freedom to save a man they had never seen, never talked to.

Only when he slid into the dark blue trousers did he allow himself to hope that his long agony was coming to an end. He was going home. He only wished Pavone was going with him.

March 17, 1973,
Palos Verdes, California

VANCE SHANNON STARED at the television set. For so many months it had been a source of pain to him, watching the debacle unfold in Vietnam, watching the miserable, long-haired peaceniks demonstrating against the United States, against their own country, by God, the worthless bunch of traitors.

But now television was an unbelievable source of hope. It had picked up the dot of an airplane in the distance, panning over the crowd of people waiting at Travis Air Force Base to greet the returning prisoners of war. Almost everyone in Shannon's family was there to greet Tom when he stepped off the plane. Nancy and V. R. were there, and so were Harry, Tom's twin brother, and his wife, Anna. Vance Shannon's wife Jill had stayed home to nurse him, as she had done for so long.

"By God, Jill, I should have gone, I shouldn't have missed this."

Jill patted him on the shoulder as she had the previous ten times he raised his plaintive cry.

"No, honey, it's best you are here. Let Tom and Nancy have their get-together, and he'll be home to see you in a day or two. After six long years, you can wait another few days."

It was not like Shannon to wait for anything. An ace in World War I, he had become one of the top test pilots in the United States, ranking with Eddie Allen, Jim McAvoy, and Vance Breese. Afterward, building on his test pilot reputation, he had started a one-man consulting firm that quickly grew into an industry legend. His twin sons, Tom and Harry, had helped, but his real forte had been in picking innovative young leaders, giving them a piece of the business, and letting them run with it. Now Aerospace Consultants had offices in eight cities and was a major force in industries no one had dreamed of when he had been flying his SPAD on the Western Front, or even when he was testing Mustangs for North American. Aerospace Consultants and its subsidiaries were a force in avionics, simulators, precision guided munitions, and the executive jet business.

At seventy-eight, Shannon was in better shape than he had any right to be. He'd survived a severe stroke, and by sheer willpower had brought himself back to the point that he was still of real value to the company he founded—at least on the airplane and engine side. Most of the rest he left to Bob Rodriquez, a twelve-victory ace in Korea, and an electronics genius who had carried the firm to new levels that he and his boys, smart as they were, could never have reached.

"I wish I could pick out Nancy in the crowd. She was wearing that fancy hat with the feather on the side, but I still can't see her. I'd love to see her reaction when Tom comes off the plane."

"And I'd really love to see Tom's reaction when he sees her and V. R."

March 17, 1973
Travis Air Force Base, California

NANCY SHANNON HELD tight to V. R.'s arm. At twenty, young Vance Robert was as tall as his father had been, six-one, and built just like him. On leave from the Air Force Academy to meet his father, V. R. searched his mother's face to see how she was bearing up.

He had been fourteen when his father, the old warhorse, had returned to the Air Force and volunteered for combat duty in Vietnam.

Tom Shannon had blazed brightly across the Vietnamese skies, shooting down four—and perhaps five—North Vietnamese MiGs before being shot down and imprisoned for six interminable years. In the meantime Nancy Shannon had soldiered on, taking on more and more responsibility with the business, pushed by both Harry and Vance Shannon, who wanted to see her occupied, her mind off the tortures they all knew that Tom was enduring.

V. R. tried to drink in everything, the surging crowd, emotions bubbling like champagne, the endless waiting as the airplane bringing his father changed from a tiny dot against the gray overcast of the sky to this huge Lockheed C-141 now slowly taxiing up to the carefully plotted area where the prisoners would be received.

It was a beautiful aircraft. V. R. noted the tail number, 60177, and the name on the nose, "City of San Bernardino." It was impossible to believe that the father he loved so much was just two hundred yards away, inside the strong white fuselage of the C-141.

The aircraft moved into position, the band played the Air Force song, and the waiting relatives surged at the velvet ropes restraining them. There was going to be a ceremony—naturally, this was the Air Force, and the returning men deserved it. Everyone had been briefed that the senior officer would get off first, say a few words, then be followed down by the others, each man to salute and be saluted and then released to the embrace of his family.

His mother's grip tightened on his arm as the big door of the C-141 opened at last. A long joyous roar erupted when the first man stepped out and said a few words. Neither Nancy nor V. R. noticed, for their eyes were fixed on the vacant spot where Tom would first appear. As each man hit the door, their hearts leaped, then fell back. In what seemed hours, fifteen former POWs, looking thin but surprisingly fit in their brand-new uniforms, had given their salutes and then been swamped by their loving families.

Finally Tom appeared, moved down the steps, saluted, and then turned to hobble toward them. Nancy dropped V. R.'s arm and raced to him, folding him in an embrace, tears flowing. V. R. walked up slowly behind her, smiling, feeling happy and strangely safe for the first time since his father had left.

March 17, 1973
Palos Verdes, California

"THERE HE IS."

Vance leaped up from his chair, grabbed Jill, and squeezed.

"He's moving a little slow, but he looks pretty good."

"Look, there's Nancy! Where's V. R.?"

Jill squeezed his arm affectionately saying, "Look, just behind him, that tall, good-looking cadet." Harry and Anna were also visible now, coming up the ramp.

By this time Tom was embracing V. R. as well, and then the camera cut to the C-141 fuselage as the next man appeared.

Vance flopped back in his chair, yelling, "Get some champagne, Jill, we need a drink. By God, I'm glad that I lived to see this day."

Jill had already popped a bottle of her favorite champagne, Korbel, and handed Vance a glass, knowing he'd barely sip it.

They basked in the glow of the television set, watching the other returning prisoners of war greet their families, sensing the tidal wave of emotion surging across the Travis flight line, senior officers weeping unashamedly, children clutching their fathers' legs, long separated husbands and wives kissing with an intense fervor.

There was a brief glimpse of Nancy and Tom walking hand in hand, V. R. following behind them, his face radiant with pleasure, and behind him, Harry and Anna, looking on with a combination of concern for Tom's condition and happiness for his release.

The scene switched and Jill said, "I hope they will never have to suffer again. I hope they will all be happy."

Vance reached up behind him and patted her arm. "We've had such a nice life and my kids have had so much trouble, it doesn't seem fair, does it? Harry has to be concerned about Anna falling off the wagon all the time; it's affected his work. You know he rarely flies anymore. Can you imagine that, a Shannon not flying? And Nancy— she's a marvel in the business, but a bone in Harry's throat. And her practically running the business will kill Tom. You know how proud he is. He couldn't take the rivalry from Bob Rodriquez; he'll never be able to stand Nancy running things, no matter how much he loves her."

Jill was stunned. Vance had not commented on the family or the business for weeks.

Obviously agitated, he went on. "And I haven't mentioned Bob and Mae! There's no way that Bob's going to be able to work with Nancy. I've created a monster, and now I'm too old to do anything about it."

He looked up at her and smiled. "Fooled you, didn't I? You thought I was out of it. Well, I am, but I'm not completely senile, not yet, and I can see the handwriting on the wall."

Jill nodded. She agreed with him completely, but didn't want to get him more excited than he was. Funny, here Vance was, pushing eighty, and absolutely right in everything he said.

"Don't let it get you down, Jill. We've had a good long run, and I may have a few more years, and I'm not going to let this bother me, no matter how it turns out. The main thing is Tom is out of that rotten prison camp, that's really all that matters to me now."

March 17, 1973
Niceville, Florida

Bob Rodriquez sat in his cramped apartment, staring at the television set, his hands gripping the grubby armrests of his chair as he watched his friend, his rival, his enemy, turn and stumble into Nancy Shannon's open arms.

Tears coursed down Rodriquez's deeply tanned face. He had known the returning prisoner of war for more than twenty years and could not believe that this gaunt, limping shadow of a man was actually Tom Shannon. He spoke aloud to himself, as he did too often nowadays. "God, how happy he must be. And Nancy and V. R., too." The sight of Tom Shannon's son reminded him of his own son, Robert Jr.—Rod, as most people called him. Rod was another precious person he had lost to his work.

Then his thoughts went to Vance, wondering how he was taking this. He wasn't in the crowd, must be home in Palos Verdes. Thank God he lived long enough to see it.

"I'll call him later—he's probably more choked up than I am."

A commercial came on and Rodriquez shut the set off. It was the one possession he prized, built with his own hands, and now carted around the country with him, wherever he went.

And he went everywhere, carrying the flag that Vance Shannon had planted so many years ago, when he ran a one-man company, flying first flights in new aircraft for a laughably low fee. Shannon's firm had grown in the post World War II armament boom, and he had brought Rodriquez in as a partner, over the objections of his two sons, Tom and Harry. Both sons were hurt that their father had violated all his previous practice by doing something without discussing it with them.

Later, neither of them—not even Tom, the more bitter of the two—could deny that Rodriquez had vastly expanded the business, taking it into disciplines that were unknown and even unknowable to the Shannons. Rodriquez combined his knowledge of electronics with an uncanny ability to find partner firms. He developed ideas such as three-axis simulators or precision weapons, built prototypes, got the government interested, and then found a bigger company to partner with. The result was a constantly growing business, with welcome streams of income coming back to Shannon's firm.

Vance Shannon had recognized his value early, even though he almost never understood exactly what Rodriquez was doing. Shannon took the firm public, and completed a series of name changes, each one reflecting its expanding scope. Rodriquez had ridden the crest of the wave and was now president and chief engineer of Aerospace Unlimited. Nancy Shannon, Tom's second wife, ran the parent company, which had been renamed "Vance Shannon, Incorporated" to honor the old man. Nancy gave Rodriquez a great deal of independence, but in the end, she was calling the shots, with the support of the board of directors.

Bob had been living at 1550 Foster Road, Apartment 1C, on and off for six months. He spent at least half his time traveling, making it increasingly tough to supervise the rapidly growing interests of the firm Vance Shannon had established for him. This apartment was convenient, about three miles from the flight line at Eglin Air Force Base, where the latest version of his laser-guided bomb was being tested.

Until three weeks ago, Bob had been living like some broken-down cold-call vacuum cleaner salesman, getting by with a mattress on the floor in the bedroom, his prized television plopped on a box in the living room. The only other furniture was a stool at the breakfast bar, where he ate miserable meals that ranged from a low of a frozen dinner to the relative high of Wheaties cereal and milk that was still fresh.

Then Mae had called, saying she was coming for one last visit. Panicking, he called Barron Rents, furnishing the place with a single order over the telephone, hoping to mask his miserable bachelor existence from her. Now he flopped back in the plaid recliner, the least offensive thing in the mud-ugly combination of cheap furniture and universal draperies. Everything was glaringly new, unmatched and unloved, and the dismal ensemble told his lonely story even better than a mattress on the floor might have.

He smiled to himself as he thought of the early days of their courtship, when Mae would have found the mattress on the floor erotic—they had made love in many other equally uncomfortable places.

A pain stabbed him as he thought about Tom being reunited with Nancy at the same time Mae was cutting ties with him. He still couldn't believe it, but he couldn't argue the point. He'd been an absentee husband, gone for months at a time, and Mae was too good for such treatment. He loved her and Rod, their seventeen-year-old son, but he was obsessed with the new weaponry he was helping create, and he let his work take precedence. Things were not going to improve. Now there was a new system on the horizon, one with possibilities that surpassed even his fervid imagination.

He didn't blame her. Mae had warned him four years ago that something had to give—and now she was serious. She had probably met someone else, it was inevitable. He couldn't blame her. He had always been faithful to her with women, but always unfaithful with work.

A mental image of Tom's face as he knew him in Korea suddenly surfaced in his mind. Shannon had been young, blond, and ruggedly handsome. Rodriquez had been top dog then, a twelve-victory ace, while Tom was a relative newcomer, eager to go to war in MiG Alley. Tom, a Marine ace in World War II, scored four MiG kills officially during the war, with a fifth victory being confirmed four years later, so he was a jet ace, too.

Later, Tom had introduced him to his father, Vance Shannon, the legendary test pilot turned industry consultant. Vance had taken an immediate liking to him, for he saw—as Tom did as well—that Rodriquez was an electronics genius, with qualities and talents that the Shannons did not possess.

For a brief while he had gotten along well with all of them, Vance, Tom, his twin brother Harry, and the rest of the Shannon organization, Aerospace Consultants, Incorporated, as it was called then. Bob liked them and had worked hard. But things changed when Vance brought him, unannounced, into the firm as a partner. Both brothers were upset, but Tom took it as a personal affront.

As Bob scored one phenomenal business success after another, Tom's enmity grew to the point that he left the firm and rejoined the Air Force. This nearly broke Vance's heart and upset everyone else, including Nancy and Harry. Tom gained some glory in Vietnam, shaping up a fighter wing and shooting down at least four MiGs. On his last mission, he was shot down and had to suffer the brutal horrors of Vietnamese imprisonment for more than six years.

The phone rang—it was Steve O'Malley, now a full colonel and working with him on the latest project.

"Did you see Tom get off the C-141?" Shannon's World War II exploits had made him O'Malley's hero well before he went to the Air Force Academy.

"Yeah, he looked a little rough, but he'll recover. He's a survivor, obviously."

"Have you talked to Vance yet?"

"No, I'm going to wait about an hour, and then call him. Give him a chance to settle in."

"Good idea. How are you coming on the presentation?"

"I've got all the transparencies done for the overhead projector, and have the notes for you to look at. This is going to be a tough sell—an unproven project, ungodly expensive, and years before we get any results. Not what Pentagon staffers like to hear."

O'Malley laughed, saying, "You got that right. If we sell this one, we should look around for buyers for the Brooklyn Bridge," before hanging up.

Both men were at Eglin to continue testing on upgraded versions of the Paveway bombs that the 8th Tactical Fighter Wing—the Wolf

Pack—had used to take out the bridge at Thanh Hoa, North Vietnam. Rodriquez had been the guiding light behind the Paveways, working on site at Ubon Royal Thai Air Force Base in Thailand to prepare the weapons for the raid. The laser-guided bombs did what hundreds of previous sorties had failed to do—destroy the bridge.

Few people other than the top military commanders had any idea of the real importance of precision guided munitions. Instead of sending a hundred airplanes to drop four bombs each, hoping that one would strike the target, you could now send one airplane, with two bombs, to take out two targets. The implications for strategy, for the budget, and for force size were immeasurable, and they were only just now beginning to be understood. One of Rodriquez's major tasks was to convince commanders that they could operate with fewer aircraft, if those aircraft were equipped with laser-guided bombs.

Now they were creating something that promised to vastly improve the accuracy of precision guided weapons, as well as create a whole new technique for navigation. In two weeks, they were going to the Pentagon to brief the Chief of Staff on what Rodriquez was calling the "Global Positioning System," a combination of twenty-four satellites and a widespread ground-based system that promised incredible navigation—and hence bombing—accuracy.

The Navy had led the way with Transit, the first satellite-based navigation system. But the Global Positioning System—GPS as Rodriquez fondly referred to it—was going to be vastly more efficient even if infinitely more expensive. It was exactly the sort of thing in which Rodriquez excelled. He wondered if Vance would be able to understand it. Harry Shannon would, of course, and so would Tom—if he would listen.

The potential for GPS was an order of magnitude more important than the new precision guided munitions. Rodriquez often used to doodle, writing GPS versus PGM over and over. When—if—they could sell the GPS concept, a whole new world would open up, not only in navigation and in bombing, but in command and control. The strength of Special Forces would be increased a hundredfold with GPS. You could conduct clandestine operations deep within unknown enemy territory with the assurance of a sleepwalker. With GPS you could do anything except perhaps win a peace.

March 20, 1973
Palos Verdes, California

JILL SHANNON GLANCED up as the big grandfather's clock chimed six times. The kids had built it from a kit when they were teenagers, before they had gone off to their service academies, Tom to Annapolis, Harry to West Point. The old clock was always fast, no matter how they tried to adjust it, so she knew she had at least ten minutes to complete laying out the table she'd prepared for Tom's first meal with them. He had specified only two requirements: no rice and no pork fat. She'd responded with a lavish buffet that went from chilled shrimp through lasagna, turkey, half a dozen vegetables and salads, and two kinds of pie for dessert. It was overkill, but she wanted overkill.

Vance had spent part of each of the last two days at Tom's place, drinking in Tom's endless flow of flying stories, with scarcely a word about his days as a POW. Now he sat companionably in the kitchen with her, watching her still-slim body move rapidly around the room.

"Tom's appetite is amazing, Jill. Nancy fixes him small meals almost every hour, the things he missed the most, and he cleans his plate every time."

"Is he bitter about how badly they treated him?"

"It's strange. You can tell he is still angry, but he's keeping it bottled up, as if it is too tough for him to bear. He's told me a few things that floored me, but for the most part he acts as if it had been a walk in the park. When he talks about prison, he talks mostly 'bout the other POWs, men he didn't meet until after they freed him, but who were legends in the prison."

"I'd like him to show me the tap code."

"He gave me a couple of demonstrations. I couldn't read it at first, he was doing it like a telegrapher, bang-bang-bang. Then he slowed it down and showed me how it worked. Pretty simple, and if it was the only way to communicate, damn effective."

They heard the front door burst open and they walked hand in hand down the long Mexican tiled hallway, Vance shedding his years with every step, Jill watching him with pride.

Tom still limped, but he moved forward strongly, giving Jill a long embrace and whispering into her ear his thanks for taking such good care of his father. He hugged Vance, saying, "Promise me one thing, Dad, no talk about me until after dinner. I've been talking all the time we've been together. It's time for you to bring me up to speed on the business."

He turned to Harry. "You, too, jump in and keep me up-to-date on what's happening. You don't have to dwell on the past, I'll pick that up later. Let's just talk about where we are and where we are going."

Knowing Tom's appetite, they moved immediately to the dining room, Vance watching as they settled themselves, showing all the elements of an old and a new family. Harry was conscientious as always about Anna, who inevitably made a point of her weight problem by eating virtually nothing when she was at table with anyone else. Anna was doing pretty well, staying away from alcohol and keeping her weight under control. But Harry looked worried. There was something going on there. He had seen the signs too often in the past. He had to be vigilant, or Anna would be off on a binge.

Nancy babied Tom, making sure he got the best tidbits and seeing that his beer glass was filled. Vance wasn't so sure about that—Tom might have some trouble handling alcohol after all he had been through. Yet there was tension there, too, and Tom, as usual, brought it right out in the open.

"Well, let's have it, Dad. I understand that Nancy is practically running things at the office now." He projected a combative embarrassment, as if Nancy was doing what Vance had expected of him.

"Well, she certainly has taken over a lot of the administrative work; Jill has taught her well. The company grew while you were gone, couldn't help it with all the wartime contracts."

It was the opening Tom had been looking for. "And I guess most of the growth was due to our wonder boy, Bob Rodriquez?"

Harry spoke up for the first time. "Good Lord, Tom, are you still chewing that old bone? Bob has been a big help, but Vance Shannon, Incorporated, and all its divisions still depend on Dad's name and reputation."

Vance and everyone else knew that wasn't true anymore. Vance was still beloved in the industry. He'd received honorary degrees from Cal Tech and Perdue, a lifetime achievement award from the Society of Experimental Test Pilots, and been enshrined in the National Aviation Hall of Fame. But he was not much of a force in the business anymore. That mantle had passed to Harry and Rodriquez.

Tom went on. "Well, I wanted to get one thing settled. In my six years as a POW, I finally figured something out. I'd been a jerk about Rodriquez, and I'm here tonight to tell you that I'm over it. I want to get back to work in the company when the Air Force releases me, and if I wind up working for Bob, it will be fine with me. And it will be fine if I wind up working for Nancy. But I want to make up for all the time I've spent away from the firm."

The stunned silence was broken only by Vance's voice. "Tom, that makes me almost as happy as I was when I saw you get off that C-141! We need you in the business, and we need everybody to get along."

"Nancy told me that Bob and Mae were splitting up. She says the problem was Bob's work obsession. What do you think, Dad?"

"No question. Bob loves her, and I think she loves him. She just doesn't want to be alone."

Nancy said, "She's not the only one."

And Jill said, "Amen."

Harry and Tom were quiet. They knew that Vance had been exactly the same, gone all the time, working seven days a week, and they, for the most part, had been following in his footsteps. Nancy had left Tom when he volunteered to return to the Air Force to fly in Korea. They got back together when he returned, but neither Tom nor anyone else knew how close she came to divorcing him when he volunteered for Vietnam. Only two things prevented her from taking action— concern for Tom's morale, and the satisfaction she was getting from the increased responsibilities Vance and Harry gave her.

Nancy smiled to herself. In a way, she had the Vance Shannon/Bob Rodriquez work obsession. It made her understand them a little better.

Tom rapped on the table, signaling for attention. They all turned to him, happy to see such a characteristic gesture surface. It meant he was already getting his confidence back.

"One thing is clear to me. We are all getting too old, and we may not age as gracefully as Dad has done. We need new blood! When Harry and I were coming up, we had contacts within the Air Force, and so we kept current. We've got to cultivate some young people, pilots, to work for the company."

Vance Shannon stirred. "Amen to that. You have anyone in mind, Tom?"

"Well, V. R. is growing up, and maybe he'll be able to join us in a few years. But we need some new people, now. Maybe we could pick up some company test pilots, guys who've been trained at Edwards, maybe, and pay them what they are worth. If we don't stay current nowadays, we'll just fall hopelessly behind."

Jill glanced around the room. Tom had struck the right note with everyone—except Nancy. It was obvious that Nancy perceived Tom's comments as a criticism, and she didn't like it.

June 3, 1973
Paris, France

THE TWO MEN watched silently as the beautifully maintained Concorde flashed by at near sonic speed, then pulled up in a sharp climbing turn that caused the crowd to gasp. Nearly 200,000 people poured into Le Bourget and except for the few gourmands who preferred drinking and eating in the manufacturer's chalets to watching the world's greatest air show, all were crowded at the fence to see what one American reporter had called "the shootout at the SST Corral."

The Concorde and the Tu-144, the world's only supersonic transports, were going head-to-head today with their demonstration flights. The press and public generally acknowledged that so far the Concorde had excelled in everything, from flying to the food served to VIPs in their respective chalets.

After their long weeks together, Alexei Tupolev, the Tu-144's designer, and its pilot, Mikhail Kozlov, were now bickering constantly, each man suppressing a consuming, subliminal anger that threatened to erupt at any time.

Neither liked nor respected the other, but in front of the endless whirl and flash of cameras they maintained a cordial solidarity, making the kinds of gestures and comments that the newsreel people expected. Kozlov would point and Tupolev would clap as the Concorde swept around, showing that they were good sports about to demonstrate their own wares.

In the cockpit of the glittering white Concorde, John Farley nodded to Andy Jones to take control. Farley had just done a series of high-speed maneuvers that brought the crowd to its feet, flying the Concorde more like a fighter than a supersonic passenger plane, turning in steep banks, rolling from side to side, and pulling up in startling climbs. Now it was Jones's turn to dazzle the crowd—and more importantly, the airline executives—with the Concorde's repertoire of low-speed maneuvers.

Tupolev nudged Kozlov with his elbow.

"Here they come again. Whatever they do, we have to do better."

The nudge triggered Kozlov's anger and, spitting, he said, "We! Let's get your ass into the cockpit if we're going to say 'we.' It will be me and my boys putting our lives on the line, and you'll be down here bowing like a ballerina."

The two men's anger had reached a peak yesterday evening when one of Tupolev's pet projects was finally implemented. Political observers from Moscow had given Alexei a severe tongue-lashing after the Concorde's demonstration of superior maneuverability. In response, Tupolev authorized a quick-fix wiring change that would override the built-in restrictions of the Tu-144's auto-stabilization computers.

Normally, the auto-stabilization system prevented a pilot from exceeding the aircraft's maneuvering limits, a prudent safeguard that protected against sudden, unexpected control movements.

Kozlov had screamed, "We've practiced this fucking air show routine for six months, and now you are going to change it because some KGB ass complains?"

"No, I'm changing because I know it's best for the airplane. It will allow you to make tighter turns at higher speeds—if you've got the balls for it. We'll change it back when it goes into passenger service."

Kozlov had walked out rather than run the risk of striking Tupolev. It was insane to fly with a change that had not been tested. The man had no idea what the consequences might be. He was maneuvering the Tu-144 at its limits now, particularly given its terrible visibility. You could barely see out of the tiny cockpit windows in level flight. In a steep climb he could see nothing, he had to do it all on instruments—no way to fly an air show.

Tupolev and his engineers had quickly rewired the auto-stabilizer to allow the Tu-144 to turn tighter and climb more steeply without overriding the pilot at the controls. It would not be safe for an ordinary airline pilot, but despite his dislike for Kozlov as a person, Tupolev respected him as a pilot and believed—knew—he could handle it.

Now they stood together silently as the huge Concorde seemed to crawl down the runway, nose high, fifty feet off the ground, rocking its wings and dipping its nose as if it were waltzing instead of flying. Then Jones slammed the throttles forward; the afterburners kicked in with huge belches of flame and a tidal wave of noise that flattened the grass, sending the Concorde up in a tight climbing turn that made the crowd go silent, certain that they were about to witness a stall, spin, and crash.

Instead, Jones pulled up to six thousand feet to begin the last twelve minutes of his routine.

Tupolev said, "You can do better at low speed. Our engines are more powerful, and the canards give you more control. Take it to the limits."

Kozlov said nothing, but bounded up the ladder into the Tu-144's cockpit like a sailor climbing rigging, knowing that his longtime friend and copilot, Sergei Blagin, would have everything ready to roll.

Alexei Tupolev watched, angered by Kozlov's shortsightedness. He had not always been that way. This, the second production model of the Tu-144, had hundreds of changes from the prototype, and Kozlov had approved all of them—except those from last night.

The Tu-144 was bigger now, it could carry 140 passengers, it had more wing area, it was improved in every way, and it was all due to Alexei. His blessed father, Andrei, had been ill for some time before his death last year. Since then, Alexei made all of the thousands of decisions, big and small, that had transformed the limping prototype into this magnificent airplane.

Kozlov, like so many others, never had the allegiance to Alexei that he held for his father. It was frustrating, unfair, uncalled for. The airplane that Kozlov was now taxiing out to the runway was Alexei's design, and no one else could claim it.

Inside the cockpit, Kozlov listened to Blagin repeat the tower's instructions. It wasn't easy—the big Kuznetsov engines hammered through the cockpit in a waterfall of noise. He wondered how the four engineers in the passenger section could take it. Something had to be done before the plane went into regular service. No one could bear that noise on a long flight. Oddly enough, on the ground, the Tupolev's engines made less noise than those of the Concorde, a point all the reporters talked about.

Kozlov responded quietly to Blagin's recitation of the checklist, his hands moving swiftly and exactly to each switch or control. What a great copilot Blagin was! He had everything ready, and even though he too was upset by Tupolev's latest changes, he maintained his usual good humor.

Lightly loaded, the Tu-144 accelerated swiftly as Kozlov advanced the throttles. Alexei Tupolev watched with pride as the afterburners kicked in and the beautiful transport launched into a steep turning climb that exceeded the Concorde's speed and angle of bank.

After three tight 360-degree turns, Kozlov brought the Tu-144 down low and fast in what he called his "worm burner" routine, racing along the centerline of runway 06, pushing the aircraft to near sonic speeds, then pulling up in another hair-raising climb that once again drew the spectators to their feet. Even Tupolev was concerned; Kozlov was giving him more than he had asked for. It was clear that the unleashed Tu-144 was far more maneuverable than the Concorde.

In a descending turn, Kozlov called for gear extension and flaps as he slowed the SST, feeding in the trim as the airspeed bled down. Out of the corner of his eye he could see Blagin looking at him nervously, his gloved hand ready to push the throttles forward to pour on the power if needed.

As the Tu-144 came across the runway, Kozlov added power to stabilize the airplane in nose-high flight, just above touchdown speed.

Midway down the runway, standing a hundred meters off to the left, Tupolev stood mouth ajar, watching his masterpiece approach at a crawl, thinking only, *Thank God it's Kozlov flying—no one else could do that.*

Seconds later Kozlov jammed the throttles forward into afterburner and the Tu-144 bounded into a tight climbing turn, turning faster and climbing at a steeper attitude than anything the Concorde had done—or could do.

Still turning at one thousand meters, Kozlov peered out of the tiny windscreen to see a French Mirage fighter on a collision course. Cursing, he dumped the Tu-144's nose. The auto-stabilization computer would ordinarily have limited the dive to at most a negative one G; instead the nose plunged down almost vertically. Kozlov instinctively heaved back on the yoke, the forward canards failed, and the right wing snapped off in a fiery explosion. Kozlov fought with the now-useless controls for the last few seconds of his life, cursing Tupolev for the stupid changes that were killing him.

The big SST broke apart as it fell, separating into incandescent chunks of wing, engines, and fuselage that rained on the village of Goussainville, engulfing homes in a deluge of flaming fuel.

Tupolev and the still-silent crowd watched the twenty-second drama climax as parts from the transport continued to fall, spreading the rain of fire and debris. There was no need for an accident investigation. He knew in his heart that he was at fault. The rewired auto-stabilization unit had caused the breakup. Six men dead in the airplane, and God only knew how many more on the ground. And all his fault, his fault alone. He should have listened to Kozlov.

He wondered if his father was watching down. He hoped not.

CHAPTER TWO

THE PASSING PARADE: Oil prices force 55 mph speed limit; Symbionese Liberation Army captures, influences Patty Hearst; Watergate scandal flourishes; Peter Benchley's *Jaws* published; Solzhenitsyn exiled for *The Gulag Archipelago*; Palestine terrorists kill 21 schoolchildren; Isabel Perón rules in Argentina; President Nixon resigns; Haile Selassie overthrown in Ethiopia; President Ford pardons Nixon; *Upstairs, Downstairs* big television hit; Jimmy Connors, Chris Evert tops in tennis.

February 2, 1974
Edwards Air Force Base, California

*S*unk deep in thought, Bob Rodriquez sat hunched in the back of the dusty staff car, worrying about today's flight. So much depended on it; for him, for his company, but even more so, for Steve O'Malley, whose career was riding on its success or failure.

As they rumbled along at the prescribed fifteen miles per hour ramp speed, they passed an almost complete catalog of Air Force aircraft— bombers, fighters, transports, helicopters—spotted along the Edwards ramp. Most of them were sitting idle, some with panels off or engine bays open, with a few attended by ground crews preparing them for today's tests. His particular interest, General Dynamics's new YF-16, was still in the hangar, waiting for its first official flight.

Rodriquez knew that the test pilot, Phil Oestricher, was already there, making the minute preflight inspection that he always conducted, talking quietly with the GD mechanics who had inspected everything twice already, but understood Phil's interest and had no objection to their work being so intently surveyed. O'Malley would be walking right behind him, double-checking the double check.

"Jesus!"

The startled driver glanced back in the mirror to see Rodriquez slapping his forehead.

"You OK, Mr. Rodriquez?"

"Sorry, I'm just such a jerk! I promised to call my ex-wife last night and I forgot to."

The driver shrugged. Everybody was an idiot if this was all it took.

"You can call from the hangar, can't you?"

"No, not now, too late, she's on her way to New York. Maybe I can catch her tonight."

He continued to flagellate himself in the usual manner, knowing that things like this were the very reason that his beloved wife Mae was divorcing him. Who wouldn't divorce an insensitive clod like him?

As he neared the huge hangar, he began to reflect on O'Malley and his presence here today. Instead of being on the line at Edwards, O'Malley was supposed to be on the Hill, flogging the GPS program, doing the hard-sell work he hated, visiting congressional staffers, reminding them of the program's possibilities, but, more important, pointing out to them how many jobs it would create in their congressman's district. That was the critical element; the staffers wanted their man reelected, to protect their own jobs, and that meant getting votes. The only real way to get votes was to demonstrate that the congressman was serving his district well when it came to the pork being dispensed from Washington.

Nobody knew this better than O'Malley's boss, General Richard V. Wyatt, the Vice Chief of Staff. Wyatt had been a strong opponent of O'Malley's last crusade, the so-called low cost fighter that had led to the YF-16. He had resented O'Malley's unorthodox—but successful—advocacy of the concept. Wanting to keep O'Malley firmly out of the airplane acquisition business, Wyatt had set up a special office in the Pentagon, with O'Malley reporting directly to him. This had benefited Rodriquez, for O'Malley was as effective working on the GPS program as he had been on the lightweight fighter, as it was now being called. The name had changed as costs had risen.

But everyone knew what the new assignment meant. O'Malley had raised so much hell about getting a lightweight fighter that Wyatt was determined to see that he was never promoted again. Ironically, if O'Malley had failed, if no lightweight fighter had come into being, his previous record would have made his promotion to brigadier general certain within the year.

The hangar doors were open now, and a tug was pulling the gleaming YF-16 out. Rodriquez saw Oestricher in the cockpit, with O'Malley walking along at the wing tip, making sure that it cleared the hangar doors that were at least forty feet away. Oestricher's head was down in the cockpit. An image came to Rodriquez of the instrument panel and switches. They were already worn, shining metal gleaming through the paint. It was amazing how quickly an aircraft's cockpit aged—outside it might look brand-new, gleaming in the sun; inside it was always tattered and torn.

Although Rodriquez had spent many hours working on this very sophisticated aircraft, he never tired of looking at it. The YF-16 had an exotic beauty, with its sensuous blended wing-body design. The wing itself had a computer-controlled variable camber that combined with flaperons to take full advantage of the relaxed stability character-istic. There were other advances as well, including a wing strake on the forebody that generated a vortex lift.

Few airplanes embodied so many advances in a single package, and he had a proprietary interest in one of the most important of these, the "relaxed" static stability/fly-by-wire control system. In simpler terms it meant that the YF-16 was deliberately designed to be far more unstable than previous aircraft, a factor that, when controlled by com-puters, gave it an unparalleled maneuverability. The fly-by-wire sys-tem was distrusted by many, but years of experiments made Rodriquez sure that it was the system of the future. As multiple computers were introduced into new designs, it became essential to take the fly-by-wire approach.

Rodriquez had seen the YF-16's competition, the Northrop YF-17. It, too, was a beautiful aircraft, and a worthy competitor. But it used two engines, and that doomed it with the lightweight fighter crowd.

Asking the driver to wait, Rodriquez walked over to O'Malley, shaking his hand and saying, "Man, you shouldn't be here. Wyatt will skin you alive when you get back."

"It don't matter, son, it don't matter; my ass is grass with Wyatt anyway, and I might as well enjoy my last days in the Air Force."

Seeing Rodriquez's stunned look, O'Malley went on. "They have given me the word, no stars for a wiseass like me. I might as well get out while I'm still young. I don't want to be one of those gray-haired colonels still running the halls at the Pentagon after they've got their thirty in."

Rodriquez was shocked. From his days as quarterback at Academy to shooting down MiGs in Vietnam, O'Malley had been a comer. Tom Shannon had predicted that he would be Chief of Staff someday.

"Jesus, Steve, after your career, how can they do this to you?"

"Easy, if they can do it to John Boyd, they can do it to me. I'm not political enough. I stepped on too many toes helping set up the Fighter Weapons School at Nellis. Then working with the fighter mafia just about finished me off. All that, and then backing this beauty—" He gestured at the YF-16.

"Forty-second" Boyd had been one of the great fighter pilots in the Air Force, and a far-ranging thinker. He earned his nickname from his standing bet that he could beat any opponent in a simulated dog-fight in less than forty seconds. Rumor was that he never lost his bet. But Boyd had an unfortunate personality, unlike O'Malley, who was a charmer. Rodriquez could see how Boyd might trip himself up, but never O'Malley, who now flashed his famous smile, saying, "Bob, you were an ace in Korea, flying F-86s against MiGs, and I tell you this air-plane is going to be the weapon of the future, not because it's inexpensive, but because it is good! It has all the relative quality of the F-86 and all the relative practicality of the MiG-15 wrapped up in a super-modern package. So far everybody's been talking about this as a cheap supplement to the F-15; I tell you that it's going to have capabilities beyond the F-15 and do it for half the price."

O'Malley was talking Rodriquez's language now—he had always maintained that the YF-16 was going to be more than just an air-to-air weapon, because he knew the electronics were coming that would turn it into a multi-mission aircraft. And that meant instead of building a few hundred YF-16s, General Dynamics would ultimately build thousands of them—all carrying the advanced pulse-doppler radar Rodriquez had developed at his firm.

The roar of the YF-16's Pratt & Whitney's F100 engine rose and Oestricher taxied out, flipping them a salute as he went by. It had been a stroke of genius on the part of the General Dynamics team to use the same basic engine that powered the McDonnell Douglas F-15, for it solved many development problems. It also made the Air Force happy because it simplified logistics and maintenance.

O'Malley stood watching as the heat from the F100 engine turned the tarmac behind the YF-16 into a shimmering mirage of lakes, then said to Rodriquez, "General Dynamics is going to make a fortune selling these to foreign air forces. There ought to be some way that we can build a company to cash in on the foreign sales."

Rodriquez nodded. They were on the same wavelength. It wasn't that he had gone as far as he could go with Aerospace Unlimited—the future was bright there for him. The problem instead was that he had taken Vance Shannon, Incorporated, as far as he could take it, given the management it had now with Nancy Shannon—Tom's wife— running it. Nancy had grown tremendously as a businesswoman, but her ego had grown with it, and she was determined to steer the firm in new directions. To go farther, to get into the really futuristic side of aviation that he knew was coming, he needed to be completely on his own.

They watched Oestricher roll smoothly onto the runway.

O'Malley said, "Let's hope this goes better than last January."

Rodriquez winced at the memory. On a high-speed taxi test, the fly-by-wire system—*his* fly-by-wire system—had been calibrated incorrectly, making it too sensitive to control inputs from the pilot. Oestricher's initial movements of the controls got out of hand, rocking the aircraft so violently that the tail plane was damaged. In an amazing demonstration of test-pilot savvy and courage, Oestricher elected to take off rather than to try to brake to a halt and perhaps roll the aircraft up into a ball. Aware of the problem, he handled the controls with the delicacy of a surgeon during his six-minute flight, making a normal landing. His quick analysis and skill had saved the airplane and the program.

"No repeats!"

Oestricher roared past on his takeoff roll, breaking ground exactly where O'Malley had computed, then took the YF-16 out of the pattern to fly to the restricted test area. The two friends returned to their

conversation on the prospects for a new business centered on servicing
the foreign companies that would be lining up to purchase the production versions of the YF-16.

"Do you speak any foreign languages, Steve?"

"I can get by in French, and I know a little Russian, but that won't
be much help. How about you?"

"Spanish, naturally, and German. Between us we'll cover most of
the bases, although the people we want to talk to will almost all speak
English."

"Don't forget Japan; we'll have to find someone who can speak
Japanese."

"We'll concentrate on NATO first. They are going to have to replace a whole lot of F-104s over the next ten years, and the F-16 will
be the one they want. We just have to come up with the services that
they need and General Dynamics won't be in a position to supply."

Steve shook his head happily.

"It sounds great, but we'll be spread thin. We need to get a couple
of young guys to come on board and do the grunt work. The way the
aircraft industry is closing down, we ought to be able to hire a couple
of test pilots."

Rodriquez nodded in agreement.

"Let's go slow, one at a time, and make sure they are compatible
not just with you and me, but with each other. I know what it means to
work in a company where someone doesn't like you. It's hell!"

O'Malley nodded. He knew exactly how tough the fights between
Rodriquez and Tom Shannon had been over the years, no matter how
Bob tried to avoid them.

They sensed activity on the field and saw that Oestricher had entered the landing pattern. Almost ninety minutes had gone by and
they had not moved from their spot by the runway. Oestricher set the
YF-16 down gently, and then taxied past them, oxygen mask off, a big
grin on his face.

O'Malley said, "No troubles this time; I can tell by his expression."

"Let's go back to L.A. tonight; we can talk some more about our
business then—and figure out how I'm going to break the news to
Vance. I hate to do it, but it's now or never."

February 8, 1974
Palos Verdes, California

THE LONG MEXICAN tiled hallway of Vance Shannon's house glistened from the drinks Jill spilled as she ran to the laughter roaring from the study. She sighed, planning to clean it up later and hoping no one slipped in the meantime.

"Look at him, there he is," Rodriquez yelled, happier and more excited than anyone had seen him in months. He was pointing to Bill Pogue, the pilot on the Skylab 4, just pulled from the Pacific splashdown.

Vance's faithful old DuMont television set had died at last and Rodriquez had replaced it with a huge color set that he had built himself, one component at a time, most of the work done late at night in lonely motel rooms on his endless road trips.

"Eighty-four days and one hour in orbit; can you believe that? That's a new record. They must be weak as cats now that they're back where there's gravity. Look, there's Pogue again, waving."

Rodriquez had known Pogue in Korea and then again when he was flying with the Thunderbird aerobatic team. He respected him both as a pilot and a scientist. He went on: "People are so fickle! Skylab is amazing, an actual orbiting space station, with scientists in place for experiments, but it just isn't getting the attention it should. I think beating the Russians to putting a man on the Moon has spoiled the American public."

He glanced around the room. Once it had been a tightly knit family but now they sat divided, as if they were rival dodgeball teams. On the right-hand side, near the fireplace, were the "airplane guys." Nancy sat with her arm around Tom. His twin brother Harry was next, with his wife, the always difficult Anna. Opposite them, ranged in a short semicircle of chairs, were the "electronic guys"—Rodriquez, with his estranged wife Mae and their son, Rod, and Steve O'Malley, a friend to both sides but Bob's colleague and potential new partner.

Plopped right in the middle, accessible to both groups, was Vance Shannon, almost eighty now, but still far sharper than he had been a few years before when he'd suffered a stroke. A long convalescence and some unusual "occupational therapy" had rehabilitated him. The therapy came in the form of telling his personal history to a writer. The process sharpened his memory and raised his energy levels, for the writer, Warren Bowers, knew so much about him that he could always supply a name or a date to spur Shannon's memory. Warren was there as usual, fading into the background, his tape recorder going and pencil flying as he made notes on a yellow legal pad.

Shannon sat hand in hand with Jill, his second wife and third love. Jill tried to be neutral, she loved everybody in the room, but she concentrated on keeping Vance happy. The unrelenting tension between the two groups sapped his strength and hers. It was a relief to have the familial feeling momentarily restored by the miracle of the Skylab 4 flight.

Ironically, it was prosperity that divided them. Fifteen years before, they were a small, close-knit group, beset by the ordinary domestic problems found in every family. They worked together toward a single goal, furthering Vance Shannon's personal creation, his consulting firm. Then called Aviation Consultants, it was a relatively small company, but much respected by aircraft manufacturers. Since then it had expanded into a huge entity with offices in every city where there was a major defense contractor. Much of the expansion had come from Bob Rodriquez's relentless genius in exploiting the revolution in electronics. The rest had come from the compression of the aeronautics industry as it consolidated into fewer and fewer big firms. Each consolidation brought about layoffs that inevitably reduced expertise. This in turn forced the surviving companies to hire consulting firms, causing Vance's well-respected company to prosper.

As happy as they were about the successful return of the Skylab crew, the series of four Skylab flights had deepened the family schism. Tom Shannon's wife, Nancy, was now running the parent company, Vance Shannon, Incorporated, with an iron hand. Tom, still recovering from his long imprisonment in Hanoi, was proud of her even as he resented the fact that he wasn't doing it. Worse, he felt that if he wasn't running the company, then Harry should have been. Nancy was his wife, but she wasn't born a Shannon, and it wasn't right that she was in charge. One day, he hoped, their son V. R. would come in and take over. But that was a long way off—V. R. was almost finished with Air Force flight training and would probably make a career of it.

Despite Rodriquez's constant urging, Nancy had elected to ignore the Skylab program, insisting that it was too short term, and that she wanted the firm to diversify into other areas—particularly real estate.

This was heresy to Rodriquez, who had garnered a bonanza in contracts from the Skylab program for his division, Aerospace Unlimited. He felt that Nancy could easily have done the same if she had been more aggressive.

Vance Shannon reached over and tapped Rodriquez on the arm. "Bob, did your friend fly on all the Skylabs? How many were there?"

"There were four, Vance, one unmanned, and three manned. Each of the three manned flights had different crews. This time, my friend Pogue flew with Gerald Carr and Ed Gibson—both great guys."

Vance nodded and turned back to the one drink that Jill would allow him. The simple truth was that the Skylab didn't have wings, and that meant he was not really interested. What the hell were they doing, flying around and around, then splashing down in the ocean? It didn't make any sense.

The television commentary went on for another few minutes, the usual shots of the welcome given to returning astronaut crews, and then broke for another commercial.

Nancy spoke up, almost for the first time that day. "Bob, do you think this would be a good time to tell the folks what we've been talking about?"

Rodriquez flushed. Damn the woman. This was the worst time to bring up the coming split, but there was no way to avoid it now. He wanted to break it to Vance first, but now it was out of the question. Struggling to be pleasant, he replied, "Sure, Nancy, if it is OK with you. You correct me if I get anything wrong."

Everyone in the group looked anxious except Vance, who, as he did so often now, was gently dozing. Jill shook her head and, glancing around, took in the family dynamic. Tom looked angry and frustrated. He had always been unhappy with Rodriquez, and was more than happy to see him go. But it was becoming more and more difficult for him that his wife was now running the business that his family had created. It was not just male pride, having more to do with his general dissatisfaction with himself. His brother Harry simply looked appalled, knowing what the loss of Rodriquez's genius would mean to the firm. Harry shared Tom's resentment over Nancy's running the firm. But he accepted it, because Nancy being the boss allowed him more time to keep Anna on the straight and narrow. If he got too involved in the business, if he had to travel too much, she was apt to start drinking again. Anna was looking straight ahead, keeping her face a mask.

On the other side of the room, Mae Rodriquez was near tears. The Shannons had accepted her totally as a family member. Now the family was breaking up, just as her marriage had. Steve O'Malley looked embarrassed just to be there, sorry that he had even a tangential part in the breakup of the firm. Warren Bowers had discreetly turned off his tape recorder and put his pencil down, and was now staring intently at the huge aquarium that Jill had installed as a gift for Vance.

Nancy's voice had a triumphant lilt. "Now is as good a time as any, Bob. I don't want to let this wait until Monday. Let's get everything on the table now."

Rodriquez wasn't good at being funny, and his attempt at humor failed once again.

"Well, it looks as if I am going to be busting up this old gang of ours. It is time for me to be moving on. Steve here is going to retire from the Air Force and join me in a new venture. Nancy has been nice enough to agree to buy up some of my stock in the old company, but I've kept a good bit, and I'll always be available to Vance Shannon, Incorporated." Then with a nod to the sleeping Vance, he added, "And to the grand old man himself."

Looking immensely pleased, Nancy went on. "Thanks, Bob; that's about it. We won't go into the details of the deal right now, they are still being worked out. Bob very nicely offered to sign a non-compete agreement, but I told him that it wasn't necessary. We've worked together so closely in the past it would be virtually impossible to decide how to frame an agreement, and besides, I think the goals of his new firm and the goals of our firm are going to be quite a bit different in the future."

Jill made a quick scan of the faces. Nancy was clearly hitting the wrong note with everyone. She was glad Vance was dozing.

Nancy went on. "After we get this finally settled—and it won't be long, I promise you—I'll be making some announcements about the new directions and goals for the firm. I think you will be pleased"— and then sensing the uniform expressions of disapproval, she stumbled and went on—"at least I hope you will. I'll try to—"

She sat down suddenly, aware that something was very wrong. She had made a mistake, but was unsure exactly what it was.

Vance stirred and opened his eyes and, his voice remarkably strong, said, "I don't know, but this sounds like a complete fuckup to me."

Then he nodded off again.

There was silence.

Embarrassed, Jill said, "He must have been dreaming; you know he never uses bad language around the family. He'd be so embarrassed if he knew he said that in front of Rod."

And Tom said, "Yeah, he was dreaming—or listening."

November 19, 1974
Palos Verdes, California

VANCE SHANNON DIED as anyone might wish to do, in his sleep, without any pain. Never a quiet sleeper, Vance had become increasingly noisy in the last year, and Jill had been forced to move to a separate bedroom. She found him when she brought his breakfast coffee in, his body already cold.

Now the Shannon clan had gathered once again in the library where so many decisions had been made, the men talking quietly, being brave, the women alternately trying to be cheerful or crying to themselves. Bob Rodriquez was in Europe, but Mae was there, loyal as ever, more a part of the Shannon family now than before.

Jill was seemingly the least affected as she rushed around in her typical fashion, making coffee, getting some bakery goods out of the freezer, trying to carry on as she knew Vance would have wanted her to do. Tom and Harry were silent for the most part, conscious of how much their father had inspired them, and aware of how much they would miss him. Anna was inconsolable, so much so that she became the object of worry, not for her sadness, but for the probability that she would use Vance's death as an excuse to begin drinking again.

Nancy Shannon was obviously shaken; her voice trembled and she sat apart from everyone, a prayer book and a rosary clasped in her hands. Harry nudged Tom and said, "I didn't know Nancy was religious."

"She's not. I don't even know where she dug those out. But she is profoundly shaken. I know she loved Dad—everybody did—but this is something else."

"I think running the business is getting to her. Some of the things she's trying to do just are not working out."

Determined to diversify Vance Shannon, Incorporated, Nancy Shannon had become deeply involved in a huge shopping mall development on the outskirts of San Diego. So far nothing had gone well, and Nancy was feeling the pressure.

Tom shrugged. "I feel guilty about it, but I don't know how to help. I never followed the real estate market. I just assumed the price of everything would keep going up. She's probably not hurting on the land she bought, it's just dealing with the builders and the contractors that is killing her. Everybody is behind schedule and everybody wants more money for every change."

"That part sounds familiar."

"Yeah, it's no different than building airplanes in that respect, I guess, but she doesn't know who to trust. With Boeing or Lockheed, there are always people we know who will level with us. She's being led down the garden path by some outsiders, and she doesn't know where to turn."

"Can she just pull out, take the losses, and get back into something we are good at?"

"She can but she won't. She's changed so much since I married her, mainly because I was gone so much. My years as a POW were hard on her; she turned to work like—"

Harry finished the line for him. "Like Anna turned to booze. You can say it, it won't hurt my feelings. God knows Anna has put us all through the mill so many times that there's no harm in being frank."

"Sorry, Harry. Didn't mean to offend."

"You didn't. I'm inured to it now. But let me tell you something. Nancy's success has been tough for Anna to take. She's told me a thousand times how Nancy is a success, and she is a failure. I try to reassure her, but it doesn't work."

Tom nodded. "It has to be tough on her. It's tough on me. I feel like half a man with her running things, and you and me working for her. I love her, just as I always did, and I respect her, but it drives me nuts to have her as my boss. Especially since I disagree with what she's doing to the company."

"Well, it's a hell of a note that we're standing here complaining about our wives, when our dad has just died."

"Harry, Dad has just passed on to another better place. He's never going to die in our memories, or in the memories of many people. I don't know anyone in the industry that had more friends or fewer enemies."

"I'll drink to that. Oops, sorry, did it again."

December 6, 1974
Arlington National Cemetery, Virginia

Two WEEKS BEFORE there had been another family argument. Vance had always said he wanted a quiet funeral, and internment beside his first wife in the family plot. His second wife, Jill, had agreed, but somewhat reluctantly. She had never known his first wife, Margaret, but nonetheless felt somewhat hurt that Vance was electing to "spend eternity" next to her.

Then Steve O'Malley had popped in with news that shook them. He had made a personal call to the Air Force Chief of Staff, General David C. Jones, asking if the United States Air Force would provide a flyover for Vance's burial.

Jones, a powerful figure of a man, with dark curly hair and a commanding stance, responded, "Vance Shannon? Absolutely. Just tell me when and where he'll be buried and we'll have a flight of four overhead at the exact moment. It will be at Arlington, of course—no place else is suitable for a hero like Vance Shannon."

It took O'Malley another three days to convince the family that Vance deserved national honors rather than the quiet ceremony he had requested. Jill wanted to be more supportive, but was afraid that her motives would be too obvious. Tom, who had always been closer to his mother, resisted the idea, while Harry was neutral. He was so preoccupied with keeping his wife sober that he devoted himself only to the most essential elements of his work. After Tom had reluctantly agreed, it took O'Malley three more days to make the arrangements at Arlington. There had been a problem at first—the beautiful cemetery was already overscheduled, but another call to General Jones took care of that.

Now the family stood at graveside, no divisions among them, Jill quite beautiful in black, V. R. looking handsome in his Air Force uniform, and Rod, already five inches taller than his father, quietly standing with Mae, taking it all in.

The weather was wonderful for Washington in December, dry with the temperature edging toward fifty degrees.

Tom leaned over to Harry and whispered, "Have you ever seen so many well-known aviation people in one spot before?"

"No, not even at the Collier Trophy Dinner. There must be three thousand or more here."

Both men watched the crowd closely, picking out friends from the service, from industry, and from the various company offices around the country.

"Not much work being done today at Vance Shannon, Incorporated. That would really frost Dad!"

"No, Tom, nor at a lot of other offices as well. Dad would really be touched. And surprised. He knew he was liked, but I don't think he'd ever dreamed there would be a turnout like this."

They lapsed into silence as a general hush came over the crowd. The body-bearers, all six-footers from the Air Force Academy, another O'Malley gesture, carried the simple walnut coffin and positioned it over the grave. They stepped back, carefully unfolded the flag, and held it outstretched, taut, over the coffin.

Father Jake Callahan stepped forward. He had conducted the Mass earlier in the day. Tom whispered to Harry, "Dad wasn't much of a churchgoer. I wonder what he's making of this?"

"He liked Jake—they used to have a cognac or two, playing chess. I'm sure Dad's happy he's here. And I think Dad believed in the church; he was just too damn wrapped up in flying to be a good parishioner."

Father Callahan was brief. "Vance Shannon was a good man, beloved by his family, his friends, and his clients. He never made a promise he didn't keep; he never backed away from a challenge, and he always delivered more than he had agreed to. He was a great flyer, a fine, intuitive engineer, and a businessman almost by accident, for he never pursued the dollar; he only pursued the truth. He will be missed by all."

Callahan paused for a moment and said, "I've composed a special prayer for Vance. It is short and a little unorthodox, but it is sincere."

He bowed his head and went on. "Dear Heavenly Father, you have received the soul of a great aviator. May he enjoy his heavenly wings as much as he enjoyed his earthly wings. Amen."

There was an appreciative chuckle from the crowd, then silence as the honor guard stepped forward with their rifles at the ready. Just as the command "Fire" rang out, the air was shattered with the sound of eight jet engines as four McDonnell F-4Es roared overhead. The rifle shots were lost in the noise of the Phantoms flying over, the number three man peeling up in the heart-stopping "missing man" salute. The F-4Es disappeared over the horizon as the haunting sound of "Taps" rang out. They watched the solemn folding of the flag in silence, too moved by the Air Force's final aerial salute to a fallen comrade to talk. Finally, Harry whispered to Tom, "That must have been laid on by O'Malley. We owe him a lot for this."

Tom nodded, still choked up.

The chaplain saluted the flag and then handed it to Jill.

It was over. The crowd began to move, a hundred conversations broke out, and Tom moved over to Steve O'Malley.

"I won't forget this, Steve. Dad must be mighty pleased."

"He was a modest man, Tom, but he deserves every honor. I'm glad I could help."

Tom turned away. It was too bad that O'Malley was wrapped up in his project with Rodriquez—he'd be a good man to bring on board the Shannon family firm.

CHAPTER THREE

THE PASSING PARADE: Pol Pot begins genocide in Cambodia; U.S. Marines recapture S.S. *Mayaguez* from Cambodian communists; two assassination attempts on President Ford; federal government bails out New York City; legislation attempts to impose metric measurements on United States; 8,000 lifelike, life-sized terracotta soldiers found in China; Legionnaires' disease appears; CB radio popular; *One Flew Over the Cuckoo's Nest* wins top four Oscars; Apple Computer launched.

December 13, 1974
Luke AFB, Arizona

*F*our sleek Northrop T-38 Talons flew through the thin, high cirrus at thirty thousand feet, the flashing gray wisps of clouds imparting a temporary sense of speed. En route back from a tough training mission, 2nd Lieutenant Vance Robert Shannon felt the familiar incredulity that he was actually paid to fly this marvelous aircraft. He mumbled to himself, "It must be in the blood, in the genes."

Neither his father nor his grandfather had ever encouraged him to fly—they both knew the dangers too well, and both had lost too many friends to the business. But they were obviously happy when he chose the Air Force, and even happier when he began doing so well in flying school. Now, only days away from graduation, he piloted the number four aircraft in the formation, enjoying the T-38's responsiveness, watching Charlie St. John lead the flight with precision and anticipating an evening of dinner, dancing, and, he hoped, sex with his fiancée Ginny.

St. John had been his rival at the Academy, in flight school, and for the affections of Virginia "Ginny" Talbot. Charlie had graduated number one to his number two at the Academy and they were now neck and neck for first honors in flying school. It had been a close-run thing with Ginny, but she agreed to marry Shannon only two weeks before. Through it all, against the odds, Shannon and St. John had remained close friends, although the business with Ginny was going to make it rough. It was just as well they were graduating, going their separate ways.

As they began a left turn, Shannon noticed a puff of smoke, followed by a blue-colored flame, coming from St. John's port engine.

"Lead, check your gauges. I see flames coming from your number one engine, Charlie."

There was no reply. Instead the canopy blew off in a high arc, followed immediately by the ejection seat, with St. John hunched forward as the seat rotated, his helmet flying off. Shannon broke left, calling, "I'll try to follow him down. Call Luke and give our position."

He threw the T-38 into a tight turn thinking, *Jesus, there must have been a fire in the cockpit to have him eject so fast. I hope he's OK.*

Shannon chopped his throttles, rolled inverted, and scanned the sky below him. Off to the right, almost out of sight, he saw a black dot, fast disappearing toward the rugged mountains below.

"I'll see him when his chute opens. He better be quick about it, though."

Rolling level, Shannon checked his fuel and realized he had to get back to the field or they would be out looking for him as well. He rolled inverted again for one last scan, hoping to see the white shroud of St. John's parachute opening. Instead he caught the sudden flash of flame and smoke as the stricken T-38 dove into the ground.

Four hours later, Shannon sat in the Officers Club with Ginny, both disconsolate, both crying.

"It's impossible, Ginny, one minute he was there, flying lead; two minutes later he's smashed into the ground, dead, his parachute unopened."

Unable to speak, she squeezed his hand.

Shannon had talked to the Air Force rescue team that brought

Charlie's body back. They found St. John, still strapped into the ejection seat, next to a big hole in the ground. The seat had hit hard, making a two-foot depression, then bounced out to land a few feet away, St. John still strapped in.

"The medic from the chopper told me that it looked like Charlie was knocked unconscious when he ejected. And none of the automatic systems worked. They'll probably ground all the T-38s until they find out why the seat malfunctioned."

Ginny spoke, her voice welling with emotion. "I hope they do. Flying is too dangerous. I wish you would give it up and do something else."

He looked at her, incredulous. "Give up flying? I come from a family of flyers. My dad is an ace, my grandfather was an ace and a legendary test pilot. My uncle Harry is famous for his flying and his engineering. How can I give it up? I won't give it up, don't even think that."

Shannon's tone disturbed Ginny. "Your best friend was just killed, and you get angry with me because I want you to stop flying? This is a new side of you, and I don't like it."

V. R. bounded up, ready to walk out, then abruptly sat down and put his arms around her.

"Ginny, angel, we're upset. Charlie's death has got us both confused. I'm sorry I was angry."

"I wish I could believe you, honey, but I saw something in your eye just now that I've never seen before. I saw exactly where I stand when it comes to a choice between me or flying. It will be flying."

V. R. hugged her, knowing she was right and knowing that there was probably not going to be any sex tonight.

July 18, 1975
Sunnyvale, California

BOB RODRIQUEZ GLANCED around his office at ActOn, the company Steve O'Malley and he had founded. The name came from a phrase O'Malley used constantly: "We've got to act on this now." It didn't make much sense, but it had a ring to it that they both liked.

But what in the hell had happened? Six months before, they had opened the new facility on one of the "scientific campuses" flourishing around Stanford. His office had been a thing of beauty, with clean-lined furniture, a big conference table, and comfortable chairs. Now it swam in files and folders, endless printouts from the company's big IBM computer spilling off to the floor, every flat surface encumbered with plans, books, and odd bits of the hardware they were developing. Two huge chalkboards, both filled with numbers, one with sheets of paper draped over sensitive information, stood there, dripping chalk dust. The only neat spot was a table behind his desk where he had half a dozen photos of his ex-wife, Mae, and his son, Bob Jr. The photos brought him equal amounts of comfort in the memories and pain at his loss.

The antic disarray embarrassed him because O'Malley's office, across the hall, still looked brand-new. Of course, O'Malley was gone most of the time. General Dynamics had won the lightweight fighter competition in January, and O'Malley was pounding the streets in Amsterdam, Copenhagen, Oslo, and Brussels, the first four foreign countries who would operate the aircraft.

It was just as they had predicted. The foreign governments liked the F-16—the Fighting Falcon as the Air Force had named it—but they needed more than an air superiority fighter. Every one of them expected the F-16 to do double or triple or quadruple duty. They wanted planes for reconnaissance, for attack, even for level bombing, not just for dogfighting. ActOn was trying to be the catalyst that transformed the F-16 to their needs with a whole series of weapons packages and radar options.

Relatively new procurement requirements facilitated ActOn's efforts. Every country who bought the F-16 had it written into their contracts that they could build some or all of the aircraft in factories in their own country. There were lots of variations on the theme, ranging from building wings and tails to totally irrelevant transactions. In one case O'Malley had to arrange for a huge shipment of grain to be sent to Holland as part of the deal, and had spent two valuable weeks scouring the United States for the best way to achieve it. But for the most part, the companies were content to have their factories build components, especially those that met their specific national needs for alternate weapons systems.

It was a bonus they had hoped for, but had not counted on. When the foreign manufacturers introduced a new product—anything from a precision guided missile to a bomb rack to a transponder—ActOn was often able to see that it was snapped up by the USAF for installation on later model F-16s. O'Malley called it the "inverted cornucopia," saying you poured a little effort in the small end and huge contracts came spewing out the other.

Rodriquez knew that it was more than just luck. He had created the line of products over the last five years, and patented each one, but he was no salesman. O'Malley knew exactly how to combine a salesman's *bon homme* manner, dispensing martinis at expensive restaurants with the detailed scientific knowledge that a smart customer demanded. No matter what he was asked, he had the answer, right then, without checking with anyone, and he impressed people, gaining one contract after another. Most competing company teams used two types of people, one for the martini drinking, one for the technical details. O'Malley did both.

But everything they had planned together, all of their best estimates, was completely overshadowed by a totally new development. Four countries—Norway, Belgium, Denmark, and the Netherlands—had signed up to buy 348 F-16s for more than $2.1 billion. Every one of those countries wanted to share in the coproduction, and few of them had contacts with more than one or two of the almost fifty U.S. suppliers. They all had experience working with Pratt & Whitney and General Dynamics, but they were at a loss when it came to lower tier producers.

That's where O'Malley scored the most; he had a wide network in the United States and spent his days linking up U.S. producers with their foreign counterparts, always with a contract generated for ActOn in the process. The work kept him so busy that he was looking for a new hire who could handle the GPS side of their business.

O'Malley was back in town, and now breezed into his office, slapping a wad of papers down on top of the stack confronting Rodriquez.

"Here we are, Bob; five new contracts. Three of them are for F-16 simulators."

Rodriquez's jaw dropped. "What are you talking about, Steve? That's not our bailiwick! Nancy Shannon will go through the roof when she hears this, she'll think we are poaching on her turf."

"And we are. The reason we are is because she's let the simulator end of her business slide. After you left, there was no one there to push it. The result is she's not competitive, and I don't think she cares."

"I'll tell you who will care. It will be Tom. He's always hated me, and now something like this will infuriate him. I don't know what you were thinking of, you know all this."

"Right, Roberto, I do, and I did it deliberately. Nancy Shannon is running the company into the ground; she's lost millions on that stupid mall she got involved in, and now she's being sued for millions more. Vance Shannon, Incorporated, didn't have a prayer of getting these contracts for simulators. If I didn't bid on them, they would have gone to Link or some other big simulator outfit, pure and simple."

Rodriquez shook his head, not convinced. "Let me think about this a bit."

He glanced at the clock and said, "Let's watch the news, and see how our boys are getting along with the Russkies up in space."

The Apollo Soyuz Test Project was a sign of the growing spirit of détente between the United States and the Soviet Union. An American Apollo spacecraft, virtually identical to the one that had orbited the Moon, had launched on July 15. It was to meet the standard Soviet Soyuz vehicle, already in orbit. To join up, they needed a universal docking module to serve as an airlock and a transfer corridor between the two spacecraft. Rodriquez had helped in the design and construction of the docking module.

The first story was a hit-and-run accident in Sunnyvale, but the news switched to a fuzzy view of the American astronauts floating easily in space and grinning for the camera as they shook hands with their rather glum Soviet counterparts.

O'Malley asked, "Do you know those guys?"

"I know Tom Stafford pretty well. I haven't met Brand, but everybody's pulling for Slayton."

"Deke" Slayton had been one of the original seven astronauts, slated to fly in the Mercury program, but pulled off because of a suspected heart problem. He'd persevered, and here he was, fourteen years later, in space at last.

"You'd think there was a KGB man on board, the way the Russians are acting."

"Maybe not on board, but you can be damn sure they are on the ground watching. One slipup, one smile in the wrong place, and there would be no more cosmonaut program for these guys. They have to be careful."

The news switched to local matters again, and Rodriquez flicked the set off.

"This brings up a good point, Steve. NASA has this monster space shuttle program coming along, and we haven't been doing anything with it. It's going to be slow, but it's the future of manned spaceflight, no doubt about it."

O'Malley nodded. "Problem is, I'm like Vance; unless it's got wings, I don't like it."

"Well, the Space Shuttle will have wings; it will be the world's biggest glider, no doubt about it. But where does ActOn fit in?"

"We've got our hands full now, with more and more F-16s being sold every day, but you're right, we have to look ahead. The F-16 program will go on for years, but our edge, our entry to it, probably has peaked, and we'll need to replace it with other business. Problem is, I feel out of the loop with the Space Shuttle. We know people at NASA and at Rockwell, too, but it's not like the aircraft industry, where we know people everywhere."

Rodriquez nodded. "And don't forget the GPS. It's starting slow, but it will accelerate. Getting some Space Shuttle business might be tough, but for one thing, it would keep us out of Nancy Shannon's hair. She won't have any interest in this at all, nor will Tom or Harry. I'm more worried about these simulator contracts; it's like a declaration of war."

O'Malley, his usual cheerful smile stretching from ear to ear, said, "Don't worry about it, old son. I'll personally guarantee that there's no problem with these. I've got to go—I need to get home, get showered, and get to the airport, I've got a meeting back in Amsterdam tomorrow afternoon."

Rodriquez almost had the last word. "No more simulator contracts."

O'Malley turned. "Wrong. More simulator contracts. And wait here one second. I'm going to introduce you to somebody you'll be glad to meet."

He left the room, returning with a tall, lean young man of serious demeanor.

"Bob, I want you to meet Dennis Jenkins. He started out as an

Army chopper pilot and wound up working as a test pilot for Northrop on the YF-17. How he did that, I'll never know. But the great thing is he knows more about space than you and I and the rest of the company put together."

Jenkins shrugged his shoulders and stuck out his hand.

"I'm glad to meet you, Mr. Rodriquez; Steve has told me a lot about you. Of course I knew quite a bit, for I've been following your work in simulators and precision weapons."

O'Malley's cheerful voice broke in, "Dennis is going to be our point man on the GPS and the Space Shuttle. He's young, but he's well connected, and unlike you or me, he can write. We are going to need a whole new approach to proposals on these projects, and we need somebody who can speak the language."

Rodriquez smiled; O'Malley vouching for the man was enough for him.

"Did you two talk salaries?"

"Not yet. I told Dennis that you would be fair. I'll leave you two now, I've got to get to the airport."

For the next hour the two men talked about Jenkins's prospective projects, Rodriquez periodically pouring coffee from a seemingly bottomless silver carafe on his crowded desk.

"Where do we stand on GPS right now?" Rodriquez was more than well informed; he had fathered the program, before seeing it taken over by the services. He wanted to see how up-to-date Jenkins was.

Jenkins was cautious, formulating his words. "As you know, the Department of Defense designated the Air Force as lead on a multiservice program; they called it the 'Defense Navigation Satellite System.'"

Rodriquez nodded, saying, "Didn't they cobble together the Air Force, Army, and the Navy approaches?"

"Exactly! I never met General Ken Schultz, but the Air Force owes him a lot, because he appointed Colonel Bradford Parkinson—and I know Brad quite well—to manage the joint program to develop the GPS. Brad was able to synthesize all the various competing systems into one. He played the services like a menu in a Chinese restaurant, taking one from column A and one from column B, picking the most useful from each one."

Jenkins took a swallow from the cup of coffee Rodriquez had given him.

"I don't think anyone else could have done it. The Army, the Navy, the Air Force, all had ideas about how to do it, and they all had vested interests, of course, you know how the advocacy system works. But Brad chose to use the atomic clocks, higher orbits, the right number of satellites, and the correct frequencies for the digital signals—and melded it into what they now call the NavStar Ground Positioning System. And he got everybody to agree on what to do."

"How many satellites are going to be involved?"

Dennis hesitated again, sorting out what he knew to be classified from material that had been released.

"Ultimately there will be twenty-four, with backups, but it will take years to get them all set up. The Air Force will start launching satellites—they're calling it 'Block 1'—in 1978, and will do it for about seven years. Then there will be follow-on programs to get it up to its planned size."

"Tell me again how it's supposed to work?"

Irritation crossed Jenkins's face. He knew Rodriquez was well versed in GPS, and realized he was being tested, but resented it being on such a fundamental level. Then he recognized that this was after all an interview, that Rodriquez didn't know him, and that he was the interviewee. He smiled and said, "Well, I'm sure you know all this, so I'll give you the blue-plate special version. Ultimately there will be twenty-four global positioning satellites in orbit, twelve thousand miles above the Earth. There will be three spares. Each one will circle the Earth twice a day, and at any given time, at least four will be available for ground receivers to interrogate. The GPS receiver locates three or four of the satellites, and figures out the distance to each one. This information is used to deduce its own location. In other words, it's the old standby of navigation, trilateration."

Rodriquez had sensed Jenkins's irritation and its passing, and realized it was justified. The man knew his business; if he had known less he would have explained a lot more, trying to cover. Then an idea flashed into Rodriquez's head.

"Are they going to be equipped with detectors for nuclear explosions?"

Jenkins's voice was approving. "Not to my knowledge. That's a great idea."

"That might be our best way back into the program. Maybe you and I can work on it a little. What do you think the biggest hazards are with GPS?"

Dennis smiled. "That's easy. The budget. This thing is going to take millions of dollars over a lot of years—billions, ultimately—and it will be a long time before it proves itself. It is going to take real sales-manship to keep it in front of Congress until it's operational. Once it's up and running, though, it will be invaluable, not just for the military, for everybody."

"What are the civil applications?"

"Again, that's easy—game hunters will want them first, then when the equipment downsizes a bit, pilots will have to have it. They'll be sticking them in cars in twenty years or less. It is going to be an im-mense market."

Rodriquez shifted gears. "How about the Space Shuttle? Is it go-ing to fly, literally and program-wise?"

Jenkins was cautious again. "It's got a lot to prove. I'm worried about the glide tests, when they separate the Space Shuttle from the 747 carrier plane—that is filled with risks. But I'm more concerned in the long run about the sheer size and number of rockets they are going to use to lift an operational Shuttle from Cape Canaveral."

"The Russians use even bigger ones."

"Yes, and they blow up regularly, but no one hears about it because of the security. I wouldn't worry if they were going to launch just one or two a year, but they are talking about making up to four launches a month. I don't see how it will be physically possible."

"Cutting to the chase, do you see any way we can make money in the program?"

"Well, certainly there can be some important consulting contracts. But I think the main money might come in creating some specialized firms that could handle the problems that are bound to come up with the launch equipment, with the foam covering, with the electronic suites in Houston—there isn't any national infrastructure yet to cover this. If we—I mean if you—get in early, you can probably position yourself for the life of the Shuttle program."

" 'We' is the correct term, Dennis. You are hired, if you're willing to work for the piddling salaries we pay here. Welcome aboard. We are going to get our share of those markets and more!"

"One thing you ought to know, Mr. Rodriquez."

"Call me Bob, we're informal here at ActOn."

"I know that you and the Shannons were close friends, and that there was some kind of falling out. I don't know and don't care what it was. But I need to tell you that I was young V. R.'s instructor pilot when he was in basic flight training. It was only for about two months, but we got to be friends, and still are. It's no problem for me, but I thought you should know."

"It's no problem for me either, Dennis. I consider the Shannons as friends, even Tom, who was never very happy with me. And I admire Tom, for all he's done for his country. I like V. R., too, and I want him to remain good friends with my own son, Rod. So don't worry about the Shannon connection."

"Thanks, Bob. I'm glad to be on board."

April 6, 1976
Palos Verdes, California

"DID YOU SEE the news?"

Tom Shannon looked up, weary-eyed from working at the same desk where his father had put in so many hours.

"About what, Harry?"

"Howard Hughes is dead. He died on board the airplane that was bringing him back to the United States. According to the stories, he was a physical wreck, skin and bones, hair long, nails grown out, the usual reports on him."

Tom tossed a Cross pencil on the tabletop. He bought about ten of the chrome sets each year, managing to lose either a pen or a pencil about every two weeks.

"Did you ever meet him?"

"Yeah, one time early in the war I came home on leave, 1942, I think, and Dad had an appointment to see him. He asked me to come along, not to meet the great man but for protection."

"Protection?"

"Yeah, Hughes insisted on meeting at odd places. This time he wanted to meet down by the waterfront at three o'clock in the morning. Dad didn't want to get mugged waiting for him, and apparently he was always showing up late. When Hughes saw me with Dad, he had a fit until he saw I was in uniform. Probably thought I was a lawyer. After that he was as nice as could be, very rational, talking about the Lockheed Constellation, getting Dad's ideas on how the flight test program should be run."

"I've heard he was like that—always pleasant but only willing to talk to experts in the field, and only about their special subject."

"If there's a heaven, I wonder if he and Dad will get together up there and talk airplanes."

"If there's a heaven, it will have to have airplanes and airplane talk in it for Dad. And he'll be too busy talking to Wilbur and Orville to talk to Hughes."

They were silent for a while, both knowing how much they missed their father's advice.

"We could sure use him now."

"We'd never have gotten into this fix, if he'd been alive and well."

Tom shrugged. "It's my fault, all the way. I never should have volunteered for another tour of combat. It was stupid, just ego and being pissed off about Rodriquez. If I'd stayed here, I'd have avoided my years in the Hanoi Hilton and maybe my wife wouldn't have taken over our company."

Harry didn't comment. It was true. Tom had been foolish to go to war again, and even though he had done well until he was shot down, it would have been better for his country—and a lot better for his family—if he had stayed home.

"What are we going to do, Tom? We can't just fire Nancy. She did a lot of good for the company, too, at a time when you were gone, Dad was sick, and I was preoccupied with keeping Anna sober."

"Well, let's review the bidding. We are in deep trouble now with her precious mall and with some of her other pet diversification projects. I don't see that we can do anything but cut our losses there, just sell out for whatever we can get, pennies on the dollar, and eat the difference."

"Nancy will never stand for that. That's the whole problem, she's committed to seeing it through, no matter what."

Tom sighed and said, "The end of our fiscal year will be coming up in October, and we'll have the annual stockholders meeting. I suggest we put it to the board of directors that we get a new chairman and CEO and that we end our participation in the mall project."

"You can't do that. She's your wife. It's tantamount to a divorce."

"I don't think it will come to that. The stress of the mall situation is killing her, and she's embarrassed that she placed the company in this position. I think she would actually be kind of grateful if we forced her hand in this. In any event, Harry, it's got to be done, and it will be the best thing for her."

"Have we got the votes to make it stick? You know she has the single largest amount of stock in the company. She has spent all her income acquiring it, and she never lets me forget it."

"That's what I've been going over. If the rest of us put our stock together, we have almost as much as she has. It's a good thing that she insisted on separate holdings for you and for her, otherwise we'd be screwed. But the irony is that the key votes, the swing vote, in this will come from Rodriquez. That son of a bitch manages to be the worm in every rose, even when he doesn't intend to. If we can get him to agree to vote with us, we can remove her as the chairman and CEO and get out of this godforsaken mall tragedy."

Harry tipped back in the chair and snorted. "And why would he do that? He's been snapping up our customers right and left for the past year. I thought the simulator business was just a fluke, but he's going after all our customers."

Tom shook his head. "I never thought I'd say this, but I can't blame him. He sees what's happening to us, and if he doesn't take the contracts, somebody else will. Like they said in *The Godfather*, it is just business. Will you go and sound him out?"

"Well, it's a cinch you can't go; you've hated his guts for so long that he'd have to be a saint to do you a favor. I've always liked Bob, and always gotten along with him. And to tell you the truth, I'll be surprised if he refuses to help out on this. He's not that kind of guy. And O'Malley won't refuse. He still idolizes you, just like he did when he was a cadet at the Academy."

"They know they will be putting a rival back in business, for I swear to you, if—when—Nancy steps down, I'm going to make sure that you replace her. Then I'm going to make sure that Vance Shannon, Incorporated, gets back on top where Dad would want it to be."

Harry smiled.

"The funny thing about that is that Dad would never have wanted his company to be this big. He'd have much preferred to have stayed small, doing the things he liked to do, testing new airplanes."

Tom shook his head. "He did it to himself when he took Rodriquez in to look after the electronic end. That's what screwed things up."

"Naw, Tom, that's just a parochial view. Dad had the best of his testing world when he was young, but as he got older, aviation matured. The world changed and he changed with it; the funny thing is that he changed faster than his kids. You and I haven't caught up to his vision yet."

"The problem was, his vision was Rodriquez, and Rodriquez took us too far too fast. Again, it's my fault. If I'd been home, tending to business like he wanted me to, it never would have happened."

"Time to stop moaning and bitching, Tom. Nancy is not going to take this lying down; we better get our ducks in a row before she suspects anything. It's a hell of a note to tell you to keep this from your wife, but you'll have to, or she will hit the roof."

"I hope you are wrong, my brother, because I'm going to tell her tonight. I think she will fold if I tell her that we are united against her."

"Not tonight, Tom. Don't tell her a damn thing until I talk to Rodriquez. If you do, and she talks to him first, you and I might be out looking for a job. At our age, it won't be fun."

Harry shook his head for a moment, then laughed.

"Look at us, Tom. Nancy is about five foot four and weighs no more than 120 pounds, I guess, and we are both scared of her. We've both been in combat, you were a POW, and this little wisp of a woman terrifies us. What the hell is going on?"

"The problem is they condition us to love them and then it's all over, they win every round. They are tougher than we are. Believe me, I hope I'm right and that she wants to quit. If she doesn't we are in for one hell of a fight."

"Well, let's hope Rodriquez is willing to help."

"I've got to find him first. He's all over the map, between pushing the F-16 program, and this new thing, the Space Shuttle."

"The sooner the better."

CHAPTER FOUR

THE PASSING PARADE: Mao Tse-tung dies, estimated to have caused deaths of up to 20 million; uprising in Soweto, South Africa; United States celebrates 200th anniversary of independence; National Air & Space Museum opens; President Gerald Ford and Jimmy Carter engage in debates; Carter elected President; North and South Vietnam reunited; Israelis rescue hostages in Entebbe raid; *Rocky* wins Oscar for best picture; Soviets win 152 medals in Olympics at Innsbruck and Montreal; Cincinnati Reds defeat New York Yankees in World Series; Deng Xiaoping restored to power in China.

September 17, 1976
Palmdale, California

*H*arry, I know you think I've been dodging you, but I haven't. We've been swamped on this program, and I haven't had a free hour, much less a free day, all year."

It was easy for Shannon to believe him. Rodriquez was hunched over a portable typewriter, pecking away at a report, wearing a two-day beard and a rumpled suit, looking thin and desperately tired under the desert sun.

"I understand, Bob, and I wouldn't have hassled you, but time is running out. We've got a board of directors meeting coming up in October, and I needed to talk to you before then."

"I guess I know why. There are no secrets in the aerospace industry.

And since that short piece in *Aviation Week*, everybody is talking about the trouble Nancy is having. What can I do to help?"

Aviation Week was the world's premier aviation magazine, known familiarly as *"Aviation Leak"* for all the secrets it uncovered. It had run a half-page article on the problems at Vance Shannon, Incorporated. Nancy had been treated courteously, but they laid the facts out in a straightforward manner, and all the knowledgeable people in the industry made the correct inference: with Vance Shannon dead and Bob Rodriquez gone, the company was in trouble.

Harry's heart jumped. This was the Rodriquez of old, always obliging.

"Bob, we need . . ."

Rodriquez held up his hand. "Just a second, Harry—they're rolling her out."

The doors of Rockwell's huge Air Force Plant 42 opened, and the incredible Space Shuttle *Enterprise* was slowly rolled out to stormy applause from the crowd of two thousand, mostly workers and industry insiders, but with a wealth of dignitaries and a colorful sprinkling of "Trekkees" gathered to see their vehicle come to life. The orbiter, officially serial number OV-101, was originally going to be named *Constitution*, in honor of the United States' Constitution, but a write-in campaign from more than 100,000 loyal viewers of *Star Trek* forced the White House to select the name *Enterprise* instead.

Harry's jaw dropped. He'd seen photos of the 150,000-pound *Enterprise*, but viewing it in gleaming white real life on the familiar Palmdale tarmac was another matter.

"It's gigantic, Bob. Are they really going to be able to fly it on the 747?"

"Harry, if they can't, my company's in real trouble. Steve O'Malley, me, and our new guy, Dennis Jenkins, have been working night and day on this, letting some of the rest of our business slide, and unless this lash-up works, we are in deep kimchee."

They stood together quietly for a while, watching the team of technicians swarm around the gigantic orbiter, while another gang, photographers and television people, formed an even bigger outer ring. With its huge nose and stubby delta wings, the *Enterprise* looked like an aerodynamic throwback when compared to the variety of sleek jets that were parked around the Palmdale tarmac, all of them needle-nosed with swept-back wings.

Bob said, "In January they are going to transport it overland to Edwards; they'll mate it with the 747 there and run a bunch of test flights. They'll start off with just flying the two aircraft together, which is frightening enough, but then it will get really hairy! They'll launch the *Enterprise* from the back of the 747, and it will glide down to land at Edwards."

"Who do they have lined up for the test crews?"

"The best—Fred Haise and Gordon Fullerton form one crew and Joe Engle and Dick Truly form the other. Talk about talent! Haise was on Apollo 13, and helped engineer their safe return."

Rodriquez took Shannon's arm and steered him over to a NASA staff car sitting next to the factory entrance.

"Let's talk in here."

Harry gave him a completely frank rundown on the situation at Vance Shannon, Incorporated, sparing no details.

"She's pretty well exhausted our capital and you know how Vance never wanted to be in debt. Well, Nancy's hocked almost everything she owns, and is putting pressure on the rest of the family to do the same. Believe it or not, she actually asked me to agree to take a mortgage out on Dad's house in Palos Verdes. I told her I couldn't do it, it was just impossible to think how Dad would have felt about that. Fortunately, she hadn't even brought it up to Tom."

Rodriquez whistled. "Pretty bad. I knew there was trouble. I never thought it would be like this. How is Tom taking this?"

Harry leveled with him. "As crazy as it sounds, I think this is a good thing for Tom. He's getting his confidence back as his strength builds up, and he wants to take the reins away from Nancy. He loves her as much as ever, but it galls him that she's running the company into the ground."

"Will he object to me helping? God knows he's been pissed off at me since day one, and I don't want to get into any problems with him now. I'm too busy, and frankly, I'm fed up with it. I've got enough problems of my own without warring with Tom."

"No, it's just the opposite. He's sorry about the past, and he knows we can't win this fight without your support. You may not be bosom buddies after this, but the feud will be over, believe me."

"Let me think about this, just for a minute. And I need to talk to Steve O'Malley, first, you know. He's my partner, and I'm not sure he'll be happy with me setting up your outfit as a rival again. Our guys have been picking up a lot of your business. Making you competitive again isn't going to help our bottom line."

"I understand that, Bob. It is a hell of a thing to even ask you to do this. But I know how you feel about Vance, and the rest of the Shannons, even Tom. I'm counting on you to see your way clear to helping out and voting with us."

"What if we don't?"

"Then I think the company breaks up; Tom and I will split off, and Nancy will probably run it the rest of the way into the ground. Dad will be rolling over in his grave, watching everything he built up go to pot."

"I'll call you tonight. Will you be back in Palos Verdes or are you staying over?"

"I'm going back. I'll be in Dad's old office by about seven tonight. I'll look forward to hearing from you."

September 17, 1976
Palos Verdes, California

HARRY WAS ENSCONCED in his dad's huge leather armchair, his feet on the ottoman, his hand near the phone, waiting for Rodriquez to call.

Anna came in with a plate of sandwiches and a glass of iced tea.

"You got a touch of suntan today, honey."

"It's almost always sunny at Palmdale. I wish you could have been there to see the Space Shuttle. It is going to be fantastic. And it's just the first step."

Anna nodded, pleasantly, her lack of interest manifest. Years of falling off the wagon and then laboriously climbing back on had taken its toll on her looks and her attention span.

The phone rang and Harry grabbed it, heaving a sigh of relief when he heard Rodriquez's voice.

"Harry, I've talked this over with Steve. He's concerned that bailing you out will put Vance Shannon back in business again, and that you'll be a real competitor. He's right. I've got a real conflict of interest here."

Harry's heart constricted. This wasn't what he expected.

"Yes, I see that, Bob."

"But there's a way out. How is Shannon stock doing now? I haven't checked it in weeks."

"It's way down, Bob, about four dollars a share, down from forty-four, two years ago."

"Well, I'll tell you what. I'll sell you all my shares—I've got close to a million shares now, give or take some—at whatever the market is at close of business tomorrow. Can you raise that kind of cash?"

"You're damn right we can! Our bank will loan me the money, they already know what we plan to do. This is very generous of you, Bob—I think we'll come out of this slump if we change the management, and our share price will go back up."

"I believe that, too, Harry, but I frankly don't care about the money. I just cannot have this divided loyalty between the welfare of your firm and the welfare of our firm. And I'm not, I'm absolutely not going to cast a deciding vote that splits up the Shannon family. I'd rather sell at a loss. You guys were always too good to me, always excepting Tom, of course."

"I accept your offer, Bob, because it's the only way out for us. We have to get back to doing what we are good at, and get out of this diversification mishmash that we're in now."

"I understand, Harry, but from now on, we are competitors, and Steve and I are going to do our best to get all the business we can. If it means running Vance Shannon, Incorporated, into the ground, we are going to have to do it. We're going public this year, and we won't be calling the shots like we used to. Do you understand that?"

"Sure, Bob, that's the way it has to be."

"Make sure Tom understands. There's nothing personal about this, but from now on, it's all business, down and dirty."

"We understand. And thanks, Bob; you could have made it a lot harder than you did."

"Take care, Harry. Give my best to everybody." Rodriquez hung up.

Harry leaned back in the leather chair, happier than he had been in months. There were lots of competitors out there, but there was lots of business, too. If they could get Vance Shannon, Incorporated, back on track, they would get their share.

He picked up the phone to call Tom with the good news.

March 24, 1977
Tinker Air Force Base, Oklahoma

HALF OF THE personnel of the gigantic Tinker Air Force Base was on hand waiting to receive the Boeing E-3 Sentry, the first of the AWACS to reach the 552nd Airborne Warning and Control Wing. Not by chance, Harry Shannon and Bob Rodriquez were on board. Harry had worked extensively with Boeing on the massive thirty-foot-diameter rotating dome that sat atop a modified Boeing 707 airframe, and the Air Force asked him to be on this delivery flight. Rodriquez helped in developing the fantastic radar system that could range out for more than 250 miles to detect, identify, and track enemy aircraft in a 120,000-square-mile area. He'd also devised the massive liquid cooling equipment that the hot-running electronics required. And in the back of his mind, he knew that when GPS came along, it would enhance the AWACS's capability immensely.

It was a magnificent weapons system, and they were already calling it a "force multiplier." One AWACS could direct all the fighters in a battle, sending them where they were most needed, warning them of threats, lining them up with tankers. It was sort of like the English chain-link radar system that helped win the Battle of Britain, but airborne, so it could be sent all over the world to any battle area. The incredible thing was that it had been hotly opposed for all of its existence by people in Congress who had no idea of its capabilities, but called it the usual "billion-dollar boondoggle" for political reasons. Harry and Bob knew that it would pay for itself the first day it went to war.

The usual first flight glitches had kept them occupied for most of the trip out from Seattle—the cooling system was difficult to regulate—but by the time they were inbound to Tinker, they had a chance to catch up.

"How did the board of directors meeting go last October, Harry? Everything I've heard says it was very peaceful."

"It was peaceful on the day of the board meeting, but a nightmare on the thirteenth, the day before. Tom decided to keep Nancy out of the loop until then. She knew something was happening, but had no idea that we were going to call for her replacement. When Tom told her that I was going to take over her position, she burst into tears and had a fit of hysteria. He'd never seen her like that before, although some of us had a few times, when things didn't go her way."

"Tough on Tom, eh?"

"Yeah, it went on for about an hour, with her alternating between crying and making threats, or so he tells me. Then all of a sudden, she bursts into tears again, throws herself into his arms, and says she was glad it was over. She said she would voluntarily resign, and throw her votes, even all her proxies, whichever way Tom said."

"Must have been a relief for everybody."

"Yeah, except for the fact that I don't really want the job. I hate the paperwork involved. But Tom refuses to take it, says he's too hotheaded, and he's right. But I wish you had stayed with the firm, and you could take over. You're a lot better at this modern stuff"—he waved his hand around the equipment packed fuselage of the AWACS—"than I am."

"Tom would never have stood for that, Harry. Nancy was bad enough, I would have been intolerable to him."

They talked for a while about the Shannons, then Harry asked, "How many of these big buckets do you think they'll build?"

"Not enough—too expensive. The Air Force is talking about buying sixty-four; if it winds up with half that it will be lucky. But we'll sell a few to the NATO countries, and Japan, maybe."

"Well, I can see where your strategy for your company is better than ours. We get in on the initial production run, but you are there for the updates."

Rodriquez nodded. "Exactly, it's the same with the B-52, they'll constantly be adding new equipment to the old airframes."

Harry Shannon shook his head.

"Yeah, we're doing better at that, but we've got a long way to go. You know, this business about adding new equipment to old airframes, Bob, Dad told us exactly that so many years ago. Somehow Tom and I never got the message. We've got to shift gears faster if we are going to make it."

"That's what worries, me, Harry. We've already seen how much better you are doing. You've picked up a few contracts lately that we thought we had sewn up. The Vance Shannon name still means a lot. If you guys stick to your new business plan, you'll do well, even though the market's in a decline. And the better you do, the tougher it will be for ActOn. It is not easy as it is; we are locked into some long-term development stuff that is all outlay and no income for years."

Harry knew he was talking about the GPS system, but didn't let on. There was no way Vance Shannon, Incorporated, was getting into something as far out as the GPS, not for a while, anyway.

"Well, we blew it on the Space Shuttle. We haven't had any contracts so far, but we're working with Rockwell to help on some of the maintenance efforts down at Cape Canaveral. There should be some money in that."

"Yeah, we're looking at it, too."

They were quiet as the AWACS finally touched down, its tires squeaking on the long Tinker runway.

Then, embarrassed, Rodriquez asked, "You hear anything from Mae?"

"Nancy and Anna do. I'm glad you brought that up. Mae's been asking about working with us. How would you feel about that?"

Rodriquez bristled. "She doesn't need to work for anybody, not with the settlement I made and the alimony I pay her. I can't believe that she asked you about a job. It's humiliating."

"She didn't ask me, Bob, or Tom, she's too sensitive to do that. But she's been friends with Jill and the other two girls for years. It's sort of natural that she'd ask them for a job if she wanted to work. And she knew that Jill would go to Nancy for her. Maybe she's bored."

Shaking his head angrily, Rodriquez yelled, "No it's not that! She's doing this deliberately to embarrass me. There are a million other places she could work."

Shannon had never seen Rodriquez like this, not even when Tom used to ride him hard. Furious, hand shaking, spittle spraying from his lips, he pressed his face up close to Harry's.

"I can't stop you, but it would be a big mistake for you to hire her. How would it make me look? I can't keep her as a wife, and she goes off to work at my old company so she can work for a competitor. It's like you guys can get along with her and I can't."

Shannon didn't speak for a while. Rodriquez was ready to fly off the handle right there on the flight line. After a bit, he said, "I understand how you feel, Bob. You were first rate with us about selling your stock. We'll abide by your wishes on this. But I tell you, it won't be easy, I'll get pressured from Jill and Anna for sure, and maybe Nancy, too."

Rodriquez left without saying good-bye. It was totally unlike him. He was reacting more to Mae's asking the Shannons for a job than he had to her divorcing him.

As Shannon walked toward Base Operations, carrying his battered B-4 bag and his parachute, he whistled softly to himself.

"Thank God this didn't come up before he sold us the shares."

August 12, 1977
Edwards Air Force Base, California

FROM A DISTANCE, a stranger might have thought the two men were brothers. Both were just over six feet tall, with medium builds and blond hair bleached almost white from the desert sun. Both men bristled with unbounded energy.

"We probably shouldn't even be talking to each other!"

Vance Robert Shannon—V. R. to his friends—punched Dennis Jenkins in the shoulder as they stood in the yellow communications van, listening to the crisp, to the point communications between the Space Shuttle *Enterprise* and its 747 SCA—the Shuttle Carrier Aircraft. Registered N905NA, the big 747 had a special mount on its fuselage top to carry the orbiters, and was modified with huge square fixed surfaces on its horizontal stabilizer to compensate for the additional side area when the Shuttle was on board.

"I don't think even my old man would care and Harry certainly would not. He thinks the world of Rodriquez, O'Malley, and the rest of you ActOn warriors. Quiet now, listen. This is the big payoff to lots of testing."

The 747/*Enterprise* had already done three taxi tests and eight captive flights, testing the systems and pushing the speed and altitude envelopes. Now they were going to undertake the most hazardous test so far—the separation of the two aircraft. The 747 would pull clear, and if everything went well, the shuttle would commence a less than six-minute glide back down to the long runway at Edwards.

On board the OV-101, the *Enterprise*, Fred Haise and Charles "Gordon" Fullerton were calmly going through their prelaunch checklist, interacting as necessary with Fitz Fulton and Tom McMurtry in the 747.

Jenkins nudged Shannon with his elbow.

"Not much emotion, eh? From the tone of their voices, you'd think they were taking inventory in a hardware store instead of flying the biggest glider in history."

V. R. nodded, knowing as Jenkins did that all four men aboard the 747/Shuttle combination knew very well that their lives might all come to a blazing end in the next few minutes if the separation didn't go as planned. Anything could go wrong—some of the explosive bolts might not fire, the Shuttle might pitch down or the 747 might pitch up, and in either case a catastrophic collision could occur.

There were precedents for "piggyback" aircraft like this that went back as far as the British Shorts composite experiments in 1937, when they mounted a twin-float, four-engine aircraft on top of a four-engine flying boat. Later, the Germans had used the concept to place fighters, Messerschmitt 109s, or Focke Wulf 190s, on top of explosive-laden unpiloted twin-engine bombers. But nothing on this scale had ever been attempted—a 150,000-pound Shuttle coupled to a 350,000-pound 747. The problem was exacerbated because the two aircraft were of such different types. The four-engine 747 had a long relatively narrow fuselage and swept-back wings, while the Space Shuttle had a stubby fat fuselage and short delta wings. There had been many hours spent in wind tunnels analyzing the airflow and the probable separation paths, but until it actually took place, no one knew for sure what might happen.

Jenkins had an encyclopedic memory for everything about the Air Force's test programs and, being a fan of "Fitz" Fulton, said, "After all Fitz's done, this must seem like a piece of cake. He flew combat in Korea, test-flew the XB-70, flew the launch B-52 for almost all the rocket-powered planes from the X-1 to the X-15, set an altitude record in the B-58, my God, he's done it all."

V. R. had a touch of his father's cynicism, replying, "No matter, he's sweating right now, hoping that the Shuttle launches clean from his 747."

Fulton's voice came on loud and clear. "We're at 24,100 feet, airspeed 310. Nosing over."

Fitz pushed the 747's nose over a scant seven degrees. Haise, in the *Enterprise*, called "Launch" as he pressed the switch detonating the seven explosive bolts that held the two aircraft together.

The two gigantic planes parted cleanly, the brief wisp of white smoke from the explosive bolts vanishing in an instant. Haise raised the nose of the *Enterprise* two degrees, then entered a twenty-degree bank, letting the nose drop down to establish an airspeed of 238 mph for the silent glide back to Edwards's runway 17.

Fulton's voice came on, saying dryly, "We're clear. Shuttle launched."

Inside the Orbiter there was no conversation as Haise established a nine-degree nose-down attitude and executed two ninety-degree turns to position the Shuttle for the steep final approach.

Shannon and Jenkins were outside the communications van now, watching the white *Enterprise* dropping like a stone toward the runway.

Jenkins whispered, "Man, when they say final approach, they mean final approach—no go-around allowed."

Haise opened the speed brakes, then seconds later rotated the aircraft so that it slowed to 213 mph just as the main gear of the *Enterprise* touched the desert floor. Inside the Shuttle, Fullerton gave Haise a thumbs-up as they rolled for more than eleven thousand feet down the runway at Rogers Dry Lake, using minimum braking.

Shannon glanced at his watch. "Five minutes and twenty-one seconds. They'll have a hard time racking enough time to earn their flight pay at that rate."

The two men walked back toward Jenkins's dusty Corvette, its seats already hot from the early-morning sun.

"How on earth did you get into the test pilot school, V. R.? It seems like yesterday when I was yelling at you for overcontrolling the Tweetybird."

Jenkins had been V. R.'s instructor in Cessna T-37s during his basic training at Columbus Air Force Base.

"I'm not kidding myself a bit. If my name wasn't Shannon, I wouldn't have had a prayer. But your boss, Steve O'Malley, is an old friend of my dad's. The first thing he did was get me jobs where I built up a lot of flight time in F-4s and even some in the F-15. I flew my ass off, but I've logged about two thousand hours of fighter time, and most of my classmates barely have five hundred. He even got me assigned to instructing Israeli pilots when they got their first F-15Cs. Then he did a little persuading with people he knew who were on the selection committee for my test pilot class."

V. R. stopped, obviously embarrassed, but determined to tell Jenkins the whole story. He went on. "I don't think it's right for things to happen like this, and I'd be pissed off it was happening to someone else, but I'm going to take advantage of it anyway."

Jenkins understood. It was the way the world worked, and it was certainly the way things worked in the Air Force. Having a patron wasn't an automatic key to success—you still had to be good, to be able to deliver the goods. But having a patron opened doors that might otherwise be closed.

"You interested in being an astronaut?"

"No, not really. I'm old school, just like my granddad; if it doesn't have wings, I'm not too interested."

Jenkins nodded.

"That may change. They have some interesting programs coming up with the shuttle, they are even talking about a space station some-day. Then they certainly will try to get weapons into space."

"That might be worth something. But those long-term programs get canceled—look at Dyna-Soar and the MOL; the Air Force spent a lot of money on both, and then DOD canceled them."

Jenkins nodded. Both projects, the Dyna-Soar and the Manned Orbiting Laboratory, would have put pilots into space for military purposes, and both were entirely feasible. But each one had fallen prey to other budget needs.

V. R. went on. "And besides, there's some interesting things coming up on the flying end, and I think you know exactly what I mean."

That ended the discussion. Both men did know exactly what was meant. The Air Force was looking for some way to beat the incredible integrated air defense systems that the Soviet Union had built up in its own territory, and then farmed out to its satellites. The Soviet system included comprehensive, redundant radar sites, tens of thousands of surface-to-air missile sites, and a huge number of interceptors. The Air Force wanted to neutralize the Soviet system, and the best way to do that was to neutralize its radar. Both Vance Shannon, Incorporated, and ActOn were subcontractors to Lockheed and Northrop, respec-tively on "black" projects that were supposed to lead to that goal.

The thought struck Jenkins that Shannon really shouldn't have known anything about the project; Harry or Tom would not have told him. The only way he might know would be through the test pilot school side. He started to ask, and then stopped. It was just too damn sensitive even for old friends to discuss.

CHAPTER FIVE

THE PASSING PARADE: President Carter makes human rights part of U.S. foreign policy; Ed Koch elected Mayor of New York City; Leonid Brezhnev becomes President of Soviet Union; punk rock music gains favor; George Lucas's *Star Wars* starts new film trend; *Voyager 1* and *Voyager 2* launched, en route to Jupiter and Saturn; United States and China establish diplomatic relations; Pope Paul VI dead at 80; mass cult suicide in Jonestown, Guyana; Dolly Parton named country singing entertainer of the year; *The Deer Hunter* wins Oscar as best picture; Shah leaves Iran after tumultuous year; Ayatollah Khomeini takes over; nuclear power accident at Three Mile Island.

April 6, 1978
Palos Verdes, California

What in the world is America coming to, Tom? Did you see where Frank Borman has leased twenty-five Airbus A300s for Eastern? Can you imagine what's going on at Boeing? I can see Mal Stamper tearing out his hair."

"What's left of it! I'm more worried about what is going on with Rodriquez and that ActOn outfit he runs. They have a lot of connections in Europe because of the F-16 program. I'll bet they are tied in to Airbus, lock, stock, and barrel."

Harry Shannon shook his head.

"Airbus is subsidized by the French government, so it probably gave Borman a price they knew that Boeing couldn't match, just to buy in."

Tom, always argumentative, came back, "Yeah, but Boeing gets a lot of military contracts. That's a form of subsidy, too, though they would deny it. I hate to see a foreign airliner on American routes, but maybe it will be good for competition."

"Like you said, though, it's going to be good for competition, but it's going to be *our* competition, ActOn. I'll bet O'Malley is on this like a herd of turtles, picking up contracts, making deals on both sides of the Atlantic. We'll do pretty well with Pan American. They've ordered five hundred million dollars' worth of Lockheed L-1011s, and we stand to clean up fitting out their interiors. That's something even you have to give Rodriquez credit for, Tom, getting us into the business of doing the interiors of aircraft, not just their external equipment."

Tom scowled. "I never said he wasn't smart. But he sure wasn't smart about telling us not to hire Mae. That crossed the line as far as I was concerned."

Harry scoffed to himself. Rodriquez had crossed Tom's line so many times in the past that the business with Mae was a trifle. Harry had honored his word: Vance Shannon, Incorporated, had not hired her, but Nancy had put her in charge of one of the residual businesses that was left over from the shopping mall debacle, and she was doing well. It was essentially a real estate office, but specializing in arranging mortgages and investigating titles. Mae had learned the business in six months, and was now operating on her own and was salvaging many of the properties that Nancy had given up on.

"Getting back to the L-1011s—you know the market is not big enough for it and the DC-10, too. McDonnell Douglas is already in trouble on the commercial side, and I don't think the DC-9 can save them forever. The two companies should have merged and just produced one airplane or the other."

Tom crumpled up the sheet of paper he had been writing on and tossed it in the wastepaper basket, saying, "Two points! They were way too proud for that. I think Douglas might have done it once, but Lockheed, never. But say they had pulled it off, they had merged, which one would you have wanted to see them build?"

Harry didn't hesitate a second. "The L-1011. They call it the TriStar, you know, and it's a much more modern aircraft than the DC-10. Douglas was in a hurry to catch up, and used way too much

DC-8 technology in the DC-10. Lockheed had been out of the commercial business so long that they could start with a clean sheet of paper.
But they may be in trouble yet; the Rolls-Royce engine they chose is
not coming along as it should."

He paused for a gulp of water and went on. "You know, Tom, I
feel badly about the whole deal. Some years ago I did an analysis for
Boeing that showed clearly that the total market for a smaller wide-
body airliner was about fifteen hundred aircraft. I wish now that I had
made a stronger pitch on the subject to both Lockheed and Douglas
management."

"Harry, they wouldn't have listened. They have a lot of smart guys
in their marketing department, and there's been a lot of competition
between Lockheed and Douglas ever since the Connie was bucking
the DC-6."

"Yeah, but the big problem is that the breakeven point for either
company was about 750 aircraft. So if they divide the market
equally—which is probably what will happen—both are doomed to
lose a bundle on the project. If one captures most of the market, it
might make a little, but the other firm will be ruined. And Boeing is
doing a much better job than anyone thought selling 747s, some to the
very market that the L-1011 and DC-10 are aiming for. I still think if
I could have gotten to their top management, I could have convinced
them."

"Spilt milk, Harry, forget about it. We've got a long way to go to
get our own company on its feet, so stop worrying about those guys.
We've never done as well on the commercial side as we have on the
military side, anyway. It's time we were concentrating on some new
military projects."

Both men knew that there was a revolution in management taking
place in the United States Air Force. The Strategic Air Command was
for many years the fiefdom of the great Curtis LeMay, and he had
given SAC its character. But now, seventeen years after LeMay's departure, an erudite, soft-spoken, four-star general named Russell
Dougherty was changing things, imparting a new look to SAC management. He had shocked his wing commanders in one of his early
talks by saying, "There's nothing in your job description or mine that
requires either of us to be an unmitigated son of a bitch." It was

Dougherty's way of moving SAC from the authoritarian style that had been a necessity when LeMay had to whip SAC into shape at the start of the Cold War. Later SAC commanders had abused their authority and Dougherty saw that new methods were needed.

In the Tactical Air Command, the new mover and shaker was General Bill Creech, a perfectionist who demanded the best from everyone—especially himself. Since the Vietnam War, TAC had fallen on hard times, and it was going to take someone with Creech's drive and determination to make it an effective force again.

Tom continued. "I think we'll have an in with the Tactical Air Command. I know Bill Creech pretty well. He's not everybody's cup of tea—fighter pilots don't like to be told to shine their shoes and wear neckties all the time—but he's a hell of a leader and he knows combat. He flew 103 combat missions over Korea and another 177 over Vietnam."

"You had a lot of combat, too, Tom."

Harry never stopped trying to build Tom up. His ego, already badly deflated by his long prison stay, had been hurt even worse by his wife taking over the family business and almost destroying it. He was recovering from both shocks, but slowly.

"And that's why he'll talk to me. He's got some great new ideas. He hates the fact that we lost 397 F-105s in Vietnam. Creech is determined never to have losses like that again."

Harry looked at his brother fondly, wishing that their father could see how much strength he had regained. The more he became engaged in the business, the more he shook off the ravages of his time as a POW in North Vietnam.

Tom went on, visibly wound up, getting up and walking back and forth just as his father used to do when on to a new idea. But where Vance Shannon had walked with long, loping strides until his very last days, Tom's injuries from his POW days imparted a nautical roll to his walk.

"Creech gave a talk at one of my Air Force Association meetings. He says he is determined to see that we never again try to fight an integrated air defense system like the North Vietnamese had or that the Soviets have now. He says he wants to take away the advantage that radar and surface-to-air missiles give them. He absolutely never wants us to have to go in low to avoid SAMs, then get the shit shot out of us by antiaircraft. And he wants to take away the sanctuary that night gives the enemy. He says we used to fight all day in Vietnam, while the enemy stood down; then at night the enemy would move all their supplies, and we couldn't do much about it."

Tom was quiet for a moment, remembering his own time in Vietnamese skies, and the futile bomb runs he and his crews had made on jungle trails, risking a multi-million-dollar F-4 and two lives trying to pick off a three-thousand-dollar truck carrying two hundred dollars' worth of rice.

Harry spoke, "We've been in the antiradar business for a while, Tom, with our jamming equipment." He knew it was a mistake the minute he said it.

"Yeah, that's another achievement of our friend, our enemy, Bob Rodriquez. But that's old hat. We introduce some ECM equipment, the enemy introduces a counter, then we introduce a counter-counter. Creech wants the industry to come up with something entirely different, and the word is that the Air Force has Lockheed and Northrop working on it already in a couple of black programs."

"Black programs" were so secret that only a few people in key positions in Congress were briefed on them, and their budgets were kept totally out of public view.

Tom went on. "We've got to get in on this, right on the ground floor. One thing I think we can do is work on night-vision equipment. You know we acquired that little outfit up in Redmond, Washington. What was the name of it?"

"I remember because it was named after its founder, Richard Pierce—he called it 'Pierce the Night, Incorporated.' You think they have potential?"

"They do if we finance them, and get them the military contracts. I think they are mostly concerned with police work, hunters, things like that. If we can get them to raise their sights, look at airborne applications, we'd be on to something. I'd like to take this on as a special project, make it my kind of contribution, à la Bob Rodriquez."

"Go ahead. You can say what you want about Bob Rodriquez, but he's a great role model for taking new businesses and turning them into profit makers. Go for it."

Harry was delighted. This was exactly what Tom needed, a mission, something he could take on and claim for his own, something that hadn't been set up for him to do by Nancy or, worse, by Rod-riquez.

"OK, I'm on it. And let's get back to those black programs that we know Lockheed and Northrop are working. What can we find out about them?"

Harry was on the spot. Lockheed had called him in five years before, when the Air Force held its competition for a new aircraft that would be difficult for radar to see. The problem was that it was so secret that he could not even tell Tom without violating his oath. He had never even told his father—it was just too hush-hush. The situation was ludicrous, Tom was perfectly reliable, yet Harry was so conscious of the importance of what he was doing that he could not bring himself to give the secret away, not even to his brother.

"Well, you know Lockheed had a soft spot in its heart for Dad. Kelly Johnson and Ben Rich were always concerned about how you were doing in Vietnam. If Creech has Lockheed working on something, it has to be in the Skunk Works. Let me talk to Kelly and see if I can get something for us."

Tom nodded, and Harry felt another jerk of conscience. Even his last statement had been a bit of a lie. For some reason, Kelly was not a true believer in the new project, but Ben Rich was, and it was Ben who had hired him. Telling Tom he'd talk to Kelly was just a ruse, one he felt badly about.

Harry was about to walk out the door when he suddenly changed his mind. Tom was trustworthy, and this might be the sort of thing that would help bring him round.

"Tom, I've been bullshitting you. We've already got a handle on the project at Lockheed, and up to now, I haven't told you about it because, naturally, I'm sworn to secrecy; it's a black program. But if something happened to me, you'd need to know, and since you brought it up, I'm going to tell you. But you have to swear to me you'll never tell a soul that I mentioned this to you, not even after I get you cleared at Lockheed to discuss it. You've got to let on that everything you learn is absolutely new to you. Otherwise Kelly and Ben would come down on me like a ton of bricks and we'd be shoved out the door of the Skunk Works. Nobody, absolutely nobody, can know that I'm telling you this."

Tom was torn between being pissed off at being treated like an outsider and being elated to learn they already had an in on something he knew had to be important. He decided to roll gracefully with the news. "Of course. I'll never say a word to anybody."

Filled with guilty remorse, Harry came back to the desk and, in a low voice, said, "You know how the SR-71 is shaped. What you might not know is that its shape is not only for speed, it is also an attempt to reduce its radar signature. The shape, with the help of some of the radar-absorbing materials they used, succeeded in that. A B-52 has a radar cross section of more than a thousand square feet. Kelly cut that down to about eleven square feet in the SR-71. It was a tremendous achievement, especially at the speeds at which the SR-71 flies. By the time enemy radar picks the SR-71 up, it's already gone past, out of range."

"Yeah, but the enemy was always able to track the SR-71. They fired a lot of missiles at it. So it wasn't perfect, even though they never hit it."

"No, that's right, and worse, the Soviets spent a lot of money improving their radar network, getting their SAMs faster firing, and so on, just because of the SR-71. So what the Air Force wants is an airplane that will be invisible to radar. But it also has to be invisible to infrared seekers, and to sound detection, too. That's what we are working on. An airplane with a radar signature so low that it is virtually invisible electronically."

Tom snorted. "That's nuts. You'll never be able to do it."

"That's what Kelly Johnson thinks, too. But Ben Rich is taking over from Kelly, and he's staking his reputation on the idea. And back in 1973, the Air Force held a competition to see if a real stealth airplane was possible. They named the project 'Have Blue.' Northrop and some other companies competed for it, and Lockheed was not even invited to enter. But you know the Skunk Works, they never give up and they elbowed their way in. Lockheed and Northrop won. Then in the runoff for what they were calling the XST, the Lockheed entry was so much better than the Northrop entry that it was no contest. Northrop figured that it had to be stealthy from the front and below—Lockheed tried to make it stealthy from all angles—and they won the contest and built the prototypes. And just to give you an idea of how they regarded the airplane, the XST stood for 'Experimental Survivable Test Bed' meaning they thought it would be enough if the pilot survived flying it."

Tom laughed and Harry went on.

"It was the first plane designed by electrical engineers instead of aircraft designers; it had every stability sin in the book—longitudinal, directional, pitch-up, pitch-down, you name it. They joked that the only thing it didn't do was tip back on its tail when it was parked."

"How long have you been involved?"

"For about five years now. I'm running a very small subsection of the project, trying to speed up the construction of the test vehicles, mostly by selecting already manufactured parts for the prototypes, you know, picking the gear from a Northrop F-5, and the fly-by-wire system from the F-16, and so on. But I've put three carefully selected scientists on our staff at Palmdale, people who have tremendous math backgrounds, way beyond our capability. It takes people like that to understand what is going on."

Harry watched Tom closely. This was the sort of thing that, properly handled, might put Tom back in the saddle, directing things and making projects happen.

It was working. There was a new light in Tom's eyes as he asked, "Well, what's the theory behind it? Am I smart enough to learn if you tell me, or you too dumb to make me understand it?"

"Both, Tom. But I'll get someone in who can teach us both more about it. It won't be fun, but it's got to be done."

"Who are you thinking of?"

Harry smiled. "This will floor you, Tom, but it's V. R. He's been working the test program, even doing a little flying."

The old Tom surfaced, his face red with anger.

"Goddammit, my son and my brother in on a project, and nobody tells me! Sure, I'm just a shot-up old crock, but it looks like you could have given me a clue. How you two must have yakked it up behind my back."

"Tom, you know V. R. loves you more than anything and respects you as much as he loves you. So do I. When you get the full story, you'll see why we kept it quiet. And you'll see that I've really stuck my neck out here, tonight. This whole thing is potentially bigger than the Manhattan Project in terms of its effect on warfare. It's not something you can talk about lightly. Especially for V. R., just at the start of his career. Wait till he briefs you. You'll see what I mean."

Tom snorted, subsiding as he usually did when he realized he was making a jerk of himself.

"We'll see if I see."

December 31, 1978
Palos Verdes, California

JILL SHANNON TRIED to preserve the traditions that Vance had established, and every New Year's Eve held the same sort of party where Vance enjoyed recounting the year's events and the progress of his firm.

This year she decided to skip the business part. Nancy was still wounded from being forced out of the company's management. And worse, it was already obvious that there had been a dramatic improvement since Harry had taken over the reins.

Jill was looking forward to meeting the newest member of the family, V. R.'s new wife, Ginny. Although she had firmly resisted marriage for three years, Ginny finally gave in and eloped with V. R. the previous February. Jill understood her reluctance to marry V. R. Anybody marrying a Shannon man was going to play second fiddle to flying, and Ginny was too strong-willed for that—or so she thought. Even though V. R. was stationed somewhere in Nevada, in all the long months since the marriage he had not come home once with his bride.

So it was just as well that the Rodriquez family no longer attended, even though Mae worked for Nancy. Love of work, rather than flying, had broken up their marriage, and the last thing Ginny needed was another bad example of a ruined relationship. She had invited them all, but Bob, Sr., had not responded, and Mae had declined. Curiously, his son, Rod, accepted with obvious pleasure. He seemed determined to somehow build a bridge back between his father and the Shannons.

As always, she concentrated on the food and drink, serving Korbel champagne for those who drank and a nonalcoholic punch for Anna and Harry. This year she had started out with a Mexican theme, got overwhelmed making the tamales, and ended up having a caterer from San Diego's Old Town come in to handle everything. As she watched them setting up, she knew that Vance was looking down, shaking his head at the choice of food and the expense of having a caterer.

Jill was ill at ease for another reason. Earlier in the day, Harry had appeared with a strange little man who had a lot of electronic gear and proceeded to "sweep" the house. Harry explained to her that he was having a briefing later for Tom and V. R., and that he had to be sure the house wasn't "bugged." The term wasn't new to her, but she associated it more with spiders than spies.

The evening went well until about nine o'clock, with Ginny—five foot four, blond, and with a great sense of humor—charming everyone, particularly Tom, who seemed quite smitten with her. The only awkward moment came when Harry said that they had some business to take care of in Vance's private study, a little room off the library where he had a safe and kept his most confidential papers. He looked apologetically at Rod and said, "I'm sure you understand this is a business matter—I don't mean to be rude, but I can't invite you in with us."

"Harry, don't think a thing about it. I'm just going to talk to Ginny, drink some champagne, and have another run at the buffet."

It was apparent that he didn't mind, that he had a mission other than business there tonight, and that mission was reconciliation.

Harry went in, followed by Tom and V. R., and shut the door.

"He's a nice kid; I hope he can talk some sense into his dad."

Tom snorted and Harry went on. "As I told you, Tom, I went to Ben Rich to ask if V. R. could brief you on stealth. He told me to go to it."

V. R. was hesitant at first, not wishing to sound like a know-it-all in front of his father, an ace in two—and maybe three—wars, and a hero for surviving every nasty thing the North Vietnamese could do to a prisoner of war. But he had done the scariest flying of his life in the Lockheed Have Blue prototype, and the subject fascinated him.

"First of all, I'll give you a nonmathematician's point of view. There have been half a dozen people involved in creating a stealth aircraft. It all started with the work of a brilliant Russian mathematician who came up with the original formulas, and has no idea how we are using them. Then a genius named Denys Overholser was the first guy to understand what the Russian scientist paper signified as it applied to aircraft. He worked with Bill Schroeder, a Lockheed retiree who came up with the computer program to use the Russian's math.

"Schroeder figured out that a three-dimensional aircraft could be constructed by 'faceting,' using a series of flat panels placed so that they reflected radar waves away from the aircraft."

V. R. could tell by Tom's blank expression that he wasn't being understood. He glanced at Harry imploringly, and Harry said, "It turns out that if you build an aircraft out of flat plates that are always at thirty degrees to any incoming radar beam, you'll get a stealth aircraft."

Tom replied, "Yeah, but how the hell do you get an airplane built like that to fly?"

"That's been the problem, Dad. They came up with what looks like a paper airplane, but in three dimensions, and it would be impossible to fly it without the modern computers that react faster than a pilot can."

Harry broke in. "This is where Kelly Johnson and Ben Rich disagreed. Kelly just didn't believe you could get an operational aircraft shaped like the drawings they were using to fly. And he didn't believe the idea would work. But Ben put his neck on the line. This is his first big program on his own; if he makes it, it will be a cash cow for Lockheed for decades. But if he fails—he will be out on his ear."

V. R. went on. "And remember, it's not just the shape of the aircraft. They cover it with radar absorbent material they call 'RAM,' and it absorbs the radar energy that is not reflected away."

Tom nodded. "OK, give me a break. If all this works, how big is the airplane on the radar screens?"

"You mean how much of a radar signature does it have? Let me tell you a story. Ben Rich went into a briefing at the Pentagon, knowing he'd be asked that question. Now, he's not talking the prototypes anymore, not the 'Have Blues' as we've called them. Instead he's talking about a full-fledged fighter-bomber, equipped with missiles, bombs, whatever. When the general asked him, 'How big a radar signature does your airplane have,' Ben rolled a ball bearing the size of a marble on his desk and said, 'Here's the observability of our airplane on your radar.' Naturally, they didn't believe him. But he was right, and testing proved it. Faceting and RAM gets the whole airplane's radar signature down to the size of a marble. It's incredible."

Tom shook his head. "V. R., how dangerous is this? I don't want you getting killed flying some crazy invisible airplane."

"It's no joke, Dad. Flying these Have Blue prototypes is dangerous, no question about it. We've lost one already; Bill Park was the pilot, and he didn't get hurt, thank God. They don't have the computer capability of the full-size airplane, and there were a lot of shortcuts taken to get them in the air. But the real fighter bomber that Ben has planned won't be much more dangerous than any modern fighter. And in combat, it will be a lot safer, because the radar and the SAMs won't be able to see it. Anybody flying in to bomb an enemy will have a free ride."

V. R. laughed and said, "Actually, I'm in more danger of getting hurt by Ginny, for being away from her all the time. This thing is so secret, Dad, that they keep the remaining Have Blue inside its hangar almost all the time. When they know a Soviet spy satellite is making a pass, they keep it covered. And when they do roll it out for a flight, everyone on the field not cleared for the program has to go into a windowless mess hall and wait until we take off. Same for when we come back to land."

Tom pressed V. R. for some more details on his experiences flying the Have Blue prototypes, but they had reached a point where V. R. finally had to say, "Dad, I've told you all I can tell you. You'll learn more in a few years when all this is unclassified, but right now, I've got to stop."

With that, Tom turned to Harry and asked, "Where's the money in this? How can we profit out of this program?"

"That's the name of the game, isn't it? Right now it looks like they won't buy too many of the new fighter-bomber. It's just too expensive, and still unproven. But the ones they do buy will need lots of maintenance, particularly keeping their radar signature down. Any little thing—a gap in the landing-gear door covers, a crack in the RAM, and all of a sudden it shows up on the radar screen like a full-size airplane. So they will take lots of tender loving care between missions. I don't think the Air Force can afford to set up a full maintenance program for so small a number of airplanes, and that's where I think we can cash in. We'll subcontract to Lockheed to do the maintenance on the airplanes, wherever they are in the world. We can charge an arm and a leg, and it will still be cheaper to the Air Force than fielding its own specialized maintenance people."

Tom was still dubious. "A, the new plane has to fly. B, we have to get the contracts."

"We'll get from A to B, don't you worry, Tom. It's C, I'm worrying about."

"What's 'C'?"

"There's another stealth aircraft in the works, a bigger airplane, a bomber. And guess who's competing this time? Lockheed and Northrop again. We have to get our share of that contract, too, when the time comes."

Tom shook his head.

"I'd give anything to have Dad listening in on this, and telling us what to do."

March 12, 1979
The Pentagon, Washington, D.C.

DENNIS JENKINS WALKED slowly for a change, glad to submerge himself in the milling throng that crowded the Pentagon's mini-mall, a collection of stores that sold everything from aspirin (in big demand) to books (less so) to a wide selection of fast but not very good foods. Like the Pentagon's inner courtyard, it wasn't really away from the Pentagon, but it was different enough to offer a little escape from the long fluorescent lit corridors all jammed with uniformed figures running from one meeting to the next.

Steve O'Malley was waiting for him, wolfing down a hot dog and holding a cardboard cup of soda in his hand. Between O'Malley and his other boss, Bob Rodriquez, they kept Jenkins on the run across the country and around the world. ActOn was no longer a small company, but O'Malley and Rodriquez still ran it as if it were a mom and pop store, with their eyes on every detail.

"You heard the news about GPS, Dennis?"

Jenkins nodded. A Navy Lockheed P-3B Orion had flown from Hawaii to Moffett Field in six hours the day before, using the new NAVSTAR GPS satellite system. GPS revolutionized navigation—all the old techniques from the sextant to LORAN were now obsolete.

"It's the first olive out of the bottle, Steve. Pretty soon everybody will be using GPS. Why, they'll be sticking GPS in dog collars so you can tell where your mutt is when he runs away. Wives will be slipping GPS into their husbands' cars, so they'll know where they go at night."

O'Malley gave his trademark booming laugh and said, "Put them down in the 'future developments' file, Dennis. It'll be a little while before they shrink down that much, but you're right, it's coming."

They climbed the long ramps up toward the fifth-floor E ring, where the Undersecretary of Defense for Research and Engineering, Bill Perry, was holding a highly classified briefing.

"Do you know why Perry called this meeting, Steve?"

"I hear it's to level the playing field with the various contractors. He's going to tell everybody as much as he can about stealth research, so that there will be more competition. Right now, Lockheed and Northrop are way ahead of everybody else, and DOD wants to be sure that others can get in, so prices will come down a bit."

Smartly dressed Air Policemen were checking credentials at the door to the secure briefing room Perry had chosen. Jenkins nudged O'Malley.

"Look who's ahead of us in line. Tom Shannon and V. R."

O'Malley shook his head. "That's easy to figure out. Tom is here as a contractor to be briefed, of course. And V. R. is doing test work at Edwards, probably getting in position to fly the prototype stealth aircraft. I sort of got him on the fast track for that. Glad to see he's made captain."

They were able to exchange greetings with their competitors as they filed in to their assigned seats, O'Malley giving the "let's have a drink afterward" signal to Tom Shannon before they sat down.

Instead of the usual laundry lists of greetings and introductions, a door opened and Bill Perry walked in, moving directly to the podium, all business and intent on wasting no time.

Perry gave a brief history of the stealth program, pointing out its historical antecedents and the recent rise in research and development funding in the field. He pointed out that there was no single stealth technology, but that success lay in the proper synthesis of many technologies. Finally he admitted that there had been flight tests of some vehicles.

With that he folded his notes, said "Good day, gentlemen," and strode from the room.

The crowd was still for a moment and then there was a sudden uproar.

Tom Shannon was especially furious. "What the hell was that

about? We don't know any more now than before we came in. This whole thing was a waste of time."

He moved across the room to catch up with O'Malley and Jenkins.

"What do you think this was for, Steve? He had all of us come in, then tossed us a softball. I feel like submitting a voucher for time and travel expenses."

O'Malley shook his head as he was shaking Tom's hand.

"Tom, I don't know. The only thing I can think is that he had to get on the record about there being flight tests. Otherwise there was no point in the meeting."

Jenkins and V. R. were talking quietly.

"Tell me, V. R., do you know anything about the flight tests?"

"I'm like Sergeant Schultz, 'I know nothing.'" But it was obvious from the expression on his face that he did.

Jenkins excused himself and grabbed O'Malley's arm. He took him to the corner of the room and lowered his voice.

"There's something wrong here. I suspect one of the contractors is way ahead with stealth—but the government's afraid of giving it a monopoly. That tells me that the other contractor will win the next stealth contract—on the so-called Advanced Tactical Bomber."

O'Malley pondered this for a bit.

"We're pretty sure that Lockheed is ahead of us now on stealth; there's no hard evidence, it's just the way that the contracts are being handled. And Northrop's not getting the results it wants. So I guess the bad news is that we won't have much to do with the stealth fighter, and the good news is that we probably have a lock on the stealth bomber."

"I hope you're right, 'cause if you're wrong, ActOn won't have anything to act on in the stealth area at all."

CHAPTER SIX

THE PASSING PARADE: Margaret Thatcher, Conservative, becomes Prime Minister of Great Britain; Jane M. Byrne is first woman mayor of Chicago; Congress bails out Chrysler Corporation; Soviet Union invades Afghanistan; Sally Field wins Best Actress Oscar; "black hole" discovered in middle of Milky Way; Pope John Paul II tours United States; Mother Teresa awarded Nobel Prize; *Sweeney Todd* on Broadway; Sony "Walkman" tape player becomes fad.

June 27, 1979
Over Lebanon

V. R. Shannon jabbed his gloved finger under his oxygen mask, letting sweat trickle out, and wondered what the hell he was doing in the infamous "Battle Triangle" of Lebanon, instead of flying over the quiet reaches of Area 51 in Nevada. There he had only to fly the quirky Have Blue; here he was a no-man in a no-man's-land.

The sharp, quick communications from the Israeli Grumman E-2C Hawkeye reminded him: he was there to kill Syrian MiGs and bring back data to the USAF on the F-15's performance in combat. No one, not even his darling Ginny, knew where he was—the mission was too secret. The United States could never acknowledge that it had an active duty Air Force pilot flying combat missions with the Israeli Air Force. He carried no identification material at all—no papers, no dog tag, nothing—and he had made a not-too-cheery commitment not to be taken alive if he was shot down.

Security was strict even for security-minded Israel. He had been introduced to his suspicious fellow pilots simply as Captain S. It was pointless, because he had been the instructor pilot for two of them when the Israeli Air Force got its first F-15s. Then he had become quite friendly with Dan Shapira and Beba Hurevitz; both gave him a wink and a nod at the introduction, but said no more. The other two pilots remained polite but wary of him until the first two indoctrination flights, when he demonstrated his proficiency and his gunnery prowess. They all spoke English on the ground, but in the air language remained the big barrier despite his two-week crash course at the language school in Monterrey. There they had concentrated on flying terminology, much of it derived from English practice.

Now he was number four in a flight of F-15s, Shapira in the lead, cruising at twenty thousand feet where there were no contrails to give them away. Israel was conducting raids on terrorist bases in the areas under Syrian control, and the intercepted radio communications showed that the Syrian Air Force was active. An Israeli Grumman Hawkeye command and control airplane—a sort of "mini-AWACS"—was watching the area, alert for any reaction from Syria.

As they turned over Sidon, the Hawkeye radar operator called: "Turn to 360 degrees; two formations of MiG-21s."

Shannon knew that the MiGs were being sent to attack the Israeli F-4s striking PLO encampments. Strange war, with the F-4s being bombers and the F-15s their escort. He knew the Phantom pilots would prefer to handle the MiGs on their own, once they had dropped their ordnance. Minutes later V. R. picked up the two MiG formations on his own radar. On Shapira's command, the F-15s lit their afterburners and dropped down on the still unsuspecting Syrians.

The late-model MiG-21s, suddenly aware of the F-15s' presence, broke off their diving attack on the F-4s and turned to run. It was too late.

Heart pounding in his first combat, V. R. mumbled, "Dad, I hope I do as well as you did," and saw three MiGs already spiraling down, trailing smoke. As his accelerating F-15 moved into firing range, he locked on his target, fired his Shafir missile, and watched with satisfaction as it flew right up the Syrian MiG's tailpipe to explode. Seconds before there was a tiny camouflaged triangle of an airplane, flown by a living, breathing Syrian pilot; now there was just a big red ball surrounded by black smoke drifting above the barren landscape below.

As V. R. climbed back up to altitude, he was surprised to see his flight of F-15s form around him. The radio crackled and Shapira's voice came on: "Congratulations on your kill, Captain! You lead us back to base."

The flight back was less than thirty minutes. V. R. smiled all the way.

December 21, 1979
Edwards Air Force Base, California

HARRY SHANNON RECOGNIZED the slim, slightly stooped figure immediately. Once the maverick of swept-wing aviation, R. T. Jones was thin as ever, slightly stooped, and, Harry guessed, perhaps using a little Grecian Formula on his slicked-back hair.

"Dr. Jones, you won't remember me . . ."

"Harry Shannon! Of course I remember you! How could I forget Vance Shannon's son, after you flew me all over Europe?"

In the late spring of 1945, Harry had flown a C-47 carrying his father and the elite of American aeronautics deep into Europe to ferret out the secrets of the Luftwaffe. R. T. Jones, along with Theodore von Karman and others, had ruthlessly gone through the German engineering records, seeking whatever they could find that was in advance of American practice.

It had been a particularly satisfying trip for Jones, who had previously postulated that at very high speeds swept wings would have far less drag than straight wings, and been politely told by the National Advisory Committee for Aeronautics that he was dead wrong. Jones always felt that the NACA's negative reaction was in part because he was a self-taught engineer and did not fit the academic mold. But the German data—and German airplanes like the Messerschmitt Me 262—proved that Jones was absolutely right, and he gained his deserved stature in the engineering community as swept wings became standard for jets.

Jones said, "It was a great time. But I don't believe mankind has learned anything from the wars. Look what's going on in the Middle East. Poor people oppressed on all sides, and their sorry governments using hatred against Israel and the United States to take their minds off their poverty. What do you think of this business in Iran?"

On November 4, Iranian students under orders from the new Iranian government seized the United States embassy in Tehran and were now holding sixty-six U.S. citizens hostage. Jones's comment touched on a sensitive issue with Harry. Still outraged by the event, he forgot his usual policy of never talking politics, saying, "It doesn't make any sense. They think we are weak, because President Carter has kept chopping down the size of the military. Canceling the B-1 was bad, but it was just a symptom. You lose all international respect if the world knows you are willing to disarm unilaterally."

Jones nodded. "You'd have thought we'd have learned our lesson with Hitler. You've got to stop these rabble-rousers when they are still small, before they have too much influence."

"It will be interesting to see what the Soviet Union will do. They love to see us sucked into small wars. And they have a huge interest in the area, they have for centuries."

"We have to worry about Iraq, too. They are getting close to having a nuclear weapon, and if they have it, they'll use it—maybe against Iran, but more probably against Israel."

Both men shook their heads, silent now in their frustration, then Jones spoke, "I was sorry to learn of your father's passing, Harry."

"Yes, it was sad. But we are losing so many of the great ones now. Just in the last year or two, we've lost Willy Messerschmitt, Barnes Wallis, Bill Lear, Wernher von Braun—it is really sort of melancholy to be an engineer nowadays."

"Well, you're looking good, but you're just a kid of fifty or so, aren't you?"

"I wish—I'm sixty-one and cannot believe it. And you were born in 1910, I know, so you're ahead of the curve. And still pitching swept wings!"

Jones laughed. "No, this time, it's a swing wing. Look, here it comes now. Tom McMurtry is flying it—I hope all goes well."

Harry was there to witness the flight of the Ames-Dryden AD-1 oblique wing aircraft in the hope it would have some application to problems he was working on in a "deep black" black stealth aircraft program. Their research showed that range was a problem with stealth aircraft, and Jones's oblique wing innovation was a promising new approach.

They stood quietly as McMurtry taxied past, the two tiny jet engines putting out an ear-piercing whistle.

Harry noticed Jones shivering.

"It's cold for Palmdale, Dr. Jones; can't be much more than fifty degrees! Would you like my jacket? I'm feeling perfectly warm."

Jones shook his head, laughing. "No, I'm delighted it's cold. Those engines only put out about two hundred pounds of thrust each; the colder the temperature, the better they will perform. I wish it were freezing!"

Except for its size, the AD-1 was a perfectly ordinary-looking airplane. It had a slender clean fuselage, with a disproportionately large bubble canopy that seemed out of scale with the rest of the aircraft. The wings, designed to pivot at the center and lie almost parallel to the fuselage in flight, were narrow, very high aspect ratio, and from a quick glance had an unusual airfoil. Oddly enough, for a jet, it had a fixed tricycle landing gear.

Jones spoke up. "Look at that—thirty-two-foot wingspan, about fifteen hundred pounds gross weight—and McMurtry has flown everything from the 747 shuttle carrier aircraft to fighters. He must feel constricted in there."

Shannon nodded and Jones went on. "I opposed this test at first. We'd already proved the theory in model form, but somebody up the line insisted on a manned vehicle."

"Did you design it yourself?"

Jones shook his head. "No, the idea of an oblique wing, pivoting at the center, is mine, but Boeing came up with this configuration and it was built by the Ames Industrial Company up in Bohemia, New York. But I tell you, you can keep your eye out for a smart, up-and-coming company right here in California, run by a guy named Burt Rutan. Do you know him?"

Harry shook his head.

"Well, if you get nothing else out of this trip, go over to Mojave and tell him I sent you. I consider Burt to be the top aerodynamicist in the country now, and he combines it with a building savvy that is going to be impossible to beat. His outfit did all the detail design and load analysis on this plane."

Jones took out a tiny pair of binoculars to watch McMurtry take off.

"He cannot fool around. That thing doesn't carry much fuel."

Shannon watched as the AD-1 sped down the runway, lifted off far later than he thought it would, and climbed up to about a thousand feet.

Jones smiled at him.

"They won't do any dramatic testing today—McMurtry will just make sure it's a good airplane first. And it's not a good airplane, at least not when he gets around to swinging that wing fully back. It's going to be tough to handle. To tell you the truth, Harry, the oblique wing won't prove itself until you get to big airplanes, supersonic transports and"—he paused, smiled wickedly, and said—"stealth bombers."

Harry's mouth dropped just as a group of NASA engineers surrounded Jones and began congratulating him.

This was not good. Jones might just be guessing, but if he wasn't, there was a leak in the program somewhere. And how the hell did he know, or even suspect, that Harry had a part in the stealth bomber? This was not good.

July 12, 1980
Long Beach, California

"WHAT ARE WE doing working on a Saturday?"

"Like we don't work every Saturday and every Sunday, too, for that matter. Glad you could make it, Bob. We haven't had a chance to talk face-to-face for weeks."

They were sitting in Rodriquez's rental Chevy outside the chain-wire fence at the airport, windows rolled up, radio playing, air conditioner on in the eighty-degree sunshine, waiting for one of Steve O'Malley's longtime projects to take off. Steve had worked for years with the famous test pilot, Russ Schleeh, to sell the McDonnell Douglas KC-10 to the USAF as a tanker. After years of delay, the Air Force finally agreed to buy some.

O'Malley glanced cautiously around the interior of the Chevy; the backseat was filled with business magazines—*Forbes, Fortune*—and probably twenty different issues of *The Wall Street Journal*.

"What are you doing in this rental heap, Bob? And how come you let it get so dirty—it smells like you have a week of hamburger lunches back there."

"I don't own a car anymore. I'm in so many different cities during the course of the year, it's easier and cheaper just to rent all the time. And that stuff"—he pointed to the newspapers and magazines—"is how I make my real money. You can make money easier on Wall Street than you can in aviation, that's for sure."

"How do you know what to buy? I've got a few mutual funds, but I've no idea what they are worth. All my money is in the company."

"Big mistake, Steve. Playing the stock market is just a matter of watching the technology and picking the comers. It's really no different than what we try to do with our company, pick a technology and try to sell it. Except if you are smart, you can make a hundred times more in the stock market because you have a whole lot of people working for you, not just yourself and a few people in the company. You just ride on their backs."

"This is all new to me, Bob. When did you get interested in this stuff?"

"I've been doing it about ten years now. The divorce was a big setback, of course, I gave Mae half of everything. That's why it made me so angry when she said she had to go to work."

Rodriquez went silent, with the sullen look on his face that O'Malley had seen so often in the last year.

"Well, if you are beating the market, you're doing better than most people. The Dow Jones has been virtually flat."

"I don't buy the Dow. That's what the mutual funds do, mainly, and that's why they don't make any money. I buy shares in companies I think will do well. And, mostly they do. Anyway, I've got a lot more invested outside of our good old ActOn than I have in it, and I'm going to keep going in that direction. When I get enough, I'll jump ship and disappear."

O'Malley stared at him. It was an odd thing to say, totally untypical. And Rodriquez rarely joked. There was something behind this. He tried to change the subject.

"How is Rod doing?"

Rodriquez jumped as if O'Malley had stabbed with a needle.

"Don't mention him to me. He's sucking up to the Shannons, after I warned him about them. I think he'd go to work for them, too, if he wasn't scared that I'd cut him out of my will."

"Come on, Bob, that's nonsense! Your son is doing well with Lockheed, why on earth would he deliberately offend you? He's just being civil, that's all."

Rodriquez sat silently for a while, obviously offended, then asked, "How come you couldn't get admitted to the flight line? I thought you had an in here at Long Beach?"

"Not anymore, and it's a damn shame. I'll bet Russ and I walked a hundred miles together in corridors at the Pentagon, trying to sell the concept of a tanker that could do so much more than the KC-135, and getting a deaf ear everywhere. Now they are going to buy sixty, when they ought to be buying six hundred. But the wheels in St. Louis are pissed off at me now. You know how the rivalry goes between McDonnell brass and the poor remaining guys with the old Douglas company."

Rodriquez nodded. The five-sided wheel of the Pentagon rotated on the axle of advocacy, and it took dedicated advocates like Schleeh and O'Malley to sell a program. The problem was that not all the products being sold were as worthwhile as the KC-10, which was effective as a tanker and a cargo plane. If the advocates had good personalities and were skillful, they could sell a bad product and waste a lot of the taxpayers' money. The human factor. It was the same with the companies. The McDonnell Douglas merger had been billed as two equals coming together, but McDonnell rapidly took control of all of Douglas's activities, and there was still a lot of bad blood between the employees of the two firms.

O'Malley said, "I thought the accident in Chicago would kill the program."

The previous May, an American DC-10 crashed right after takeoff from O'Hare Airport in Chicago, killing 273 people. It brought back all the memories of the 1974 DC-10 accident near Paris, when 346 were killed.

"It damn near did! McDonnell Douglas was still working hard to fix things from the Paris crash when the Chicago accident came. I remember years ago, when we were still friends, Harry Shannon said that the DC-10 was rushed and had too much old DC-8 technology in it. I hope they caught up with the KC-10."

Nodding, O'Malley replied, "I know for sure that they did. Russ and I spent a lot of hours with their engineering bigwigs, checking out the changes they came up with after the accidents. You can never be 100 percent safe, even with the changes, but the tanker will be flying a different flight regime than the airliners. Far fewer takeoffs and landings, far less time in the air over the years."

They were quiet for a while, both men sensing the other had something he wanted to say, but was hesitating. Still stalling, Rodriquez spoke first.

"What do you think of the Iranian rescue fiasco?"

"It dooms Carter; he can't win the next election after this."

In April, the United States had attempted a military operation to rescue the fifty-odd hostages still held prisoner by the Iranians in the American embassy in Tehran.

"I understand you were called in to investigate. What can you tell me about it?"

"Bad planning, bad luck, and bad weather ruined it. They were too cocksure of themselves . . ."

"They?"

"The White House, Carter and his staff, kept interfering, wouldn't allow enough assets—they wanted to do it on the cheap, and when they ran into trouble there were no reserves."

"How bad was it?"

"Well, you know that eight men died and there were a lot of injured. What happened was that they planned to stage it over two nights, which was stupid in the first place. On the second night they were going to send in eight helicopters with troops to locate and rescue the hostages. The helicopters were to fly them out to where C-130s were prepositioned, and the C-130s would fly them to safety. Then two choppers got lost in a sandstorm and one had mechanical problems. They wound up without enough helicopters to carry out the mission. Worse luck, a helicopter crashed into a C-130—that's where the eight were killed. The shrapnel from the crash damaged five of the RH-53 choppers and they had to be left behind, filled with information that the Iranians used to run down CIA spies in Tehran. It was a complete fiasco."

"What's next?"

"I don't think Carter will try anything anymore. They won't negotiate with him, he hasn't the guts to call for a declaration of war, which is what it would take now. We'll have to wait it out."

They sat quietly now, watching the huge KC-10 ease down the taxiway, nose bobbing. This was not like a typical first flight, when there was always an escort of camera vehicles, fire engines, and communication vans. The basic KC-10 airframe had been proven in commercial service, so it was just another delivery to another customer as far as McDonnell Douglas was concerned.

Rodriquez pulled out a notebook and wrote down the date and tail number, 79-0433.

"I do this every first flight I attend. When I'm old and cranky, I'll go back in and look at the dates and the numbers, and remember how things were back in the good old days."

"You've always been cranky, Bob, you don't have to wait. Do you know who's flying it?"

"No, I'm just like you, out of the loop with the McDonnell Douglas people."

"Yeah, it's a shame. But between the GPS and the . . ."

O'Malley instinctively looked around, checking to be sure there was no one nearby. He knew the music from the radio would mask his voice—that's why they were playing it—but he still had to check before saying, ". . . stealth bomber, I don't get to cruise the companies anymore. I leave most of that to Dennis nowadays; he's a good schmoozer and he picks up a lot of good information."

Rodriquez nodded, waiting for him to go on. The conversation had finally gotten to the point O'Malley had been waiting for.

"Bob, I'm sorry to say that I think we've picked a loser in this stealth game. I'm especially sorry, because the concept tied in with so much of your work on precision munitions."

Rodriquez had been in the forefront of precision guided munitions for the past ten years. He saw PGMs, as they were called, as the only answer to the immense Soviet superiority in armor in Europe. If the Soviets ever decided to invade West Germany, on their way to the English Channel, there wouldn't be time for conventional warfare to work. There had to be target-specific bombs created, so that every bomb would kill a tank, not just one bomb out of a hundred.

"As you know, the DOD wanted an 'assault breaker' force—aircraft and helicopters armed with laser-guided bombs that could range back behind enemy lines and take out targets while they were still in their bunkers. And to do that, they asked for a stealth battlefield surveillance vehicle—they called it 'BSAX' for short—one that could loiter over the lines, invisible to the enemy radar, and pick out targets for the attack aircraft."

Rodriquez twitched impatiently. So far O'Malley wasn't telling him anything new. Most people in the business already knew, you could pick up so much, just reading the trades, if you knew what to look for. Put that together with casual conversations as you worked the companies, and it all came together.

"The DOD gave Northrop a 'pity' contract for the BSAX after they lost out to Lockheed on the Have Blue project. And Northrop blew it! Their BSAX design didn't cut it. But you know Fred Oshira?"

"Yes, he's a first-rate engineer."

"Well, Oshira saved them, he redesigned the aircraft, using totally new stealth ideas, and won a new contract for a flying prototype. They're calling it 'Tacit Blue' for some reason. I've seen the drawings, and it's an ugly bastard. Never thought I'd say that about an airplane, but there it is."

"How are they coming?"

"I've got no idea. The prototype won't fly for a couple of years. But if it's successful, it will be far more advanced than Lockheed's stealth fighter—a second generation of stealth, so to speak, third if you count the SR-71."

"Is it faceted like Lockheed's Have Blue?"

"No, and that's why I wanted to see you. Instead of facets, it's going to rely on sweeping curves in the structure and loads of radar absorbent material. That means the big bomber will probably be a flying wing, just like old Jack Northrop wanted."

Rodriquez waited for O'Malley to get to the point.

"And that's where I think we have to go. We've got to develop radar absorbent material, RAM—some that can be used structurally, some of it that just goes on easy and is durable. The stuff they have now reacts to heat in flight, and it can't take weather. A hailstorm will turn a stealth airplane from invisible to big as a barn door in just a few seconds."

"Do we have any specialists in this? This is brand-new stuff for ActOn. What's the market going to be?"

"I don't know. They are talking about buying 275 Advanced Tactical Bombers in the out years, you know ten years down the road. They'll be big, but the thing is, they will require intensive maintenance. We can't get in on the manufacturing subcontracting, not right away, but we can position ourselves for the future with new materials."

Rodriquez looked doubtful. There was something eating him. O'Malley had never seen him acting like this.

"I don't know, Steve. Sometimes I think we are too smart for our own good. We are out there, pushing GPS, pushing precision guided munitions, pushing stealth, while guys are making a fortune making nuts and bolts and spare parts. I buy stock in those types of companies, those and fast food chains, big hardware stores, and that sort of thing."

"Bob, you worrywart, I can't see you getting all worked up making nuts and bolts! You'd be out of your gourd in weeks. You're never happy unless you are on the next page, ahead of everybody else, including me. You'd rather go broke pushing something futuristic than making a fortune pushing something ordinary. Besides, the Air Force won't be the only customer. The Navy will need it for missiles and ships, and the Army will need it for missiles and tanks."

"Stealth battleships and stealth tanks. That will be the day."

"Maybe not battleships, but smaller missile launching ships for sure. And cruise missiles have to be redesigned for stealth. They are hard enough to shoot down now, but if you can give them stealth characteristics, they'll change the face of warfare."

Rodriquez seemed to sink deeper into his morose reserve.

"You know, Steve, I made a big mistake in bailing Tom and Harry Shannon out. I sold almost a million shares of Vance Shannon, Incorporated, at four dollars a share, and it's up to eight now."

O'Malley shook his head. Rodriquez had never talked about money before. Now it was all he was talking about. There was something going on with him. Still, he had always acted strangely when there was a big, tough project coming up.

"And what do they do after I bail them out? They go directly against my wishes and hire Mae."

O'Malley thought, *Ah, just as I suspected. It has nothing to do with money. He's still hurt over them hiring Mae. Jesus, how can I get out of this?*

Rodriquez went on, talking faster as he did when he was excited, a little spittle showing at the corner of his mouth.

"And now they are going to clean our clock in the stealth business. Well, I'm not going to let them. I haven't touched a penny of my money since the divorce. Like I said, Mae got half then, but my end has built back up, way up. I'm going to round up some investors and go back and make a hostile takeover bid for Vance Shannon, Incorporated. Then we'll see who hires who. Are you with me on this?"

This was the last thing O'Malley wanted, but he knew better than to cross Rodriquez when he was in a mood like this.

"I guess, Bob, if you think we can do it, but we've never done anything like this. I don't even know what a hostile takeover means. And I don't know if we have the resources to do it and keep our own business going. You know better than anyone how competitive it is in technology nowadays; you miss one thing and you're obsolete. And we've been way too rigid in our control, not delegating, keeping our hands in everything. We could take a lesson from Vance Shannon's book. You're where you are today because he delegated responsibility and authority and, best of all, control of the budget."

"That's exactly why we have to do this. We'll take them over, fire the old guys who are holding them back, and make some real money. We'll run the place like Vance used to do."

"Old guys? You mean Tom and Harry Shannon? We've got no beef with them. Tom is my hero, always has been since before I went to the Academy. And Harry has always been straight with us."

"Not so straight that he didn't OK hiring Mae. Don't tell me that Nancy did something they didn't approve of. You know better than that."

There was an edge to his voice that O'Malley had never heard before.

"You don't mean all this, Bob. You're just upset. We're not corporate raiders, we're just a couple of ex-pilots who like to make big new toys that go bang for the military."

"Not anymore. Like the old Hitler joke, no more Mr. Nice Guy; I'm going to run them into the ground, or die trying."

There it was, down and dirty.

"Well then, Bob, you'll probably have to do it without me. I don't want to get involved in something like this, not when there is so much important stuff going on in the defense industry. We could wind up spending all our money and have two ruined companies instead of one. You only have to be out of the business for six months nowadays, and you are out forever. What the hell would happen to our GPS contracts, our PGM business, our simulators, not to mention stealth?"

"If I have to do it without you, Steve, I will. You know the terms of our partnership."

The two men had a simple verbal contract. If one offered to buy the other out, he had to name a figure; if the other man chose, he could reverse the process and use that same figure to buy the first man out.

O'Malley nodded. "You mean you'll buy me out or make me buy you out?"

"You're right as usual, O'Malley. Think it over. Let me run some numbers and I'll get back to you. In the meantime, you better watch this takeoff. The KC-10 was your baby, and don't you forget it."

O'Malley turned to watch the tanker move swiftly down the runway. Maybe he'd made a mistake leaving the Air Force. Better to be a gray-haired colonel running the halls in the Pentagon than a corporate vulture trying to raid a friend's company.

CHAPTER SEVEN

THE PASSING PARADE: United States breaks diplomatic ties with Iran; Shah dies at age 60; Somoza thrown out as Nicaraguan ruler; Ronald Reagan elected President; John Lennon killed; Reagan inaugurated, Iran frees hostages; Sandra Day O'Connor becomes first woman on Supreme Court; air controllers strike; IBM personal computer marketed; Iraq wages war on Iran; AIDS is identified as killer disease; *Cats* on Broadway; laptop computers appear; Nintendo markets Donkey Kong; *Chariots of Fire* wins Oscar as best picture; the "mouse" introduced for computers; U.S. hockey team beats Russia for the gold in the Winter Olympics; *Columbia* space shuttle launched; John Hinckley attempts to assassinate Ronald Reagan; Princess Grace of Monaco dies after a car accident.

June 9, 1981
The Pentagon, Washington, D.C.

Sweat stained the back of O'Malley's shirt as he hurtled down the hallways, elbowing past idling three-stars and jumping over a long low trailer hauling stacks of unread computer printouts. It was sort of funny—everybody else ran—two-stars, one-stars, and below—but the three-stars just ignored everybody as they strolled along, their major and lieutenant colonel worker-bees awkwardly following behind, unable to run because their bosses walked. You rarely saw a four-star in the hallways.

Puffing, he thought to himself, *Here I am, not gray yet, but an old colonel running down the corridors, just like I said I would never do.*

He pulled up short outside "the Tank," the classified briefing room in the basement of the Pentagon, to check that his ID was hung around his neck, reflecting with pleasure as he always did, *But at least I'm the richest son of a bitch of a colonel running around here!*

O'Malley, as usual, arrived ten minutes too early for the meeting. He could have sauntered down, maybe had a cup of coffee, for meetings here in the bowels of the Pentagon always started late. But he ran for the sheer joy of being back in the Air Force and away from the bitter infighting between Bob Rodriquez and the Shannons over control of Vance Shannon, Incorporated.

His mind flashed back to the previous September. Bob Rodriquez had not yet made a formal offer to buy him out, but O'Malley knew that his partner was neglecting ActOn business to fly around the country, gathering support for his planned takeover raid on the huge business Vance Shannon had founded. Then, early one Saturday morning, Rodriquez turned up at his little two-story house in Manhattan Beach. Steve's wife Sally (the bane of her life were the inevitable bad jokes about Sally O'Malley—she was born Sally Brennan) was at church, and he wished he'd gone with her.

Rodriquez didn't fool around, going straight to the point, refusing an invitation to come in—he just stood on the little porch, feet spread in a pugilist's stance, face intent with barely suppressed emotion.

"Steve, I've gathered support all around the country from enough shareholders to have ActOn make a buyout bid to take over Vance Shannon, Incorporated. Are you with me?"

"You know how I feel about that, Bob. You are going to force me out of our company. I won't participate in a hostile bid on a friend's firm."

"They are not my friends, and if they are your friends, you are no longer my friend. It's just as well that you get out now. Can I assume that you will abide by our verbal agreement about a buyout?"

O'Malley was tired. He knew this was coming, and resented it.

"Of course, Bob, I'm offended that you would even ask. What is your offer?"

"Fourteen million cash. For every share you own. That's about twenty percent over the market value, if you figure it out."

O'Malley had already figured it out; now he tried to figure out how he could get out of the situation. He stalled, trying to see if there was any way he could come up with enough cash for a counteroffer.

According to the terms of their agreement, if he could raise fourteen million, beg borrow or steal, he could buy ActOn out from under Rodriquez. And he could do that by selling his own shares. It would depress the market, but not by twenty percent. So he could sell his own shares to generate the money to buy Rodriquez out.

But there was a fundamental problem. ActOn without O'Malley would prosper; ActOn without Rodriquez would probably curl up and die. Even running around the country, fighting to get control of Vance Shannon, Incorporated, Bob was getting more business for ActOn than anyone else could.

"Do Tom and Harry know what you are trying to do?"

"Yes, I kept it secret for a while, but there was no way I could get the support I needed without them knowing. They know."

"Well, I accept your offer, but I'm telling you now that I oppose what you are doing, and I'll support Harry and Tom to the end. You are making a big mistake, and worse, an unnecessary mistake, for all the wrong reasons."

"Spare me your philosophy, Steve. You've been a big help in getting ActOn running, but now it's time for you to go. Help them if you want, I don't give a damn."

Rodriquez, always the soul of courtesy in the past, didn't even nod good-bye, spinning on his heel to sprint down the curved concrete path to his rental beater.

Steve walked back into his house and made two phone calls. Harry Shannon answered the first one.

"Harry, if Tom's there can you get him on an extension?"

"Steve, good to hear from you. Tom's out with Nancy at church. He hasn't missed Mass since he's been back from the Hanoi Hilton; says he owes a lot to the Lord."

"We all do, Harry. I guess you know what Rodriquez has been doing?"

"Yeah, it looks like a proxy fight. I hate to see it, but it's having a good effect on Tom. He's a fighter, you know, and he's always wanted to get Rodriquez in his sights. This thing is a tonic for him."

O'Malley let out a sigh of relief.

"That's great. And you tell Tom that Bob has bought me out, lock, stock, and barrel. I refused to take part in the raid."

"Great, we'll hire you today!"

"No thanks, Harry, and good luck. I've got other plans."

And Harry had nailed it. "I'll bet your next phone call is to Lew Allen!"

O'Malley laughed at the memory. Harry was exactly right. His next call was to the erudite Chief of Staff, General Lew Allen, begging to be recalled into the Air Force on some special assignment. Allen, after giving him a long lecture about the evils of the military industrial complex's revolving door, had orders cut, recalling him and assigning him to his own staff in the Pentagon. And as much as Sally hated moving out of California and back to Washington, she was happy for him.

Their one point of difference was his attitude toward money. Selling his share of ActOn had not only freed him to do what he really wanted to do—get back in the Air Force—it lined his pocket with millions of dollars that he promptly invested in government bonds. Not much return, but safe so that he didn't have to worry about it. And, to Sally's dismay, he insisted that they live mostly on what he earned as a colonel, just to stay part of the Air Force crowd, buying a tract house in Annandale, near the beltway, rather than something more expensive close in. O'Malley wanted his decisions evaluated on their merit, not his bank account. He liked the Air Force life, and he knew that he could never get back in the swing of it if he flashed a lot of money around.

The Air Police guard outside the door to the "Tank" suddenly stood up, and O'Malley turned to watch the group of beaten-looking colonels and generals filing out—their briefing must have gone badly.

The guard smiled sympathetically and said, "Your turn in the barrel, Colonel O'Malley."

Inside the oppressive, ill-ventilated Tank, there was a long center table, surrounded by rows of chairs that reached backward and up to the dimly lit ceiling. O'Malley put his hastily prepared briefing on the podium and checked through his vue graphs one more time. Nothing was deadlier to a briefing than an out-of-place vue graph.

It was good being tight with the Shannons again. If he hadn't had the close connection with V. R. Shannon, he'd never have the inside information he had on these celluloid sheets, the documentation of the air drama over Iraq. He had sponsored V. R.'s early assignments, and V. R. had proved himself. Now Tom Shannon's son was being shuttled around the Air Force from one tough job to another, alternating between the stealth programs and liaison work with the Israeli Air Force.

The latter was not a one-way street by any means. The United States was supplying the Israeli Air Force with aircraft and ordnance, but Israel was developing its own armament industry and perfecting some combat techniques for the F-16 that the USAF could use.

He smiled with pleasure at the thought that it was his airplane, the lightweight F-16, which the Israelis had used with such deadly effect against the Iraqi nuclear facility at Osirak.

The room stirred as the Chief walked in with his small staff. Unlike most previous Air Force Chiefs of Staff, Lew Allen had never seen combat or even served overseas. But he was a giant intellect, a scientist, and exactly what the Air Force needed now that President Reagan was committed to expanding the armed services. Tall, bald, wearing a heavy set of glasses, he gave a friendly professorial nod and O'Malley began his briefing with the usual courtesies before launching into the first vue graph.

"As we all know, the Iraqis used French fiscal and engineering assistance to build the Osirak nuclear facility, with the clear intent of producing nuclear weapons."

O'Malley tapped on the image with his pointer and said, "The Iraqis planned a forty-megawatt light-water nuclear reactor in place at the Al Tuwaitha Nuclear Center. It is about eleven miles southeast of Baghdad. Construction began in the late 1970s. The initial name for the reactor was Osiris, after the Egyptian god of the dead. The French renamed it Osiraq, to combine the name of the god and the country into one."

He called "Next" and the unflappable Master Sergeant Dave Menard flipped the chart, showing a map of the area. He had worked with Menard, an airplane history nut, in the past, and was glad to have him with him now. No incorrect charts, no upside-down tables, with Menard.

"The Israeli government engaged in intense diplomatic activity trying to stop the Iraqis from proceeding with the development of a nuclear weapon. France declined to help; it was actively engaged in providing the Iraqis weapons in exchange for oil. Italy also refused to intervene, for much the same reason, oil."

There was a general murmuring in the audience—O'Malley could not make out the discussion, but assumed it was comment on France's continuing opposition to Israel.

"The Israeli Cabinet was informed that a shipment of ninety

kilograms of enriched uranium rods was being sent by France to Iraq. They knew that as soon as the rods were placed into the reactor, the danger of radioactive fallout from an attack would be unacceptable. A decision was made to attack the reactor before it went 'hot' to avoid excessive fallout. In consultation with his cabinet—and against some bitter internal political opposition—Israeli Prime Minister Menachem Begin ordered the Israeli Air Force to eliminate the facility. The Israelis believed that Iraqi nuclear weapons would be fatal to their existence. Begin reportedly said that 'he will not be the man in whose time there will be a second Holocaust.'

"Next vue graph, please.

"The Israeli Air Force attacked on 7 June 1981, using six McDonnell Douglas F-15s for escort and eight General Dynamics F-16s for the attacking force."

He called "Next," and said, "First takeoffs were at 15:55 local time—that would be 12:55 Greenwich. They launched from Etzion Air Base in the Negev, the closest Israeli air base to Iraq. The force flew over Jordanian, Saudi Arabian, and Iraqi airspace at about 750 feet altitude to make the attack. There is unconfirmed word that Jordan's King Hussein was vacationing in Aqaba. He reportedly saw the low-level Israeli aircraft flying over and personally tried to phone Saddam Hussein to warn him of a probable attack. Fortunately for the Israelis he could not get the call through.

"Next vue graph, please.

"Here is their route—660 miles at low level, popping up at 17:35.

"Next one, please.

"The actual attack took one minute and twenty seconds. This photo is from the last F-16 to attack, and shows that the reactor is in ruins, its concrete ceiling caved in. The Iraqis had been caught by surprise, and their antiaircraft defense was ineffective.

"Next one.

"Each F-16 carried two unguided Mark 84 two-thousand-pound bombs, with time-delay fusing. They also carried external tanks, which was a potential problem.

"Next chart.

"The external tanks were not designed to be jettisoned while the airplane was still loaded with Mark 84s; fortunately, they dropped them over the Saudi desert without incident. When they were about to enter Iraqi airspace, they dropped down to about one hundred feet. Two F-15s stayed with them as close escort; the other four climbed in different directions in Iraqi airspace to create a diversion, and to engage any airborne Iraqi aircraft. Such an engagement would have been fatal to the Israeli planes, as they did not have enough fuel to enter combat and get home.

"At 17:35 Israeli time, about twelve miles out from the nuclear reactor, the F-16s climbed to seven thousand feet. They acquired the target, and dove at about six hundred knots indicated, releasing their weapons at thirty-five hundred feet. The airplanes had about a five-second separation between them; all bombs hit the target, but two failed to detonate. All the Israeli aircraft immediately climbed to altitude—forty thousand feet, I understand—for the trip home."

O'Malley nodded to Menard to shut the vue-graph projector off.

"Any questions, sir?"

There was a dead silence; until Allen spoke, his staff would stay quiet.

Finally Allen stood up slowly and said, "There's been adverse political reaction to the strike all around the world. We've been helping Iraq in its war on Iran. I know you aren't a political analyst, Steve, but your briefing shows you have sources. What's your take on this?"

Caught unprepared, O'Malley hesitated, then said, "Let me comment on the technical aspects first. The mission was brilliantly executed by the top pilots in the Israeli Air Force. They pulled it off without having to use in-flight refueling. Probably no air force in the world, besides our own and the RAF, could have done it."

He paused, still frantically gathering his thoughts.

"But politically it's a mix. Inside Israel, everyone's delighted with the short-term results. But some are worried that Israel is blinded by the Holocaust syndrome. Others are worried that the Iraqis will just start over, and this time bury the facility so that it cannot be attacked."

Allen interrupted him. "I didn't mean your take on Israel. What is your take on the effect on the United States?"

"We'll probably never have to fight Iraq; but if we do, it's better for Israel and the U.S. for them not to have nukes. And better for the Iraqis as well."

Allen nodded, stood up, and strode out, his staff following.

Menard looked up. "Good briefing, Colonel, all except for that last part."

"You mean about us fighting Iraq?"

"Yeah, like that will ever happen. We've got the Israelis there to clean their clocks."

"You may be right, Dave. I hope you are."

December 31, 1981
Palos Verdes, California

TOM SHANNON SAT at his father's big desk, laboriously typing a letter he was going to stuff into the envelopes of his Christmas cards. They were all signed, and would be going out the following Saturday, weeks later than his usual early November sending.

"This is the first year I've ever put a letter in the Christmas cards, but so much has happened, and I had to explain why I'm late. I hate being late. It makes you look like you are only sending out cards to people who have already sent you one!"

Harry responded, "You've got a lot to tell them, Tom. Just the big fight with Rodriquez alone would fill a couple of pages. And then you have to hit all the things that affected the company this year; at least with your old business friends."

"The fight with Rodriquez was just like combat, Harry. If you turn away from an attacking fighter, you are dead. You turn into him, guns blazing, and you have a better chance. It worked with Zeroes, it worked with MiGs, and it worked with Bob Rodriquez."

Harry watched his brother with pride. Eight years ago he had come home, literally a beaten man, savaged by more than six years as a prisoner of war in Hanoi. He was starved, his broken bones had not healed properly, and no one knew the extent of his psychological scars.

The first few years of his recovery were slow, in part because of the extent of the trauma, in part because of the death of his father, and in part because he felt emasculated that in his absence his wife Nancy had become chairman and CEO of Vance Shannon, Incorporated. He loved her, but he didn't want to work for her, and he resented the fact that neither he nor his twin Harry was running his father's company. He even resented Harry not taking over, just because he was preoccupied with his wife Anna's drinking problem.

All that changed when Nancy ran the company almost into the ground with failed real estate ventures. She called it "diversifying," but it almost gutted the firm until he and Harry engineered a coup to take over the company. In the process, Harry took over as chairman of the board, giving the CEO position to Tom. Then, in September 1980, Bob Rodriquez had openly announced his intention to acquire enough shares to take over Vance Shannon, Incorporated.

The announcement had been like an electric prod to Tom, who had never liked Rodriquez. He was yearning for combat again, just as in the old days when nothing could keep him from volunteering to fight in Korea or Vietnam. He couldn't fly fighters anymore, but he could sure as hell take on Rodriquez.

He insisted that Harry take over the role of CEO and then began a series of nationwide tours, soliciting votes from the major stockholders in Vance Shannon, Incorporated. Most of the individuals he saw were old friends, often retired employees from the firm. But he did his best work at the many mutual funds that held substantial amounts of Vance Shannon stock in their portfolios.

Coming home, he told Harry, "You wouldn't believe it, little brother, the mutual funds regard our company as the most stable in the industry. It gives them a toehold in aerospace without the risk that most companies have."

"What's their take on ActOn?"

"They have less confidence. They know Bob's brilliant, but they are worried about the last year's performance—it was OK, but not like the previous two years. And of course, we did better last year."

"I had no idea we were that popular."

"No, neither one of us ever paid any attention to the bean-counter side of the business. Some of it is halo effect from Dad's name. But just thank goodness we had good people, and that they didn't lose faith when Nancy put us in the nosedive. In fact, a lot of the mutual funds came in when we were in a slump, figuring they would profit when we recovered. And they have."

"What do they say when you tell them Rodriquez is going to buy us out?"

"That's the tough part, Harry. They like ActOn, too, but they think Bob is making a mistake trying to buy us out. They run charts on us, they run charts on everybody, and they think that ActOn and Vance Shannon are both big enough and different enough to prosper. They don't think there's much to be gained by a consolidation of the two firms."

"Do they know it's just revenge that's motivating Rodriquez?"

"No, he's selling it as a 'merger of two equals' and telling them he can cut out a lot of duplication if he acquires control."

"For 'duplication' read 'Tom and Harry Shannon.'"

"You're right of course, but he doesn't say that. We've got a reputation, too, and that would hurt his chances. And when I tell them what the problem is, they sit up and listen. It will probably hurt ActOn in the long run. A lot of them I talk to are suspicious of Bob's judgment."

The battle with Rodriquez was a tonic for Tom. The more difficult it became, the more he enjoyed it, traveling around the country and doing a lot of flying in the company Learjet, always with an instructor pilot, but still in the left seat, making all the decisions, and even regaining his instrument flying proficiency. Concentrating on the gauges was a relief from the tedium of the business details he used to woo the stockholders.

Matters came to a head at a special stockholders meeting that Rodriquez insisted on, even specifying the time, date, and place—9:00 A.M., Wednesday, October 7, at the big Vance Shannon hangar at the Los Angeles International Airport. Rodriquez knew that it would be difficult for a lot of the small shareholders to get to the hangar in rush hour and that most would be at work on a Wednesday. He believed he controlled enough votes to win, but wanted to make sure.

The hangar was carpeted with folding chairs, anticipating a large turnout of stockholders, and an improvised stage was built, with two podiums, desks, and chairs for the two respective teams. Tom and Bob did not speak or shake hands. Each man sat near his podium. At the appointed hour, Rodriquez rose and addressed the sparse audience. Relatively few stockholders had managed to get through, but the press was well represented. After some formula words of welcome, Rodriquez came to the point.

"This meeting was called to announce ActOn's determination to purchase Vance Shannon, Incorporated, for $250,000,000. This represents a premium of about 20 percent over the current price of thirty-four dollars, and is believed to be in the best interests of the shareholders."

There was a stunned murmur from the press, and an audible gasp from the audience of stockholders. The price was considerably higher than had been predicted.

Rodriquez went on for a few moments, saying the expected things about consolidation, economies, growth, and future prospects, then turned, nodded to Tom, and sat down.

Tom walked slowly to the podium. Harry noted that his limp seemed a bit more pronounced than usual, perhaps a bit of gamesmanship.

"Mr. Rodriquez has made his declaration. I will now make Vance Shannon, Incorporated's declaration. We decline his offer. Instead we are making an offer of $300,000,000 for ActOn, and have secured the necessary funds to prosecute this strategy today."

There was another gasp from the crowd as Rodriquez stood up shouting, "You cannot do that, Shannon!"

Tom walked to Rodriquez and stood looking down at him. Even though his beating in Hanoi had cost him the erect posture he'd carried since the Academy, he still towered over his old friend and longtime enemy.

"We can, and we will, Bob. I have the money pledged already, and I have the necessary votes. By the way, Bob, I doubt if you've had time to play any of the new video games. I suggest you look into Pac-Man; that's what we're calling our business strategy—'the Pac-Man defense.' You could look it up."

Tom turned back to the microphone and said, "Ladies and gentlemen, we will now take questions from the audience, before proceeding to a vote on the two issues before us."

Rodriquez stood up.

"There won't be any questions and no vote is necessary. I withdraw ActOn's offer to purchase Vance Shannon, Incorporated, and I'll see you in court, Tom Shannon."

Tom picked up his microphone, walked forward to the edge of the platform, and said, "Ladies and gentlemen, this will take a bit of time to sort out, as you can imagine. I'm sorry Bob called you out here on a wild-goose chase. We'll be getting back to you shortly with the time and date of a new stockholders meeting, with a complete agenda and a more convenient location."

A week later, ActOn announced that it was being acquired by the Allied Corporation. Bob Rodriquez was severing his connection with the firm.

Tom looked up from the typewriter.

"You pretty much know what I'll tell them about Bob's attempted takeover and our Pac-Man defense, where the goal is to eat up the other guy before he eats you up. Well, we ate him up first! But jog my mind about what's happened recently in the industry that affected us."

"Well, it's not good material for a Christmas card, maybe, but we lost a lot of the giants in the industry this year. Just think of it—Don Douglas, Jack Northrop, and Juan Trippe all went west earlier in the year, all within a period of about sixty days."

"Yeah, and the ejection seat guy, James Martin, he died around then, too. I'll throw them all in with a line of condolence. What else, something upbeat."

"How about Boeing's response to Airbus with the 757 and 767? We have contracts to do the interiors on about thirty of them already. And NASA got two operational Space Shuttle flights off; that helped our maintenance subcontracts at Cape Canaveral."

"Good! And there were those crazy guys who flew the balloon across the Pacific. We don't make any money out of that, but they deserve a salute, anyway."

"It's a bit of a downer, but you might mention Lockheed has finally bit the bullet and is going to phase out the L-1011."

"No, that's too gloomy. They lost a bundle on it, and poor old McDonnell Douglas is in worse shape on the DC-10, just like you said it would be. I have to hand it to you, Harry, you called that one."

"Well, getting back to upbeat, McDonnell Douglas flew its first jump jet—the AV-8B."

"That's a keeper. I love that name 'AV-8B'—reminds me of the old McGuffey AV-8 that Dad test-flew back in the thirties—you know, the one powered by a flat-head Ford V-8 automobile engine."

"The new one has a little more than 80 horsepower, I believe."

The two brothers batted the year's news back and forth for another hour before Tom finally gave up.

"That's it, two typewritten pages; I have to have three hundred copies made, and I'll be stuffing envelopes all New Year's Day."

They were quiet for a while.

"What do you think Dad would say if he knew how deep in debt we were willing to go to scare Rodriquez off?"

"He knows. I've got the feeling he's looking down here all the time. And as much as he hated debt, he would have approved. Even though Bob was his pick, he never would have stood for a takeover."

"Have you talked to Mae since the big stockholders meeting?"

"No. Nancy said she was embarrassed by the whole thing, just wants to forget it. She's dating a nice guy now. Bob's a thing of the past."

Harry shook his head.

"I doubt it. I think Bob's round the bend. I think he'll be back to make trouble for us, and for Mae."

May 1, 1982
Tonopah, Nevada

THERE WAS STILL plenty of light and the temperature had dropped ten degrees from the daytime high of seventy-three. V. R. Shannon knew that he could use all the thrust he could get on any takeoff in Lockheed's super secret "Senior Trend" aircraft. Called the F-117A, it was a full-scale development version of the aircraft Shannon knew would revolutionize the way wars were fought.

It had not been easy. The whole concept had been contested from the very start. Kelly Johnson, the doyen of Lockheed engineers—indeed, the doyen of all aeronautic engineers—had protested bitterly that the awkwardly shaped stealth fighter would never fly well. That was just the start of the problems that Ben Rich and his team had to endure—and were still enduring.

The two "Have Blue" experimental prototypes had flown a total of eighty-eight flights, but both had crashed and now lay buried at a hidden spot in the Nevada desert. Fortunately, in both crashes the pilots, Bill Park and Ken Dyson, had survived. V. R. had flown the second prototype on a number of occasions, and it was always chancy, like balancing a pool ball on the point of a cue stick. There was simply too much stealth in the design—and not enough aerodynamics.

The Have Blues had taught Lockheed a great deal, however, and earned it a contract for five full-scale development versions and fifteen production aircraft. These were not simply scaled up versions of the Have Blue, although they followed its general outlines and its faceted shape. The second Have Blue had been covered with radar absorbent material, and it was soon painfully obvious that the so-called RAM was difficult to work with.

But the big problem was with openings, whether for the landing gear or the refueling probe or a simple access panel. When they were perfectly sealed, they didn't present anything for a radar beam to reflect from, but if they were not perfectly aligned, they multiplied the aircraft's radar signature by hundreds of times. There were manufacturing problems as well. In many cases, normal off-the-shelf avionics could not be used because of the awkward, angular shape of the aircraft. Instead, they had to be custom built to fit within the faceted contours of the bulging fuselage. This drove costs up and made maintenance difficult.

The full-sized F-117As were much bigger and heavier than the Have Blues. Engine thrust was way up, of course. Where the Have Blue's J85 engines, borrowed from a Navy trainer, had about three thousand pounds of thrust, the production aircraft had GE F404 engines with about eleven thousand pounds of thrust. It needed every ounce, because the new airplane, at fifty-two thousand pounds takeoff weight, was more than four times as heavy as the Have Blue. The weight, combined with the less-than-aerodynamic shape of the airframe, made aerial combat problematic.

V. R. went over his briefing notes. It was a two-part mission, with the first part being fairly simple. He was to take off, fly to the nearby bombing range, and after being cleared in, make a practice bomb run and then a real run. He would be dropping the newest version of the Paveway III laser-guided bomb. The bomb had a small marking charge in it, and they would be checking the accuracy of his drop, but that was not the test's primary purpose, which was to see how much the quick opening missile bay doors increased the airplane's radar signature.

The drop made the flight something of a family affair. Bob Rodriquez had developed the Paveway III laser system when he was still part of the Shannon organization. His dad's friend, Steve O'Malley, had been a principal proponent of the F-16, and his uncle Harry had selected the F-16s fly-by-wire system as an "off-the-shelf" item for the black jet. V. R. had participated in both the Have Blue and FSD portions of the test.

The second part of the flight was more critical. Another "black" project was testing the effectiveness of Soviet fighters against the F-117. After the bomb drop, he would be "attacked" by a MiG-23, captured months ago by the Israelis and now flown by an expert USAF pilot from the aggressor squadron at Nellis. The F-117A was not really a dogfighter, and the probability of it entering combat carrying an air-to-air missile was slight, given its value as a stealth attack airplane. Still, for this mission, they had simulated a combat load of a Sidewinder heat seeking missile for the dogfight sequence. Given the MiG-23's superior speed and maneuverability, it wasn't going to be much of a fight.

As V. R. waited for takeoff clearance he ran his eyes over the crowded instrument panel, reflecting that the drop in temperature here was not nearly as bad as the drop in temperature at home. Ginny was furious with him. Instead of getting an assignment as a flight instructor at Nellis as he had promised, he had opted to stay with the stealth program. Offered a pilot's position in the 4450th Tactical Group, a highly classified new unit scheduled to receive the production F-117As for operational use, Shannon had agreed, knowing that he was reneging on a promise to Ginny to get a more conventional job with more conventional hours.

He had handled it badly. He never should have promised to look for a "conventional job," not that many flying jobs in the Air Force were conventional, anyway. But this way he had gone back on his word, disappointing her. It was a dumb thing to do, but he had no choice. He had to fly this airplane, in combat, and help prove what he'd been working on for so long.

As he did so often lately, he'd gone to his father for advice.

"Dad, I don't want to put you on the spot, but I know that you and Mom had a lot of problems concerning your flying. It looks like I'm getting into the same boat, with Ginny."

He went on to explain the situation, telling him that he had to make up his mind within the week, or he couldn't volunteer for the 4450th.

Tom Shannon stood up, walked around his desk, and put his arm around V. R.'s shoulders.

"Son, I made a lot of mistakes in my life and the worst two were volunteering to go back to combat in Korea and then in Vietnam. Both times I bitterly disappointed your mother. She never had any idea about how I felt about it; she just considered me to be another crazy flyer like my dad. Now Harry, he's different. He sacrificed flying for Anna. He's a better man than I am."

As his father paused, V. R.'s stomach contracted. He was going to get exactly what he didn't want: advice to pass on flying the stealth fighter, and going along with Ginny's wishes.

"But I'll tell you, Son, you've got to do what your gut tells you. I think your gut is telling you to say no to Ginny and yes to the stealth fighter. And if I'm right about that, that's what I'm telling you, too. There's an old western movie cliché, where the hero says, 'A man's got to do what a man's got to do.' But corny as it sounds, it's exactly right. It's your life, and if you've got that damn fighter pilot bug in you, you have to do what it tells you. I think Ginny will stick with you. She loves you."

It was exactly what V. R. wanted to hear, and confirmed his decision. All he had to do now was convince Ginny it wasn't the end of the world.

He knew she had a point. It was tough for her to spend all week in Las Vegas, waiting for him to come home. And it was dull for him, too. Except for the flying, life at Tonopah was excruciatingly boring. Monday through Friday was spent in studying the aircraft and preparing for test flights. If they were lucky, they'd log some daytime flying in a Vought A-7. Most of the time they spent skulking indoors, trying to absorb as much knowledge as they could about the complex systems that governed the aircraft. Then on Friday night they flew home to Nellis, 140 miles to the southeast, in a Key Air Boeing 737, coming back early Monday morning. On the way from Tonopah to Nellis, they labeled the 737 "the honeymoon express"; on the way back, Nellis–Tonopah, it was "hangover special."

The tower called, "Scorpion 3, cleared for take off."

Shannon advanced the throttles swiftly, and the black jet rushed forward, its strange triangular shape not unlike a huge paper glider. During the initial takeoff roll it felt more like a sports car accelerating than an aircraft taking off. Once airborne, a cartridge plugged into his AP-102 computer flew it to its destination far better than he or any other pilot could have done, picking the optimum route considering terrain, wind, defenses, everything. It made him feel a little superfluous, but his hands never left the controls at any time.

As the F-117A lifted off he gave a quick sigh of relief. Less than two weeks before, Bob Riedenauer, a Lockheed test pilot, had crashed on takeoff. The aircraft had rolled inverted, hit the runway, and then slid backward for hundreds of feet, all because the flight control wires had been installed in reverse. It had been going on since the beginning of flight—where they used to attach the aileron or elevator cables backward, now they had found a way to foul-up electronically.

The two GE F404 engines sang sweetly, putting out their eleven thousand pounds of thrust as he climbed swiftly to twenty thousand feet, before leveling off. V. R. monitored the progress on the moving-map display, his hands still resting lightly on the stick. The F-117A followed its preprogrammed path, integrating the information from the navigation and flight management system, changing altitude and airspeed as necessary to put him over his entry point at exactly the right moment.

Shannon went through the routine calls for entrance to the bombing range as the program set up his pattern. He was joined by an A-7 chase plane, there to photograph the Paveway III's separation from the aircraft. On the ground, half a dozen different systems would monitor the change in the F-117A's radar signature when the missile bay doors snapped open and shut.

The controller on the bomb range cleared him to drop and the A-7 moved into position, to the rear, and slightly below his altitude.

V. R. monitored the system as the target became the next waypoint for the computer. He waited, watching his Infra-Red Acquisition and Detection System—IRADS-crosshairs position themselves over the target. Two infrared sensors—the Forward Looking Infra-Red (FLIR) and the Downward Looking Infra Red (DLIR)—put the target's image on his central cockpit TV display.

The two infrared units were the only equipment on the aircraft that were not passive, so they had to be carefully controlled, and used only for a minimum amount of time. If not, the enemy defenses could track back to the aircraft. V. R. used the forward-looking set to acquire the target; as he drew closer, it was automatically handed off to the DLIR. All V. R. had to do was keep the crosshairs on the target, making minor adjustments as needed via a small button on the throttle.

He watched the crosshairs closely, checking his altitude and airspeed, and selecting "ARM" on the master arming switch. His aircraft's laser designator lit the target and the DLIR picked up the reflected signal. V. R. felt the missile bay doors snap open and shut as the Paveway III dropped. His laser designator illuminated the target with a laser spot about eighteen inches in diameter, and the Paveway sought it, correcting for wind all the way right down to impact on the target, a much mangled Soviet T-72 tank carcass.

It used to be rare when the bomb range controller called back "Shack," meaning a direct hit. Now it was rare when he did not. But the missile's accuracy was not at question so much as the radar signature when the missile bay doors opened. V. R. wouldn't know those results until he returned.

The A-7 pulled away just as the MiG-23 came into view, closing at twelve hundred knots. The range controller came back on saying "Fight's on" as the two fighters passed each other, then arced into turns, the MiG climbing, the F-117A holding its turn, slowing down. V. R. knew he couldn't outspeed the MiG, so he tried to get both their airspeeds down where the F-117A wouldn't be at so much of a disadvantage.

The MiG hurtled down past him, V. R. peeling to the right just as the aggressor pilot was about to fire. The F-117A, surprisingly agile given its total disregard for aerodynamics, decelerated further, dropping down to two hundred knots, as V. R. made another tight 360-degree turn.

As the MiG shot by, climbing for another pass, V. R. skidded the F-117A to the right, jammed his throttles forward, and lifted his nose for a snap shot with his Sidewinder. To his surprise, the virtual image of the missile reached out and hit the MiG-23's symbol just as ground control called, "That's a kill, Scorpion 3. Fight's over."

The MiG pilot's voice came up, obviously disgruntled but trying to hide it.

"Good shot, V. R.; I let you off easy this time."

Surprised at the turn of events, Shannon peeled away for the landing back at Tonopah. Everything had worked well this time, but it was all virtual combat, no one was really shooting at him. He knew that if there was a next time, the MiG-23 would play it differently, and he'd never get a lucky shot like that in again.

But it was really unimportant. The F-117A wasn't a dogfighter and never would be. It was a bomber, designed to go in unseen. And here the F-117A was invisible to the local radars, but who knew what the enemy was developing? The whole stealth thing had started from a Russian scientist's paper. It was hard to believe that they wouldn't have a countermeasure up their sleeve. And if the missile doors revealed its presence, it was only stealthy part of the time. Just one exposure might be enough to give an alert enemy a shot with a barrage of SAMs.

Ah, that was in the future. In the meantime, he had his own little war going on with Ginny.

CHAPTER EIGHT

THE PASSING PARADE: Palestine Liberation Organization agrees to withdraw forces from Lebanon; Henry Fonda dies at age 77; U.S. banks lower prime interest rate from 17 to 11.5 percent; Pete Rose sets an at-bat record of 12,365 surpassing Hank Aaron's previous record; China pledges to seek reunification with Taiwan by peaceful means; Ingrid Bergman dies at age 67; *Hill Street Blues* wins six Emmys; Epcot Center opens; John DeLorean arrested for possession of cocaine; Dow Jones industrial average continues climb; Great Britain defeats Argentina in Falklands War; Leonid Brezhnev dies; Vietnam Veterans' War Memorial dedicated; Cosmonauts Berezovoy and Lebedev land safely after a record 211 days in space.

October 9, 1982
Palos Verdes, California

*A*lways the philosopher in the family, Harry Shannon put his hands behind his head and stretched out on the long, low leather couch in the familiar library of his father's Palos Verdes house. Tom was at the desk, working, valiantly trying to balance his checkbook, and V. R. was due to arrive any minute.

It would have made financial sense to sell the house—the market was booming, but sentiment prevailed and all the Shannons used it as a neutral spot where they could discuss business away from the office environment. It was also a guest house for V. R. and Ginny, and for so many of their friends who dropped by that the neighbors jokingly—or maybe not so jokingly—suggested that they take out a hotel license.

It pleased Harry how the tenor of their meetings had changed so completely in the last year. Tom, now fully engaged in running Vance Shannon, Incorporated, was still savoring his triumph over Rodriquez. He had emerged from the shadow of his harsh treatment in Hanoi to be exactly like he had been in his youth: eager, energetic, and always combative. Nancy had accomplished an almost equally miraculous transformation, going from the hard-hitting—if often wrong—chief executive officer to a supportive role as Tom's administrative assistant, doing his bidding, offering advice only when asked, and all without rancor. She seemed genuinely pleased to have given up the hard decision making, and was basking in both Tom's recovery and his sincere appreciation for what she did.

Harry mused to himself, *Nobody would believe it in a soap opera or a movie. She went from top dog in a tough business to loving, supporting wife in a matter of days.*

Nancy's ill-advised handling of the business was still too sensitive for conversation, however; no one ever mentioned it in her presence, and even when, as they inevitably did, things came up on the real estate fiasco she'd become embroiled in, Tom and Harry kept it as quiet as possible, always trying to shield her from further embarrassment.

There was an equally large change in V. R.'s behavior, and in the way he was treated. Tom loved him fiercely, of course, but up until about a year ago, he had looked upon him as his son, highly successful, but his son still. As proud as Tom was of V. R., it simply had not occurred to him to treat him any differently than he had in the past as a pleased, proud father.

The change came not because of V. R.'s meteoric rise in rank—he was being promoted regularly in advance of his Academy colleagues. Instead it came as Tom was cleared to learn more about the important work V. R. was doing with the latest plane in the Air Force arsenal, the top secret "black jet," the Lockheed F-117A. Thanks to Steve O'Malley's influence, V. R. had been in on the stealth program almost from the start, and few of the other pilots flying the operational aircraft had the depth of engineering background that he did. Consequently, he was called on to work with Lockheed's Skunk Works and even with

Vance Shannon, Incorporated, on some of the tougher problems being encountered.

Harry was aware that the connection between V. R. and Vance Shannon, Incorporated, was suspect. Someone—naturally he suspected Bob Rodriquez—had written letters protesting what was termed an "egregious conflict of interest situation" to Ben Rich, to Colonel James Allen, the incredibly competent commander of his unit, the 4450th Tactical Group, and to the Secretary of Defense. All hell had broken loose for a couple of weeks until everyone was satisfied that V. R. was a staunch defender of the Air Force's interest, and not that of Vance Shannon, Incorporated. The letters had phony signatures and addresses and, strangely, had not been sent to the press. That was the main reason Harry thought it was Rodriquez. He was clearly trying to hurt the Shannons, but was still patriotic enough not to want to hurt the still-secret stealth program.

"Tom, have you ever wondered how everyone has been able to keep the F-117A secret so long?"

His twin looked up from his checkbook and bank statement, hopelessly at odds with each other, as always.

"It's amazing. Nothing else in this industry has been kept a secret for a minute, but they've been flying F-117As out of Tonopah for a year now, and no one has said a word. Somebody's been doing something right for a change. And not all night flights, either, like it used to be."

The front door burst open and V. R. thundered down the hall in his flying suit, boots clattering on the tile, then erupted into the library with a big grin, Harry's ancient battered B-4 bag under one arm, and a six-pack of Budweiser in his hand.

"Dad! Uncle Harry! Good to see you."

They embraced and Tom reached up and rubbed the silver oak leaves on V. R.'s shoulders.

"Man that looks good, V. R.! Congratulations. You're going to be Chief of Staff someday if you keep going at this rate!"

Harry reached over and rapped on the big carved wooden table.

"Don't say that, Tom—that's what you used to say about Steve O'Malley, and look what happened to him."

They caught up on family business for a few minutes, Tom warning V. R. that Nancy was going to pressure him about having some children.

V. R. grew serious. "OK, Dad, but tell her not to say anything to Ginny. We've been trying for the last year, and no luck. We've got a whole bunch of tests to do now, to see what the problem is. The last thing she needs is some advice from Nancy on having kids. She feels inadequate already. And as for me, if I find out that I'm firing blanks, I don't know what the hell I'll do."

Then, unconsciously assuming a new, more formal posture that went with his new role in the family, he said, "Let's get down to business. You remember the test I flew last May on the missile bay doors? The results were a disaster. When the bay doors open, the entire stealth capability is lost, just for seconds, but for that time the airplane appears as big as an F-15 on the radar screens."

Tom and Harry nodded. They had been working the problem from two approaches. One of their subsidiary companies had spent thousands of hours and hundreds of thousands of dollars designing mechanisms to open and shut the missile bay doors more rapidly. The problem was that the missile or bomb required a small but irreducible amount of time to separate from the aircraft and clear the doors. No matter how fast the doors opened and shut, there was still the time requirement needed for the bomb to clear.

V. R. went on. "I've got an idea that I wanted to run by you before I propose it to my boss and to Ben Rich. It's not gung-ho offensive, and that's why I'm hesitant about it. And what I'm going to tell you is way more than top secret. You are both cleared, but you cannot let this go farther than this room, not even to the people you have working on this problem, until I tell you so. I'm sure you understand. Or you will when I'm finished.

"First off, we've got all kinds of radar equipment on the bombing ranges, at the base in Tonopah, at Nellis, and elsewhere. The information we're getting back is that we are not as 'stealthy' as we thought— that under certain conditions we can be acquired by a SAM site. And this means we are going to need to operate with jamming support— and we are damn short of that."

V. R. popped open three bottles of beer and handed them around.

"Well, here's where I think we are. We've got the missile bay doors opening and closing as fast as possible, and we've got the launch trapeze operating as fast as possible as well. I don't think we'll get any more improvement in that area. So we've got an unsolvable problem, unless we look at it differently. Here's what I'm proposing. We hook the radar homing and warning system—the good old RHAW gear—to the bomb system. If we are being painted by enemy radar, we don't open the missile bay doors, and come back around for another run, letting the escort jammers do their best to suppress the radar site that is painting us. It means wasting some run-ins, maybe, but it is better than getting hit by a missile."

Neither Tom nor Harry spoke. This was a new approach, and an unusual one for it was, as V. R. had warned, defensive in nature. It could mean that some bomb runs would be aborted and have to be repeated—always risky.

Tom spoke up. "If your RHAW gear could speak direct to the jammers, it could give them a fix on the radar causing the problem. And maybe to the local AWACS as well; they could vector some Wild Weasels in to take out the radar site."

Wild Weasels had the toughest assignment in the Air Force. Always "first in and last out," the Wild Weasels' job was to attack the SAM sites and clear the way in for bombers. In essence, they had a shoot-out with the SAMs, trying to kill the SAMs before the missiles killed them. Their losses had been staggering in Vietnam, with the pioneering crews paying the heaviest price. Even today, only the toughest, most competent crews could handle the duty.

Harry spoke up at last. "I think that's brilliant, V. R., and Tom's idea is great, too. No reason we cannot get it to talk to the jammers and the AWACS simultaneously with its stopping the missile bay doors from opening. And I don't think it suffers from being a defensive idea; the whole idea of stealth is basically defensive, anyway. This is the sort of thing Bill Creech will go for in a minute. And Ben Rich, too."

"OK, if you think so. I'm going to go back to Tonopah today and propose this, and Dad, I'll fold your suggestion in as well, as my idea. When it gets back to you, it's news, you understand? I don't want any more letters saying I'm doing what I'm doing—talking to my dad for advice. And talking to you, too, Uncle Harry."

With that, V. R. turned and headed out the library door, leaving his untasted beer on his dad's desk. Tom picked up V. R.'s beer and glanced at Harry.

"You not drinking yours, either?"

"No, I don't want to go home and have Anna smell it on my breath. She really doesn't care if I have a drink, but I'm just more comfortable doing without. I couldn't take another round of her falling off the wagon."

They sat comfortably, not talking for a while, marshaling their thoughts. They didn't get to meet face-to-face as often as they should, and they always tried to bring each other up to speed. Both men knew that the company had grown so much that they needed to delegate some of their responsibilities, but the turnaround from Nancy's disaster had been so recent and so remarkable that they hated to do so.

"It's been quite a year, Harry. The company's doing well, we've got most of Nancy's obligations taken care of, Bob Rodriquez has fallen off the face of the earth, and V. R. is a roaring success. I just hope that he gets his marital issues solved."

"Does anybody ever do that? They'll survive, just as Dad did, and we are doing. I just hope there's no war, and that V. R. can move on to less dangerous flying."

"That'll be the day. A young guy wants danger; you know how that is."

"You more than me, Tom. I always thought I wanted to be a fighter pilot, but I kept flying other types. You wanted to be a fighter pilot, an ace, and that's what you were. It takes all kinds."

"You were in combat; it takes more guts to sit there in a B-17 and let the Messerschmitts and the flak have at you than it does to try to sneak up on a Betty! But things don't change. Just look at that young kid, H. Ross Perot's son. He's wealthy, got a tremendous family business, and what does he go and do? He and his copilot, Jay Coburn, become the first to fly around the world in a helicopter. I read the story on it, and there was plenty of danger involved, particularly when they had to land on a container ship at sea to refuel."

Harry nodded. "They picked the exact right time; until the jet engine came along for helicopters, it would have been out of the question. There's a market we ought to take a look at. Not building helicopters, but getting more into the maintenance side of the business."

"You're right. Perot and Coburn were smart enough to see that the Bell Jet Ranger could just do the job, even though there wasn't much margin for error. It took some guts to do it. But there's something in young guys that makes them want to test themselves. Look at the Falklands War. I was talking to the British air attaché in Washington a few weeks ago, and he said that there were fistfights among crew members scrambling for an assignment to go to war."

"Probably the same thing on the Argentine side. Just a bunch of young guys panting to go shoot and get shot at."

Tom laughed. "Shooting is better. Getting shot at is no good."

"You don't have to go to war to get shot at today! I understand that some of Braniff's stockholders were threatening to shoot somebody at Braniff or at the Federal Aviation Administration, somebody."

The government, in its wisdom, had deregulated the airlines in 1978, trying to get more competition into the business. Braniff International Airways, for years one of the most progressive and innovative airlines, had expanded too far too fast and went too deep in debt. In May, they shut down, leaving employees, stockholders, and customers desolate.

"They won't be the last, Tom, you wait and see. This deregulation thing will change the whole picture of airlines. Old companies will be failing and new companies will be starting up."

"Is that something you would like to get into? We've got some capital building up, we could hire some of the top hands and start an airline of our own."

Harry hesitated. He had to work up to this in the right way, get Tom interested, and then lay the kicker on him.

"Way too risky, especially in today's climate. But I'll tell you what. I think we could consider starting a business where we buy airliners— some used, maybe some new—and lease them back to the airlines. Form a separate corporation, use mostly the bank's money for finance, and base it somewhere in southern California, say at Mojave or somewhere, where the land's relatively cheap and the climate is good for outdoor storage."

Tom balked in his familiar way, brow wrinkling, shoulders hunching up, fists clenching.

"I don't know. Sounds like we're getting into banking more than airplanes—we don't want to repeat the real estate fiasco."

"No, I've been looking into this. There are some people doing it already on a small scale, here and in Europe, too. But if deregulation goes like we think it will, it would be perfect. The old companies will have to get rid of their airplanes, probably for a dime on the dollar; the new companies won't have any money to buy airplanes, and we could be there to lease them. Save them the capital expense."

"It's intriguing, Harry, we've got to do something. Can we run it by the board of directors and get some insight?"

"I'll get it on the agenda. I know they'll say what you just said, 'It's like real estate.' But it's not. Its airplanes—buying them, selling them, maintaining them. And it's civilian business, so if the Reagan spending boom stops, we'll have some balance in our business."

"Let me think this over, Harry. I'm inclined to go along on it, but I get goosey every time I think about how close we came to shutting up shop over the real estate deals. We're just nicely back on our feet, and I hate to tip the balance. Not only that, we are spread thin; we'll need somebody to manage it for us, someone we can trust."

"We'll be careful. And the board has to approve. We've got some smart people helping us. And I've got an idea about who could manage it. You won't like it, of course."

"Well, why pick someone I don't like? Half the industry's being laid off nowadays; there are a ton of people to choose from."

"Yes, but the guy I've got in mind is good—and it would be good for us to have him. Bob Rodriquez, Jr., is available. Rod's looking at the consolidation within the industry and wants to get out from Lockheed and into a smaller firm, someplace he can have more say."

Harry watched the familiar series of expressions march across Tom's face as he struggled for control. Finally, he stood up and hunched over his desk, saying in a low, measured voice, "Are you serious? Do you have any idea of the repercussions this could have on us with his dad, wherever he is? And as nice as the kid is, do we know he'd be loyal to us? Look what Bob tried to do to us."

"Tom, the kid has been working to smooth things over for the last few years. He has a good head, not as sharp as his dad, but a good heart. I think we'd be smart to bring him into the company. More than that—if his dad surfaces, we'd be smart to bring him back into the company. I wish I knew where he was."

"You are a glutton for punishment. Rodriquez tried to take over this company; he would have fired us if he had."

"There was something wrong with him, Tom. I talked to Steve O'Malley about it. He was convinced Bob was having some sort of nervous breakdown. But after all he did for Dad, after all he did for us,

I'd be happy to have him back on the team. And getting his son on board might be a way to do it."

"Have you talked it over with V. R.? You're always in cahoots with my son, you've probably talked to him about it before you talked to me."

"Absolutely! He has the best read on you of anybody. And he told me that you'd turn red, get mad, and then finally see the sense of it."

Tom slumped back in his chair. "He was right, as usual. It's a pain in the ass having a kid who's smarter than you are. And I also know what you're thinking."

"What's that?"

"What would Dad say about it?"

"I know what Dad would say. Go for it, he's a good kid."

CHAPTER NINE

THE PASSING PARADE: The Washington Redskins defeat the Miami Dolphins 27–17 in Super Bowl XVII; crippled nuclear-powered Soviet satellite Cosmos 1402 enters the atmosphere and disintegrates, Eubie Blake, ragtime composer and pianist, dies one week after his hundredth birthday. Sally K. Ride becomes first U.S. woman astronaut; Korean Airline 747 shot down by Soviets; terrorist explosion in Beirut kills more than 300; United States invades Grenada; Bell telephone system broken up; Democrats nominate Walter Mondale and Geraldine Ferraro as presidential and vice presidential candidates; Republicans renominate Reagan and Bush.

September 10, 1983
Mojave, California

*T*he weatherman was right; it must be a hundred degrees already."

Harry looked closely at Tom, who was obviously unwell. The eighty-mile drive from Los Angeles should have taken an hour and a half. Instead, they had spent three hours on the road because Tom repeatedly had them pull over so that he could try to relieve himself, apparently without much success. Tom was both touchy and taciturn about his health problems since coming back from the Hanoi Hilton.

"Let's cut this short, Tom. Young Rodriquez will be here at noon, and we'll leave as soon as he shows us around."

"No, I'm OK. We've got a lot of dough invested in this and in Rod. I want to see how it works."

The Mojave flight line was busy, despite the heat, with an assortment of aircraft not to be found anywhere else. Tied down along taxiways were long fleets of woebegone-looking Boeing 707s and 727s, along with Douglas DC-8s and a handful of the slick Convair 990s. There was a strange-looking biplane, a Soviet Antonov Colt, parked with them. The forlorn airplanes had the bleak look of animals too sick to be slaughtered. Windscreens and windows were covered with plastic, engines were stopped up by wooden intake guards, and the tires were gradually going flat. Airlines that were still operating took the care to paint over their company livery, vainly trying to hide their distress. Smaller companies and those that had gone belly-up left their old colors intact, fading in the desert sun, their once-famous names a reproach to an industry in the agonies of deregulation.

Tom and Harry called their new leasing company AdVanceAir, in honor of their father, and of the more than one hundred airplanes scattered around the field, they owned twenty-three. Harry's choice of Bob Rodriquez, Jr., to run the firm was a happy one, for he was a natural salesman like his father, and besides the twenty-three airplanes on the field, he already had another forty leased out to airlines around the world, each one churning out profits for AdVanceAir. In all the long history of the many Shannon companies, there had never been such a quick and abundant return on their investment.

"I tell you, Tom, this is a gold mine, but it won't last. We've beaten the competition to the punch, but there will be others jumping in as soon as they see how well we are doing."

Pale, Tom stepped into the shade of a hangar, leaning against the door.

"Well, we're paying Rod plenty; his job now is to stay ahead of the competition." He hesitated, then went on. "How are you coming with your wild-goose chase?"

Harry flinched. He knew that Tom thought that he was both crazy and perhaps even disloyal to be looking for Rod's father. The elder Rodriquez was Tom's old enemy, an aggressive entrepreneur who had tried to take over their company a few years ago and failed.

"No luck, Tom. I hear some crazy things, that he's running drugs, that he's working for the CIA, or that he's dead. Don't mention any of that to Rod, for heaven's sake."

"No, I may be old and tired, but I'm not stupid yet. Does Rod ever talk about him?"

"No, he's never mentioned him except in the most casual way. He knows the problems his dad caused, and he's grateful to be working with us."

Tom grumbled something about being sentimental patsies, and then gathering his strength, walked on toward a dust-laden MiG-15 that sat near the hangar among a collection of older jet fighters—a Lockheed F-80, a North American F-86, and, curiously, a rare Douglas F4D Skyray.

He walked around the MiG, panting. "This is the first one I've ever seen on the ground. Ugly little bastard, isn't it? Mean in the air, though. Tough. But who the hell would set up a museum out here?"

Harry watched him with concern; Tom's face was red, but he wasn't sweating in the hundred-plus-degree heat.

"I think they keep them in flying condition, Tom, for some special projects and for movies. Let's go back to the car and get the air conditioner on. I've about had it with the heat. You wait here and I'll drive it over."

"No, I can make it."

They walked slowly back to the car. Tom waited outside, breathing heavily, until Harry got the air conditioner going and the temperature down, then slid gratefully onto the Cadillac's broad front seat. They watched as the doors to Burt Rutan's hangar opened and a tiny little white airplane was rolled out.

Tom said, "That's a strange-looking bird."

"Yeah; canard surfaces, swept wing. It's all fiberglass composite structure, you know, supposed to be easy to build."

A tall, lean man scrambled into the cockpit and fired the engine up. Moments later the airplane was gone, disappearing to the northeast.

"Harry, I'll bet that was Dick Rutan. He was a great pilot in Vietnam. Flew the 'Misty' fast FAC mission." Then, grumbling, he went on. "If Rod is late, maybe we ought to just go back. Let's wait until noon; if he's not here, we'll just cut out."

At noon precisely a yellow Mercedes 380SE whirled up in a cloud of dust; Bob Rodriquez, Jr., hopped out of his seat to open the door for his mother Mae.

Harry glanced at Tom to see how he was taking this. To his surprise, his brother seemed to be pulling himself together, obviously pleased at seeing Mae again. He wondered if Tom regarded Mae as an ally, since she had divorced his longtime foe, or whether he was just registering pleasure at the sight of such a beautiful woman.

Rod stood by diffidently as Mae embraced each of the Shannons in turn.

"Mae, you are as beautiful as ever. I thought Tom's eyes were going to fall out when you stepped out of the car."

Their rare conversations with Mae were usually one-sided, for while she could ask about Nancy, Anna, and V. R., they could never ask about her former husband. Mae never tried to conceal the fact that she still loved him. She just could not endure his workaholic lifestyle. Talking about him with her was just too painful.

Bob Rodriquez had dropped out of their lives without a word of farewell. He had placed all of his cash—an immense amount after the sale of his ActOn stock—and his enormous stock portfolio in a trust managed by an old friend at the Bank of America. There were many sightings of him, but Harry's investigations had proved that most of these were false. The most improbable story, but one that Harry was almost convinced was true, was that Rodriquez had been killed on a tiny island in the Bahamas. The story was that the aircraft, an ancient Cessna 310, was overloaded with marijuana, and he had crashed making an attempted forced landing. His body was never found, but there was enough identifying material to conclude that it had been Bob. Yet it was hard—almost impossible—for Harry to believe that Rodriquez, a twelve-victory MiG ace in Korea, an ardent patriot, and independently wealthy, would descend to drug running. There was no reason for him to do it, unless he was somehow undercover, working for the government.

Harry had kept Rod posted, but on the condition that none of it could be revealed to Mae, simply because he wasn't certain himself. When he found incontrovertible evidence that Bob was either alive or dead, he would of course let them both know. Until then, he was not going to pass on any wild conjectures to Mae.

It was evident that Rod was eager to tell them some good news, and ushered them inside AdVanceAir's more than modest office, a prefab building hauled from some construction site and nestled against the side of a World War II hangar. Tom looked around uneasily at the office furnishings, clearly culled from some used furniture store, enjoying the welcome cool breeze provided by two wheezing, dripping, window air conditioners. Rod brought out some bottled Pellegrino water from an ancient refrigerator, poured it into reasonably clean glasses, and smiling, watched them settle into the folding metal chairs around the old table. Then he walked to a portable blackboard, covered with a sheet, and said, "Let me fill you in, military style, with a good old-fashioned briefing."

He removed the sheet, revealing a stack of cardboard posters. The top one read simply, "AdVanceAir Leasing: Creating Instant Airlines Around the World."

Nodding to Tom and Harry, he said, "And that is what your foresight has done: built an airline manufacturing machine. I use this room and these beat-up briefing charts to tell potential customers how they can use us. I could be fancier and use a projector and slides, but I'm trying to impress everyone with our economy of operation. That's why the office is this clunker of a building and why I've chosen this beaten-up furniture. I'm trying to sell economy and profit, not just airplanes, and the economy starts here."

Harry and Tom exchanged glances. This was the exact opposite of another important side of their business, fitting new airliners and business jets with luxurious interiors. In those offices, everything was beyond sumptuous, from the furnishings to the beautiful women whose task it was to see that every client felt like a movie star.

Rod went on. "We're not dealing with a rich clientele. We're working for the most part with young hustlers, guys who worked for airlines that have gone belly-up since deregulation. They know that low prices sell tickets and that you cannot get low prices with fancy extras. Here's what we offer them."

He tapped the first line of the next chart.

"We will sell airplanes if anyone wants to buy, and we'll sell them cheaper than they can get them anywhere else. Only about ten percent of our business comes from sales, and that is good, because we make more money from leasing the planes."

He tapped the second line of the chart.

"Our real moneymaker is leasing the aircraft, with one or even more crews; we pay their salaries and allowances, we take care of the maintenance and insurance. In turn, the people doing the leasing—the so-called lessee—pays a guaranteed amount for a guaranteed amount of hours. The lessee pays the fuel costs, landing fees, crew expenses, and all the miscellaneous costs."

Rod looked at them, beaming.

"What this means is that an airline can be set up with a minimum capital investment; all the money they raise can be used for operating expenses for the first two or three years, until they get on their feet. We really are in the business of creating instant airlines."

Tom started to say something but Harry put his hand on his arm, nodding for Rod to go on.

"There are other ways to make money, too; we'll do any variation on the lease the customer wants, as long as we are sure of making a good margin of profit. For example, we have what we call a 'damp lease.' That means we provide the aircraft but no cabin crew. Or we can give them a 'dry lease' meaning that we don't provide insurance, maintenance, anything. But our bread and butter is the full lease."

Tom couldn't be repressed.

"Sounds good, but where on earth do you get the crews lined up and trained? How do you handle the maintenance?"

"We get them from the same source as the airplanes, older airlines with high cost structures that are going or have gone belly-up. There is an enormous pool of crews and maintenance facilities available. We have a huge file of applications on pilots, flight attendants, flight engineers, mechanics, you name it."

He paused, took a drink of water, and went on.

"Remember, these aren't people who were fired for incompetence, these are the people whose dreams of retirement imploded when big carriers like Braniff collapsed. They are eager to go to work, and appreciate the chance, even though the salaries are nothing like they earned before, and the benefits are minimal."

"But how about the maintenance? We have some maintenance capacity in our company, but it's mostly geared to business flying."

"The beauty of it is that major airlines are still struggling to survive. They are trying not to do a Braniff and are cutting back flights and flying time. That means they have excess maintenance capacity, and are willing to run twenty-four/seven just to get our business. In fact, we are in a position to get concessions on maintenance rates because they want our business—we give them a transfusion of ready cash they are dying for."

Harry spoke up. "That's got to be good politically; they may hate us for putting up rival airlines, but at least we're giving them something back."

Mae spoke up for the first time, surprising everyone but Rod.

"It is more than that, Harry. They are looking to the airlines we service as a model for cost cutting, for sure, but it's tough on them because of all the built-in union agreements they have on pilot's pay, hours worked, and so on. More importantly, they look on us as a negotiating instrument when it comes time to deal with the unions. They hold us up as an example of why they have to cut personnel slots and cut wages, and the unions don't have much of a defense against that."

Rod spoke. "Mom's been helping me out. She learned so much in the real estate business and she has a fine eye for contractual detail. I'm going to show you some return on investment projections that we are making for the year, and then ask your advice."

He pulled out the last chart and said, "As you see, if things continue the way they have, and I know that they will, you will have made something like a forty-two percent return on your investment this year. Next year it should be closer to fifty percent because of some particularly sweet deals we have coming up with foreign airlines— Africa and Southeast Asia, mainly. Farther out, it will probably decline, but I don't think it will ever go below thirty percent, and if it does, we'll be looking into something different. I've got some handouts here that you can ask your bean counters to look at. It lays it all out, down to the last dime."

Harry and Tom were impressed. Rod had repeatedly assured them that things were going well, but they had no idea that their leasing scheme was prospering on this scale.

Tom said, "What in the hell do you want advice from us for? You've got the program knocked, as we used to say in cadets. I can tell from the look on Harry's face that he's as amazed and as pleased as I am."

"Well, here's the advice I want. My mom, your friend Mae here, has been in this from the start, advising me. She has her real estate business well in hand, and a good set of managers to run it. I want her to come here full-time and run this operation, because I've got some other things I need to do."

He looked meaningfully at Harry and went on. "I'll still be here to work with her most of the time, but I've got to carve out some independent work time for myself. When I do, I won't take any salary from the company."

Harry knew immediately what he meant. Rod wanted to join him in finding out what happened to his father. It took Tom a bit longer to catch on. When he did, he flushed and said, "OK, I understand. I don't approve—you know my problems with your dad, but I know you have to do what you have to do. After a performance like this, what can I say?"

Harry said, "You say yes, like I do. Welcome aboard, Mae, and keep up the fantastic work."

They spent another twenty minutes discussing details, but Tom was paling, and Harry wanted to get him home. Before he left he said, "Rod, I'm proud of you doing what you are going to do. I want to help. Come see me in Palos Verdes and let's see how we can work together on your project."

Rodriquez was glad that they were going to let Mae substitute for him and grateful for the offer of aid in finding his father. He knew that Harry had spent a lot of time and money on this already, and he might have objected to cooperating.

"I will, Harry. And thanks. And when the time is right, thank Tom, too. I know what this cost him."

December 31, 1983
Palos Verdes

THERE HAD NOT been so much emotion in the old-fashioned tile-roofed Palos Verdes house since Tom's return from Vietnam a decade before, when he was a newly released—if more than battered—POW. But there was an enormous difference. Then Vance Shannon had been the invalid given a new lease on life because his son was home from the wars, not well perhaps, but home. Tom's presence had been a tonic to him and certainly made his last days happier.

Now the reverse was true. While the family gathered in the library, discussing Harry's bombshell, Tom lay near death in the master bedroom, not so much fighting for his life as quietly accepting his condition. Day by day, his heart condition grew worse, and both he and the family had refused any radical treatment.

With so little time left to him, Tom didn't need to know that Bob Rodriquez was alive and well. Four long months of investigation by Harry and Rod had gone nowhere. But the team of professional detectives working for Harry had at last verified that the elder Rodriquez had neither been killed in the crash nor was he a renegade dope smuggler. Instead, the crash had been a cover story for a new assignment. The detectives didn't know—or were not telling—what the new assignment was, but it was more than enough that they now knew that Bob Rodriquez was alive, well, and working in an honorable, if very dangerous profession.

Tom was sleeping quietly, and Nancy and Harry walked down toward the library.

"You are right to keep this from Tom; there's no way it could make him happy, and it might well upset him. I think he derived some satisfaction from the idea that Bob was dead, and that he had met an unhappy end."

He squeezed Nancy's arm.

"Yes, and you know that wasn't like the old Tom. Somehow I think he distilled all his resentment of his torture as a POW, all the years he lost in Hanoi, into his hatred of Bob. When he was a younger man, he would have shrugged off any unhappiness about a business deal, even the attempted takeover; it just wouldn't have mattered that much to him. But he was so badly treated by the Vietnamese that he just couldn't take the problems with Bob."

"It's strange, he never said anything against the Vietnamese as a people; he did talk about the evil guard—what did he call him, Rabbit?—once in a while. But somehow I think Tom began to see Rodriquez as the sum of all bad things; it was easier to hate a known, visible target."

There were tears in Nancy's eyes as she said, "I hope he finds some peace, now. He's been through so much."

The rest of the family was gathered in the library where there had been so many New Year's Eve celebrations in the past. It had been Vance Shannon's custom to gather the clan, put out a noble buffet, and recount the year's happenings at his business. For the most part these had been happy occasions, for there were only a few years when either a slump in business or outside events dampened the mood. Tonight there was an unusual mixture of sadness over Tom's decline and euphoria over knowing that Bob Rodriquez was not only alive, but that his reputation was untarnished.

There was plenty to be happy about in terms of the results of the family's widespread business holdings. Despite having retired, assuming a chairman emeritus role, Harry now acted as the pater familias. He had the firm's chief financial officer prepare a brief survey of the firm's achievements as a preview of the coming annual report. He said to Nancy, "This is so different from the early days. Dad would get up and say something like 'Well, we made a little money last year, but we're going to have to watch our Ps and Qs this year,' and that would be it. Now I've got a sixteen-page two-color brochure to hand out, and I only understand about half of it."

Nancy nodded. Curiously, she understood the brochure very well, for it was a sixteen-page reproach to her time as head of the company. No one had intended it that way, and perhaps no one else saw it, but she realized that the company she had run almost into the ground was now prospering as never before. It hurt, but she said nothing. She had ruined the evening on a few of these year-end briefings in the past. She would not ruin tonight's.

Harry stood up, surveying the room. There were about the same number of people there, but the mix was different. Three seminal figures were missing, of course: Vance, Tom, and Bob Rodriquez. And the disposition of the room had changed. Where once there had been an unconscious grouping of "friends of Tom," and "friends of Bob," there was now a homogeneous mixture of family and friends. It reflected the corporate new look of Vance Shannon, Incorporated, with its many divisions and associated companies. Rod was there with Mae, representing the incredibly successful AdVanceAir Leasing firm. Dennis Jenkins waited quietly. He was now president of SpaceVisions, the former ActOn company. It had been a subsidiary of Allied Aviation briefly, until Dennis gained enough shares to make it a private company once again. He sat next to Anna—who was not drinking, hadn't been for almost three years now. On the other side of the big fireplace sat the newly minted Brigadier General Steve O'Malley, talking earnestly with Tom's grief-stricken son, V. R. And quietly in a corner, taking no notes, but taking it all in, was Warren Bowers, who was working on a second volume of Vance Shannon's biography.

Harry stood up, causing Anna to wince as he tapped on his Waterford crystal champagne glass with a spoon.

"Welcome again, everyone, to the annual Vance Shannon Memorial debriefing."

They laughed, knowing that Vance would have writhed at such a remark.

"We'll keep this short, for obvious reasons tonight. I've given you all the first draft of what will be the company's annual report; there might be some changes, but this is close enough, and you'll see that Vance Shannon, Incorporated, did very well indeed, as did our new subsidiary, AdVanceAir Leasing."

There were subdued cries of "Hear! Hear!"

"I'd like to propose four toasts, tonight—that ought to be enough to get us oiled up. Then we'll talk, as Vance would have done, about the big events of the last year and what might be coming up in the future. Then I'll throw it open to questions and comments. Nancy keeps reminding me that the cold food on the buffet is getting warm, and the warm food is getting cold, so I'll be quick about it."

He raised his glass and gave the toast that Vance always started out with, a reminder of his days flying combat in World War I: "To those who have gone West."

They sipped at their champagne, with Anna and Harry, as always, drinking club soda.

Then he said: "To a great American hero, Tom Shannon."

Nancy looked at V. R.; both their eyes were filled with tears as they drank.

"To another great American hero, who did so much for his country and for this company, and who will be back with us soon, we hope—Bob Rodriquez."

There were more murmurs of "Hear! Hear!" and Rod reached over and kissed his mother Mae.

Finally, Harry raised his glass again. "And last, to the man who started this family and these companies, an ace, a test pilot, and a magnificent leader—Vance Shannon."

There was a spontaneous cheer as they drank.

Harry, emotional, waited a moment to gain control of his voice and then said, "Now, let's look back. Who has any comments they'd like to make on the year?"

V. R. stood up. "First, let's give Steve O'Malley a round of applause for his first star! For a guy they said was washed up as a colonel, he's done pretty well."

It was true. O'Malley had been a fast burner, but run into a bureaucratic brick wall that seemed to doom his Air Force career. He'd stepped into civil life briefly, made a fortune with Bob Rodriquez's help, and then wangled his way back into a slot at the Pentagon where his talents were recognized.

O'Malley waved, and nodded across the room to his wife Sally, who was sitting with V. R.'s beautiful blond wife, Ginny. Both women watched the room with wary amusement; both were "pilot's widows," with their husbands gone most of the time. Both had more than once teetered on the edge of getting a divorce before they finally realized that they were hooked and that there might be worse things than being married to a pilot.

O'Malley said, "Congratulations on what looks like a great year. I know it's obvious but I want to remind us that we owe a lot to Ronald Reagan, who stopped Carter's unilateral disarmament and started making America strong."

V. R. said, "Roger that! It was about time, too! The stupid press makes fun of him about his Strategic Defense Initiative, calling it Star Wars and stuff, but the practical fact is that he's going to spend the Soviet Union into the ground. They will never be able to keep up with what we're doing. Mark my words, with things like starting the B-1 program, adding fighter wings, adding missiles, Reagan is going to win the Cold War."

The room went quiet. V. R. was young, but his statement was exactly the caliber of the predictions that Vance Shannon used to make, and Vance was rarely wrong. Suddenly the crowd looked at him in a new light. V. R. was now the heir apparent, even though he was solidly locked in to an Air Force career.

Rod spoke up: "V. R., I hope you are right. Dennis here has been saying something similar for months. That there is really light at the end of the Cold War tunnel."

Jenkins said, "Right on, V. R. And look on the commercial side. Boeing built almost two thousand 727s before they stopped production and they just rolled out their thousandth 737. I'll bet they build five thousand 737s before they're done. And the Soviet Union cannot keep up there either; they are building some good-looking airliners, but they just don't match the economics of a Boeing product. Their engines suck up too much fuel, they need too much maintenance."

O'Malley broke in. "They are better at shooting them down. Did you read their account of shooting down the Korean Airline 747? It was simply murderous bureaucratic incompetence."

They were quiet and Mae spoke up. "Steve, you must be pretty happy about the way the F-16 has gone. How many have they built so far?"

He smiled. The F-16 had been his pet project, one that had run him into the career minefield because his boss had opposed it.

"Number one thousand has rolled out. They are going to make a lot more before that line ends."

Rod nodded happily. He hadn't said much, but he had a point to make, and he wanted Warren Bowers to take note of it.

"Folks, it's been a great year, and next year will be better. But things are changing. Vance Shannon was in on the start of the jet age, and he told my dad that they had witnessed only the first two stages. The first stage had been based on the novelty of the jet engine and the speed it provided. That's why the Boeing 707, the Douglas DC-8, the Caravelle, and the rest of them were so successful. They made flying easy, fast, and comfortable. And safe, too. Vance said the second stage would be based on size—and he was right again with the 747, the Lockheed L-1011, and the Douglas DC-10. They made flying relatively cheap; it wasn't any faster, and it was a lot less comfortable, but it brought air transport to the masses on an economic basis."

Suddenly flushing, he said, "And my dad told me about the third phase of the jet age, the one we are just entering now. It is one that our firms will be able to take advantage of, if we play our cards right. The third phase is going to be based on ever more economical engines and on cleaned-up aerodynamics. You'll see huge engines with 60,000 and 100,000 pounds of thrust, and more."

He stopped and turned to Harry. "Harry, you remember telling me about watching Dick Rutan take off in his little fiberglass airplane?"

"Sure, Tom was amazed by it, just as I was."

"Well, that is, in microcosm, the future. You are going to see exotic aerodynamics, exotic materials, and another whole generation of engines that will carry us into the twenty-first century and beyond."

There was a general silence, for two reasons. This was the first time Rod had ever made a prediction like this, and he sounded just like his father—which was promising in the extreme. The second was concern over whether a change of this scope was really in the best interest of their firms.

O'Malley finally broke the silence.

"I agree with you, Bob, but there's another development just over the horizon. Nobody's figured it out yet, but it has to be faced. And that is hypersonic flight. We've got the Concorde going, and lots of fighters are supersonic, but the next step has to be not just going three times the speed of sound, like the SR-71, but getting up there in six or eight times the speed of sound."

There was silence again and Mae finally said, "Steve, you never say anything unless you are pretty well convinced of it. You've got some insight, from something, probably a classified project that we don't have. But just hearing you say it makes me believe it."

Harry said, "That's enough for tonight! We've gone from a World War I toast to hypersonic flight. Now let's just see if we can make it all the way to the buffet table, where I'll at least know what I'm doing for once."

October 18, 1984
Edwards Air Force Base, California

MAJOR GENERAL STEVE O'MALLEY and Dennis Jenkins walked slowly out of the debriefing room, shaking their heads. It had been one hell of a debriefing. The prototype North American B-1B had landed at 2:38 P.M. after a three-hour and twenty-minute flight from the plant in Palmdale.

"Steve, this was pretty damn good for a first flight on an airplane as complex as the B-1B. There were only a couple of delays before take-off, the flight systems worked fine, and so did most of the avionics."

Jenkins's morose expression did not change. "That's easy for you to say; you're not responsible for the radar—and it didn't work at all."

Both men wandered out toward the flight line where mechanics were still swarming around the huge bomber. Unlike the ill-fated B-1As, which had been painted white, the number one B-1B, serial number 82-0001, was painted in two shades of gray and a dusky dark green, giving its long nose and swept wings an even more sinister look.

Jenkins sighed. "Christ, this has been a long time in coming. I don't think any bomber anywhere has had the development time or the mission changes this one has."

It was true. The program had started in 1961, when the Air Force was looking for a replacement for the B-52, then already 19 years old. It continued on for the next sixteen years under a variety of names and stupid-sounding acronyms—subsonic low altitude bomber (SLAB), extended long range strike aircraft (ERSA), low altitude manned penetrator (LAMP), and finally advanced manned precision strike system (AMPSS).

The Secretary of Defense, Robert S. McNamara, had tried to kill it many times, once by demanding that the Air Force stretch the General Dynamics F-111 into a bomber, the FB-111. In April 1969, the aircraft finally received a decent designation, the B-1A, and a contract was let for North American Rockwell to build 244 of them. Four B-1As were built, the first one flying in December 1974. After three years of testing, President Jimmy Carter, in the midst of a frenzy of unilateral disarmament, canceled the program, saying that with the new air-launched cruise missile, it wasn't needed. This was an outright lie; the ALCM, as it was called, was early in its development and was no substitute for a bomber that could penetrate enemy defenses.

Jenkins went on. "You were right about Ronald Reagan. When he ordered the B-1B into production, he saved the Air Force. This airplane has tremendous potential, and the B-52 design is thirty years old now."

Both men knew that the B-1B was not as ambitious an airplane as its predecessor, the B-1A. It was not as fast, but it had far better stealth qualities.

O'Malley said, "Dennis, the nature of war is changing. The one hundred B-1Bs we're going to buy will saturate the defenses of the Soviet Union better than the B-52s can do. But it's more important that it's adaptable. We'll be able to use the latest in GPS navigation, and meld that into our precision guided bombs."

"I agree. But what do you mean when you say the nature of war is changing? The Soviet Union is still our main enemy; we still have to claw through their radar, their SAMs, their fighters."

"Yeah, but the Soviet Union is on its last legs. I just hope it doesn't go out with a suicidal launch of intercontinental ballistic missiles. They've been stuck in Afghanistan since 1979. They are setting the Muslim world on fire. Look at all the incidents around the world, the hijackings, the killings, the explosions. And look how we are reacting to them. The Iranians made fools out of us by capturing our embassy in Tehran. And now last year, in Beirut, they bomb our embassy in April, and blow up the Marine barracks in October. What do we do? We protest and we walk. They killed almost 400 people and we flee the scene of the crime."

"What the hell can we do; it's just a bunch of fanatics, not the whole Muslim world. You can't declare war on the fanatics and kill people wholesale."

"The hell you can't. Germany was run by a bunch of fanatics, the Nazis. And Japan was run by a bunch of fanatic militarists who ordered Pearl Harbor bombed and then declared war on us. And we sure bombed the hell out of *their* people. We had to—they were passive about the fanatics, and the fanatics were trying to kill us. It's the same thing here."

Jenkins shook his head and stayed silent. O'Malley was a brilliant guy, but this seemed to be off base.

"I know it sounds nuts, Dennis, but I'm running the trend lines out ten, maybe twenty years, and it looks to me like we're going to be fighting entirely different kinds of wars. We'll be looking to kill individuals, or maybe small groups, not armies. No army blew up the barracks in Beirut, just a bunch of terrorists. No army is going to blow up the New York subway system, or set off a little nuke in D.C.—it'll be a small gang of terrorists."

It was hot on the tarmac at Edwards, and they stood sweating in the shade of the swept wing of the number one B-1B. They were alone— all the mechanics and technicians had gone in for supper.

"Steve, you don't talk like this as a rule. This is the first time you've ever mentioned anything like this to me."

"Or to anyone else. I'm just getting used to the idea."

"Well, be that as it may, something caused it. And I've got a damned good idea it was something you found out about Bob Rodriquez. You probably cannot tell me what it is, but there's something going on here that is totally strange."

"You're right, as usual, Dennis, and not only am I going to tell you, I have to tell you. Something fatal could happen to Bob, and we'll never know about it, and nobody would ever reveal anything. Something could happen to me, for that matter, and I want somebody able to tell the family what he's doing when the time comes. You can't tell them now, it's too secret; talk about deep black, this is deepest indigo, you can't get any more classified than this. And I'd be court-martialed if anyone knew I told you about it. But I'm going to because I know you'll keep it to yourself. If something happens to me, later on, you'll be able to pass the word on to Mae and Rod, and to the Shannons."

O'Malley stood up and walked around the airplane, scanning the tops of the wings on the off chance that there might be someone he hadn't seen still there. He came back and said, "OK. Here it is. Bob Rodriquez had been running drugs, working for the FBI. His looks and his Spanish language talent made him a natural. Apparently he was so fed up with the Shannons and Mae and the business that he volunteered for undercover work, just to get away from it all."

"I figured it had to be something like that. Bob was a patriot."

"That he was and is. Then something bigger came up. They needed someone who could infiltrate some of the terrorist networks they were uncovering. They faked the accident in the Bahamas where he was supposed to be killed, and put him into an intensive course in Arabic language and culture. His size and his coloring made him a natural. Bob wasn't really a linguist, but apparently he did well in school, and now he's working inside some terrorist organization. I don't know where, and I don't want to. I just hope he can survive, and somehow get back to a normal life back here."

"So this was how your theories got started. Did you meet with him?"

"Yes, one short two-hour meeting, in the back of a van parked out in West Virginia. He was so hungry for news, real news about Mae and Rod that we talked about them most of the time. But he told me that the terrorist threat was real, and that their ultimate goal was to defeat the United States, not in face-to-face combat, but by destroying our economy with terrorism."

"Not bloody likely."

"Don't discount it, Dennis. I think we've got a real fight on our hands, because the terrorists are radical Muslims who are making the whole Muslim world—a billion and a half people—dance to their tune."

"Frankly, Steve, I think you are wrong. In the first place they are terribly poor. In the second place, they are militarily inept; look how Israel has cleaned their clocks every time."

"They almost succeeded in 1973; it was a close-run thing. If we hadn't bailed Israel out with an airlift of supplies, the Arabs would probably have won. And the Israelis would probably have used their nukes. No telling what might have happened then. Believe me; this is the threat of the future."

Jenkins mulled it over for a while and said, "Steve, you haven't really convinced me, but I've known you long enough to know that you are usually right. This tells me that we've got to look into changing our weapons and our tactics for a totally different kind of fight. At the same time, we can't let down our guard. We both think the Soviets are going down the tube, but some lunatic might decide to take us down with them, and we have to be able to prevent that."

"I wouldn't have said a word to you, Dennis, if I didn't know you'd keep it as secret as I have to."

They walked in silence back to the edge of the flight line, where O'Malley had parked his staff car.

"It's a damn shame, Dennis, that we cannot all get along. Look what's happened just this year—the Space Shuttle's working beautifully, we fired off an antisatellite missile, and Reagan is calling for a space station to be built. It's good in the civil market as well. We've got twin-engine airliners, 757s and 767s flying the Atlantic, and that crazy Burt Rutan has a round-the-world nonstop, non-refueled airplane being built. It could be a lot of fun if we could get away from the wars."

"We've gotten away from the wars; it's just that the wars haven't gotten away from us."

CHAPTER TEN

THE PASSING PARADE: Uranus examined by *Voyager 2* space-craft; space shuttle *Challenger* explodes after launch; President Marcos forced out after twenty-year reign; Nazi service of Aus-trian President Kurt Waldheim revealed; nuclear accident at Chernobyl power plant causes immense damage; Reagan's "Star Wars" policy rejected by House of Representatives; Jonathan Pollard convicted of spying for Israel; legislation bars hiring illegal immigrants; Margaret Thatcher elected to third term as Prime Minister; huge earthquake hits Los Angeles; Rudolf Hess found dead, strangled, in prison; huge 22.6 percent drop in value of stock market on "Black Monday," October 19; *Les Misérables* wins eight Tony awards.

April 14, 1986
Off Land's End, England

V. R. Shannon was still not comfortable in the airplane, and he didn't like flying with another man in the cockpit, his weapons systems officer. The F-117A Nighthawk in which he had accumulated six hundred hours wasn't as fast or as long-ranged as the General Dynamics F-111F he was flying tonight, but he was used to its quirks, and he flew it solo. This was different. His hands didn't yet go automatically to the needed switches, and he had to sort out the emergency procedures that applied to the F-117A when he needed to correct something in the F-111F. Yet like all the F-111 pilots, he relished the ease with which he could sweep the wings, extending them for low speed operations, sweeping them back to go supersonic. It took all the guts he had, though, to fly hands off while the automatic terrain-following radar guided them at low levels—three hundred feet or less, through valleys and over mountains, day or night, without regard to weather. And while he had absolute confidence in his weapons systems officer, Captain Charles Waple, he knew that the confidence was not reciprocated. Yet.

Major General Steve O'Malley had dragooned V. R. from his job as operations officer with the 415th Tactical Fighter Squadron a year before, pumping him up with his radical theories on the nature of the terrorist threat and the need to strike a blow. Steve's wife, Sally, had called V. R. two months earlier. They were both worried that Steve was going to scuttle his career with his continual focus on the threat of Muslim terrorists. This ran counter to the pervasive, time-honored thinking within the Air Force that the main threat was the Soviet Union. And once again Steve was making powerful enemies in the Pentagon, people who resented his having left the Air Force, made a fortune in industry, and then returned to be put on an apparent fast track to four-star rank. V. R. had talked to him in early January, when O'Malley was visiting Lakenheath, checking on their readiness.

"General, you know that Sally and I had a long conversation about you. She's worried that you are about to shoot yourself in the foot with this terrorist business, just like you did with the F-16."

O'Malley grinned. "And who was right about the F-16? I was. And I'm right about this, no matter what they say in the Pentagon. I'm getting some traction with the idea, too. Look what the bastards have been doing to us."

Intuitively, V. R. couldn't believe that O'Malley was right. The Soviet Union seemed like a much more impressive threat—it could wipe out the world in an hour, even if it chose to sacrifice itself in the process. Yet O'Malley was smart and it was hard to deny his logic. The worst was the truck bombing of the Marine barracks in 1983, but since then the terrorists had launched attacks on airports in Rome and Vienna, and exploded a bomb on a TWA airliner—it was a miracle that the plane had not crashed. In April, they had attacked a Berlin discotheque, killing American servicemen.

O'Malley had gone on: "There have been three thousand attacks around the world just in 1985, and everybody is trying to pretend they didn't happen. Meanwhile, the Soviet Union is a rust belt, sinking in its own waste. We've got to stop these Muslim fanatics, and the top guy right now is Qaddafi, in Libya. He's a smart-ass, and Reagan knows we need to squash him."

So there it was. All of the planning was directed at a joint Air Force/Navy strike at five targets in Libya, in cooperation with friendly NATO countries. That had gone sour in early April, when France, Germany, Italy, and Spain not only refused to cooperate in a strike, they denied passage of U.S. warplanes through their airspace. Some friends.

Now the fleet of eighteen F-111Fs—Aardvarks they called them because of their long, pointed, slightly turned-up noses—was en route on a round-trip flight (they hoped) of sixty-four hundred miles that would take thirteen hours and twelve in-flight refuelings. The F-111's three targets were in Tripoli, while Navy carrier planes were hitting two sites in Benghazi. A fleet of twenty-eight McDonnell Douglas KC-10 and Boeing KC-135 tankers flew with the strike force.

It was relatively quiet in the cockpit of Lujack 34, his call sign. There was no radio chatter and the airplane flew well on its autopilot. These were special versions of the F-111, with powerful Pratt & Whitney TF30 engines, each putting out 25,100 pounds of thrust and giving a top speed of Mach 2.2. Best of all, they were equipped with the new and highly classified AN/AVQ-26 Pave Tack bombing system.

Pave Tack was sort of a modern Norden bombsight both in importance and in secrecy. It had been one of Bob Rodriquez's last contributions to precision bombing. He had developed a system that gave high-speed tactical aircraft the ability to acquire, recognize, and attack tactical targets during day, night, and some adverse weather conditions. Building on Bob's earlier designs, Pave Tack used an imaging infrared sensor and laser designator/ranger for navigational updates, target acquisition and recognition, and weapon delivery.

V. R. had gone through a conversion course at Cannon Air Force Base, immersing himself in the big swing-wing F-111F and its complex electronics. Now he had about two hundred hours in the aircraft, and was the low-time man in the 48th Tactical Fighter Wing. He didn't have to wonder what Chuck Waple thought about that.

Especially on this mission. They had launched from RAF Lakenheath at 17:36 GMT, and their first night refueling—in radio silence, of course—had been from a big McDonnell Douglas KC-10—the first time anyone in the 48th had refueled from that aircraft. And it was thirteen long years since the last wartime flights in Vietnam. Very few people in the formation were combat veterans. V. R. had been blooded, flying secretly for Israel and scoring a victory over a Syrian MiG. No one in the squadron knew this, although it would have helped V. R.'s new-guy position to have told them.

The tankers helped the fighters navigate at 26,000 feet and 450 knots. The fighters clustered next to their "mother tanker" in such tight formation that radar controllers on the ground could see only the tankers on their screens as they charted an extremely accurate course, skirting all NATO airspace. Four EF-111F Raven electronic warfare aircraft flew with them, ready to blank out enemy radar, communications, and SAM launching electronics. Grumman had modified a dozen F-111s into electronic counterwarfare aircraft. The crews called it the "Spark-Vark" and reveled in its advanced equipment that included GPS navigation gear.

They would need the EF-111s. V. R. and the rest of the 48th pilots felt they were on a crapshoot, facing a duel with the sophisticated Soviet surface-to-air missiles that were part of the expensive Libyan integrated air defense system. There were Soviet spy ships in the Mediterranean, watching for an attack they knew was coming. The same governments that denied overflight also harbored Soviet operatives eager to pass information on to Moscow. This night would really test the F-111F—and the 48th TFW.

O'Malley had balked at the instructions to have eighteen F-111s make the attack; he thought the element of surprise would be lost. He knew that the long route and the multiple refuelings would increase the chances of a mishap by orders of magnitude. But he had been overruled by Secretary of Defense Caspar Weinberger, who wanted a significant amount of bombs dropped on the target. The only concession they made was demanding that the Air Force and Navy aircraft attack simultaneously, to maximize any element of surprise that remained.

Time droned by for the F-111s, with the almost hourly stimulation of in-flight refuelings keeping the crews awake.

"Tony, how are we doing? Will we meet the rules of engagement?"

Waple's sleepy voice came back. "No problem, Skipper, if we get down and manage to identify the targets. All the equipment is functioning perfectly. You just have to fly down the chute at the right time and the right speed."

The right time was now. V. R. and the other F-111Fs descended to two hundred feet, releasing their bombs precisely at 02:00 hours local Libyan time. V. R.'s target was the Tripoli airport. They got confirmation on the target and Waple's twelve Snakeye parachute-retarded Mk 82 bombs, five hundred pounders, destroyed an Ilyushin IL-76 transport and tore up some revetments. As V. R. pulled up he saw a flash in the distance, and thought, *Oh-oh. Someone just caught the golden bb.*

The combined Navy and Air Force assault was over in ten minutes. Libyan resistance was light, and seemed confused and inaccurate. By morning they'd have the reconnaissance photos to tell how much damage had been done. He was content. They had hit their targets, and maybe they had Qaddafi's attention. Now he hunkered down for the long flight back, more of the same, plowing along, excitement subsiding, doing the air refueling drill, and wondering what O'Malley would think about the raid.

And wondering when he would get back to the 415 TFS, the Nighthawk—and Ginny. He thought for a moment and reflected, *There's my problem. I've got things in the wrong order.*

November 23, 1987
Mojave, California

STANDING OUTSIDE THE dingy office, Rod nodded at Harry and smiled, saying, "Looks like it's going to be an all-male family reunion."

"They missed a bet. They expected it to be hot and here it's a pleasant sixty degrees."

Both men recalled a previous visit, one that had tested the late Tom Shannon's will and courage with its heat. Tom had passed away on New Year's Day, 1984, quietly in his sleep, just as his father had done.

"The temperature's not the only thing different; we've got a bit of a crisis on hand with AdVanceAir Leasing, as you know. Do you want to start, or should I?"

Harry smiled. "Well, let me start with a general discussion, find out what everyone has been doing. I know everyone wants to hear from V. R. how the Libyan raid went off. And I know O'Malley is going to give us a pitch on how rotten the Muslims are—you can't avoid it when he's around. Everybody else will want to have their say, too. When we've finished chewing the rag, you give your pitch first, because I know you have nothing but bad news. I've got mostly good news, so I'll finish on an upbeat note."

They went through the fragile door, twisted almost off its hinges by a hot Mojave wind last summer. Inside, the rest of the group, all Shannon intimates and all investors in AdVanceAir Leasing, kept up their buzz of conversations.

For years they had met at the traditional New Year's Eve party at the Shannon house in Palos Verde. Last year, everyone was spread all over the world, and Harry canceled the party. This year Harry and Anna were planning a three-week cruise over the Christmas holidays. But today's business was so urgent that everyone agreed to move the meeting date up, and coordinate their schedules to meet at Mojave. O'Malley was at Edwards on business so V. R. caught a flight down from Tonopah to drive over with him. Dennis Jenkins had picked up Warren Bowers in Santa Monica and drove out with him and Harry.

The dreary mélange of used furniture—folding metal chairs, padded office chairs with missing casters, a bench—was pushed around into a circle as Harry stood by the cloth-covered briefing board. He noted that the cloth was black this time—Rod had a puckish sense of humor.

"Good morning, all. Sorry the ladies didn't see fit to make it, but we'll take them all out to dinner tonight to make up for it. We've got about forty minutes of business to conduct, give or take a quarter of an hour, but first I know we all want to hear from V. R. about Operation El Dorado Canyon, when he and his F-111 buddies put the fear of God into Qaddafi."

Steve O'Malley gave out a hearty "Hear! Hear!" and they smiled. He had slipped the idea for the raid into the back door of the White House Military Office. A buddy who flew Air Force One dropped the idea casually to one of Cap Weinberger's staffers, and it had taken off.

V. R. stood up, smiling, gave them the story of the raid, then turned to O'Malley, saying, "General, you know the results better than I do. Why don't you tell us all what really happened."

Beaming, O'Malley said, "Well, even though the tangible military results were not all we wanted, the psychological results were. In short, we scared the shit out of Qaddafi, that's for sure. There's been a definite decline in hostile actions from the Muslim organizations Qaddafi was funding. He himself was reported to be virtually incapacitated for days after the raid. He disappeared for twenty-four hours. He likes bombing others, but isn't so crazy about being bombed himself. You know that he claims that his daughter was injured. I'm only sorry that it was her and not Qaddafi himself."

O'Malley paused and went on. "The rules of engagement inhibited the attack. It is damn hard to get a positive target I.D. in that environment. Only four of the F-111s—V. R.'s was one of them—got definite target identification. Six had to abort because of aircraft problems, and seven flat missed their targets entirely. One put a bomb near the French embassy."

Dennis Jenkins yelled "Hear! Hear!" and got a laugh.

"But we got a lot of pointers for improvement. For the next A-rab we go after." O'Malley was quiet for a moment, then said, "We were also lucky. The Libyans didn't put up anything like the defense they should have been able to do with the equipment they had on hand. You know they had at least three thousand Soviet technicians there—they must all have been drunk. We lost one airplane, as you know. They claim it was shot down by a SAM, and maybe it was, but it could have been just pilot disorientation."

V. R. spoke up. "You said it, General." V. R. never presumed on their friendship to call him Steve. "It was pitch-black, the flak was limited but coming up on all sides, and we had to jink around. It would have been easy for someone to lose their orientation and go in."

There was some back and forth, the usual banter among friends, then Harry called on Dennis to talk. "What's going on in your world, Dennis?"

"Harry, you've got the CFO's report in your back pocket there, so I won't comment on the business. But I would like to say that NASA seems to be slowly recovering from the loss of the *Challenger.*"

They were all quiet. Not a man in the room could forget where he was when the ghastly news of the January 1986 Space Shuttle disaster had burst over the networks.

"When do you think they'll fly again? Or do you think they'll fly again?"

Dennis shook his head. "They'll fly again, for sure, but not until they've gone over everything another thousand times. They are shaken that such a trivial seeming thing—a rubber O-ring—could have caused such a tragedy. It will be two years, maybe three, until they fly again. But they will fly. NASA is committed to it, and so are the astronauts."

Jenkins went on. "The *Challenger* got the year off to a bad start, but there were some high spots later in 1986 that have to give you hope for the business. Lockheed kept on churning out C-130s—more than eighteen hundred now, and no sign of the line stopping. We had the first flight of the McDonnell F-15E. It is one hell of a strike fighter, and it's going to be around for a long time. And maybe the cheeriest news of 1986 started out here in Mojave. Dick Rutan and Jeana Yeager made it around the world, nonstop and un-refueled in the *Voyager*. That was some deal, you have to admire them—Dick, Jeana, Burt, the whole crew."

V. R. nodded in agreement. "That was a lot riskier than bombing Qaddafi! Every time I watch their takeoff roll, I get goose bumps. They looked like they were going to buy the farm right there at Edwards."

Harry spoke up. "We'll hear a lot more from them. Burt Rutan already has a series of designs in the works, all totally unlike anything we've seen before. He's a genius, just like Dad said he was."

Surprisingly Warren Bowers spoke up. "What about '87, Dennis? Anything worth while mentioning there?"

Jenkins smiled. "Well, the funniest thing was that kid, what was his name, Mathias Rust, flew a Cessna into Moscow and landed in Red Square."

There was applause and O'Malley called out, "Don't let that fool you. They had him under surveillance all along, and could have shot him down, but after all the bad publicity about shooting down the Korean Airliner, they didn't have the guts to do it. But it does show that there are cracks in the Soviet system."

Dennis nodded and went on. "We're getting some competition in fighters. The Brits and the French have the Typhoon in work, and the Swedes have another hot little fighter, the Saab Gripen; I don't know how they do it, a tiny little country staying up with the rest of the world."

O'Malley, always a trifle chauvinistic, said, "They do it with American technology. That's a G.E. engine they are using, and they are arming it with Sidewinders and Mavericks, all good G.I. issue, built under license."

Jenkins said, "Agreed, but be that as it may, they'll be competition, and the market for fighters gets tighter every year as their price goes up. Remember what Norm Augustine predicted: someday every dollar in the Air Force budget will go to buy just one airplane."

"Anything else before we get down to business?"

Jenkins spoke again. "Let's hear it for the B-1B. Most of us saw it at the rollout, and this year it set a whole bunch of world records. Steve, V. R., you probably know Bob Chamberlain? He and his crew set more than a dozen world records in the B-1B on July Fourth. That airplane has come a long way, despite all the critics."

Harry waited a moment, looked around to see if anyone else was going to talk, then said, "Now brace yourself. Rod is going to give us the bad news."

Looking more than a little sheepish, Rod went to the easel and pulled the black cloth off, folded it as carefully as if it were a funeral flag, and waited while they digested the single sentence he had grease-penciled on the sheet. It read:

Of 128 new low-cost airlines created after deregulation, only 37 are still operating.

"You'll remember that I told you that AdVanceAir Leasing was in the business of creating instant airlines. What I didn't know, and couldn't tell you, was that deregulation was in the business of creating instant bankrupt airlines."

Dennis said, "I'm just a minor stockholder in this group, but what does it mean to us?"

"As you know AdVanceAir stock is not publicly traded; we were going to go public last year but I'm glad we waited, otherwise we would have cost a lot of people a lot of money. What it means is that the big cash-flow projections and the big profits we predicted for 1987 are just not going to happen. We've actually been pretty lucky—of the twenty-seven airlines we have leased airplanes to, only seven have failed, but another ten are shaky. I think the remaining ten are pretty solid. I'll pass out some hard figures for you, but here's the long and short of it. We're just about going to break even this year, but next year we will lose money because we'll have the expense of flying back to Mojave all the aircraft that are sitting abandoned because their airline has gone belly-up. There are about sixty of them, and unless I can peddle them, they will all have to be brought to ferry-flight status and flown back here for storage, waiting for business to pick up."

Bowers, not a wealthy man by any means, had most of his investment placed with AdVanceAir. There was a tremble in his voice as he asked, "Is that going to happen?"

"I can't tell you, Warren. The only thing I can tell you is that on my mom's advice, I hedged on this happening. She had me use some of our surplus cash to buy positions on the Boeing 737 and Airbus A320 lines. If the demand for those airplanes picks up, the buying options will be like gold. I think it's enough to keep us in the black all through 1988 and maybe longer. By then the effects of deregulation should have dampened out, and we should be back in business."

Warren looked blank. "I have no idea what you are talking about. What is buying a position? What is a buying option?"

Rod said, "It's common practice. You put money down early in a production cycle on an airplane that's supposed to be delivered a year or two or more later. Then if an airline comes along that's desperate for new equipment, you can sell them your place in the line at a profit. If not, and we stay in business, we can lease the new airplanes to customers."

Obviously distressed, Warren murmured, "I sure hope so."

Rod went on. "And I'll tell you something else. Unless Boeing gets organized, the A320 is going to clean the 757's and 767's clocks! The fuel efficiency numbers for the airplane are fantastic, and it looks like the public is really going to like the interiors."

O'Malley said, "Isn't Boeing going to compete with a new design? They have to, otherwise they are helping create a monster competitor."

Rod said, "No, it looks like they are going to stand pat and just upgrade the 737. It is a terrible strategy and the old-line guys at Boeing, the guys who saw the company bet on the 707, the 727, the 737, and the 747, are going nuts! They can't stand the idea of another company making a better airplane."

Dennis Jenkins was always up on the inside news and said, "Apparently the new top brass in Boeing is saying that it is time to stop trying to run the company like a model railroad, and always spend the money on new equipment. Instead they are going to concentrate on shareholder return. Personally, I think it's a fatal strategy."

There was a general murmuring—all were Boeing fans—and Harry said, "Well, Rod's given us the bad news and I hope that that is as bad as it ever gets. The good news is that the rest of Vance Shannon, Incorporated, performed better than the market; every share you held in the company last year has gone up in value by about 30 percent. That's better than almost any aerospace company stock in the business, and it speaks to the values Dad instilled in the company and in us. I just wish he and Tom were still here with us."

Harry passed around the draft copies of the annual report for analysis. He felt fairly comfortable. No one, except perhaps Warren, had been unduly shaken by the bad news from AdVanceAir and the profit and loss statement in the annual report would ease most of their discomfort.

As they read, he surveyed the group, admiring their boundless source of energy and talent, and realizing how well they represented the aviation industry. From the start, aviation had demanded the utmost from its people, often even their lives. It was no different now. With a sense of nostalgia, he remembered those long gone years when he and his twin brother Tom were young, trying to expand their father's business. They would have given a lot to have had people like these to work with then. He was just glad he had them to work with now.

CHAPTER ELEVEN

THE PASSING PARADE: U.S. Navy mistakes Iranian airliner for hostile aircraft, shoots it down, 290 dead; George H. W. Bush elected President; compact discs outsell vinyl records for first time; defeated Soviet Union leaves Afghanistan; antidepressant Prozac introduced; tunnel ("Chunnel") under English Channel under way; eight-year Iran-Iraq war ends; Lucille Ball dies; *Exxon Valdez* releases huge oil spill in Alaskan waters; Chinese students rebel in Tiananmen Square; Oliver North guilty in Iran-Contra affair; Mikhail S. Gorbachev becomes President of Soviet Union; Cincinnati Reds star Pete Rose banned from baseball for gambling; Colin Powell appointed first African American Chairman of the Joint Chiefs of Staff; huge earthquake in San Francisco; Burma becomes Myanmar; Deng Xiaoping resigns leadership; Communist bloc begins to disintegrate; Berlin Wall torn down; Romanians revolt, kill President Ceausescu.

November 22, 1988
Palmdale, California

Steve O'Malley grabbed V. R.'s hand and said, "Congratulations on those eagles, Colonel; you're getting to be a pretty hot rock in the promotion department."

V. R. returned the grip, grinning with pleasure, saying, "I've been lucky. I've had some friends—you being the best of them. And being the son of an ace and the grandson of Vance Shannon has helped a lot. I don't know how long it will go on, but I'm going to ride it out."

O'Malley nodded at the closed hangar doors of Northrop's Palmdale facility, saying, "They are sure doing this differently than the F-117! Imagine having an open rollout like this before the airplane even flies."

"I think there are a couple of reasons for it. We could keep the F-117 pretty well hidden—"

O'Malley interrupted, "Pretty well hidden! There wasn't any public announcement of the Nighthawk until about ten days ago. I never knew anything that was kept so secret so long."

"We were lucky, but I'm glad they let the public in on it. It will make things easier, you know, routine flights in daytime, and all the rest. But the B-2A is so big, they couldn't hide it, and they couldn't just test it at night. And as you know better than me, its cost is soaring, so they need some hype to strengthen its position in Congress."

O'Malley said, "Well, no surprises. Congress never stops shooting us in the foot, grandstanding for votes. It played its usual game of cutting back procurement as costs rose, and surprise! Unit costs go up. They knew going in that the research and development costs were astronomical—they had to be to get an airplane this advanced. It would have averaged out for the original 135 aircraft program, but if they do what the insiders say they are going to do—cut back to just twenty airplanes—it means each B-2A is going to cost more than two billion dollars apiece. The press and the antimilitary types will have a field day with that."

He wanted to say more, that the B-2A program was billed for hundreds of millions of dollars of even more highly classified "black" programs, but he could not, not even to his old friends. Dennis Jenkins slid in beside them in time to comment on O'Malley's last remark.

"There's not much in the way of press here today—can't be more than fifty people. For a big event, they've really limited the media. We're lucky to be here ourselves."

It was true. Normally a rollout like this called for all the bells and whistles a public relations department could devise and everyone with any remote connection to the program was invited. If you supplied the plastic envelopes that held the nuts that went on a starter assembly, you got an invite, because invitations translated into promotion and into votes. Today there were only about five hundred spectators, all arranged in the bleachers facing the hangar. Everyone was a heavy hitter in government, business, or the military, but there were not many of them.

"It looks like they are walking a tightrope between wanting to court Congress and not antagonize the press."

O'Malley shook his head, saying, "No, it's more than that. Northrop and the Air Force are extremely sensitive about the shape of the aircraft's trailing edge. That's why they've positioned the bleachers the way they are. You watch, they will open the hangar doors, roll the aircraft out, and keep the rear of the aircraft away from public view. It's just good sense."

The crowd was a little restless. Security had been tight and some people had been in their seats for almost an hour, and these were people who didn't have an hour to spend. The airfield seemed strange, for instead of the typical roar of aircraft taking off, it was dead quiet. All takeoffs and landings at Palmdale had been suspended for the rollout. Fortunately the temperature hovered around 70 degrees instead of the summertime 105.

"What's going on in your world, Dennis? You keeping your eye on the Russkies for us?"

"You have to hand it to them, gents. Their Space Shuttle looks pretty much like our Space Shuttle. They named theirs 'Buran'— means 'snowflake' they tell me, a hell of a name for a shuttle. I've seen some videos that were smuggled out to us, and it looks pretty good. They had the guts to launch it and land it unmanned!"

Jenkins and V. R. exchanged looks. O'Malley never wanted to hear anything about the Soviet Union's progress nowadays—he was becoming more than ever focused on what he called the "Muslim threat."

Just to prod him, V. R. said, "Yeah, and I saw some film of their new bomber, the Tupolev Blackjack. It looks like our B-1, but it's much bigger. They'll probably make a lot more of them than one hundred, to boot. And I heard they flew the Tu-154 on hydrogen. Imagine that!"

O'Malley snorted and said, "Well, you watch that hangar door. They are going to roll out something shortly that will make the Russians weep! There's no way they have anything like it, not now, not for twenty years. This thing is a miracle."

All three men knew it was, for all had some hand in it, and they sat together companionably, lost in their thoughts.

O'Malley had been an ardent supporter within the Air Force and on the Hill with Congress, and for reasons of his own. The airplane was sold as a solution to the magnificent Soviet air defenses, and it was that indeed. But O'Malley saw it as something else, a silent sentinel that could fly unseen and undetectable anywhere in the world. With its uncannily accurate precision munitions, a single B-2 could take out multiple small targets.

The targets O'Malley had in mind were special and unprecedented. To him the entire Muslim world, all the one and one-half billion of them, was dancing to the tune of a handful of fanatic leaders, men such as Osama bin Laden, Abul Nidal, and others. He knew that these leaders had large organizations, but that their infrastructure was fragile, and that much—perhaps everything—depended upon their messianic leaders. He saw the B-2 as an instrument of divine justice, able to take out these leaders with a single strike that did little collateral damage. If the terrorist cells were the hydra-headed enemy they were said to be, the B-2 was the perfect sword to remove their multiple heads.

And it would be even better if another of his programs could be kept from view long enough to bring it into existence. There was hard evidence that the rogue states—Iraq, Iran, North Korea, others—were hardening their weapons facilities where they were developing nuclear, chemical, and biological weapons of mass destruction. These sites were scattered and either located in mountain tunnels or buried under tons of desert rock. In either case, no conventional weapon could reach them. The standard nuclear weapons in the arsenal would cause too much collateral damage. So O'Malley had seen to it that there was adequate "black" money secreted in the B-2A program to develop "mini-nukes." These were small bunker-busting bombs that the B-2 could carry. These mini-nukes would have a small yield, perhaps only one-tenth of one percent of a kiloton—but would be effective against the embedded factories. A test of a dummy of one version, the B61-11, showed that a nuclear warhead could survive plunging through hundreds of feet of rocky soil before detonating.

Virtually no one within the departments of State or Defense saw the Muslim threat as he saw it. In part this was based on bad intelligence. Jimmy Carter had gutted the "humint," the human intelligence gathering capability of the agencies. As a result, O'Malley had to dissimulate, backing the B-2A on the basis of its deterrent value, while knowing that another, more important mission would be covered as well.

It wasn't hard for him to do, for the huge bomber, with its 172-foot wingspan and 350,000-pound gross weight, was a magnificent weapon, one with which the Soviet Union could not cope. It was designed to be invisible to radar and heat-seeking devices, and at a little distance, virtually invisible to the eye.

V. R. was nostalgic. The airplane about to rolled out was replete with techniques, systems, and devices that the various Shannon firms had participated in over the years. The first was the standard in-flight refueling system that Harry Shannon had helped develop with Boeing after World War II. Then there was a quadruple redundant fly-by-wire control system that Bob Rodriquez had pioneered and that O'Malley had backed in the F-117A. One small division of the firm had helped develop the incredible "cotton gin" method of applying the radar absorbent structural material that permitted the B-2A to have its flowing, radar-deflecting contours. Perhaps most important, there was the family of precision guided weapons that Bob Rodriquez had developed over the years.

The thoughts led him to wonder where Bob was; it was something that they knew he was alive. It would have been great to have him here at this rollout, to see the fruit of his work. He should be up on the speaker's platform, ready to take some bows; instead he was somewhere in the Middle East, apparently. Privately, V. R. thought that Bob must somehow be in contact with O'Malley—he was probably the source for much of O'Malley's information on the Muslim terrorists, or at least the source for O'Malley's consuming concerns.

Dennis Jenkins's thoughts were quite different. He knew that the basic argument for the B-2A was that instead of sending a thousand bombers to take out one target, you sent one bomber to take out sixteen or more targets. The secret was stealth, and where the F-117A was all angles and facets, the B-2A had a sinuous flowing beauty. Its basic titanium structure was wreathed in a smooth-flowing jacket of radar absorbent material, its lines unmarred by any fins or rudders. Like the F-117A stealth fighter, it provided the radar screens with a target smaller than a hummingbird.

But Jenkins worried that advancing technology might solve these stealth secrets. He lived in fear that someone—the Soviet Union, the Chinese, perhaps even some completely improbable enemy such as India or France—might decide to emasculate the stealth programs with some new anti-stealth device. Or they could take a simpler, more direct approach, an openly aggressive act such as a massive strike against our satellite systems.

The United States had opted to have a high-tech military force, small, volunteer, and elite. The American war machine functioned beautifully by weaving the information derived from extraordinarily expensive satellite systems. The satellites provided brilliant communications, unparalleled intelligence, magnificent weather forecasting, and unbelievable navigation capability. They were all tied to command and control platforms that could direct small forces to exactly where they were needed. It was expensive, but it freed the mass of the American public from worrying about defense. All Americans had to do was see that 4 percent of the Gross Domestic Product was spent on defense, and spend the rest of its time enjoying its unprecedented affluence.

Satellites could be taken out. An F-15 with a special missile had proved that back in 1984. The experiment had promptly been discounted, and the program shut down, not because it failed, but because it was too successful, a too-powerful lesson for any enemy.

Not that the satellites had to be shot down one by one. Any of the more advanced nations in the so-called nuclear club could detonate a series of nuclear missiles in space to take the satellite systems out. There would be no way for the United States to recover. Each one of the satellite systems took hundreds of billions of dollars and decades to build and launch. There was very little redundancy in most of them, and none in some. If they were attacked and destroyed, the United States would immediately find itself incapable of conducting military operations, and with a current force too small even to defend itself.

This was the spot where he and O'Malley fell out. Jenkins felt that the space race still had to be won. The first step in the victory would be deploying aircraft with laser beams powerful enough to destroy any ballistic missile upon launch. The second step would be putting these weapons into space, so that there would be a continuous global, twenty-four-hour coverage against attacks on the satellites, or for that matter ballistic missile launches against surface targets. It was Star

Wars squared and he knew it—but he believed it was the only means of protecting the country on the comfortable if dangerous path it had chosen.

A band began to play as the hangar doors opened. The B-2A remained in the background, almost invisible against the dark interior of the hangar. When the doors were fully opened, a tug drew it out into the sunlight toward the bleachers, which were arranged in a V-shape that matched the sweep of the B-2A's leading edge.

It was a jaded crowd, filled with high-ranking officers and top industry executives. Most of those attending had been to a dozen rollouts and first flights. There was absolute silence for almost a minute and then a roar of approval as they saw how incredibly sophisticated the airplane was.

Jenkins said, "Too bad Jack Northrop didn't get to see this. I know they told him about the airplane before he died, but he would have loved to see this beauty on the ramp. And too bad your granddad isn't here, V. R.—he'd have loved it, too."

Jack Northrop had been the American flying wing pioneer. His XB-35 and YB-49 flying wings were promising, but stability problems ruled out their procurement. It was a program that Vance Shannon always lusted to work on, but never had the chance. He had always regretted it.

The band stopped playing and as the first speaker moved toward the podium the unmistakable sound of a Lycoming flat-six engine droned over the field. Every eye on the field turned up to fasten on a slowly circling Cessna 172.

Jenkins said, "He said he was going to do it, but I didn't believe it."

O'Malley, red in the face, yelled, "Who the hell is it? What's he doing over the field? It's got to be restricted today."

Jenkins laughed and said, "It's Mike Dornheim of *Aviation Week*. He was watching the NOTAMs, the notices to airmen, and said that if there were no airspace restrictions over the field, he was going to get a photographer and fly over. By golly, this will be the scoop of the century. Somebody screwed up; he wouldn't violate a restriction, I know him too well."

O'Malley stormed away, furious, yelling back, "They don't call it 'Aviation Leak' for nothing, but this damn near amounts to espionage. I'm going to have his head for this."

V. R. shook his head. "I think Steve needs a vacation. He never used to be like this; ten years ago he would have laughed and seen it for what it is, a news story. There's no way they can keep the shape secret once they've rolled it out in public like this."

O'Malley's mental state was now too often the subject of their conversation.

Jenkins said, "He's burning himself out on this terrorist stuff. I would have thought that the raid on Qaddafi might have quieted him down, but it's just the opposite, he's more wrapped up in it than ever."

"Dennis, if he would just be a little discreet about it! He never minces words, you know, and that hurts him with the smoother types. Do you think you can tip him off? I can't say anything, we're good friends, but there's still the difference in rank—I just can't shake that off. I can kid around, but there's no way I can come to him and essentially reprove him."

"I've tried, but he's a true believer, there's no way you can shake his opinion on this."

The crowd was beginning to thin, and they talked of business and family matters.

"How's Ginny doing? Has she ever gotten used to you being away all the time?"

"She's paying me back. When I told her that I was going to Guam for six weeks, to set up for a deployment, she told me she was going to Europe. She went to Switzerland first and is in France now, then she's going back to London for a few days. She'll be coming home on the twenty-first, just in time for Christmas. I just hope I'm back in time. If not, there will be hell to pay, for sure."

December 21, 1988
Approaching Lockerbie, Scotland

THE MIXTURE OF frustration and apprehension that gripped Ginny Shannon on every flight was beginning to fade. She had a late start when the bags she'd left in the Cadogan Hotel's checkroom couldn't be found for almost an hour. Then the taxi ride to Heathrow was the reverse of the usual nightmare. Instead of the cabbie speeding, she had a punctilious driver who stolidly maintained posted speeds despite Ginny's pleas for him to hurry. The lines at the airport were longer than usual, filled with the usual strange mixture of people and costumes, sounds and odors. Still she made it on time, and once on the airplane, her carry-on stowed and seated on the aisle, things went relatively well. The scheduled 6:00 P.M. takeoff was delayed only about twenty-five minutes—not unusual at Heathrow.

The high-spirited antics of some excited college students—from Syracuse, apparently, and coming back from an overseas study program—annoyed her. *I must be getting old,* she thought. *A few years ago, that would have been me, annoying someone else.*

During the climb out, she wondered as she had so many times what it was about flying that so captivated V. R. and all the Shannons. She had flown with V. R. often enough in smaller planes. The Shannon firm owned a fleet of aircraft ranging from single engine Cessnas to Learjets and V. R. had checked out in them all. They had flown from Santa Monica to Palm Springs in a Bonanza, and once, from Burbank to D.C. in the Learjet, with V. R. letting her sit in the right seat and actually handle the controls. On every flight, everything had been a serious matter of delight to V. R. He simply reveled in everything from the preflight to the instructions from Air Traffic Control as if they were some kind of Mardi Gras treat. And when airborne, en route, he seemed to become a breathing part of the airplane, admiring the scenery, pointing out traffic to her, and in general behaving as if they were enjoying some vastly entertaining party. She had never liked any part of it but pretended to, to please V. R. Now locked in the aluminum tube of the 747's fuselage, flying seemed to her as it always did, no different than being trapped on a crowded New York subway train.

Ginny usually drank very little, but this had been a revenge trip, taken only because V. R. was off again on one of his many temporary tours of duty, this time to Guam. She had toyed with the idea of simply showing up in Guam to surprise him, and decided against it, choosing to visit Paris and Geneva instead. Time, circumstance, and inclination had led her to drink wine not only every day, but with every meal but breakfast. It made her feel guilty, for the Shannon family had been cursed by Anna's long and usually losing battle to alcoholism. V. R. rarely took more than a sip of beer, no matter what the occasion, and he often bemoaned the fact that his uncle Harry had never reached his true potential because so much of his time was spent caring for Anna. Nonetheless, now she was looking forward to the first drink service, trying to decide between what she thought she should have—sparkling water—and what she wanted—a Jack Daniel's on the rocks.

The passengers on board the Pan American Clipper *Maid of the Seas* had reached that usual state of anticipation when level-off was imminent, when seat belts could be unfastened, drinks would be served, and the initial rush to the bathrooms could begin. Forward, in the spacious cockpit, the flight crew was beginning to relax and enjoy the ineffable sense of joy and accomplishment that flyers felt—and Ginny could not understand.

Captain James MacQuarrie scanned the instruments with satisfaction. As they leveled off, he called for cruise power and, responding to the ground controller, said, "Good evening, Scottish, Clipper 103 at flight level three one zero." His first officer, Raymond Wagner, added: "Clipper 103 requesting oceanic clearance."

Alan Topp, an air traffic controller in the Prestwick Scottish Area Control Centre, watched his radar screen, where Clipper 103's passage was like every other airliner's, a routine green square starting its march across the Atlantic, one of scores of similar squares he had monitored that day. At 7:01 P.M. he noted that the aircraft was on its prescribed course of 316 degrees, flying at a ground speed of 434 knots, just as it should have been given the forecast winds.

In the next instant, a Semtex plastic bomb concealed in a Toshiba radio cassette player exploded in the Clipper's forward baggage hold, tearing out a twenty-inch hole that began the instant progressive destruction of the aircraft. The green square disappeared from Topp's screen as the 243 passengers and 16 crew members, some already dead, plunged earthward toward the quiet town of Lockerbie, Scotland. Burning debris, torn parts, and mutilated bodies would kill 11 more innocent victims on the ground. Ginny was spared the horror of the plunge, killed instantly by flying debris.

December 2, 1989
Tonopah, Nevada

THE CHANGES IN V. R. Shannon's personality and especially his proficiency had not gone unnoticed. Only the week before, the commander of his 37th Tactical Fighter Wing, Colonel Toby Tobin, had pulled him aside and questioned him about how he was feeling. Tobin had observed him preflighting his aircraft and clearly saw that V. R. was not as engaged in the process as he should have been. Tobin had also noticed how obsessively Shannon talked about his hatred of the Muslims, and how the world was endangered by them.

The latter was certainly understandable. His wife had almost certainly died at the hands of a Muslim terrorist, probably a Libyan national. And Tobin knew that V. R. felt guilty that he had flown the raid against Qaddafi, as if that had somehow predisposed fate to take revenge against him by killing Ginny.

V. R. was his deputy, clearly being groomed to command the unit when the time came. If his work hadn't been so important—and if they didn't have an important mission coming up—Tobin would simply have grounded him. Instead, he did something he hated to do—put a superior officer on the spot. He used a secure line to call Steve O'Malley, a three-star now, but an old friend.

"Can we talk off the record, General?"

"Yes, if you drop the General. Call me Steve and spit it out."

"Steve, you'll probably spit me out after this, but I'm worried about V. R. Shannon. He's become as convinced that the Muslims are our main enemy as you are."

O'Malley grimaced. "Are you saying that he's getting to be a nutcase like me? Look, I know everybody—well, most everybody—thinks I'm an alarmist over the terrorists, and the last thing I need is V. R. stoking the fires. But it's understandable. First of all, he loved his wife, and the terrorists killed her. Second, he's right just as I am—the terrorists are the biggest threat America has ever faced. What's he doing that scares you? You wouldn't call me if he was just shooting his mouth off."

Tobin filled him on the loss of technique that he had perceived in V. R. over the last thirty days, emphasizing the apparent lapse in his preflight. You didn't dare overlook anything in the F-117. If something as minor as the door of the in-flight fueling receptacle was not perfectly flush, the airplane shed its stealth like a snake shedding a skin. Just flying the airplane was no more difficult than flying any modern jet fighter, but flying it in stealth mode was entirely different.

O'Malley said, "The main thing is this: do you think he's safe to fly the 117? If he's dangerous, pull him off. It will hurt him because flying is the only thing keeping him sane, but you can't afford to let him kill himself or someone else."

"I'm not going to ground him, not yet anyway, but I am going to wire-brush him to get his attention. I'm scheduled to brief him on his efficiency report this week and it is going to shock him. He's never had anything but perfect ERs since the Academy and I'm going to bump him down a notch in two or three areas."

"That's pretty drastic, Toby. You'll knock him out of the running for his first star if you do that. The competition is too tough nowadays to have anyone not walking on water be considered."

"Well, I'm going to show him what the situation is now. If he shapes up, I'll revise the ER before I submit it. But he doesn't need to know that."

"Well, it's a plan. But before you go, Toby, let me tell you, he's not wrong about the Muslims. They are after us. I've got a young guy, Seffy Bodansky, advising me on this. It is real. We have to change the way we do business. In the old days, when somebody attacked us, we sent in the Marines, we went to war. Nowadays we send for the cops and sue in an international court. As a result, the Muslims are laughing at us."

O'Malley did not mention that he had more direct and dire news that he had from a trusted, impeccable source: Bob Rodriquez.

Tobin reverted to a formal tone, anxious to stave off O'Malley's lecture on the Muslims. "Yes, sir, General O'Malley. I'll keep that in mind."

O'Malley sensed the change in tone, realized that he was preaching again, and slammed the phone down, saying, "You'll see."

December 19, 1989
Approaching Rio Hato, Panama

IN TWO DAYS it would be a year since Ginny died. V. R.'s eyes scanned the instruments constantly, but by rote; where once he flew as part of the amazing F-117A, now he was like most pilots, a guider, a watcher, someone superimposed on this magnificent weapon, not part of it. Where once his nerves and muscles had been an integral part of the Nighthawk's fly-by-wire system, where his brain had been seamlessly integrated with the aircraft's computers, now he was like an unsure cowboy atop a fractious horse.

It was Ginny's death, of course, that intervened. He could not look at the night sky without wondering if that was the last thing she had seen. He could not endure the muted glow of his instrument panel, knowing that another glowing panel had flown her out to her death. Every flight used to be a soaring, soul-stirring aesthetic experience. Now flying was a penance, a painful anodyne that somehow kept him from shooting himself in the agony over Ginny's loss. He no longer loved to fly, but he could simply not endure anything less demanding of his consciousness. He had become a menace when he drove a car, his relentless sorrow so preoccupying him that he didn't even notice the angry bleat of horns as he breezed through stop signs or swerved from one lane to another, without regard to traffic.

It was not that he thought less often of Ginny when he flew. It was instead the relentlessly demanding nature of flying the F-117A that forced its way into his consciousness, forcing the thoughts of Ginny to the background, still there, but subordinate to the need to keep the aircraft flying well.

He had to keep thoughts of her in the background tonight, for this was the Nighthawk's long-awaited combat debut. The United States had grown weary of Colonel Manuel Noriega's increased belligerence. The drug dealer and money launderer had seized power in Panama in 1985, and since then busily expanded his businesses as he expanded Panama's military forces. President George Herbert Walker Bush had declined going to the United Nations to settle the issue. Instead he authorized Operation Just Cause, designed to capture Noriega with minimum cost to the U.S. or to the Panamanians.

V. R. was flying in Bandit 27, the number two position in the lead element of a six-ship strike force of Nighthawks. The element was led by Major Greg "God" Dammers in Bandit 23. Their mission was to drop bombs close enough to disorient—but not kill—Noriega's troops at the Rio Hato barracks, so that they did not oppose a parachute landing by Army Rangers.

He knew he should have been leading the flight and he knew why he wasn't—Tobin had lost confidence in him. He grew angry, not with Tobin, but with himself. With Ginny gone, the only thing important to him was his job—and he was failing in it. And after seeing his ER—the worst he had ever received in his career—it would not have surprised him if Tobin had left him off the mission entirely.

Strangely enough, the ER, with its almost deadly certainty of killing any chance he had of being promoted to brigadier general, didn't bother him. It had been fair. Tobin was right, he wasn't doing well. But the possibility of not having flying to shield him from the pain of Ginny's death filled his heart with fear.

Tonight's raid was not as long as the strike on Libya—but long enough. The F-117As needed to tank up from their two accompanying KC-10A tankers at least five times for the round-trip. V. R.'s target was a Panamanian army base at Rio Hato, just sixty-five miles southwest of Panama City. It was the least important of the two missions, another sign of Tobin's lack of confidence. The other four Nighthawks were tasked to support the special operations forces who were to capture Noriega himself and bring him to justice.

There had been so many briefings that even V. R., with his attention diverted, knew the mission by heart. At Rio Hata there was a big barracks complex where Battalion 2000, some of Noriega's elite troops, was quartered. The mission planning called for the Nighthawks to drop two BLU-109 bombs, not on the barracks, but in the open field beside them. On the last briefing Tobin had jokingly called their two-thousand-pound bombs "the world's biggest stun guns" for they were designed not to kill the sleeping soldiers, but simply stun them so they could not react to the simultaneous parachute landings by the U.S. 2nd Ranger Battalion. The bombs were fused to explode on impact to make the most noise and do the least damage possible.

As zero hour approached, V. R. felt more comfortable. He had gone through the preliminary "switchology" as they called the long checklists that prepared the aircraft to drop. The only thing that bothered him was an unusual last-minute switch in the target coordinates.

Dammers began his attack, and V. R. followed; intuitively he knew that something was wrong, they were much closer to the coast than the briefings had called for. The bombs released, the doors opening and closing almost instantly, and the two Nighthawks pulled up for the long trip back as gunfire lit up the sky. Apparently the "stun-gun bombs" had failed, for the sky erupted with small-caliber gunfire as the Panamanians tried to fight off the attacking paratroopers.

As he headed back toward the first refueling track, V. R. reproached himself. If he had been himself, at the top of his form, if he had been doing what he should have been doing instead of wallowing in despair, he would have caught the error and corrected it. Now it looked like they had dropped their bombs far from the Rio Hato barracks. He hoped they hadn't killed any innocent civilians. Worse, they had smeared the F-117A's reputation. People were already calling it an expensive failure; a half-dozen articles by congressmen had "proved" it was a waste of money. Now he and Dammers had made them right and placed the whole stealth program in jeopardy. What the hell difference did it make that the enemy couldn't see you coming if, when you got there, you couldn't hit the enemy?

Sweating, stomach constricted, V. R. realized that Tobin had been exactly right when he told him that he had to make a decision. He was either going to be a flyer or a mourner. He couldn't go on doing both. Now maybe he had the worst of worlds—Ginny was gone forever and he had flown himself out of the Nighthawk program.

CHAPTER TWELVE

THE PASSING PARADE: The Internet is created; Nelson Mandela freed in South Africa; Hubble Space Telescope launched, flaws discovered; Oliver North's conviction overturned on appeal; Dr. Jack Kevorkian assists in suicide; Johnny Carson departs *The Tonight Show*; Baltic countries declare independence from Soviet Union; Iraqi troops seize Kuwait; East and West Germany reunited; Poland elects Lech Walesa President; Judge Clarence Thomas accused of sexual harassment; smoking banned on domestic airplane flights; Soviet Union disbanded, eleven separate republics form Commonwealth of Independent States; Boris Yeltsin becomes President of Russia; Mount Pinatubo erupts in Philippines, Clark Air Force Base covered in ashes.

August 3, 1990
The Pentagon, Washington, D.C.

*B*y God, you were right! Hussein isn't kidding around. Iraqi troops have already overrun Kuwait. It's just as you said, there's been no resistance worth mentioning—the Kuwaitis were asleep at the switch."

Steve O'Malley beamed across his desk at a man he had not seen for a decade, a man whose looks did not seem so much to have changed as intensified. Bob Rodriquez had always been fit, and now his thin wiry musculature spoke of long years of effort and denial. O'Malley knew that Bob was over sixty, but his dark hair and beard were barely flecked with gray. His face was lined and his eyes were almost lost in the habitual squint imposed by desert life.

Once staunch friends and business partners, they had fallen out when Rodriquez had attempted a hostile takeover of the firm Vance Shannon had founded. Shortly after the takeover attempt failed, Rodriquez disappeared into a murky world where rumors ranged from his death in a dope-smuggling flight to totally improbable stories of his working for the CIA. Now, tan and unusually dapper in a light tan summer suit, blue shirt, and red tie, Rodriquez seemed almost frail, dwarfed by O'Malley's imposing desk.

One of his several phones rang and O'Malley excused himself to take the call. Rodriquez sat there, uncomfortable in his Western clothes, nervously playing with the plastic visitor's tag affixed to the lapel of his suit. He had started out the morning early, giving two briefings at the State Department. O'Malley had picked him up and drove him to the Pentagon, where he had briefed twice again, once to the Joint Chiefs and once to a group of top Air Force officers specializing in Middle Eastern affairs.

Now he wanted more information from O'Malley about his ex-wife, Mae, his son, the Shannons, and all the rest of the people he had forsaken. O'Malley had already given him some of the most significant details on the ride over from State, and thoughtfully had a huge album of family pictures ready for him. It was not enough, he was hungry to know more.

O'Malley's enthusiasm about at last coming to grips with the Muslim world in combat was very evident, and it troubled him. Rodriquez had spent more than eight years in that world, first perfecting his Arabic, then using his business acumen to gain commercial credibility. The CIA had started him out small and tentatively in a business he knew well, air-to-air missiles. He had provided contacts first, then moved into the illicit shipping of key parts. As he became known and trusted, he expanded into banking operations. With CIA approval, he had laundered millions of dollars for terrorist groups.

It was a double-edged sword. The money he laundered was intended to do harm to the Western world. The CIA believed this danger was more than offset by the intelligence he provided on the terrorists and their likely targets. He never tried to infiltrate a terrorist cell—it would be extraordinarily difficult for any non-Arab. But his dark complexion, facial features, and surprising language skills had enabled him to function in the terrorists' world, where, as everywhere else, if you followed the money, you got to the source of the problem. He was a conduit to many sources, from a simple, dedicated jihadist seeking immortality with a suicide bomb to the intricately layered corruption of Saudi royalty.

Rodriquez thought O'Malley's attitude was simplistic. O'Malley's solution was a massive attack on the Muslim world, one that would generate such damage and such fear that the Arab national and religious leaders would be forced to seize control of the terrorist movement and end it. Yet Rodriquez, even after his years of intimate acquaintance with Islam, could not offer a better solution. The masses of the Muslim world were passive, and the fanatic minority dictated not only religious policy, but secular political policy. In many ways it was not unlike Germany when the Nazis took over in 1933. Even among the Nazis the number of fanatics was comparatively small, but they exerted such control over their party, and over the nation, that they were able to force the world to go to war.

O'Malley slammed the phone down.

"You've flew with the 1st Tactical Fighter Wing, didn't you?"

"We called it the 1st Fighter Interceptor Wing in those days—a great outfit."

"We'll have the whole wing, forty-eight F-15s, in Saudi Arabia by the end of the week! If we don't, your pal Saddam Hussein will scoop up Saudi Arabia like he's copped Kuwait."

Rodriquez was silent, for O'Malley was probably right. Iraq had borrowed billion of dollars from Kuwait to finance the bitter eight-year war with Iran. Instead of paying its debt, it now claimed that Kuwait had been slant-drilling oil from Iraqi fields. The huge Iraqi army was poised on the border of Saudi Arabia, with nothing to keep it in check—yet.

"This couldn't be better from my point of view. This puts their intentions out in the open, and we can hammer them as hard as we want."

Rodriquez said, "It may not be easy. They've got the fourth largest army in the world, and their air force has had lots of experience."

He was dissembling by habit. Rodriquez did not have much respect for the bulk of the Iraqi forces. Saddam had imposed a Sunni regime upon a Shiite majority, and there was dissension in the ranks. His most valuable troops were in the Republican Guard. The rest were more suited to police work than an armored campaign. The Iraqi Air Force had at times fought fairly well against the Iranian Air Force, but would not survive for two days in action against the American Air Force.

O'Malley frowned. "We're still in a bind. If he launched his attack today, there's nothing to stop him from taking the most important Saudi Arabian oil fields. He won't have to go all the way to Riyadh. But we've got to get enough forces over there to stiffen the Saudis' spines, and we've got to get the United Nations on our side for once. It's not going to be easy."

He paused and went on. "This is where the congressional penny-pinching hurts us. We don't have the sealift or the airlift to fight a full-fledged war in Iraq. It will take us six months to build up, just because Congress has cut back on the funds we need for logistic support."

Rodriquez said, "We're stepping off a cliff here. If we station large American forces in Saudi Arabia, the Arab world may well rally to Iraq's side. Certainly the Muslim fundamentalists will. But there's no way out. Iraq owes Saudi Arabia twice as much as it owed Kuwait. The only way Saddam Hussein can salvage his country from the expenses of the war with Iran is to seize the Saudi oil fields as well."

O'Malley looked kindly at Rodriquez, wondering how much he had suffered all these years, and what privations he had endured to get the information the CIA needed. He represented the best in "humint"—human intelligence. As the United States' intelligence-gathering capability had increased through satellites, "humint" had been de-emphasized. Now it was something the country badly needed and almost totally lacked.

"Bob, you were brought up as a good Catholic boy, just like I was. How was it living as a Muslim, performing their rituals? What kind of insight did it give you into Islam?"

Rodriquez was silent for a while. Finally he said, "Steve, I was a fallen-away Catholic, so I'm probably not the one to make a comparison. Islam would function better as a religion if the Muslim world was not so bitterly impoverished, if there was not such a tremendous difference between a very few obscenely rich families and the hundreds of millions of poor people. There's so much corruption, and they waste half of their assets by treating women like slaves."

O'Malley leaned forward in his chair, saying, "Exactly. Let me read you something that Winston Churchill wrote, back before the turn of the century."

He picked up a walnut plaque from his desk and showed Rodriquez the bronze engraving. Then, reluctantly, ashamed that he needed them, he put on his recently acquired reading glasses and read:

"How dreadful are the curses which Mohammedanism lays on its votaries! Besides the fanatical frenzy, which is as dangerous in a man as hydrophobia in a dog, there is this fearful fatalistic apathy. The effects are apparent in many countries. Improvident habits, slovenly systems of agriculture, sluggish methods of commerce, and insecurity of property exist wherever the followers of the Prophet rule or live. A degraded sensualism deprives this life of its grace and refinement; the next of its dignity and sanctity. The fact that in Mohammedan law every woman must belong to some man as his absolute property, either as a child, a wife, or a concubine, must delay the final extinction of slavery until the faith of Islam has ceased to be a great power among men.

"Individual Moslems may show splendid qualities—but the influence of the religion paralyses the social development of those who follow it. No stronger retrograde force exists in the world. Far from being moribund, Mohammedanism is a militant and proselytizing faith. It has already spread throughout Central Africa, raising fearless warriors at every step; and were it not that Christianity is sheltered in the strong arms of science, the science against which it had vainly struggled, the civilization of modern Europe might fall, as fell the civilization of ancient Rome."

O'Malley removed his glasses, and placed the plaque reverently on his desk, saying, "Churchill wrote that in his book *The River War* in 1899. It is as true today as it was then. Perhaps even more so, for now they have access to means they've never dreamed of before—not just swords for cutting off heads, but nukes for cutting off cities."

Rodriquez shook his head. "I wish you were overreacting. I've met many interesting and worthwhile Arabs, people I would like to have as friends, but their system is corrupt. Their treatment of women is abominable. And life is so miserable for the masses that a bright, healthy young man can choose to die as a suicide bomber and think it is a smart career move. The poverty leverages religion so that the fundamentalists, the fanatics, can turn it into a weapon of self-destruction."

O'Malley said, "Bob, I've got a raft of photographs and clippings for you to take with you. But I've got to ask you, what are your plans now? Is your cover still secure?"

Rodriquez shook his head. "I think I could go back to Egypt and reopen my business there without too much difficulty. But frankly, I'm sixty-two and too old for this. Some time I'll tell you what I've gone through. Right now I'm going to concentrate on spending time in the United States, making amends to some of the people hurt even though I loved them. I know Mae won't have me . . ."

O'Malley put up his hand. "Don't say that, Bob. She never remarried, and she could have in an instant if she had wanted to."

Rodriquez's deeply tanned face seemed to change color and he choked before going on. "But I can see my son, and try to make up with him what I've cost the family. And the Shannons, too. I was crazy, trying to hurt them because of Mae. I wouldn't recommend spending weeks alone in the desert to anyone—but it does give you time to think. I'm still in pretty good health, and although I know Tom Shannon is long dead, I can apologize to Harry and the rest of them."

"You won't have to apologize, Bob. They know you were disturbed. I've never heard any of them, even Tom, say anything bad about you after you left. They were worried, they figured you were . . ."

"Off my rocker? They were right."

"Well, yes, that's right. They knew you well enough to know that something had happened to you mentally. And much later, when we finally got word that you were doing something important, they understood. They assumed you had recovered or were recovering, and doing like you always did, immersing yourself in your work. Can I ask a personal question?"

"You might as well, we're carving at my heart right now."

"How are you fixed for funds?"

"Steve, I've got no idea. I left everything with a trustee at the Bank of America, telling them to be conservative. I'm probably very wealthy, I should be. And if I'm not, what the hell, I'm old, but I can still work. Somebody needs a camel driver somewhere, I'm sure."

"I figure the Shannons will have more than one camel for you to drive."

January 17, 1991
En Route to Baghdad

THIS WAS IT. Tonight the stealth fighter was going to prove whether Ben Rich or Kelly Johnson was right. Johnson had died just the previous month and was considered by many to be the greatest aeronautical engineer of the twentieth century. He had always insisted that the F-117A was a mistake, that its angular-faceted shape was an aerodynamic monstrosity. He felt it would never be useful as a warplane. Fortunately Ben Rich, another improbably creative engineer, knew, for one of the few times of his life, that his longtime mentor was wrong.

V. R. Shannon fervently hoped Rich was indeed correct. He'd taken the Nighthawk into combat once before, in Panama, and things had not gone as well as he wished. Tonight they were beginning Operation Desert Storm, attacking one of the toughest integrated air defense systems in the world. They would prove—or disprove—the value of stealth once and for all.

His Nighthawk was one of the ten Lockheed F-117As of the 415th Tactical Fighter Squadron that had rumbled down the runway at 0022 hours. His fellow pilots called the isolated field at Khamis Mushait in Saudi Arabia "Tonopah East" for its sixty-eight-hundred-foot-high elevation and the uncanny similarity of the surrounding mountains.

The Nighthawks were one part of a simultaneous one-two-three punch designed to take out Iraqi air defenses. At sea, mixing the past and the future, a battleship and two cruisers stood by ready to launch Tomahawk surface-to-surface cruise missiles. At the same time, Task Force Normandy, a lethal joint strike force of Air Force Pave Low and Army Apache helicopters, was ready to attack key air defense positions deep in Iraq. All three of the assault units were pathfinders, opening the electronic gate to Iraq for the heavy assault forces—B-52s, F-15s, F-16s, and many others.

The first refueling had gone well. The tankers, airborne since just after midnight, orbited dangerously close to Iraqi airspace, just as they had done so many nights before, always with the intent of lulling Iraqi defenses. Tonight would be a night just like any others for the Iraqis—until the attack began.

The three strike forces were but the tip of the massive United Nations' spear. At other bases all across Saudi Arabia and other supportive nations in the Gulf, hundreds of fighters, bombers, reconnaissance, electronic countermeasure, and support aircraft were airborne. A flight of Boeing B-52Gs was inbound from Barksdale Air Force Base in Louisiana, flying the longest combat mission in history, ready to fire their air-launched cruise missiles at Baghdad. The crowded decks of huge Navy aircraft carriers in the Red Sea and the lower Persian Gulf were alive with action as they prepared for the assault. AWACS aircraft, another of Bob Rodriquez's great contributions, orbited just as they did every other night, also looking perfectly routine to the sleepy Iraqi observers, but ready to orchestrate the attack.

There was an hour to go before bombs away and V. R. had to force himself to think of other things than the capability of Baghdad's air defenses. Israel's 1981 attack on the Osirak nuclear facility had so enraged Hussein that he funded the creation of an amazingly sophisticated defense system. It was conservatively rated as seven times more powerful than the system that had defended Hanoi during the Vietnam War. The critical command and control facilities were buried underground, his aircraft were in shelters designed to withstand a nuclear blast, and there were more than seven thousand antiaircraft guns and sixteen thousand surface-to-air missiles, most of them deployed around Baghdad.

It was tough to think of "other things" and not think about his beloved Ginny. Her death over Lockerbie, Scotland, gave this mission a visceral touch, for he knew that Saddam Hussein funded terrorists. He had not recovered from the loss and lived a monastic life, centered only on flying, and on revenge. To him, as to O'Malley, the war against the terrorists was a personal one.

To escape thoughts of Ginny, he forced himself to think briefly of Kelly Johnson, again hoping him to be wrong about the F-117A, but mentally praising him for all he had done for the nation. Johnson's U-2s were part of the attack team tonight, and the newest Air Force fighter, the Lockheed F-22A, had just won the fighter competition over Northrop's F-23A. Others had fathered the F-22, but Johnson had fathered the Skunk Works culture that made it possible. On a more personal note, Kelly had been solicitous about both Vance and Tom Shannon, and had helped V. R. on more than one occasion.

Tonight was going to be tough. He had two pinpoint targets in Baghdad that he had to identify in quick succession with his forward-looking infrared system. He would have to track the first target, designate it with a laser beam, and release the bomb with the downward-looking infrared system. Then he had to make a thirty-degree turn, and repeat the act a few seconds later on the second target. All the while he had to fly the aircraft, watch out for missiles, and be sure that all of the things that kept the Nighthawk stealthy were functioning correctly.

V. R. had been in Iraqi airspace for thirty minutes when a pitch-black Baghdad loomed ahead. He eased his fighter in broken-field turns around the effective range of the defensive radars just as a halfback would elude tacklers, then acquired his first target, the huge telecommunications center that had been dubbed the "AT&T building" by planners. He kept the crosshairs of his laser designator on the building that served as the central communications center for the Iraqi war machine. At precisely the correct interval, the weapons bay snapped open, and a two-thousand-pound GBU-27 Paveway III laser-guided bomb streaked toward its target, diving toward a tiny spot of laser light fixed on the roof of the building. The bomb burst through the laser spot, plummeting into the building and destroying it. The world knew before V. R. did that his mission was a success for all radio communications, including those of CNN, ceased immediately.

Pumped with adrenaline, certain that he had already proved the Nighthawk in combat, V. R. turned immediately toward his second target, another slightly smaller communications center. Once again his crosshairs stayed locked on until the Paveway released to plunge with an eerie accuracy into the communications center. Exultant, V. R. immediately headed for his post-strike refueling from a waiting tanker. Then there would be the long trip back to Khamis Mushait, for landing. As his excitement ebbed, he realized how glad he was that Kelly Johnson had been wrong and that Bob Rodriquez had pioneered the Paveway III. Stealth and precision guided munitions—this was the

188 WALTER J. BOYNE

way to fight the war. As he flew back the adrenaline rush of the attack was slowly succeeded by a building fatigue. Underneath these sensations, there was one constant, a percussive Bolero-like beat signaling his aching, never-ending memory of his dead wife Ginny.

June 12, 1991
The Pentagon, Washington, D.C.

As V. R. Shannon moved down the corridor of the E Ring toward O'Malley's office he shuddered. Unless he played his cards right, he'd soon be working here, trapped in the five-sided building with thousands of others day in and day out, doing damn little, if any, flying.

A young major flew out of O'Malley's office, caught sight of V. R.'s chest full of ribbons, and came to a respectful halt.

"Colonel Shannon? I'm Doug Culy. General O'Malley's waiting for you. Let me take you right in."

O'Malley's back was turned to the door, and as usual he was on the telephone, speaking rapidly to someone about yesterday's crash of the Bell-Boeing V-22 Osprey. The tilt-rotor craft was intended to replace helicopters, but was caught in the usual congressional debates that surround every new weapons system.

"I don't give a damn if no one was hurt; this is serious, they are attacking this program every day, and I've got to have some answers as to why it crashed. And I want them today, by three o'clock."

He slammed the phone down and whirled around in his chair, a grin breaking out when he saw Shannon standing by the door.

"Come on in, V. R., great to see you."

They chatted about their families for a moment, and O'Malley said, "Before we get down to the real business of the day, I've got some numbers to run by you. One of my staffers took these numbers out of Buzz Moseley's report, and I'm pretty sure they are right, but my staffer's drawn a conclusion I'm worried about and I want to see what you have to say."

O'Malley leafed through a mound of papers on his desk and came up with a blue folder. Inside was a single sheet of paper, and he read, "F-117As flew 1,271 missions during Desert Storm. F-117A pilots averaged about twenty-one missions each. On the first night, the F-117A force represented only 2.5 percent of the attacking force, but hit 34 percent of the targets."

He paused and said, "Now here's the kicker: 'The F-117As demonstrated that stealth aircraft can be flown without electronic warfare aircraft in attendance on all missions except those into the most heavily defended areas.'"

V. R. sat up straight. "The first numbers are good; I flew twenty-one missions myself. But the conclusion is dead wrong. The F-117As need electronic jamming on every mission; if they don't have it, someone is going to get knocked down, surer than hell."

"Why do you say that? You didn't get hit, none of the stealth fighters took a hit."

"No, but it was just a miracle that we didn't fly into a golden BB after the first night. They were shooting at random. But the thing that spooked us was that they were already doing some pretty clever things with their radar. It was obvious that they were trying to track us, and if the war had not ended when it did, they would probably have figured it out. That's why we need jammers."

From the look on O'Malley's face, V. R. knew he'd said the wrong thing.

"There was the real problem. The idiots ended the war without getting Saddam Hussein! We'll be back there fighting in another ten years, and this time it will be even rougher. I know what happened, some wise guy came up with a great sound bite—'the hundred-hour war'—and the White House went for it. What a crock this is. This is going to be an open invitation to terrorists to go to Iraq for training and for funding. Hussein will do anything to get revenge for this. We should never have let him off the hook."

Shannon was quiet. He knew the next subject would be Muslim terrorism, and it was way too painful for him still. He burned with a fierce hatred for the terrorists, but O'Malley was over the top so much that the scuttlebutt was that he'd never get his fourth star.

He was wrong. O'Malley, his face florid with rage, said, "The Air Force hammered the Iraqis into the ground; it was the most successful air campaign in history. And the Army, with its grandstanding 'Hail Mary' sweep through the remnants of the Iraqi Army, is getting all the glory. The Air Force is being treated as a support arm, for Christ's sake, when it won the war on its own. All we needed the Army for was to round up the prisoners."

Shannon didn't speak. When O'Malley was wound up like this, there was no need.

"Well, we are going to show them. We are going to put on a PR campaign that will have their heads swimming. And you are going to lead it."

O'Malley pressed a buzzer on his desk and Major Culy literally ran in.

"You met Doug outside, probably. Anyway, he's going to take you down to the colonel's assignment section, and let you talk over your next job. I know you don't want to come to the Pentagon, nobody does, but face it, you are coming. And you are coming to work for me. There's no sense in creating the finest Air Force in the world if nobody knows about it."

Shannon stood up, indignant. "Don't make me fly a desk, General! You can't do that."

"Don't worry about flying a desk. You are going to be my lead man on every new airplane the Air Force is buying from the F-22 to the C-17 to the V-22. And you are going to be telling the world exactly what the Air Force did in Iraq and what we can do with the new equipment. Don't argue with me, you've cherry-picked your assignments up to now; now it's time to hunker down and do some work the Air Force wants you to do."

There was nothing V. R. could say to that. He had been given one prime assignment after another, and been promoted faster than anyone in his class at the Academy. It was payback time.

January 1, 1992
Palos Verdes, California

THE SHANNONS WERE getting old, and while their New Year's Eve parties had never been very wild, even staying up to midnight was a challenge, so Harry had changed the celebration to a brunch on New Year's morning, and it seemed to make it easier on everyone.

Lieutenant General Steve O'Malley had flown in yesterday and spent the night in the house, sleeping in Tom's old room. Anna had fussed around changing sheets, dusting, making sure that the bathroom was stocked with everything from toothpaste to dental floss, intent on doing something useful. Now Steve was holding court in the library, laughingly chiding Harry, Bob Rodriquez, Dennis Jenkins, and even poor old Warren Bowers for their lack of faith in him. Nancy Shannon was, as usual, absent. Soon after Tom's death she began to travel, and now almost never came to visit them. There had been no arguments, no reproaches, but Harry felt that she was just too embarrassed over the way she had handled company business, and was seeking to escape.

He knew the feeling. Riding herd on Anna all these years had taken its toll on him, and in his heart he envied Nancy.

"Come on, admit it! You believed I was bonkers when I told you the Soviet Union was on the way out, and that the Muslims were the new enemy. I've seen those looks, those taps on the side of the head."

It was true. Most of the group—V. R. Shannon excepted—had thought O'Malley was overreacting when he diminished the Communist threat and warned of the threat of Islamic fundamentalism. The Soviet Union had been fighting the United States in the Cold War since 1945. It had an incredible force of nuclear arms, including intercontinental ballistic missiles that were more powerful, more accurate, and far more numerous than those of the United States and its allies. It had a powerful scientific and industrial complex that had led the space race for many years. The Soviet Army was by far the most powerful in the world, with more planes, tanks, and artillery than any possible United Nations combination.

Mae Rodriquez, her eyes shining, sitting with her ex-husband Bob on her left and their son, Rod, on her right, holding both their hands, had long believed in O'Malley and she wanted to egg him on, see him enjoy himself. She said, "How did you know, Steve, when no one else did?"

O'Malley laughed. "I'll tell you who really knew—Ronald Reagan and Cap Weinberger. They knew that if they spent enough money on defense, the Soviets would bankrupt themselves, and they did!"

Grinning, O'Malley didn't go into the other factors that he knew counted. First was the utter failure of the Communist economic system, so complete that food had to be rationed in Moscow for the first time since World War II. Then there was the rise and fall of Mikhail Gorbachev, who let the genie of democracy out of its Soviet bottle with economic reforms and an unprecedented openness. His plan backfired as modern communications enabled the Russian people to see, for the first time, how impoverished their system was.

Still, it had happened so quickly. The Soviet military had indeed been devastated by the efficiency of American operations in Operation Desert Storm, and realized that they were hopelessly far behind and could never catch up, given the rust-bucket Soviet economy. Then one political event followed another. Hardline Communists sequestered Gorbachev in an attempt to force him to reintroduce Stalinist methods of government, but the public rebelled and the military refused to go along with the coup. Then individual members of the federation began to declare their independence—the Baltic states first, then Georgia, the Ukraine, and others. Boris Yeltsin led the way in Russia itself, informing the United Nations that it was no longer a part of the Soviet Union on December 24. Then, fittingly, given the suppression of Christianity by Communism, on Christmas Day, December 25, Gorbachev resigned as President of the Union of Soviet Socialist Republics, televising an emotional, ten-minute speech explaining how freedom of speech had prevailed. The following day, the Soviet flag was hauled down at the Kremlin.

But O'Malley was not about to deliver a history lesson, nor was he willing to stop chewing his old bone of Muslim aggression.

"Let's not get too cheerful. The Muslims are going to succeed for the very reason that the Soviets failed. The Soviet Union had systematically destroyed religious faith, and when things got bad, the people had nothing to cling to. The Muslims live and breathe their faith, and they are already so poor that nothing worse can happen to them. That's why they are so dangerous, that's why we've got to figure new ways to beat them. They are going to be a lot harder to deal with than Russia—I tell you in ten or twenty years we are going to be looking back and wish that good old Joe Stalin was running things in Russia and that the Soviet Union was our big enemy."

As he stopped, everyone in the room turned to look at Bob Rodriquez. One of the few Americans who had actually lived life as an Arab, working undercover for the CIA in Egypt, Syria, Iraq, and Afghanistan, Rodriquez believed as O'Malley did. Despite his instinctive sympathy for the average Arab individual, he was aware that militants had captured the initiative within the Arab world, and that basically O'Malley's gloom and doom forecasts were correct.

Rodriquez said, "Look, folks, I'm just back from a long crazy time. I've got to admit that I think Steve is right about the threat, and I don't have any solution for it to offer. It's a matter of time. If we would get maybe twenty or thirty years to deal with the problem, to set up some huge sort of Marshall Plan to help the Muslim economies all over the world, maybe we could change things. Steve always says that is the false twist the fanatics put on religion that is the problem, and they get away with it because of the absolute poverty. He's right. If you are a twenty-year-old man and know that you'll never have a decent job, that you and your family will always be scraping by, one day at at time, and that people in the West are living well, driving big cars, and so on, you are bound to hate them. Then some fanatical Imam comes along and convinces them that heaven awaits them if they kill an infidel. And men like Hussein and Arafat make use of them, pay their families a bonus if they die in a suicide bombing. It's hard for us to understand, and impossible for them not to understand—it just makes good sense to them."

Mae squeezed his hand.

"That's enough, Bob. Let's stop thinking about what bad might happen and tell these wonderful friends of ours about something good that is going to happen."

Everyone looked at Mae knowingly. The looks on the three faces of the Rodriquez family had given everything away from the moment they came in, but everyone had carefully avoided comment, wanting Mae to have the pleasure of making the announcement.

The three stood up, Mae's arms about Bob and Rod, and she said, "Bob and I are going to remarry next month. We are going to be a family again . . ." Mae burst into tears and both men, short, dark, intense Bob, and the taller, grinning Rod kissed her.

Harry stood watching the happy group, remembering the many times that the extended Shannon family and their friends had celebrated the New Year in the old Palos Verdes home. It had not always been so happy. He noticed Warren Bowers scribbling furiously in his inevitable notebook. Warren had finished his two-volume biography of Vance Shannon, and said he was now working on a novel about a fictional aviation family.

Harry smiled to himself. "If he's writing about the Shannons he won't need much fiction; most of the facts in this family have been hard to believe."

CHAPTER THIRTEEN

THE PASSING PARADE: Presidents Yeltsin and Bush formally proclaim end to Cold War; United States lifts trade sanctions against China; secession of Bosnia and Herzegovina leaves rump Yugoslavia of Serbia and Montenegro; first antismoking patch, NicoDerm, marketed; the "Teflon Don" John Gotti convicted; Hurricane Andrew ravages Florida; Atlanta loses to Toronto in World Series; Bill Clinton elected President, Democrats control Congress; Dr. Mae C. Jemison becomes first African American woman astronaut; Prince Charles and Princess Diana to separate; Bush pardons former Reagan officials accused in Iran-Contra debacle; author Vaclav Havel elected as President of Czech Republic; terrorists cause huge explosion at World Trade Center; Branch Davidian religious cult attacked by federal agents; final episode of long-running television sitcom *Cheers*; Israel and PLO sign a peace agreement at White House; women allowed to enter combat in U.S. military; White House lawyer Vincent W. Foster, Jr., commits suicide under mysterious circumstances; China violates nuclear moratorium; North American Free Trade Agreement approved by House; war clouds build in Balkans once again.

July 25, 1992
Edwards Air Force Base, California

*I*t was clear, dry, and only ninety degrees, comfortable weather for Edwards in the summer, but both men were hot and sweaty in their flight gear. Sprawling under the wing of their McDonnell Douglas

F-15E, they watched the efficient fuel service and waited for the obligatory visit from the base commander.

"Unusual that he's late—something must be up. Hope nobody's in trouble."

Steve O'Malley went on. "I told them I didn't want any honors or any fuss; this is a private visit, just you, me, and a few guys from flight test. They know we've got to get back to D.C. as soon as possible."

V. R. nodded. In the past few months he had begun to experience again the contentment that a fast cross-country flight formerly gave him, when the airplane doesn't break, when the weather is good, and, most of all, when you are flying away from the current problem. Trouble was that this time there was a problem on both ends. On April 25, a Lockheed YF-22A had crashed, and the media had picked up sensational film footage that showed the fighter sliding, wheels up, along the runway, flames and sparks shooting out. The aircraft was flown by Lockheed's chief test pilot, Tom Morgenfeld, an old friend of Shannon's from the F-117A program. Fortunately Tom wasn't injured nor was the plane totally destroyed. It would never fly again, but it could serve in some ground testing.

The crash set off all the antimilitary critics, who immediately claimed that the YF-22A was—as always—"a billion-dollar boondoggle" and had to be canceled or the nation was lost. The same uninformed critics immediately began blaming the pilot, the hardware, the software, all without any basis in fact.

O'Malley and Shannon were there to get the first solid analysis of the accident from professionals, and that would have been enough work for either one. The problem was that they had flown from the scene of another, even more controversial crash. Just five days before, a Bell-Boeing V-22 Osprey had crashed into the Potomac, during a demonstration at Quantico Marine Air Base. The V-22 was a technological gamble, combining the forward speed of a turboprop transport with the vertical lift and descent capability of a helicopter. Instead of a conventional helicopter rotor, it featured a tilting wing, which moved to rotate the huge propellers from forward flight to vertical flight as needed. The concept had been around for thirty years, and tested for most of them. Now it looked like it was moving into the realm of the practical.

Everyone wanted a weapon with this capability, especially the

Marines, who were dependent upon high maintenance—and dangerous—twenty-year-old helicopters for their vertical lift. But the Osprey was expensive, and had a troubled history, with one crash in 1990. No one had been hurt then, but it made the program's future precarious. Its critics called it the "Killer chopper-plane," a nickname that made O'Malley grind his teeth.

Then, on July 21, the fourth prototype crashed at Quantico Marine Air Base. Its backers had set up a special ceremony to demonstrate the V-22 and a large number of congressmen and government officials, most of them already for the program but with some opponents, included. There was also a huge media turnout—anything having to do with the controversial V-22 was news.

Overloaded with the hubris that often surrounds new prototypes, the Osprey was supposed to make a high-speed pass across the field, low and hot as if it were a jet fighter, then pull up and make a vertical landing in the helicopter mode. Instead, with everyone watching, the right engine of the V-22 burst into flames, and it dropped five hundred feet into the Potomac River. Tragically, all seven Marines aboard were killed.

O'Malley had originally been a backer of the aircraft and had seen to it that the funds needed to acquire fifty CV-22s were in the Air Force budget. But in recent months he had become doubtful about the ultimate success of the program, and was in a difficult position. If he declared himself against the program now, it might well kill it, and he knew the Marines were totally committed to obtaining it. Yet if he continued to support it, when he had legitimate doubts, he would be doing both the Air Force and the Marines a disservice. Cost estimates had risen from thirty-five million to an incredible eighty million per airplane. The investigation into the V-22 crash was just getting under way when he was called to Edwards to hear the findings on the YF-22 crash.

As they waited beneath the wing, Shannon said, "It's strange about aircraft numbers. The B-47, C-47, and P-47 were all great aircraft. There's never been a great aircraft carrying 22 as a number."

He looked up, saw the look on O'Malley's face, and went on. "Until now. The F-22 is going to be a great fighter, and maybe so will the CV-22 be a great transport, or helicopter, whatever it is."

"For Christ's sake, V. R., don't make a dumb statement like that in front of anybody else. I know what you mean, but things are so tough in both programs now that it would only take a stupid idea like that to kill them."

An hour later they were in a classified briefing room, their sweat congealing under the frigid air-conditioning, watching a long series of videos recording the F-22 accident and listening to a clinical analysis of the probable causes.

O'Malley knew the stakes were high. The aircraft had been under development since 1981. At the moment there were almost twenty billion dollars invested in the program. Before it was completed and some six hundred fighters delivered, there would be many billions more.

If it went well it would be worth it. The production F-22 was already superior to every fighter in the world by orders of magnitude. It was stealthy, maneuverable, and able to cruise supersonically without using afterburners. Best of all, its electronic suite dominated the air battle, able to kill enemy aircraft before they knew the F-22 was there. But the program was proceeding slowly. The briefing officer, an intense young lieutenant colonel named Gordon Raynor, called for a ten-minute break and O'Malley leaned over to Shannon.

"You know what worries me? It's the software. We are ten years into the program now, and there are already millions of lines of code; in another ten years there will be even more millions. How can we integrate them all? How can we foresee all the glitches? Sometimes I wish we'd never gone to computers, and simply stuck to rods and pulleys and round dial instruments."

Shannon knew this was just talk. O'Malley had been the leading proponent of fly-by-wire aircraft, but there was something in what he said. With hardware, you had certain definable parameters that could be measured and tested. With software it was different, there were indefinable problems lurking within any system, and these multiplied themselves at the inevitable interfaces. In older aircraft, the relationship of components could be portrayed as a pyramid tree of alternatives. In software architecture, the pyramid trees became huge interlocking forests, with interlocked branches and roots that were only dimly hinted at—and some were never seen until it was too late. The big problem was that assumptions made early might be perfectly correct—at that instant in time. Ten years later, other totally unforeseen events rendered the assumptions wrong—and caused software glitches.

O'Malley went on. "Ten to one, they will call the F-22 accident 'pilot error' when all the votes are in." He hesitated for a moment and said, "At least no one will be able to say that about the Osprey accident, not the way that sucker was burning."

O'Malley's brow furrowed and he sat back in his chair. He had backed both programs with all the power and influence he had in the Pentagon and with Congress and now both were in jeopardy. He wasn't concerned about his reputation—he'd retire soon, and he had more than enough money so that he would never need to work if he didn't want to. But he worried about having helped sell the country two bills of goods, two weapons systems that promised too much and, of course, cost way too much.

"You know, V. R., it was easier in your granddaddy's day and in your dad's day as well. Everyone knew the ground rules, the new fighters appeared like clockwork every two years or so, and you could design, build, test, and get them in operational service in maybe five years. Now you can spend a career on a design, spend thirty years preparing something, and have it fizzle out."

It was unlike O'Malley to be pessimistic. He always saw how lemons could be turned into daiquiris, especially when everyone else agreed that he was totally wrong.

Raynor came back in, gently called the room to order, and said, "I'm going to pass out a complete package that gives you all of the mathematical analysis behind our conclusions. But I want to give a simple summary, one that can be used with the public, if you like, and one that doesn't depend upon any formulae."

With that he signaled to the projectionist and a slide appeared on the suspended movie screen saying:

1. The accident was caused by pilot induced oscillation (PIO).
2. A PIO exists when the airplane attitude, angular rate, normal acceleration, or other quantity derived from these states is approximately 180 degrees out of phase with the pilot's control inputs.

O'Malley erupted, screaming, "Goddammit, you are blaming the pilot for this, and you don't know for sure if he caused it! Of course it's PIO; we've had PIO since Orville and Wilbur flew at Kitty Hawk; we had it on the first taxi hop of the F-16. But that doesn't explain why a top pilot like Tom Morgenfeld would induce it on the YF-22!"

Raynor was visibly distressed.

"General O'Malley, I'm not blaming the pilot. When you go into the equations you'll see that PIO was inevitable, given the weight, speed, and center of gravity of the airplane. The parameters were such that the software dictated the PIO."

"Then why call it PIO? Call it SWIO, software induced oscillation."

Raynor said, softly, "General, I think you know the answer to that far better than I do. The public will understand if a pilot makes a mistake flying a brand-new, super-hot fighter. It won't understand if there is a mistake in ten years and twenty million lines of code of software, with all that it implies."

Raynor's reply was on the mark, and O'Malley sat down, a sickly smile on his face, saying, "Colonel, you get an A plus for this. I'm sorry I yelled at you. I'm sure Tom Morgenfeld understands as well."

"He's on board with the findings, General O'Malley."

All during their long trip back to Washington, O'Malley mentally berated himself for overreacting to Raynor's conclusions. They had done exactly the right thing. They were locked into a Frankenstein monster of a software program, and there was no way out except to test it until it was right, no matter how long it took, or how costly it was.

Shannon understood O'Malley's dilemma. On the trip out, they talked almost continually on the intercom, catching up on Air Force and family business. Now, going back, he was glad that O'Malley was preoccupied. It gave him a chance to think about his own future. He had at last begun to reconcile himself to Ginny's loss. He didn't plan to begin dating again. That just wasn't possible for the time being. But at last he was shedding the black dog of depression that had hung about his neck, and he could concentrate on his job, being O'Malley's go-to guy for special projects.

It was an ideal assignment. O'Malley, no longer allowed to fly solo because of his rank, kept him on call for missions like this. He got to fly all he wanted, and could even deal himself into Red Flag once a year, so he could stay up to speed on his combat flying. And that was his goal in life. He might be getting over Ginny's loss, but he would never get over his hatred of the fanatic Muslims who killed her and all the others. When he flew in Red Flag, no matter who the opponent really was—Air Force, Navy, aggressor squadron, whatever—in Shannon's mind there was a Muslim in the cockpit, and his goal was to kill him.

October 1, 1993
Arlington National Cemetery, Virginia

THEY WERE EARLY, as always, and sat in V. R.'s rental car, a Hyundai of all things, awaiting the ceremony. Jimmy Doolittle, one of America's greatest and most popular aviators, had passed away on September 27 at age ninety-six. Now he was going to be interred next to his beloved wife, Jo, in Arlington. She had preceded him in death by five years that Jimmy had found to be so very lonely.

The large crowd was informally falling into small groups, each one representing the era from which they first knew Jimmy. The largest and most impressive were the Doolittle Raiders, the now-grizzled veterans who had flown with him as young men on his history-making April 18, 1942, bombing raid on Tokyo. Other groups, even smaller, with older men, most in wheelchairs, represented Jimmy's racing days, when he had booted the red-hot Gee Bee racer around the pylons to win the Thompson Trophy. Still other groups were made up of those who had known him in industry, or served with him in the Eighth Air Force. But a surprising number were young people who could only have known him by reputation.

O'Malley pointed to them, neatly dressed, standing quietly, and said, "I'm glad to see the younger people here. You know Jimmy's death received a lot of media coverage, but it was nothing compared to the news space they devoted to Jerry Garcia, when he died. It makes me angry— here is Doolittle, a hero who had served his nation brilliantly in combat, a scientist who had insisted on the United States having hundred-octane gas during World War II, a leader in the industry, a racing hero. And here was Garcia, a musician, famous, but a doper, and his death got ten times the coverage. It doesn't make sense."

Shannon smiled. There was no way that O'Malley was going to understand the "Deadheads." But there was truth in what he was saying.

Doolittle's contributions had been so tremendous for the nation, and while Jerry Garcia was a talented, personable guitarist, he was in no sense a hero.

For the past year, the swift pace of events had separated the two old friends for months at a time, and there was much to catch up on. Both had seen too many funerals at Arlington, and Shannon checked his watch to be sure they would have time to walk to the little chapel where those closest to Doolittle would make their farewell remarks.

"We've got a few minutes. What's the latest on the V-22?"

Frowning, O'Malley said, "It's tough. They've figured out the crash was due to hydraulic lines fracturing and causing the fire, and they are in the process of completely revising the hydraulic system. It will cost millions, of course, but they have this super-high-pressure system and they need to be sure that the lines don't fatigue. But that's the least of the problems in my mind."

"Oh-oh. That doesn't sound good."

"It's not. You're an engineer, and I know you'll understand this, but I'm not sure there's any way to get this across to the public in a palatable way. We've got to be able to sell the idea that we solve the problem—and we can, it will just take time—but I'm afraid there will be a knee-jerk reaction that this is the final straw, and the program will be canceled."

"You haven't said what it is."

"I know it, dammit, V. R., just wait a minute. It's tough to formulate without a blackboard and some drawings. But here it is, and it is a fundamental problem in all tilt-rotor designs. As the V-22 descends vertically, its wing is tilted up so that the propellers act as helicopter rotors. Each wing pushes the airflow away from half of its respective rotor. The faster it descends, the greater the vacuum, resulting in less lift. They're calling this the 'vortex ring state.' If one rotor loses more lift, because of the way the pilot maneuvers the V-22, it can flip the aircraft over. It can happen so suddenly that there's no recovery, and no way for the crew to escape."

"Any hope to control it, General?" V. R. still called Steve "General" even in informal situations like this.

"Sure, we'll beat it if we can keep the program alive long enough, and get enough money to sustain it. But it is dicey, especially since there's another computer software glitch."

"Software's going to kill us!"

"It's like the old pre-women's lib joke about wives, you can't live with them and you can't live without them."

O'Malley saw a veil of pain flit across Shannon's face and realized he had goofed.

"Sorry, V. R. Bad analogy." He hurried on. "As with any system, the V-22's complex computer software sometimes goes down. There's a backup computer that takes over in 2.5 seconds. That's quick enough in a fixed-wing aircraft, but it's fatal in the V-22 where you absolutely have to keep the rotors in synch. If you don't, it can flip over in an instant. We've got to get the backup online in a second or less, or we're in trouble."

Both men were silent. The Osprey was a lot more survivable than conventional helicopters because it was more difficult to detect or engage. It was much faster, and had five times the range of the older helicopters. The Marines liked it because the V-22 could pick a route that would give the landing party surprise and protect it against antiaircraft fire, whereas the shorter-range helicopters sometimes had to go right through a high-threat area. But unless these flaws were fixed, it would never see production.

"How did we get in this position, General? We've got two world-beating weapons systems, and it's taking forever and the U.S. mint to get them to the troops."

"Sometimes I think we're not doing what Jim Webb always told NASA, 'Don't let the perfect be the enemy of the good.' We've got a lot of hobby shoppers, advocates always wanting to improve things. Maybe the procurement system's just too big, too complex now."

O'Malley pointed to the clock on the dashboard and they got out, joining the long line filing into the Fort Myer chapel. The Air Force Chief of Staff General Merrill McPeak was there, solicitously seeing that the grand old man of the space program, General Bernie Schriever, was escorted to his seat. As they glanced around they realized that if aviation had a royalty, it was here, paying homage to Jimmy Doolittle.

The two men were silent during the rest of the simple but moving ceremony. The horse-drawn gun carriage, the empty saddle, the measured pace all might have seemed incongruous for Jimmy Doolittle, who had led his nation in both air and space since 1917. But in the dappled sunlight of Arlington, among the hush of the crowd, each person obviously involved with his or her own memory of Doolittle, it seemed perfect.

The ceremonial rifle volleys and the always plaintive taps brought emotions almost to a peak. There was a parade of modern aircraft, F-16s, F-15s, a B-1, followed by the puttering roar of a North American B-25, the once-powerful bomber in which Doolittle had bombed Tokyo. The ultimate salute was four F-16s sweeping across in the moving "Missing Man" formation, the number three aircraft peeling off and upward toward where everyone knew Jimmy Doolittle was looking down at them.

O'Malley's elbow nudged Shannon. With tears in his eyes, he said, "Gets me every time. What a tribute that is, to Doolittle, and to everyone else who's gone West."

Later, as they drove back to Andrews Air Force Base, Shannon asked, "Do you think we have more Doolittles coming up the pike?"

O'Malley nodded. "You wouldn't think so, given all Jimmy did, but I guarantee that we do. It's really incredible. We've got a pure volunteer force, and it is the highest caliber of people in history. We're so strong in our noncommissioned ranks that other countries cannot believe it. And our officer corps is strong, too. Sure, there are more Doolittles out there. It will just take time and circumstances to reveal him. Or her."

December 31, 1993
Palos Verdes, California

"WELL, IT LOOKS like the big annual Shannon New Year's party has dwindled down to just us."

Harry and Anna Shannon sat in the center of the big round oak dining-room table. Bob and Mae Rodriquez sat on their left while Dennis Jenkins and Warren Bowers sat on their right.

Warren, always politely inquisitive, asked, "Where is everybody?"

Mae Rodriquez spoke up. "Our son is in Ireland, trying to work out an even more comprehensive deal with Ryanair in Ireland. They are sort of like our Southwest Airlines, but not nearly so popular. Rod has some ideas he hopes will change their image—and make a lot of money for AdVanceAir Leasing."

Bowers's face changed perceptibly and they laughed. He had steadfastly invested in AdVanceAir, and seen its stock rise and fall. Despite good advice on diversification from Harry and others, Warren had stuck to it, convinced that in the long run, AdVanceAir would pay off for him.

As was usual of late, Bob remained silent, basking in the glow of being back with Mae again. They were obviously happy. Rodriguez had "come in from the cold" and, instead of immediately plunging back into business, had set about spending all of his time completely oriented on Mae, trying to make up for the years when he had dropped completely out of sight, and even more, trying to make up for the hard years before their marriage had broken up. Mae continued to run AdVanceAir with their son and managed a successful real estate firm on the side. At her urging, Bob was now slowly easing back into business, doing some consulting for Paul MacCready's Aero-Vironment, and investing in a small company that made radio-controlled model aircraft.

Mae said, "Tell them about your project for Paul, Bob. It's not classified, and I think they'd be interested. Warren especially!"

They leaned forward as Bob took a drink of wine to give him time to think. Part of the project was top secret; part was unclassified, left as a cover in case someone got wind of the testing going on near Pasadena.

"Well, you'd have to see it to believe it." He paused for a moment as he said, "For that matter, you'd have to see Paul to believe him. He's so soft-spoken and so intense; sometimes when he talks to you he just slows down his delivery until it's almost painful, and then you realize that he's time-sharing with you, he's thinking about another one of his projects while he's talking to you. What he's done, from human-powered flight to solar-powered flight to wind-powered generators, is just incredible."

They watched him shedding years as his enthusiasm took over, looking just like the Bob Rodriquez of twenty years before when he had been fired up over every new project.

"Now we have tiny remote control model planes, no bigger than a sparrow; they can carry cameras and remote sensors, and you can use them just to have fun, or the military can use them to gather information. They are electric-powered, of course, so they are virtually silent."

That much was safe; what he couldn't tell them was there were even smaller versions, some no bigger than a butterfly, that could be flown deep inside an enemy fortification, a bunker, a mosque, anything, and record everything going on. It was a miracle of miniaturization.

"I'll bring one down next time we meet, and you can fly it. It's much easier than flying a big radio control plane—most of the flying is automated, all self-controlled, everything is already canned on a tiny chip."

There was a buzz of conversation, a pause, and Jenkins spoke up.

"What about Steve O'Malley? I thought he'd be Chief of Staff by now."

"So did we all, Dennis, but he was just too forceful, stepped on too many congressional toes. I think the Air Force wanted him, but they knew he'd have trouble getting confirmed. He was too outspoken about the terrorist threat, and a lot of people just don't want to hear about it."

Warren put on his historian's hat, saying, "It might be just as well. Curt LeMay was the best air combat commander in the world with the Strategic Air Command, but he was stifled as Chief of Staff. Just didn't have the personality for it."

Jenkins said, "That's what's so surprising. Nobody is more charming than Steve O'Malley—except when he's on the case of something. I think he stubbed his toe finally with the F-22 and the V-22. Both great projects, but they are taking too long to get operational. Nobody can back programs like that for so long and not be tarnished."

Rodriquez asked, "What are his options?"

"I think he'll serve as long as they'll let him; he's carved out a niche of his own, and he's too valuable to retire. He's got plenty of money, of course, and that's been part of the problem—a lot of people resented that he had both wealth and rank."

Anna sat quietly as always, embarrassed by so many memories of the past when her drinking had caused so many problems. Finally, as if she realized she had to contribute somehow to the conversation, she asked, "Where is V. R.? I wish he would meet another woman. It's been a long time since he lost his wife."

It was an awkward question. Everyone was worried about V. R.; he was entirely too focused on getting revenge for Ginny. They all believed that her loss and O'Malley's obsession with the terrorist threat had changed him.

"He's over in the Middle East, flying Operation Northern Watch, you know, suppressing any Iraqi flying, making sure that Hussein doesn't kill any more Kurds, all that sort of thing."

Harry saw that Anna realized she had not said the right thing—again. He patted her hand, and glanced around the table. They all admired him for tending so faithfully to Anna for all these years. And he had tended to her. But not faithfully. For, what was it, twenty-seven years now, his life had been made sweet, useful, and fulfilling by another woman, a perfect lover, his own true love. And he would see her tomorrow, as he did each Saturday, and she would be undemanding, understanding, and amazingly, given their ages, exciting. She made his life worthwhile. He hoped he made her life worthwhile in return.

CHAPTER FOURTEEN

THE PASSING PARADE: Sarajevo (where WW I started) pounded by Serbian heavy weapons; Los Angeles jolted by major earthquake, scores die; Aldrich Ames, most damaging spy in U.S. history, arrested; Hutus begin slaughter of hundreds of thousands of Tutsis in Rwanda; Nelson Mandela wins 60 percent of votes, elected President of South Africa; O. J. Simpson arrested in murder of wife and her friend; Hubble Telescope confirms existence of black holes; strike in Major League Baseball cancels World Series; the United States asserts influence in Persian Gulf with armed forces; Republicans sweep House and Senate races; Russians attack secessionists in Chechnya; Japanese earthquake kills more than 5,000; United States gives $20 billion aid to bail out Mexico; American terrorists blow up federal building in Oklahoma City; increase in fighting in Bosnia and Croatia; O. J. Simpson found not guilty by L.A. jury; assassin kills Israeli Prime Minister Yitzhak Rabin; Dr. Bernard A. Harris is first African American astronaut to walk in space.

August 29, 1994
Palos Verdes, California

Over the years Vance Shannon's home in Palos Verdes had been changed from a family residence to a sort of high-level hostel for the various members of the Shannon clan as they migrated through the area on business. As a part of a larger plan to induce Bob Rodriquez to become more active in the family firm, Vance Shannon, Incorporated,

Harry Shannon had asked Bob to supervise the enlargement of the Palos Verdes house, equipping it with the latest in video, film, and audio equipment. The ostensible purpose was so that highly classified briefings could be held there without any risk. The real reason was to have briefings that would intrigue Rodriquez and lead him to once again infuse the firm with some of his old genius. Harry and Steve O'Malley had discussed the idea for months, and today's meeting was part of their master plan.

Remodeling the house suited Rodriquez, who was enjoying his new freelance status immensely. For the last year he had spent part of his time working on Paul MacCready's black projects and part just dabbling in things that interested him. The house was a project that appealed to two of his many interests—hands-on construction and an elaborate installation of the most intricate electronic gear available.

Surveying the scene, Harry shook his head in wonder.

"Can you imagine what Dad would have said about this? He spent hours in here in silence, going over drawings and technical specifications, and now you've turned it into an electronic paradise."

"It's more than that, Harry. I didn't just install the stuff you called for, I brought in experts from your firm to modify the acoustics of the room. It is totally soundproof and it has been hardened so that nobody will be able to use any kind of electronic eavesdropping equipment to detect what's going on in here."

Rodriquez was breathing hard, and Harry watched him critically.

"You had a physical recently, Bob? Seems to me like you're puffing a bit."

"Well, it's hard for an iron man like you, seventy-six and fit as a fiddle, to understand, but some of us old guys are not in the best of shape."

Harry considered that for a while. It wasn't surprising that Bob would have health problems, considering the tough, demanding covert life he'd led.

"You didn't answer the question. Have you had a physical?"

Bob smiled. "Yes, and for a good reason. I'm going to start flying again, and they passed me with flying colors. I'm about ten pounds underweight, and they told me to stay that way if I could. But next week I'm going to start checking out in the company planes. I'll begin with the Cessna Caravan and work my way up to the Gulfstar V. I've cleared it with everyone, they told me no problem."

"That's great news. I stopped flying when they put me on Xanax a few years ago, and I miss it. I still fly with a check pilot, of course, and that's what I'd advise you to do as well."

Rodriquez didn't say anything. He'd fly with a check pilot until he was current; after that, he'd be damned if he wouldn't do his own flying.

Harry read the message on Rodriquez's face and smiled. It was the kind of response he wanted.

"Are we ready to go for the big meeting? O'Malley wouldn't have called us all here if it wasn't something important."

"When is he getting out? He's gone as far as he can go as a four-star, and they cannot keep finding special jobs to keep him busy."

"No, I think they will. He can stay in for another three years at least, if they still work things the way they used to. After that they might make him an Assistant Secretary or something—anything to keep his knowledge and energy in the Pentagon."

Harry paused. This was dangerous ground. O'Malley had left the business world and returned to the Pentagon because of Bob Rodriquez's crazy determination to take over Vance Shannon's firm many years ago. All that was past history now, but he knew Rodriquez didn't like to be reminded of it.

So it was quite a surprise to him when Rodriquez said, "It's surprising how many lives I fucked up over time, isn't it? Tom's, maybe Nancy's, Mae's, Rod's, Steve's, probably Dennis, and maybe even you and Anna. I'm the one they should have put on Xanax, and they should have done it years ago."

His tone was casual but it was evident he meant what he said. Harry tried to smooth it over. "That's all in the past, Bob. You did what you had to do. We've all got demons driving us—look at Tom, look at Anna, look at me, for Christ's sake, nobody's perfect. Nancy's a perfect example, she had her own demon and damn near ran our company into the ground. Nobody's perfect."

Rodriquez said nothing, just stared at the wire-splicer he still held in his hand.

Harry went on. "In a way it might have been a good thing. Our companies actually got stronger because of your opposition, and God knows what you did for the country while you were undercover. They don't hand out the Presidential Medal of Freedom to trouble-makers."

Rodriquez nodded, saying, "That's the hardest secret I've ever been asked to keep. I want to tell everybody, and of course I can't."

Two months before, in a secret ceremony at the White House, William Jefferson Clinton had awarded the Presidential Medal of Freedom, the nation's highest civilian award, to Rodriquez. The only people attending were O'Malley, Mae, Rod, and on Rodriquez's special plea, Harry Shannon. Clinton was his usual charming self, pointedly remarking that while he could not say what the medal was being awarded for, he could tell those present that it was much deserved, so much so that even as well as they knew the recipient, they could never imagine what he had done.

"Someday you will be able to tell, and that will clear up everything for everybody. I'm glad Mae was there; it gives her some insight that she probably needed."

Rodriquez stood up abruptly. "They're due here in about ten minutes, and that crew is never late. I'm going to wash up."

O'Malley had asked that all the central figures of what the industry called the "Vance Shannon gang" be present, and if possible, he wanted them to be able to stay over a day.

Nine minutes later the door burst open and they filed in with the precision of aviators and the deference of longtime friends, each urging the other to go ahead. V. R. Shannon and Rod led the way, V. R. slapping his uncle Harry on the shoulder and Rod unashamedly embracing his father in a long hug. Dennis Jenkins trailed after them, and the rear was brought up by an unusually boisterous Steve O'Malley, holding a videocassette over his head and yelling, "Behold the future, gents, I'm going to let you in on the hottest new weapon in aviation. But only after I give you some big news and a stern lecture."

Rodriquez had spared no expense on turning the library into an electronic studio and there were more than a dozen leather recliners to choose from. Harry had already put out a few beers, knowing they would be passed over for the most part, and a larger set of bottled water and soft drinks.

O'Malley didn't waste any time.

"You'll probably remember what Norm Augustine called 'The Last Supper'?" Augustine was chairman of Martin Marietta and one of the most articulate men in the industry.

Harry, V. R., and Dennis nodded. Bob Rodriquez said no, and his son stayed silent, not wanting his dad to be alone in not knowing something of pretty general knowledge.

"Well, briefly, back in 1993, the Secretary of Defense, Les Aspin . . ." He paused while the usual groan went up—Aspin was no friend to the military. "Moving right along, Aspin and Bill Perry invited the top aerospace people in the industry, informing them that they could expect at least a 40 percent reduction in defense spending in the future. The word was: consolidate, merge, or get out of the industry, because DOD wasn't going to pay for overcapacity."

O'Malley paused to drink from his water bottle and went on. "The budget had already declined from $600 billion in 1988 to $300 billion in 1993, and the companies were already hurting. Both Aspin and Perry were brutally straightforward. They said that they needed only one contractor for bombers, two contractors for rocket motors, two for tanks, one for submarines, and so on. The message was clear: the party was over."

There was a general silence as each man sought to determine the import of O'Malley's story to his own activities. O'Malley went on. "The trend to mergers started a year ago in March, when Lockheed acquired the General Dynamics fighter facility at Fort Worth."

They all knew this one was close to O'Malley's heart. He'd been a big proponent of the F-16, and he followed its success with a parent's pride.

"Dan Tellep, Lockheed's chairman, told me how that one came about. Bill Anders, the astronaut and chairman of General Dynamics, had come to him with a stunning proposal: he was asking to buy the Skunk Works. Bill was worried that GD lacked the engineering capacity to generate a follow-on project to the F-16. Dan refused, of course; the Skunk Works is part of Lockheed's legend. Then Anders floored him, saying, 'Well, how about Lockheed buying our Fort Worth facility? I'll sell it to you for less than the value of the orders we already have on the books.'"

They laughed and O'Malley went on. "Dan said it took him about thirty seconds to realize what a great franchise the F-16 would be, and suddenly, almost fifty years after the F-104, Lockheed was back in the fighter business."

He looked around the room and said, " 'The Last Supper' started a feeding frenzy. You remember that Martin acquired G.E. Aerospace in 1992, and Northrop swallowed up Grumman in March of this year. They call it Northrop Grumman, but it spells the end of Grumman except as a name. Tomorrow, they plan to announce the formal merger of Lockheed and Martin into the new Lockheed Martin Corporation. Norm Augustine calls it 'a marriage of equals' and the money boys on Wall Street are calling it a marriage made in heaven."

O'Malley was a good stage manager, and he let the idea sink in. There were some individual conversations and finally V. R. spoke up. "General, what effect is all this going to have on Vance Shannon, Incorporated?"

Dennis Jenkins was usually quiet, just taking things in, but this time he said, "And how about SpaceVisions?"

"These are exactly the questions I wanted you to ask, and I've got the answer in this videocassette. But you both know that your firms benefit every time there is a big merger or consolidation, for the first step is always to cut costs and reduce staff; this means they have to go outside for some contracting help. But the main thing is that this merger forces a change of focus on the whole industry. Just look at who is wrapped up in the F-22, the only fighter program the Air Force has—Lockheed Martin, Boeing, and two engine companies. That's the ball game for the next few years, even if Boeing or McDonnell Douglas wins the joint strike fighter competition. Even though the field is dwindling down, we'll see some more mergers in the near future—Northrop Grumman is already on the prowl, and you can look to some bidding wars between it and Lockheed Martin. Unless there's a radical change we might see Northrop Grumman/McDonnell Douglas or McDonnell Douglas/Boeing or any combination of those famous names. It will just depend on the fit."

Harry spoke up for the first time. "None of them will fit like Lockheed Martin; that's a perfect dovetail. Maybe McDonnell Douglas-Boeing might make it, because McDonnell is mostly military business and Boeing is mostly civilian. Its new 777 is a knockout, first airplane designed entirely using a computer."

O'Malley nodded. He had set them up perfectly for his purposes.

"As strange as it seems, the success of the 777 is a paradigm for the stuff I'm talking about. The old process of building mock-ups, prototypes, and a series of test vehicles is over for commercial aircraft, and it has to be over for other projects, too. Let's put this merger stuff aside for a minute. I mentioned the Lockheed Martin merger because it is a macro thing in the industry. We all know the players, and it looks like a good deal—for them and for the country. But where does it put the little guy? Out in left field."

There was a murmur of agreement.

"Bob, you told me this room was perfectly secure. Any precautions we have to take?"

"Not a one. This beats the Pentagon's tank any day for security."

"And for ventilation, too! So let's run the tape. There is no audio—they wouldn't release the audio to me yet—but let's watch it and I'll try to answer your questions when it's over."

Rodriquez selected a back-projection format, and they sat quietly as the screen darkened, ran through the grainy black and white flashes of unedited tapes, and suddenly flashed on "Top Secret," "General Atomics Corporation," "July 3, 1993."

No one besides O'Malley and the senior Rodriquez had ever heard of the firm before. Rodriquez had some contact with them in connection to his work for MacCready.

The first image was of a long runway. It could have been any one of a dozen abandoned World War II auxiliary landing strips that studded the desert between Los Angeles and Edwards.

O'Malley was virtually crooning as he said, "This is the airport at Adelanto—the name of the town means 'progress' and that's what you're about to see."

What looked like an updated version of the old Ugly Stick radio-controlled aircraft rolled uncertainly to the center of the runway and waited there, vibrating.

It wasn't a pretty aircraft by any stretch of the imagination. The long nose had a bulge at the very front where a real airplane would have had a canopy, then tapered back. The slender wings drooped slightly, and the skinny spring steel landing gear seemed as if it was made from piano wire. The undercarriage was barely able to keep the slab vertical surfaces, drooping with a forty-five-degree anhedral, from touching the concrete. In the rear, a high revving engine drove a pusher propeller.

V. R. spoke up. "Looks like an anorexic VariEze!"

O'Malley smiled, knowing that every modern design owed something to Burt Rutan even if he didn't have a direct hand in it.

They watched as the strange little aircraft accelerated, the camera taking in a worker, clad in T-shirt, shorts, and white baseball cap, giving it scale. Another man, obviously in Army uniform, was at the side of the runway, also filming the takeoff. The drone then lifted off, climbing swiftly as models do and quickly establishing a pattern for landing. It flew back to the runway, seemed to drift to the left, corrected, touched down on the left gear first, then slammed its nose wheel down. It was over in a few minutes.

Jenkins spoke up, almost for the first time that day.

"That's it? We've been flying drones since Kettering's Bug in World War I! Reginald Denny made them for target practice, and we used Ryan Firebees in combat. What makes this special, Steve? And how could it possibly be connected to space?"

"Dennis, this is the future, pure and simple, for little firms who want to stay in the business. The Air Force is going to stop putting pilots in harm's way and getting their ass shot off, like Tom Shannon did more than once. This one is going to be called the Predator—I've got dibs on naming it—and it is the start of a revolution. And it is related to space because it can be controlled via a satellite relay."

Harry could not conceal his incredulity. O'Malley was usually right, but this seemed to stretch the point.

"Who was that guy in the Army uniform?"

O'Malley came as close as he ever did to blushing.

"I hate to say it, but this started out as an Army program. They don't know it yet, but I'm going to steal it right out from under them. This project should belong to the Air Force!"

Shaking his head, Harry went on. "You are going to steal this airplane to fight with MiGs?"

"Not with this, no, that's what the F-15s do now and the F-22s will do later. But when we've established air superiority, we'll fly these unmanned aerial vehicles—UAV is the preferred acronym right now—over enemy territory, day and night, and we'll pick off anything that moves. Just let a camel driver try to move across from one oasis to another and we'll nail him cold. But later, ten years from now, twenty maybe, we'll be ready to start building real combat vehicles that will take on the MiGs and whatever else they throw at us."

V. R., always a pilot at heart, asked, "Will you be using other airplanes to guide these? Who flies them?"

"Pilots will fly them but from the ground. Here's the thing to remember. I didn't just show you an airplane. I showed you a system. Behind that little dude of an airplane is an amazing tapestry of technology that weaves in satellites, lasers, infrared, television, GPS, and everything else in the market today. And tomorrow we'll be adding precision guided munitions to the mix. Pilots sitting in specially equipped trailers will fly them, maybe from a local site, maybe from thousands of miles away, it doesn't matter. With satellite communications, everything is real time, no matter what the distance on earth."

"Steve, I don't want to sound negative, but you are talking about fighting MiGs and bombing, when it seems to me that the best this thing could do would be to carry some electronic sensors and maybe do some photo reconnaissance."

"Harry, I know you think I get carried away and I do. But I know in my gut that this is the way to the future. It just makes sense: have an air force that establishes air dominance, then do your control and your fighting with unmanned vehicles."

"How does this thing perform?"

"This is a prototype, Dennis, but let me give you what the specs are for the production version."

He pulled a yellow Post-it from his pocket and read, "Endurance: forty hours; cruises at about seventy knots; wingspan forty-nine feet; length twenty-nine feet, max takeoff weight just over a ton; the engine is a 101 horsepower four-cylinder Rotax, just like they are using in the ultralights."

The forty hours seemed to make an impression. If you can loiter over a battlefield for that long, you stifle the enemy's ability to move. Yet there was doubt on everyone's face, except for Bob Rodriquez, Sr.

Young Bob Rodriquez, Jr. voiced their thoughts. "Come on, General, we're sweating out the F-22, with supercruise and stealth, and you're touting a throwback. It's not even jet-powered, it probably can't climb above fifteen thousand feet."

"Don't you worry, Rod, there will be unmanned jets in the future, and stealthy ones, too. That's why I'm saying this is the future for the little guy, the companies that cannot produce the F-22s. I'll bet you that in a year's time there will be firms all over the world producing things like this."

Bob Rodriquez, Sr., was not noted for his humor, but he stood up, assumed Al Pacino's stance and voice, and said, "Just when I thought I was out, they pull me back in."

As the room broke into laughter, Harry Shannon flashed a look of gratitude to O'Malley. The man had done much for his country and much for the Shannon family. Getting Rodriquez on board at Vance Shannon, Incorporated, would be the key to the firm's future.

April 5, 1995
Duluth, Minnesota

"What's that old joke about first prize being one week in Duluth and second prize being two weeks?"

They were eating a huge breakfast at the "Original Original" Pancake House, preparing themselves for another day of meetings with the small but professional crew at the Cirrus Design Corporation plant at nearby Hermantown. Two days before they had witnessed the first flight of the revolutionary Cirrus CR20, a hot little four-place aircraft with a host of modern features.

His mouth full, Dennis Jenkins chewed slowly, then said, "This is the first time I've ever had scrapple. And the last."

"I'm too old for traveling in cold country like this, Dennis, but I'm not too old to appreciate a real treat." Harry Shannon helped himself to the rest of the scrapple, looked around, and then said, "You know there might not be a Cirrus or a lot of other airplanes if it hadn't been for the way Ed Stimpson pushed the General Aviation Revitalization Act through Congress last year."

He paused, and Jenkins could see that he was troubled. Something was bothering him, and it was the lot of the aviation industry.

Harry said, "I still feel uncomfortable about coming out here to see the first flight and pretending that we want to buy an airplane. We've never done anything like this before."

Jenkins laughed, saying, "Harry, if you want me to believe this is the first industrial espionage Vance Shannon, Incorporated, was ever involved in, I'd have to say I don't believe you. It's just that this is the first that you've been the lead man on it."

Shannon winced. His father's company had been Simon pure when it came to avoiding even the appearance of industrial espionage. But in the later years, as the company grew bigger, he knew that it had gone on.

Jenkins continued. "And it's partly true. If this airplane is as good as it looks and as they say it is, we could add it to our combined fleet."

"That doesn't make much sense, Dennis. Since we brought Space-Visions in as part of Vance Shannon, Incorporated, we've had to get rid of a half-dozen planes. I don't know what you were doing over there, but you had about twice as many airplanes as you needed."

"Yeah, but we don't have any like the Cirrus. There aren't any airplanes like the Cirrus."

It was true enough. Cirrus Design Corporation had started out building the VK-30, a radical pusher-engine kit plane. It had been pretty well received, but the company founders decided to make a play for the big time, moved their plant to the Duluth Airport, and brought out a clean, four-place light plane with some radical features. Of composite construction, the airplane featured a glass cockpit and, most intriguing of all, a ballistic parachute system designed to lower the entire aircraft to the ground in the case of in-flight difficulties.

"Were you at Oshkosh last year?"

Jenkins nodded, saying, "I never miss the EAA Fly-In if I can possibly help it. I shouldn't have gone last year, but I'm glad I did, for as soon as I saw the Cirrus on display there, I knew we had to have one. And I knew we could profit from its technology."

"Do you think there's any chance that we can buy them out? Everybody in my family has always itched to get into the aircraft manufacturing business, and somehow it never came about. This would be a good way to start."

"No chance. I've talked to the two principals, brothers, Alan and Dale Klapmeier. They are determined to beat out Cessna in sales in their field."

"That's not ambition, that's chutzpah! If and when Cessna sees them gaining on them, they'll put out a new product and snuff them."

"I don't think so, Harry. These are two determined guys, with a vision, and they know how to build a team. I think their slogan 'Plane Genius'—that's 'p-l-a-n-e'—says it all."

"Well, what can we use from them? We've got Rutan's outfit, Scaled Composites, if we want to contract out some composite construction work. We can license the Ballistic Recovery Systems from Boris Popov's company, just like Cirrus does, if we want to use a parachute for one of the unmanned vehicles we're doing."

"We don't want anything from them but their business model. Combining our two companies made a lot of sense from a balance sheet standpoint, but it made us way too big. You don't see it so much because you are not around as much as you used to be, and I'm glad for you that you are not. But making decisions is tough for us now. Despite everything we do, there are too many committees, too many design reviews, too many everything. I want us to blueprint how Cirrus operates, and set up a new company, small, to do the drones."

"Unmanned aerial vehicles. Not drones. Repeat: unmanned aerial vehicles."

Jenkins could tell from the tone in Harry's voice that he had touched a nerve.

"You are right about that, Dennis. We are too damn big. I hate going even to the annual stockholders meeting, a bunch of strange faces sitting around, pretending they know something about the industry."

As Harry grew older he thought more often about his father, and how he had run his still tiny business.

"I know I sound like a broken record, but Dad would never have put up with the setup we have now. I think you are right. If we set this new company up along the lines of Cirrus, or whatever, who is going to run it? You?"

"No, I'm locked in with more than I can handle at SpaceVisions. We've got stuff coming down the line that is fantastic, and you know I've always been smitten by the idea of manned spaceflight. I can't shake my fascination with the Space Shuttle, even though it's old hat to the public by now. No, I was thinking of making it a Rodriquez team project. Have Bob Sr. act as Chairman, and Bob Jr. run it as CEO and President. Leave Bob Sr. to do the thinking and the planning on unmanned vehicles, and not just air vehicles at that. We will need them on land, on and under the water, and out in space as well, for exploring Mars and wherever we can get to."

Harry didn't speak for a moment.

"Have you talked to them about it?"

"No, but I know Rod feels like he's a fifth wheel at AdvanceAir. Mae is running the leasing programs brilliantly, and I think he'd jump at a new gig. And I think Bob would be gratified to be able to work with his son on a new project."

Harry shoved his almost-empty plate away and finished his fourth cup of coffee.

"Tell you what let's do. Let's go over and talk to those folks at Cirrus and buy you an airplane. I know you are dying to get one, and we might as well save time by putting our order in now. Then let's level with them, tell them we admire what they are doing, and would like to have our team Rodriquez come out for a visit to see how they work. We'd pay them a fee, of course—why should they take time to help us out pro bono? And if it turns out the Rodriquez boys don't go along with our idea, I'll hire some young whippersnapper and take over the project myself."

As Dennis was paying the check he considered Harry's last comments. Everything was great until the line about hiring a whippersnapper and taking over himself. That was the last thing he should do at his age—it wasn't going to be easy to set up the new firm and keep it as simple as the folks at Cirrus had done. He wasn't even sure if Bob Rodriquez could handle it. But it had to be done, and Harry was not the man to do it.

For his part, Harry walked outside into the welcome, if brisk, fresh air immensely satisfied with himself. He had worked with Steve O'Malley for months to bring Bob Rodriquez back within the Vance Shannon, Incorporated, fold, only to find that he was no longer the same man. It was difficult for Bob to work with others. So much had happened to him during his long lonely years as a covert agent that he no longer worked well within a big corporation. Harry had always respected Dennis immensely, the man had led ActOn successfully, made SpaceVisions into a real contender, and was now a tremendously valuable asset to Vance Shannon, Incorporated. Now this new track was going to be his biggest challenge. He was channeling Rodriquez's talent into a new environment, one where he might be able to function as he did in the past, and he was adding Rod to the equation. Without having said a word, both men understood that as talented as the younger Rodriquez was, his real value would now be in allowing his father to put his extraordinary vision to use, unfettered by the bureaucracy inevitable in a big corporation. Stuffed with a big breakfast, looking forward to the prospect of a flight in the new Cirrus airplane, Harry felt uncommonly content with himself. When Jenkins came out through the door, Harry slapped him on the back and said, "Not bad for a couple of geezers, eh? Coming up with a new strategy! Let's hope we can sell it to the Rodriquez boys."

"And to the Cirrus boys."

October 11, 1995
Air Force Academy, Colorado Springs,
Colorado

THERE WERE TWO lines passing in front of the Academy's officers club. From left to right, a long series of three- and four-star generals were filing into the third Corona meeting of the year. From right to left, a handsome buck led four does on a gourmet tour of the Academy's azalea plants. Both lines seemed to be enjoying the beneficence of the weather, dry and fifty-five degrees.

The tri-annual meetings dated back to 1944, and had long since proved themselves to be the best conduit of upper-level information and insight. The series of presentations crossed all the command boundaries, and everyone had a chance to say their piece, on the spot, and in the presence of the Chief of Staff. For the Air Force, the Corona meetings were remarkably free of protocol, and everyone was encouraged to speak up, even if their opinion ran counter to the prevailing philosophies.

Three hours later, just before the lunch break, Lieutenant General Harry Matarese had just concluded a compelling briefing on unmanned aerial vehicles.

General Ron Yates, commander of Air Force Materiel Command, commented, "We've been able to resolve so many of the flight control issues with UAVs so that they are much more reliable now.

I think it's time that we really evaluate unmanned aerial vehicles as a combat system."

From the other side of the room, Lieutenant General Carl Berry spoke up. People turned to him, for Berry was usually somewhat reticient, but when he spoke it was always worth listening to. Berry was the deputy chief of staff for command, control, communications, and computers, the heart of the AWACS and JointSTARS programs.

"We are now able to combine surveillance and reconnaissance very effectively into our command and control systems. I think we can link anything that develops in UAVs right into the existing architecture. No problem."

General Mike Loh, first commander of the new Air Combat Command, stood up. A big man, almost massive in impression if not in size, he was normally outspoken and occasionally boisterous. Now he stood for a moment before softly saying, "Given that we are getting new munitions—sensor fused, what-have-you—and that we have good lightweight missiles, the Hellfire for one, maybe it's time we look at a combat UAV."

There was the dead silence that occurs when a really big idea pops up, and then the room erupted into a hotbed of noise, with everybody wanting to chime in.

In the back of the room, sitting quietly, Steve O'Malley felt a glow of contentment. There is nothing like having a good idea confirmed by a roomful of three- and four-star generals.

CHAPTER FIFTEEN

THE PASSING PARADE: Terrorists kill hundreds in Sri Lanka and in Israel; 110 killed in ValuJet crash in Florida; Ella Fitzgerald dies; terrorists kill 19 servicemen at U.S. base in Saudi Arabia; Yeltsin reelected Russian President; Prince Charles and Princess Diana divorce; Flight 800 crashes in mysterious circumstances off Long Island; Taliban capture Kabul; Clinton-Gore team decisively beats Dole-Kemp ticket; Madeleine Albright becomes first woman Secretary of State; UN picks Kofi Annan as Secretary-General; Israel agrees to give up much of city of Hebron; Deng Xiaoping dies at 92; first sighting of Comet Hale Bopp; Tiger Woods wins Masters golf tournament; exploration of Mars by remote spacecraft begins; Dolly the Sheep cloned; China takes over Hong Kong from British after 156 years; American terrorist Timothy J. McVeigh receives death sentence for Oklahoma City bombing; Mother Teresa dies at 87; FBI declares Flight 800 crash not caused by sabotage.

August 10, 1996
Mojave, California

*T*he thermometer in the shade by the trailer read 85, but to Harry Shannon it seemed like 110. In contrast, Bob Rodriquez, only about a decade his junior, was oblivious to the heat, running around the exterior of the partially completed building in a new sport coat, already oil-stained and torn at the pocket.

Must be his years in the desert, Harry thought. *He's like a camel, drinks a huge quantity of water in the morning, then goes till noon without another taste*. He took another hit on his bottle of Poland Spring and went back inside the completed office area where air-conditioning had dropped the temperature to a crisp seventy-two degrees. He sat in a leather chair, wondering why he had ever agreed to such a stupidly obvious name as RoboPlanes for their new company.

There was a reason of course. Rodriquez had suggested it, and Harry was doing nothing to dampen the man's overwhelming enthusiasm for their new project. Rodriquez's trip with his son to the Cirrus plant had inspired them, and they plunged into two concurrent programs, either one of which would have been enough for ten people. They began designing a whole series of new remote-controlled aircraft, ranging from tiny models derived from Bob's experience with Paul MacCready to huge drones that were to fly halfway around the world and remain on station for days. Simultaneously, they designed their new plant, contracting out the actual construction, but staying on top of it every minute of the day.

This morning they were going to have an informal review of their progress for Harry, Dennis, and the newly retired Steve O'Malley, just back from his retirement ceremonies in Washington, and aching to go to work.

O'Malley, a four-star general, had become the target of increasing attacks from the left wing, who knew of his antiterrorist feelings. They dug into his past and picked out any of his decisions that could possibly be construed as "conflict of interest." Completely ignoring all his invaluable contributions, they pilloried him as the "revolving door general." No one who knew him believed it, and the Armed Services Committee declined repeated requests for special hearings. Nonetheless, his effectiveness was diminished and to his wife Sally's relief, Steve elected to retire. The administration immediately offered him an Assistant Secretary position in DOD, but he refused. Enough was enough.

The retirement left Steve in a rough position. To avoid the very thing he had been accused of, conflict of interest, he had invested all of his substantial fortune in a blind trust, with instructions to purchase nothing but U.S. Treasury bonds regardless of the economy. He had missed the gradual rise in the stock market, and the bond return had varied over the years. Nonetheless he was still a wealthy man, and he was free now to invest as he chose. But he knew that if he went to work for an existing aerospace company, or even invested in one, the media hounds would be on his back. But pledging his assets to a start-up venture like RoboPlanes was relatively safe. It would be months, years maybe, before they attracted any attention, and by that time his retirement would be old hat. Despite his wealth, he absolutely could not stay idle, and he was willing to risk it all on the new project. His wife thought he was quite off his head, but she had thought that for all the years of their marriage and was content that it was so.

Rod came up to him and said, "General, this is quite a difference from my old construction shack I used for AdVanceAir Leasing, isn't it?"

"It's Steve to you and everybody else from now on, Rod. I had a great career, but I'm a civilian now, pure and simple." Waving his hand at the building he said, "Catch me up on everything. You know I've stayed out of things until I was retired. How big is this thing going to be anyway?"

"It's going to be huge, maybe fifty thousand square feet, maybe bigger. We are designing it as we go along. Every new drone we've come up with has caused some changes, but because the building's design is modular, we can accommodate it. We are going to build it as we go, sizing it to the aircraft we build. We're going to do the whole thing under one roof, then roll them out the door to the runway. The only problem we have here is radio interference; there's so much crazy stuff going on at this airfield that we're probably going to have to find some remote spot, well away from Edwards and Mojave, to do the test flying."

"One thing—let's stop calling them drones. The buzzword term now is 'unmanned aerial vehicle' and the acronym is UAV."

"UAV. Sort of rolls off the tongue. Drone does have a bad connotation. But what will the feminists say about using 'unmanned'?"

"We'll hear from them, or the politically correctistas, that's for sure. Do we have any contracts yet?"

"It's incredible. We have a seven-million-dollar backlog, and we've not officially opened the doors yet. Actually it's a good thing we're not ready, as most of the contracts are coming from foreign countries, and of course we have to clear them with DOD and State and God knows who else."

O'Malley's eyes narrowed. "Which countries are buying?"

"Our biggest order is from Israel, and that's the one that will probably get approved first. But we have orders from the three P's as we call it—Pakistan, Peru, and Poland."

"Well, you are going to have to be careful about selling to Islamic nations such as Pakistan. You don't want the technology getting into the wrong hands."

Rodriquez sensed O'Malley's anger.

"The orders from Pakistan are for gunnery targets—not much more sophisticated than you can buy in a model shop. Poland wants some pretty fancy stuff, and it's hard to understand."

"Well, they've been a battlefield through the centuries—can't blame them for wanting new technology. And it's affordable. What are they buying?"

"We've got some beautiful designs for their infantry and armored divisions to use. You shoulder-launch them, and they have television and infrared cameras. They fly out maybe ten or fifteen miles, survey the landscape, and point out any troop concentrations, tank parks, or what have you. Peru has a different requirement, they want to suppress the drug trade on its eastern border. They want big, long-range aircraft, able to clear the Andes at relatively high altitudes and then have a very long loiter time over the lowlands to the east and the Altiplano to the southeast. They have a huge frontier, hitting Ecuador, Colombia, Brazil, Bolivia, and Chile. We've got the designs down, but no prototypes built."

The younger Rodriquez went on: "Here is what has amazed us. There is an emerging civil market that has fantastic potential. The country is so well trained now on computers and video games that high technology can be embraced at the local level. We're getting inquiries from police and sheriff's departments, search and rescue outfits, health departments, fire departments, forestry agencies, and so on for all sorts of UAVs. The beauty is that we can customize our basic products at very little cost to whatever the customer needs. In ten years, I predict we'll be doing 50 percent, maybe 80 percent, of our business with non-military customers."

As O'Malley paused to digest this, Bob Rodriquez, Sr., walked up and put his arm around his son's shoulder, his common practice. O'Malley and Harry often speculated that he was trying to make up for all the years he had been gone.

"Harry's inside—the heat gets to him, and I think he remembers how it took its toll on Tom. He said he wanted to talk to us about the Ranger. Let's go see what he's got for us."

The Ranger was the latest in the series of RoboPlanes designs that Rodriquez had created in the last year. Almost as a joke, they were following the practice of the old line aircraft manufacturers in Great Britain who used the first letter of the name of their companies as the first letter of the aircraft they built—Hawker Hurricane, Supermarine Spitfire, Handley Page Halifax. For RoboPlanes, they had already designed and flown the Rocket and Rascal. Now they were at the RoboPlanes Ranger, and beginning to see that alliteration was not all it was cracked up to be.

Steve nodded, saying, "I'm worried about Harry. He seemed depressed earlier, and that's not like him, not even after all he's been through."

Harry was waiting by the model of the Ranger, a sleek, saucer-shaped, jet-powered aircraft, thinking, *It's going to be stealthy—except for that jet engine.*

They all grabbed comfortable seats and Harry said, "Gents, I wanted to get you together today because I received some bad news last night. Our old friend Hans von Ohain called me from Dayton. He'd just received word that Sir Frank Whittle had passed away."

No one said anything. All of them knew Ohain quite well, but Frank was older and had not been as accessible as Hans.

"What I'm going to tell you is obvious, but most of you, save Bob Sr. here, are too young to really grasp it. Life goes by so swiftly! Frank Whittle—what a man. The only time I remembered to call him Sir Frank was when I was in his presence—best not forget it then. But Frank crammed two or three lifetimes into his eighty-nine years, and still life went by too swiftly for him."

Harry paused, seeming to search for the words.

"I remember in 1978, when Tom and I went to a symposium put on at Wright Patterson; they brought in Whittle and Ohain to tour the base, and then talk to the engineers. It was incredible. Both men get credit for inventing the jet engine, and Ohain's flew first, but Hans deferred to Frank all the time, and Frank not only enjoyed it, he expected it. They both gave short talks, just reminiscences, but then they had a question and answer session. In about ten minutes, they were not talking about how they invented the jet engine, and instead were engaged in heated discussions on the latest topics in the field, disagreeing with each other, disagreeing with the engineers, but totally absorbed in the process. Both men realized that they had revolutionized the world of flight and that was not enough for either one, they wanted to press on, to carry their ideas out to the maximum extent."

Harry waited again, watching their faces.

"Let me give you a little history lesson. There've been three major phases so far to what people are going to call 'the jet age.' The first came from Ohain and Whittle inventing the jet engine, of course. That started a wild run on ever newer jet engines, as power, reliability, fuel consumption, everything improved. That lasted for about a decade, but then came the second phase, when aerodynamics began to catch up. The engineers accepted that they were going to get new generations of more powerful engines, so they turned to fine-tuning aerodynamics so that the power could be used. Thus we saw Whitcomb's area rule come into play, working just on decreasing drag through efficient design and making full use of the power. They came up with ever more drastically swept wings, and then swing wings, to have the best of both worlds. To accommodate the speed range, they engineered sophisticated engine inlets. Airfoils were improved, and they found ways to have slots and flaps unfold from a wing so that it turned from a narrow blade into an umbrella. Nobody knows better than this group how the computer helped, bringing in the fly-by-wire era. Some things didn't work out—they tried to reduce laminar flow with slots in the wing that sucked in the boundary layer. It worked, but it was too expensive. And all the time, engines kept improving, too, particularly in thrust and reliability.

"Then the very things they had done in the past, sophisticated engines and airframes, meant that aircraft were much more expensive and had to be used longer, and operators began looking at aircraft as platforms and not as replaceable bits of hardware. So the third phase began, keeping aircraft flying longer by improving the onboard equipment. That's why we still have B-52s flying as first-line aircraft, and why we can use 707 airframes for everything from command and control to the NECAP aircraft, with their ultimate nuclear authority on board."

He was quiet for a moment. Nothing he was telling them was new, but he knew they had probably not considered things in the light he presented the ideas.

"Now we have a chance to ride the crest of the fourth phase, the unmanned era. I want to see us get so involved in this new crazy science of unmanned vehicles that we ignore the rest that's going on with our bigger companies. We've got good managers running things, the backlogs are huge, we're making a profit—but I for one am getting stale. RoboPlanes—and we've got to change that stupid name sometime—is the future, not only here on Earth, but for planetary exploration. There's no point in putting a man on Mars until we've got all the information we can by using unmanned vehicles. But that's just part of it."

Harry was rarely emotional, but he was clearly moved, and his friends leaned forward, wondering if he was going to reveal some illness or some other bad news.

"I'm an old crock, I realize it. But you've got to listen to me here. Don't reject this because it's coming from a geezer. I've thought this through, and I'm going to tell you that we have a chance here to go way beyond anything anyone has done so far with unmanned vehicles. We have a chance here to be pioneers in hypersonic flight. We can lead the industry, if we get started on it, invest in the research, and spend the money on facilities. I think RoboPlanes is going to be a gold mine, turning out aircraft and licensing other people to build them. But RoboPlanes can lead the way in hypersonic aircraft if we make up our minds to do it. It means a hell of a lot of experimentation, it means getting involved in scramjet engines, it means waiting maybe fifteen or twenty years to get a return on investment. But we are the ones to do it, and I say we get started now."

He sat down heavily in a chair and busily drank from his water bottle while surreptitiously wiping his eyes with his fingers.

No one said anything. This was a totally new direction, different in every way from all that they had been planning for months. This was not starting a new venture or spinning off a company. This meant a total shift in their efforts from almost everything they had done in the past. It was risk-filled—no one knew what either the commercial or the military prospects might be. And here was old, conservative Harry, throwing them out the challenge of a lifetime.

O'Malley spoke in a soft, measured voice, most unusual for him. "You know that there are already some R&D contracts out there. Boeing is working on hypersonic stuff."

"Well, it's not exactly new. Lockheed built hypersonic projects back in the fifties—called it the X-17."

"They used rockets. They also built the X-7 back in 1951, using ramjets. We'll probably have to use rockets, too, for test and for launch, but I think Harry's talking about air-breathing engines."

Bob Rodriquez, Sr., stood up, flushed with excitement and suddenly looking younger than his son.

"You're damn right he's talking air-breathing, and he may not realize it, but he's talking manned, too. There's enough of this unmanned crap for everybody, but if we do it, let's do it with a functional hypersonic aircraft, one that can do a mission with a man flying it."

O'Malley chortled, saying, "That sounds exactly like Kelly Johnson talking. He hated building experimental aircraft; he wanted a mission for everything they built. And so do we. Let me get on my soapbox for a minute."

The noise level had risen a little, but it got quiet in a hurry. Steve O'Malley liked to joke, but they could tell this was deadly serious. He said, "Gents, we've done a lot of flying and fighting—old Harry here flew B-17s in the great war. His brother Tom was an ace in two wars and maybe in three; Bob was a top ace in Korea; V. R. has done his bit, some of which he can't tell us about. But all the past wars and all the future wars and all military affairs, including airpower, involve height, reach, and speed. Height gives you the view, the view gives you awareness, and awareness lets you capitalize on speed, giving you opportunities.

"Reach enables you to hold an opponent at a distance, so you can hurt him, and he can't hurt you. This goes back to David and Goliath, and you remember, David used an aerospace weapon, a missile, to win his fight.

"Speed enables you to take action quickly. Sun Tzu said, 'Rapidity is the essence of war,' and it still is. Aviation combines height, reach, and speed, and hypersonic aviation involves all three to an absolute optimum. With hypersonic vehicles, especially manned hypersonic vehicles, a handful of assets will be able to control combat anywhere in the world on a moment's notice. It is the perfect addition to the use of our command and control systems, the perfect instrument for our satellite systems."

There was a general silence as everyone digested O'Malley's comments.

Rodriquez asked, "What are we talking about when we say hypersonic? Do we mean like the X-15, maybe Mach 6.0 tops? Or the Space Shuttle, orbiting at 17,500 miles an hour or so? Or in between?"

There was no response and he went on. "Let me look at it. More than Mach 3.0, for sure, at least Mach 6.0, maybe Mach 8.0; I think that will be about the limit, but let me take a look at it."

The numbers didn't really mean anything to them yet. They would not until they translated into dollars and schedules and capabilities. As they sat there, mutually stunned, O'Malley suddenly bounded up, grinning, and said, "One last word. This setup is perfect for me. No conflict of interest with anybody. We can start out here with a blank slate, and do it all right here on our brains and our guts."

The always soft-spoken Dennis Jenkins said, "And our money. Count me in."

August 1, 1997
Long Beach, California

As an Air Force officer, Steve O'Malley had systematically disguised his wealth, driving the same kind of cars and living in the same style homes that his peers did, trying to avoid making anyone working just for the adequate but less than sterling Air Force salary feel jealous. Now, as a civilian, he tossed his money around with reckless abandon. He gave Sally free rein to build and outfit a home in La Jolla and she was already talking about another one in Colorado. His only demand was a seven-car garage to house his exotic and antique automobiles. The jewels of his collection were Vance Shannon's 1937 Cord and an F355 Ferrari. The Cord had been a gift from the Shannons, a thank-you for the extra effort he had gone to in arranging Vance's funeral at Arlington. He paid almost 50 percent more than the sticker price to get the Ferrari. Both cars were Sunday drivers. He called his new Mercedes S600 his "beater," something to get him to work and back.

"You know, Roberto, it was just seventeen years and about one month ago that you and I were sitting right here in your filthy rental car, watching the first flight of the KC-10. Now we're sitting in this little jewel—twelve cylinders, no less—in air-conditioned comfort, watching one of the saddest scenes in aviation history."

That meeting, so many years ago, had affected the lives of both men and their families. Rather than participate in the hostile takeover that Rodriquez was proposing, O'Malley decided on the spot to get out of the industry and somehow wangle his way back into the Air Force. Rodriquez, after a spectacular confrontation with Vance Shannon, Incorporated, and an equally spectacular failure, had left the industry as well, going off to a still-unreported career in the black world of covert intelligence.

Obviously moved, Rodriquez intently watched the activity going on at the huge factory building. Workmen had already dismantled the old McDonnell Douglas sign, and still in plastic wrapping, the new Boeing sign was ready to be installed.

Rodriquez said, "I think Boeing's making a mistake, just absorbing the McDonnell Douglas company, erasing its name like this. McDonnell and Douglas were two of the greatest names in the industry, and when they merged, they combined them."

"I guess Boeing-McDonnell-Douglas is too big a mouthful. In any event, that's the decision. The funny thing is that so many of the top spots are going to MacDac people that it looks like McDonnell Douglas bought Boeing, using Boeing money." O'Malley had a set of insider connections throughout the industry and always had "the word" even before *Aviation Week* or *The Wall Street Journal*.

"Well, it may not be as good a fit as Lockheed Martin, but Boeing's civil line and McDonnell Douglas's military line are good complements. I'm sort of surprised it got past the Justice Department."

"No, I read the decision on it. It said that McDonnell Douglas's civil business was down the tubes, and there was no prospect of reviving it. Apparently their production problems kept them from spending what they needed to on research. There was no way they could win in the wide-body market and the DC-10 crashes hurt them badly. They just couldn't compete with Boeing on the civil side, and losing the F-22 competition killed them on the military side."

Rodriquez reached into the Mercedes's glove box and pulled out the thick owner's manual, flipping through it.

"You know this is sad, too. The Cadillac used to be the pinnacle of cars, and now it's the Mercedes. I wonder if the same thing is going to happen with airliners."

"You talking about Airbus Industries?"

"Of course. Their A330 is cleaning up on Boeing's 757s and 767s. I'd never have believed it, but the operators see advantages in an all Airbus fleet that Boeing isn't providing."

"Well, at least there is plenty of business to go around. Everyone is predicting the need for maybe fifteen thousand new airliners over the next twenty years, and neither company will expand to build them all—too risky. But Boeing's chips are riding on the 777 now. If they cannot reestablish themselves in the market with it—you'll see Airbus as number one in the industry."

"An *infamia*! We ought to be number one in everything, cars, planes, whatever!" Rodriquez realized instantly that he had made a mistake—this would set O'Malley off on a terrorist rant.

"You're right, Bob, but the way we are handling the terrorist threat, it looks like we've lost our national will. They are plotting to destroy us—they want to kill every one of us, for God's sake—and we are just going along, being politically correct, afraid to call a spade a spade."

Rodriquez scrunched down in his seat, knowing he was in for at least a fifteen-minute diatribe. He listened for a word that would enable him to break in, to get O'Malley back on track. Finally it came as O'Malley went on, saying, ". . . and another thing. We've got to fight them asymmetrically, just as they are fighting us, we've—"

Rodriquez broke in. "We're starting that, with our UAVs. But it will be the hypersonic manned vehicle that will be the key weapon. We'll have to be able to shut down everything from potential truck bombers to missile launches, using UAVs as spotters and a manned hypersonic vehicle to kill them."

It was enough. Embarrassed, O'Malley realized he was ranting and flushed.

"Sorry, Bob. I know this is an obsession with me. And I know I've gotten to V. R., too. I've got to put a lid on it, especially around people who've heard me out a half-dozen times."

"Steve, don't worry about guys like me, but you've got to cap it when you are with people you don't know. I happen to agree with you—I've lived in the Muslim world, and I believe in the threat you are talking about. But for doing business, even with the military, you've got to keep it more balanced. Otherwise they write you off as a kook—and our ideas with it."

O'Malley started the car, backed up slowly, then drove away in silence. "Dammit, Bob, seventeen years ago you and I had our falling out here. Then I thought you were the nutcase. Now here we are, seventeen years later, and I'm the nutcase."

"No, my friend, when it comes to nutcases, you are not in my class. I was fighting an ego problem. All of you think it was Mae's rejecting me. That was part of it, but a lot of it was the Air Force sending me home, and keeping me from being the top ace in Korea. At least that's what I thought then. It was a nervous breakdown, I guess, just too much work and too little self-esteem. But you are different. You see what's in the future. You just have to control your passion, and you've got to help V. R. control his, too. His obsession with the subject comes from his wife's death in the Lockerbie explosion. Yours is more reasoned, so you have to help him sort things out."

O'Malley nodded, realizing it was strange that unlike either Rodriquez or Shannon, he had a stable married life, and that was due solely to Sally's common sense. Being married was tough anytime; being married to an aviator was virtually impossible. He decided he'd give her the OK on the Colorado house just to compensate for all she had put up with during the Air Force years.

March 15, 1998
Palos Verdes, California

"WELL, WHAT'S THE bad news?"

Steve O'Malley strode into the room, filling it up as he always did with sheer personality, dismayed to see Bob Rodriquez and Dennis Jenkins looking so downcast.

"We got all varieties for you, Steve. First, have you heard that our old friend Hans von Ohain died two days ago?"

"No, I'm sorry to hear that. What a guy! I knew he wasn't well, but hadn't heard from his wife Hanny for weeks. Hans was the finest gentleman you'd ever meet. Everybody who knew him just loved him. He'll be missed by all."

"It's been a bad year for heroes—Tony LeVier last month, who knows who next month."

"It's just a factor of aviation's aging. It's been ninety-five years since the Wright Brothers flew so it's not surprising that the pioneers are going. Twenty years from now, it will be the space pioneers, the astronauts, turning up their toes. But something else is bothering you or you wouldn't have sent me the 'get here or else' message."

"Steve, I don't know how I'm going to break this to Harry, but our big meeting back in August of 1996, when we decided to go into not only unmanned vehicles but to begin dabbling in hypersonics, has about blown up in our face."

Rodriquez spoke up. "We were naïve, pure and simple. I've been doing a ton of research and just came back from a week in D.C., talking to the guy they call 'Dr. Hypersonic,' Dick Hallion. He gave me a briefing that curled my hair."

Jenkins looked at O'Malley and shrugged. They both knew that Rodriquez always talked in a pessimistic way, even when he was feeling optimistic about something. It was the way he covered his bets and kept his enthusiasm from swaying somebody else.

"Well, we've all been looking into it, we all know a bit about it, but what did Dr. Hallion say that has you ready to throw in the towel?"

Rodriquez shook his head. "I'm not talking about throwing in the towel, but I am talking about getting all of us, especially Harry, to recognize the risk. We are behind the power curve in making UAVs of any size. We can compete in the smaller, hand-launched area, but the bigger stuff, like the Predator or the Global Hawk, is way beyond our capability. They have too much of a head start on us. I've been able to get us some subcontracting work from the primes on both of those projects, and I think we'll have to be satisfied for the time being with that. Between that and the little airplanes, we'll about cover our operating costs at Mojave. But the hypersonic field—I'm not sure we can compete anywhere."

238 WALTER J. BOYNE

"What did Hallion have to say?"

"Let me get to that—first let me take you through the history of hypersonic flight, it's a lot more intensive than we thought. He gave me a slide show and I'd like to run it for you."

As Rodriquez reached over to start the slide show he said, "The first thing that we have to grasp is so damn obvious that I'm amazed we all didn't just know it intuitively. Hallion showed me that there have been two long-term sets of experience in hypersonic flight—one in air and one in space. It wasn't till he laid out this chart that I grasped the full implications of hypersonic history for the first time. I felt so stupid!"

A colorful chart popped up starting with 1940 at the base line and stretching out until 2010 on the right. Midway up the chart, a series of fifteen hypersonic test vehicles was listed, some hypothetical, some hardware, and ranging from the Sänger-Bredt through the X-15, and all the way out to some projected experimental projects that were just black asterisks, indicating they were classified.

Below the line of test vehicles were listed, in chronological order, aircraft that had gone supersonic or hypersonic, and ranging from Yeager's X-1 through Lockheed's X-7 to the XB-70 to the Space Shuttle.

Above the line of test vehicles were the hypersonic vehicles that had operated in space, from von Braun's V-2 through the ICBMs through a whole series of experimental efforts, with the last of these being black asterisks. Two sweeping lines served to bring the hypersonic air and space efforts together.

"Hallion says that we're at the point where we can integrate all the air and space experience of the past into a new series of vehicles that will give us global hypersonic flight."

O'Malley studied the chart and said, "I'm familiar with most of these, but what is the Sänger-Bredt?"

"Eugen Sänger was married to Irene Bredt. Both were Austrians and both were fantastic mathematicians. They conceived of a plane they called the *Silbervogel*—Silverbird—in 1938, for Christ's sake! They saw it as a space transport or as a global strike aircraft, launched from a monorail. Launched by a rocket, it would use its own rocket engine to gain enough speed to enter orbit. When its speed decayed, it would glide down and 'bounce' off the atmosphere, to gain altitude again. They calculated a fifteen-thousand-mile range with an eight-thousand-pound bomb load."

O'Malley whistled. "That's just like the Dyna-Soar concept, the X-20!"

"Exactly; there was a lot of Sänger-Bredt inspiration in the Dyna-Soar, but not too many people picked up on it. I certainly didn't. Too bad that neither one was ever built."

Rodriquez went on through the slides, each one a bit more complex than the preceding one. He didn't have to do much explaining, the slides spoke for themselves, and they said that hundreds of millions of dollars had been invested in developing hypersonic flight, and that on balance, many of the experiments had achieved remarkable success.

When he had finished he said, "Hallion told me that the very wealth of data gained in all these experiments is a double-edged sword. On the one hand it is invaluable to anybody researching hypersonic vehicles. On the other, the number of experiments has blunted enthusiasm, and led most people to think that there's no point in pursuing hypersonic flight for the present. This is despite the fact that the Space Shuttle goes hypersonic every flight."

Rodriquez pressed the advance button and another chart came up. It was titled "The Culture of Complacency" and showed a brief saying, "Hypersonics?? But there's no customer demand! No requirement! No market need!"

Rodriquez said, "That's what we are faced with, gents: a project that's been through the mill for seventy years, if you go back to the Sänger-Bredt, and an unfavorable climate of opinion. Even among the military, there are only a few forward-thinking guys who want to spend money on hypersonic aircraft. From the financial side, that is perfectly understandable. From the scientific side, it is inexplicable!"

O'Malley had been uncharacteristically quiet, but now said, "That's bullshit. Maybe that's so now, in the United States, but do you think America is the only one interested? Do you have any idea what a hypersonic cruise missile, a stealthy hypersonic cruise missile, in the hands of a rogue state, would do to the Navy? It would move it out of littoral waters, and maybe right out of the ocean. We couldn't even enter the Mediterranean! We'd have to back off from Taiwan and from North Korea. Just the threat of a hypersonic cruise missile would destroy our credibility overseas. They aren't dumb. They know a hypersonic cruise missile would do to us what the threat of stealth and precision guided munitions did to the Soviet Union—just dry up our military capability."

He paused, breathing heavily, and said, "There's no way we'll get a program through Congress, not with all the staffers trying to parcel out jobs to their own constituents. And if it goes to the services, we'll be dead in the water. The Navy won't want to hear of it because it won't want to spend the money on a defense system. The Army won't be interested, period. And the Air Force, my beloved old Air Force, would hobby shop it for twenty years before it got the hardware delivered. This is something we're going to have to do ourselves. We'll have to present the government with a fait accompli, just do the design, test and manufacture, and hand them workable weapons, hypersonic UAVs and manned hypersonic strike aircraft. We can make it happen, no matter what the eggheads say about the prospects."

"You are right, Steve, and it's not all black. Hallion told me that in 1995, the Air Force Scientific Advisory Board said that in ten years we should have Mach 8 scramjet cruise missiles, and that by 2020, we should have scramjet orbital vehicles with a speed of up to Mach 18."

O'Malley shook his head, saying, "That's what they said, but that's not what anybody's paying to see happen. I don't think we are one step closer to either of those goals today than we were in 1995. And that's the beauty of it for us."

The others looked at him, surprised.

"Look, guys, I take this as a statement of need, one that we can fill. Bob, how much of this massive data is available to us?"

"Practically all of it is in the public domain, except for the current classified stuff."

"That means we can catch up, and with some insight, start where everybody else has left off. We just have to focus. We can talk about this later, but I see three projects that we need to develop. The first is a hypersonic cruise missile, and the second is a defense against it. The third is a manned rapid response tactical air vehicle, a scramjet cruiser with maybe a Mach 15 capability."

"What sort of time frame, Steve? We've got a lot of money in the till, and the parent companies will keep generating funds if we can sell it to the stockholders. But this will eat it up fast. The government

couldn't keep funding some of the projects, like the National Aerospace Plane."

"Dennis, we'll probably go flat broke on this, all of us, but it's too
damn challenging to turn down. Timetable? How the hell do I know?
But what the hell, let me throw out a schedule for you. We'll fly the
first hypersonic cruise missile in 2005, fire the first antihypersonic
cruise missile in 2006, and roll out the prototype—roll out, not fly—
the hypersonic cruiser in 2007. That gives us ten years to do what
everybody else has failed to do in eighty years. We cannot do this like
NASA, and we cannot do it like Boeing or Lockheed Martin. We are
going to have to out-Rutan Burt Rutan! We'll take the Cirrus business
model, pump it up with Rutan's engineering techniques, and build this
whole new technology right here in Mojave. If we can do it, the government will buy the product and we'll recoup. If we don't, we'll all be
looking for greeter jobs at Wal-Mart."

Jenkins looked stunned, then suddenly brightened, saying, "Steve,
I'd think you were nuts if we didn't have Bob Rodriquez here to apply
his genius. Look back at the past—precision guided munitions, GPS,
AWACS, every damn thing imaginable. Bob, this can be your greatest
achievement, after all you've done this will be the one they'll remember. And we'll be with you all the way."

Rodriquez smiled and said simply, "We can do it."

CHAPTER SIXTEEN

THE PASSING PARADE: Pope John Paul II visits Cuba; White House scandal erupts, with President Clinton accused of relations with intern Monica Lewinsky; Italian ski cable cut by low-flying U.S. Marine aircraft; ethnic Albanians in Kosovo targeted by Serbs; FDA approves Viagra; Theodore Kaczynski sentenced to four life terms; atomic tests conducted by India in spite of worldwide furor; Terry Nichols gets life sentence for the Oklahoma City bombing; U.S. cruise missiles hit suspected terrorist bases in Sudan and Afghanistan; U.S. budget surplus largest in three decades; House impeaches President Clinton along party lines on two charges, perjury and obstruction of justice; Clinton orders air strikes on Iraq; George W. Bush elected President.

July 26, 1998
Mojave Airport, California

Warren Bowers was feeling pretty full of himself, pontificating about the Rutans to a captive audience of Harry Shannon, Steve O'Malley, Bob Rodriquez, and Dennis Jenkins.

Bowers was for many years the chronicler of the Shannon family, and his two-volume biography of Vance Shannon, *The Frequent Friendly Flyer*, had received rave reviews and was on *The New York Times*'s Best-seller list for several weeks, hitting the number four spot before edging down. The book also strengthened Warren's hold on the affection of the Shannon family. With sales almost as great as those of Chuck Yeager's biography, Warren was propelled from writing articles for obscure airplane magazines to being a well-respected literary figure.

Yet success had not changed him, for at the frequent meetings of the "Shannon gang" as they were referred to by industry insiders, he remained for the most part just the fly on the wall, recording what was going on for future books and articles.

Today, however, he was a central figure in the small gathering of RoboPlane officers at the Mojave Airport, and he let himself run large, dominating the conversation, and conveying more information and enthusiasm about the Rutans than anyone needed to know.

He was an expert on the subject. In the course of his writing he had often interviewed Burt Rutan, and the tall, friendly, articulate design genius enjoyed talking to him. Then he had engineered an unlikely business meeting for Dick Rutan, when the latter was raising funds for the projected global circumnavigation, nonstop and unrefueled, of the radical *Voyager*.

Warren had written extensively about the first round-the-world helicopter flight by Ross Perot, Jr., and Jay Coburn in 1982. He parlayed his friendship with Ross Jr. into a face-to-face interview with industry magnate Ross Perot for Dick Rutan and his fellow pilot Jeana Yeager. This put him further in the Rutans' good graces, and he followed up by writing the best book thus far on the epic 1986 round-the-world trip of the *Voyager*. Bowers's even-handed treatment of Dick and Jeana's sometimes tumultuous relationship further established him as a family friend.

Thus when the Shannon gang expressed an interest in observing the first flight of Rutan's fantastic new *Proteus* aircraft, they asked Warren to get them an invitation.

"Burt says he's happy to have you here, and will be glad to talk to you as long as you want—on another day. He's so wrapped up in the details of the first flight that he won't have a chance to spend time with you. And he sends his respects to you all and, as he said, 'particularly to the memory of your father, the great test pilot Vance Shannon.' Those were his exact words."

The group exchanged glances, but Warren was on a roll. Not talking often made him unstoppably loquacious when he did. As they listened, they watched the relatively small group of engineers and technicians moving methodically around the *Proteus*, the largest all-composite aircraft any of them had ever seen. Like many Rutan designs, it featured tandem wings with dual tail booms and an exceptionally elegant long fuselage.

O'Malley said, "That's either the ugliest airplane I've ever seen or the most beautiful. I can't make up my mind. The fuselage is arched more than the Connie's was. Has to be intended to carry big external loads."

Jenkins added, "It looks like some prehistoric carnivore, but I vote for beautiful."

Looking slightly miffed at the interruptions, Warren went on. "As you may or may not know, Burt started his firm, the Rutan Aircraft Factory, in 1974, but he had been building airplanes designed for the homebuilder for years. You know the line—VariViggen, VariEze, Long-EZ, and a whole bunch of one-offs, including the *Voyager*. He was so successful, and so much in demand for engineering consulting work, that he formed Scaled Composites in 1982."

Beaming, convinced that he had their attention again, Warren took a pull on his water bottle, wiped his mouth, and said, "Scaled Composites has gone from one big project to another—the Beech Starship, the Predator agricultural airplane, the Pond Racer. But more than that even, he's inspired competition, forward-looking engineers who venture into composite construction and radical configurations. Some big-time companies, Beech, of course, but giants like Airbus Industries, too, are placing more and more emphasis on composites."

Warren checked the faces of his captive audience, happy to believe that they were still hanging on every word, but missing the dull cast their eyes were assuming. Being the focal point was unusual for him, and he made the most of it.

"But today, you are going to see one of Burt's greatest advances in aerodynamic design. When you see the *Proteus* fly—"

Bob Rodriquez couldn't stand any more and interrupted him. "I looked up 'Proteus' in my thesaurus. It can mean 'Greek sea god' or it's the name of the second largest moon of Neptune or it's a rod-shaped bacterium you find in urinary tract infections. Which one was Burt thinking of?"

The sarcasm transformed into a blissful introduction as it sailed over Warren's head. "Good question! You know, in 1989, the Voyager 2—the spacecraft, not Burt's airplane—discovered the second largest moon of Neptune, and it was named Proteus. That's where Burt probably got the idea. But more . . ."

The sound of *Proteus's* two Williams International FJ44-2E engines starting up caught even Warren's attention, and he turned to watch.

"What do you think that thing weighs, Steve?"

"I don't know—maybe twelve thousand pounds fully loaded. Those two Williams jets put out about twenty-three hundred pounds of thrust each. That and all the wing area—must be close to five hundred square feet—means it will have a real altitude capability, if not a blazing top speed."

With the rest of the crowd, they lapsed into silence as the *Proteus* taxied out to the runway, seemed to hesitate for just a few seconds, and then almost hopped into the air after an incredibly short takeoff run. Then like a gleaming white and very streamlined pterodactyl, it turned out of the pattern for its test hop. The "Shannon gang"—minus Warren, who had gone off to talk to some of his friends at Scaled Composite—squatted under the well-worn wing of a DC-3 parked on the apron.

Rodriquez spoke. "It's funny, the *Proteus* doesn't look anything like Paul MacCready's designs, but both companies are working from the same premise: using composites and lightweight construction to get high altitude, long duration missions."

Jenkins said, "We won't go wrong if we draw on both teams for ideas for UAVs, but I don't see much in either one yet on hypersonics."

O'Malley added, "Talking about UAVs—the *Proteus* could be used as a UAV with no problems. There's a world of room for equipment on board, and you could store another ton, maybe more, underneath."

Harry Shannon was quiet, obviously troubled as the temperature rose rapidly toward the hundred-degree mark.

"This has been good, but I've got to get back to the car and turn the air conditioner on. The one thing that troubles me is not what we've seen, but what we didn't see. If we are interested in hypersonic flight, it's a damn sure thing that Burt is, too. If he's not, somebody, NASA or industry, will be tasking him to get interested. I'd like to find some way to work with him, but we don't have enough to offer him yet. Plenty of money, yes, but we've got to get some definition to our projects, and then maybe go to him."

He nodded to Steve who immediately left with him toward the Mercedes, already idling, air conditioner on, in anticipation.

Rodriquez said, "I worry about Harry. You know how Tom went; I'd hate to see Harry do the same thing."

Jenkins said, "Me, too. I think he's worried about having led us all into some kind of dead end, between the UAVs and the hypersonic research. Coming out to see the *Proteus* sounded like a good idea, but I'm not so sure now. I think Harry sees Rutan as too advanced for us to compete with."

"Maybe so, Dennis, but I get the opposite feeling. As a kid I used to come out to Mojave here and just bum around. Over the years I watched as it turned into this center of research. Dan Sabovich, a really good guy, took over a closed-down Marine base and nurtured it into this premier civilian flight test facility. It's had more crazy airplanes and more old warbirds than you can imagine. Then Sean Roberts established the National Test Pilot School! Talk about balls. Sean had a lot of flying time in a lot of airplanes, maybe fifteen to sixteen thousand hours, but he didn't graduate from a test pilot school himself. Now it's the only civilian test pilot school in the world, and has the respect of even the great centers like Edwards. Then there was Bob Laidlaw and Flight Systems, and the Rutans—they've all helped to make this place great."

Jenkins took this in, absorbed by the lore and by Rodriquez's intensity. He said, "And your point is?"

"All these guys succeeded and they started out with far less than we have. They had nowhere near the money—we've got practically inexhaustible funds if we are prudent. And look at the baseline of information we have to draw on. It's endless, monumental. The problem will be sifting through it and getting the relevant data. And as much as I admire Burt, and Paul MacCready, and some of the other giants, I think we have as much talent available to us."

"You're right, of course, Bob. I think the first thing for us to do is get back in the car with Harry and pump him up a bit, then go have another skull session on laying out a schedule for our first scramjet engines. We've got the UAV line pretty well in hand, as far as we can go with it. We just needed to cut some metal and burn some kerosene in a scramjet. We don't care if a few of them blow up on the way—Frank

Whittle used to laugh about standing in the lab, with his jet engine about ready to come apart. He's probably looking down now, thinking what a bunch of wusses we are."

"Frank would never have said 'wusses.' 'Namby-pambys' maybe, but never wusses."

October 5, 1998
Cape Canaveral, Florida

DENNIS JENKINS LET himself into the small condo he maintained in Cape Canaveral, put the small stack of groceries away in the cabinets and the refrigerator, and heaved himself into his one major luxury, a massaging recliner that he'd bought on impulse from a Sharper Image catalog, and never regretted.

As the programmed massage began to ease the muscles knotted from driving too far and too long in his Corvette, Jenkins contemplated the two manuscripts that loomed in great stacks. One, on his desk, was a scholarly history of the Space Shuttle program, grand achievements, warts and all. The other, on modern aircraft and the advent of genuine foreign competition, rested in part on a card table and part spread over the floor.

Looking at it, he estimated he was about a year behind on the Space Shuttle, and two, perhaps three years behind on the modern aircraft book.

"And worse, I'm putting myself farther behind. Every time we advance at RoboPlanes, with either UAVs or hypersonic vehicles, my book gets more out-of-date."

He considered the Space Shuttle book first. Three of the four remaining space shuttles—*Endeavour*, *Columbia*, and *Discovery*—had flown in 1998, making a total of five flights. It was far short of the optimistic planning of the early years, but it was still adequate for the current missions. In June, the *Discovery* had docked with the Russian Mir Space Station, offloaded almost five thousand pounds of supplies, and for the first time in history updated its navigation data with data from the Global Positioning Satellite system. It took Andrew Thomas from the Mir, after he had spent a record-setting 130 days in its cramped confines. This was the sort of thing he had to record, in detail, so that it wouldn't be lost to history.

The *Discovery* flew again in October, deploying and retrieving the Spartan-201-05 free-flyer, and doing test work in preparation for servicing the Hubble Space Telescope. These difficult and important experiments were largely overshadowed by the return to space—after more than thirty-six years—of Senator John Glenn.

Who knows, he thought, *maybe they'll be selling tickets to rich tourists next.*

Much more had been done, not least the long overdue selection of Eileen Collins to command a Space Shuttle flight in 1999. An Air Force lieutenant colonel, Collins had earned her right to command the hard way, through work, skill, and lots of flying time. But of course the press ran away with the idea of her being a woman, instead of her being the best for the job. A woman as space shuttle commander, a senator returning to his astronaut days—that's what sold papers.

It was understandable. But that was why his book had to be different, a meticulous, day by day, minute by minute, problem by problem, success by success, failure by failure account of an incredible program of which the world had no real idea. The Space Shuttle itself with its launch system, controls, stringent training, and unbelievable human factor requirements were all so amazingly complex that they were simply outside the ken of a layman. They were difficult to comprehend, and there was no need for the average person to know about them.

Sadly, the days when the first seven astronauts had won the hearts of the American public were long over. Now astronauts were doing far more difficult tasks under equally dangerous circumstances, and the public registered little or no interest. They watched the liftoff and the landings, and pretended to be grateful if there was no accident, when, Jenkins suspected, for many, disappointment was the real emotion.

The other book was perhaps an even greater challenge. Airbus had emerged as a formidable competitor to Boeing, a story in itself. But there were other factors now. Based in Brazil, Embraer was turning itself into one of the world's leading aircraft manufacturers simply by creating one efficient, salable product after another. Canada's Bombardier was doing the same thing, building aircraft that American businesses and airlines bought with pleasure because they were tailored to the new operating modes. In Europe, Dassault was continuing its dazzling series of designs, and four nations were combining their talents to produce the Eurofighter. Even tiny Israel was competing, and it looked like Russia was coming back with new designs.

Then there was China, doing now exactly what Japan had done after World War I. It was absorbing foreign designs, participating in their manufacture, and learning every day. Within months, the first Chinese-built McDonnell Douglas MD 90 would fly. There was no beating the Chinese combination of brains, energy, and low labor costs. They were going to be a player, perhaps the biggest player besides the United States, maybe even bigger than the U.S. In ten years, maybe twenty, at the outside, there would be Chinese designed and built airliners operating all over the world. They already had a good handle on fighter planes.

Jenkins was tired. The work on the UAVs had been relatively relaxing, but every day that they progressed into the hypersonic field, the work became mentally and physically more demanding. It was so damn challenging, so interesting, that they were all, even Harry, working long days, sometimes pulling "all-nighters" like a bunch of freshmen in college. So far the results were elusive. Periodically, just often enough to keep their interest at a peak, they seemed on the verge of some breakthroughs, but so had everyone in the past who delved into hypersonic flight.

He toyed with the idea of getting to work but quickly switched to having a black label Johnnie Walker on the rocks. Work could wait for a few hours.

December 28, 1998
Over Northern Iraq

MAJOR GENERAL V. R. SHANNON felt at home for once. As always, his F-15E Strike Eagle was seemingly flying itself—it was a stable platform that turned refueling into a breeze and every landing into a grease job. He knew that young Bob Dorr, an up-and-coming major, was in the backseat, monitoring his every move, and while it irritated him, he was grateful. V. R. got to fly so little lately that it made sense to have a proficient pilot on board—and the regulations called for it.

The Iraqis, increasingly recalcitrant under the bloody-minded Saddam Hussein, had attacked Kurdish villages earlier in the year, using helicopters and some fixed-wing aircraft. In response, the United States, the United Kingdom, and Turkey agreed to Operation Northern Watch, creating a no-fly zone that sealed off Iraq by air from the 36th parallel to the north. Shannon now commanded the 38th Air and Space Expeditionary Wing, operating out of Incirlik, Turkey, and tasked to suppress all Iraqi air operations in the no-fly zone.

Shannon no longer flew as often as he wanted because budgetary cutbacks had reduced flying hours, and he always felt he was "stealing time" from younger pilots when he flew. Yet periodically he had to fly, just to stay current in the aircraft and to keep up his knowledge of what was really going on.

Letting down could be fatal. Three years before there had been a totally sad friendly fire incident, when two F-15s had shot down two U.S. Army Blackhawk helicopters through a series of preventable errors. Shannon was determined not to have any repeat on his watch.

Still, it was tedious work. The crews flew hundreds of hours every month putting time on the airplanes, but not getting the intensive training they needed. There were some valuable by-products, of course. The flights enabled dossiers to be built on Iraqi capabilities, and target folders were already prepared for virtually every SAM and radar site from Baghdad north. For Shannon, however, it was galling—there were targets below, lethal surface-to-air missile sites, radar installations, all set to attack, all manned by Muslims—and he could only overfly them.

Dorr's voice came over the intercom. "Skipper, we've got some SAM activity going on down there. Looks to me like they are getting set up to fire for real." The Iraqis always went through a drill when the coalition aircraft appeared, but the electronic equipment on board the F-15Es and especially on the more distant AWACS aircraft could detect just how serious the efforts were. Sometimes it was just a proforma exercise—Shannon could mentally see the Iraqi soldiers listlessly going through the motions—but sometimes they went almost to the brink of firing, with all the right switches thrown and the only remaining task the order to fire. This was one of those times.

Adrenaline rushed through Shannon, and he became instantly alive, one with his aircraft. From their position he knew the missiles were the two-stage SA-3s that NATO had given the strange code name "Goa." The Soviet Union had shipped thousands of SA-3s to client nations throughout the world, and Iraq still had a massive supply. Shannon alerted the three other Eagles in his flight, knowing they had already probably picked up on the signals themselves. His call was followed instantly by an alert message from the AWACS aircraft orbiting to the north.

He asked Dorr, "Have you got them painted? Let's not use the HARM missiles; let's save a little money and drop the Paveways on them."

He was dissimulating and knew that Dorr knew it. The HARMs were deadly effective against the radar, but today he'd asked that his ordnance load include the GBU-15s that were more lethal to personnel.

It pleased him that his Paveways had been brought into being by Bob Rodriquez over a long and difficult time. Essentially a two-thousand-pound Mark 84 bomb fitted with a laser guidance system, they cost about $245,000 each—about the same as the HARM missiles. But they produced far more collateral damage, and would take out the enemy soldiers at a far greater distance than the HARMs could.

"They are firing, Skipper—there's one, two, three of them away." Dorr's voice did not betray the lethality of the threat—the SA-3s were far more formidable than the SA-2s used by North Vietnam. The highly maneuverable Goas were capable of Mach 3.5 speeds and had a built-in television camera with a fifteen-mile range to close in on their targets.

Shannon threw his fighter into a steep diving turn to the right, swinging his head to the left to see the rest of his flight following. It was a technique as old as the Vietnam War—keep the SAMs in sight, dive under them, and force them to try to maneuver beyond their capabilities.

"I have the SAMs visually, all three. Let me know if they fire any more."

Dorr, straining under the G forces as Shannon tightened his turn, grunted, "Noo mooore soo faar."

The F-15E's dive carried them below the smoke-streaming SA-3 missiles that would either turn so sharply that they broke up or would fly on aimlessly until they self-destructed.

As they jointly went through the procedures, Shannon marveled at his own composure. He was about to do what he lusted to do most—kill Muslims like those who had joined together to kill his wife. Still, he contained his emotions, moving flawlessly through the long series of steps that would enable his laser-guided bombs to reach their targets.

Shannon raced through the procedures to set up the bombing system, touching the computer screen quickly to enter his commands, Dorr following him through even as he scanned his own screens for more SAMs. They were vulnerable now, making a wide sweeping turn to come in toward the target and only ten thousand feet above it.

The thought *no different than Nintendo* went through his mind as it had a hundred times before as he punched ACCEPT, ACCEPT, FLY into the custom arming screen. Still effortlessly, strumming the controls as if it were a familiar guitar, he brought the video screen up on his number two multi-screen display. His gloved finger selected the Target Infrared button to pull up the LANTIRN pod targeting screen. Designed for use at night and in bad weather, it contained a combination laser designator and range finder. With it, a pilot could detect the target and attack it in a single pass.

He could hear Dorr's heavy breathing, and pressed the F3 key to check Dorr's screen despite knowing that if he was off track, Dorr would tell him quickly enough. Shannon pressed the Air to Ground ARM screen, arming the two GBU-15s, then switched back to the targeting view.

He picked up the target as his screen displayed the SA-3 site, making out the launch setup, the SQUAT-EYE search radar, and the LOW BLOW guidance radar. Shannon estimated there would be perhaps forty people within the lethal blast area; he wished there were more. Destroying the equipment wouldn't do Saddam Hussein much harm; he had plenty more in stock. But killing the men manning the site would give Shannon the satisfaction of revenge. As the seconds flew by, Shannon selected his target with his mouse; the aircraft heading and the bomb-drop countdown immediately appeared on the HUD, the heads-up display. Now the target was being automatically tracked, integrated into the aircraft systems.

Shannon fine-tuned the target designator, letting the autopilot keep the aircraft exactly on course. He alternated between the two displays, playing with the target's infrared image, watching the countdown proceeding on the HUD, listening to Dorr's countdown. Then five seconds before release, he pressed the button on the joystick, allowing the computer to drop the bomb at exactly the right instant.

When the bomb released, the time to impact appeared on the screen; at twenty seconds before impact, Shannon pressed the ARM button, turning on the laser. He knew the bomb was locked on to the laser, the laser exactly illuminating the target.

Dorr yelled, "Direct hit," as they swept on in a sharp turn. Shannon glanced down at the huge plumes of smoke coming from the target.

"The rest of the flight must have hit a SAM storage depot. This was a good run."

They leveled out and began to climb, heading toward the distant KC-135 tanker that was orbiting, waiting to refuel them.

Shannon let the image of the explosions run through his mind, thinking that it was some small payback for the loss of Ginny. He wanted more. The old saw that revenge is a dish best served cold flashed through his mind—*What bullshit*, he thought. *Revenge is best served in a hot blast of bombs.*

CHAPTER SEVENTEEN

THE PASSING PARADE: Newt Gingrich replaced by Dennis Hastert as Speaker of the House; ten members of International Olympic Committee expelled for bribery in site selection; King Hussein of Jordan dies; President Clinton acquitted of impeachment charges by Senate; Bertrand Piccard and Brian Jones make nonstop balloon flight around the world; the Yankee Clipper, Joe DiMaggio, dies at 84; Czech Republic, Hungary, and Poland join NATO; Serb attacks on ethnic Albanians prompts NATO air strikes; Dr. Jack Kevorkian guilty in second-degree murder trail; two suspected bombers of Flight 103 handed over by Libya; fifteen killed in Columbine High School shooting, including two shooters; eleven weeks of NATO airstrikes force Serbs out of Kosovo; Taiwan openly challenges China's "One China" policy; John F. Kennedy, Jr., wife Carolyn, and sister-in-law Lauren Bessette killed in airplane crash; Colonel Eileen Collins becomes first woman to head a space shuttle mission; Vladimir Putin becomes Prime Minister in Russia; world population reaches six billion; General Pervez Musharraf seizes power in Pakistan; copilot deliberately causes crash of EgyptAir airliner, killing 217; first spacecraft launched by China; Islamic terrorists hijack Indian jet; Hillary Clinton enters race to become senator from New York; NEAR spacecraft orbits an asteroid; Internet stock boom busts; stocks plunge; widespread computer disruption from "I Love You" virus; former Indonesian President Suharto arrested for abuse of power, corruption; Sinn Fein agrees to disarm, Great Britain restores parliamentary powers to Northern Ireland; Saddam Hussein revives missile program; Bashar al-Assad becomes Syrian President, succeeding his father; Concorde crash kills 113 near Paris; Republicans choose Bush and Cheney; Democrats pick Gore and Lieberman; Milosevic overthrown in Yugoslavia; terrorists kill seventeen U.S. sailors in atack on U.S.S. *Cole*.

June 1, 1999
Over Kosovo

V. R. Shannon felt like a fraud, a stowaway watching Operation Allied Force unfold, even though the fantastic crew on the AWACS airplane treated him like a king. Somehow, in the twenty-four hours between the notice of his coming and his arrival, they had set up a special chair and console arrangement so that he could be switched from screen to screen and from audio channel to audio channel so that he would constantly be in on the unfolding airpower assault as it happened.

Major Hank Myers kept apologizing for the lack of action.

"We've pretty well beaten them down, sir. Over the last nine weeks, NATO's put up more than thirty thousand sorties—that's almost five times what we did in Operation Deliberate Force in Bosnia in 1995. We've even got the Luftwaffe down here—the first time German planes have been in combat since 1945."

It was about time. The war in Kosovo had been going on for weeks, and almost a million refugees had been forced from their native lands. For some unfathomable reason, airpower had not been used effectively or in mass. As a result, the goal of throwing the forces of Slobodan Milosevic out of Kosovo had fared badly. The Serbs were tough fighters, brilliant in their use of terrain, adept with fobbing off dummy tanks and fake bunkers to draw fire. But finally, at some command level, a decision had been made to get on with the war, and on March 24 a force of more than one thousand NATO aircraft began an unrelenting air campaign that was now paying off.

Shannon was there as an observer, gathering information to report back to the headquarters, USAF, upon his return. He would much rather have been in the cockpit of a Nighthawk or a Strike Eagle. But those days were gone. Rank and age had turned him into what he had always derided, a "chairborne warrior."

His participation in this war was ironic. NATO, and of course,

principally, the United States, was fighting to free Muslims from op-
pression. He would do everything he could to carry out his duties, and
he knew that the ethnic minorities that Milosevic was trying to wipe
out were largely innocent people. But they were Muslims, and Muslims were in his mind inalterably identified with terror. He knew that
only a few fanatics carried out the acts of terror, but he blamed the
Muslim majority for being passive, for being intimidated by the minority.

The glowing radar screens were quiet, and while there was a steady
traffic on the radio, it was muted, obviously only routine transmissions
going on. Shannon was lost in thought. *It was the same in Germany. The
Nazis were a minority, and they were the fanatics who started the war, who
killed the Jews. But that didn't stop us from attacking the German people who
allowed the whole sordid mess to happen. We bombed German cities day in and
day out trying to eradicate the fanatics. We should be doing the same thing now
with the Muslims. Sad as it is, unjust as it is, we'll have to kill non-fanatic
Muslims to get them to control the fanatics. There is no other way. We—*

Myers tapped him on the arm and pointed to a blip on the radar
screen at his left.

"That's a U-2, sir. We call it 'the Dragon Lady.' "

Shannon nodded, his mind going back to stories his grandfather
told of Kelly Johnson and Tony LeVier and their arguments about
how to fly the prototype U-2. Good Lord, that was in 1955, forty-four
years ago. And the U-2s were still flying. They were doing different
missions now, not flying the long secret overflights as Gary Powers
had done. Instead they were loaded with all kinds of sensors and
linked to a whole galaxy of satellites, command and control aircraft,
fighters, and bombers. Instead of being a lone star in the distance over
the horizon, gathering information on film to be viewed later, they
were now like the central gear in an enormous clock of capability,
sending real-time information to centers for analysis that resulted in
real-time bombing action.

Shannon had flown in the two-seat version of the U-2 not long
before, and could remember how uncomfortable his pressure suit was,
and how noisy it seemed, with the sound of his own breathing, the
hum of avionics, and, just once in a while, a muted gasp from the engine, as if it too were starved for oxygen. And it was of course. The

single General Electric F118-GE-101 turbofan engine was at full throttle, ingesting a minimum amount of fuel with the thin air.

He pictured the pilots in their U-2s, busy with their computers and sensors, their tiny cockpits pressurized to 29,500 feet, and breathing the throat-drying 100 percent oxygen to maintain the equivalent of an 8,000-foot pressure altitude.

Myers touched the radar screen again, unaware that Shannon was reading and understanding the information as swiftly as he was.

"Watch this, sir, it's going to happen fast. He's acquired a target, some enemy aircraft parked on a dirt road under some heavy overhanging trees. He is sending the position to the CAOC"—then remembering that Shannon was a four-star but not necessarily up on the acronyms, Myers went on—"the Combined Air Operations Center in Vicenza, Italy, via satellite."

Shannon nodded, not wishing to seem impatient, grateful for Myers's concern, realizing that he might misunderstand the steady stream of audio and visual information.

Myers said, "We get the information as well, of course, and we just alerted a flight of orbiting F-16s just south of the area. If—and I'm sure it will—CAOC authorizes a strike we'll give the F-16s the go-ahead."

Less than thirty seconds later, Myers said, "There it is—they have approved the strike."

Two minutes later Myers turned to him, saying, "They hit the targets; looked like old MiGs to them but full of fuel. A good run."

While Myers talked Shannon put himself in the F-16's cockpit, vicariously sharing the thrill of the target acquisition, the run in, the concern for antiaircraft fire, and the pleasure when the bombs hit their targets. Nowadays precision guided bombs rarely missed.

The AWACS went on in its long lazy orbit, and Shannon once again had time to think. Bob Rodriquez and the Shannon family firm had done a lot to make this mission possible. Bob had contributed mightily to the precision guided munitions program, to the GPS, and to the AWACS as well. Going back a bit farther, Harry Shannon had been behind the Boeing boom refueling concept that was still being used every hour of every day. And of course, Steve O'Malley had virtually fathered the F-16 program years ago. All in all it was a family night.

Myers came back to his chair, saying, "Would you like me to go over the mission with you again, sir? We have it on video, we can run it through if there's anything you're not sure about."

Shannon just smiled. "No thanks, Major Myers. I have a pretty good idea of what happened tonight. Better than that, I've got a good idea of what it took to get to where we are tonight. Thanks for all your help. You can just let me vegetate here for a while."

Looking pleased at the thanks, but obviously happy not to have to keep babysitting a four-star, Myers wandered forward to take his place at his regular console, winking at his partner as he sat down.

"I think most of it went over his head. But he's a pretty good joe for all that."

October 19, 2000
Mojave, California

THE COMPANY NAME remained "RoboPlanes" partly because they had been too busy to change it, and partly because it provided a plausible cover for the research activities that now preoccupied the firm. The building itself had grown like some self-perpetuating modular monster, section after section being added, while six miles away, in a fence-enclosed facility, the early, small-scale test engines were roaring night and day.

Bob Rodriquez had gone through the mounds of hypersonic data, picking clusters of ideas just as a vintner harvests selected grapes for a special bottling. And he had gone through the vast complex of Vance Shannon, Incorporated, doing the same thing with engineers and scientists, dragging them off vitally needed, profitable projects from all over the country, and sequestering them in the RoboPlanes complex. In the process he had infuriated company managers everywhere, and oftentimes the engineers and scientists themselves were unhappy.

Until they got on the job, and saw what a monumental task and what a significant opportunity they had been given. No one had to come on an involuntary basis, but it was much like a domestic Operation Paperclip, the celebrated program at the end of World War II that brought brilliant engineers such as Wernher von Braun to this country. The people Rodriquez induced to come found the Mojave area to be rather austere, particularly if they had come from eastern facilities, but the challenge of the work was rich, and so were its material rewards. Bob's wife Mae was brought in to create a luxurious (if still basically modular) housing complex, with first-class schools for the children. Mae used subsidies to lure wonderful first-line stores to the area. Totally unlike anything ever seen before in Mojave, they were intended to keep RoboPlanes's employees happy, but benefited the entire county and soon were paying for themselves. She brought in ethnic restaurants, Thai, Vietnamese, even Burmese, to give a civilizing effect.

The combined costs of the effort were staggering, and even all of Harry Shannon's managerial efforts could not convince the board of directors and stockholders that there would ultimately be a payoff. Instead, Harry, V. R., Steve, Bob, and Dennis pooled their fortunes and borrowed to their maximum capability to take the company private once again. The process took an agonizing ten months to complete, but it salved their consciences. No longer did they have to fear that they were dealing falsely with the stockholders.

Incredibly, there had already been totally unexpected spin-offs from the pursuit of both scramjet and UAV technology. These were already bearing a sufficient burden of the expenses to keep Vance Shannon, Incorporated, earning at roughly the same level as it had in the past. Their very earliest experiments with the scramjets had led to patents in ceramic technology that were directly applicable to cooking ware. These patents had been purchased by two different commercial firms, one foreign, one domestic, and the royalties were already rolling in. And just as young Rod Rodriquez had predicted, the civil demand for UAVs was growing exponentially. The damn things were so cost-effective—they didn't draw a salary, required minimum maintenance, and effectively multiplied a police force or a forestry unit using them by an order of ten or fifteen. If an airplane crashed in a deserted area, a single UAV could search the area, home on to its emergency beacon, use GPS to pinpoint the spot, and remain overhead for hours so that the rescue parties could come directly to it. The police used the same sort of surveillance for tracking stolen cars, staking out a suspect's hideout, or simply providing a presence. The sound of a RoboPlane overhead quieted a lot of gang and narcotics activity on the streets, for they knew that it carried real-time television images direct not only to police stations, but to the local police cars. Periodically, the frustration level would rise, and someone would take a shot at the UAVs, but none had been lost so far. Perhaps not surprisingly, the media had caught on to the corny RoboPlane name, and it had become a generic for civilian UAVs. Rodriquez initially favored trying to protect the copyright, but soon they were in the same position as Xerox had been with other copy machines. It didn't matter who made the copier, people called it "Xeroxing" and that was it. The final convincing straw was the prevalent rumor that a film was being made called "RoboPlanes" and featuring an android UAV that somehow falls for a good-looking woman detective. RoboPlane's lawyers had sent a letter of protest, but there was no reply and Rodriquez, occupied with the challenge of hypersonic flight, told them to forget about it.

Their UAV experimentation had led to some totally new concepts in streamlining as well. The trucking industry had leaped upon their developments with glad cries. Unimaginably, some of the same principles that applied to a fifty-pound UAV could be extrapolated to the cab and the undersurfaces of an eighteen-wheel truck, cutting drag and resulting in substantial fuel savings. These fairings had a side benefit for the truckers, for they provided a space where some quarters, quite luxurious compared to the usual truck-stop motel, could be fitted.

Harry had long since realized that these benefits were just the iceberg's tip, for the engineers and scientists that Rodriquez had dragooned into the UAV and the hypersonic programs had a wide variety of interests, and each one sought to apply what he or she was learning to their previous company projects. The more they worked, the more they explored, the more derivative products there would be. The most bizarre example so far had been a totally inexplicable spin-off that made the inventor rich and added to RoboPlanes's coffers. It involved a new and better pop-top for cans, and derived from a valve they were developing for the scramjet. Another huge surprise was the television sale of remote control models. Harry hated the huckster part of the business, but there was no denying the comfort it provided the bottom line.

There were far fewer successes with the furious level of scramjet experimentation. The local facility had proved inadequate, and a newly built one, located fifteen miles away in the desert, was testing the larger engines. The move was necessary, for even the most elaborate mufflers and diligent buffering could not silence the incredible shrieking noise of scramjets operating in the wind tunnels. Even worse, frequencies far too high to be heard caused a violent nausea for anyone not wearing the proper ear protection. Everyone at the new facility—a combination of large and small supersonic wind tunnels and engine test bays—wore both earplugs and helmets, but still suffered from the fatigue induced by the incredible panoply of noise. There was an odd side effect, totally unexpected, on automobile and truck tires, which suffered internal fatigue and sometimes failure from the high-frequency vibrations.

Bob Rodriquez, Sr., had already made his morning round of every building in the facility, a habit he had picked up from Ben Rich at the Skunk Works. Like Ben, he bounded into each group with a grin and a new joke, and like Ben he absorbed in a glance how the group was doing. Facial expressions and body language often told him more than the endless stream of memorandums, and he had long since identified the players who made things happen, even in this super-select group.

Much of their progress had been made possible by early decisions that happened to work out. Had they failed, the project would probably have been abandoned by now. Working with O'Malley and Jenkins, Rodriquez established a series of goals for their missiles fleet. Among these were that most of the family would be stealthy, including the cruise missiles, the anti-cruise missiles, and the unmanned aerial vehicles. For the most part, stealth for the manned hypersonic vehicle would be provided by speed. It would be so fast that when it was picked up by radar, it would already be too late for an enemy to react. Then they decided that while they would use engines from established manufacturers—rockets and jets—for the missiles and the unmanned vehicles, they would create their own power-plant system for the manned hypersonic vehicles. Finally, and most difficult, they decided that if at all possible they would not use a rocket booster on the manned hypersonic vehicles, but instead use a combination fanjet/scramjet engine. The goal from the start was that their vehicle would take off and land under its own power—no drops from mother planes, no engineless glides back to landing.

The basic simplicity of the scramjet engine continually amazed and frustrated the Shannon team, Rodriquez in particular. The very name "scramjet" infuriated him for its cuteness. It was a stretch for an acronym, standing for Supersonic Combustion Ramjet. A scramjet engine consisted of an inlet, a combustion chamber, fuel injectors, and a thrust nozzle. The scramjet engine ingested air at supersonic speeds, allowed it to flow around a fixed nozzle where fuel was injected, combustion occurred, and thrust was produced. The designs that spoke to Rodriquez were all "waveriders," meaning that the underside of the vehicle formed the intake and the nozzle of the engine. The waverider was an exciting shape, a speedster riding its own shock wave like a surfboard riding the monster waves on Oahu's North Shore. He had investigated reams of data, and in the previous three months had worked himself all the way back to some canceled projects. They gave him some insight for a totally new, if very high risk, approach, and today his task was to sell the rest of his team on the concept.

Rodriquez walked into the conference room, ordinarily spic and span, but this morning littered with empty coffee cups and papers from the all-night meeting that had just ended.

"Thank God nobody smokes anymore. This place would be intolerable if they did."

Rodriquez quickly tidied up the smaller conference table, placed three chairs around it, and deposited one of his files at each position. As he finished, Jenkins and O'Malley walked in, both looking pleased with themselves, but both obviously very tired.

After the usual greetings and inquiries, Rodriquez said, "Harry is under the weather, but told me I had his proxy to vote for whatever we decide here."

Harry attended fewer and fewer of their meetings. The new enterprise initially gave him both energy and strength, but the intensity of the program was beginning to sap his vitality. They knew he was going to the doctor, getting checkups, but Harry was closemouthed about such private matters. They guessed that something was wrong.

"Before we get started, Dennis, Harry told me to congratulate you on the hundredth flight of the Space Shuttle."

The Space Shuttle *Discovery* had launched after delays, and encountered difficulties almost immediately when their rendezvous radar failed. They docked manually with the International Space Station and successfully transferred their main cargo, key building materials.

"Tell him thanks, but I'm not personally responsible. When you consider they had planned to make the hundredth flight in 1979—not 2000—it is not too shiny."

O'Malley said sadly, "What is shiny? I'm still in shock from the second Osprey crash."

On April 8, the Marines had been simulating a search and rescue mission with two V-22s near Marana, Arizona. Descending swiftly, perhaps two thousand feet per minute, the right rotor of the second V-22 stalled, rolling the airplane over and plunging 245 feet to the ground. Nineteen men were killed, and the program was once again under risk of cancellation.

"It was the typical vortex ring state incident. But there may have been some interplay with the rotor-wash of the other V-22. I hope they sort this one out fast, otherwise the program might go down the tubes."

Dennis Jenkins, always upbeat, said, "Steve, there is lots out there that's shiny. Boeing's got its Airborne Laser 747 flying, and that is a big leap forward. They delivered number four thousand of your favorite airplane, the F-16—what a coup acquiring that program was for Lockheed—a gold mine! The Joint Strike Fighter competition is under way, and both the Boeing and the Lockheed Martin entries look pretty good."

Rodriquez snorted. "Well, maybe Lockheed's looks good; the Boeing job is funny-looking. But I'm sure it will fly well."

It was true—the Boeing entry had a peculiar, snub-nosed look that was uncharacteristic of the firm's usual comely designs. The Lockheed Martin JSF naturally looked much like the F-22.

O'Malley, casting around for something to make his "not shiny" remark valid, said, "Don't forget the Concorde crash near Paris! That's hardly shiny."

Rodriquez gently tapped on the table.

"Enough of the griping, guys. Look in your folder. We've had far too many meetings on this, and I'd like to get agreement today so that we can start cutting metal on our Big Baby."

Rodriquez had given each of their projects nicknames— "Deathblow" for the hypersonic cruise missile, "Little Slicker" for the anti-cruise missile, and "Big Baby" for their manned hypersonic vehicle.

O'Malley didn't like the practice and said so. "Look, Bob, you can call it anything you want, but we've got to have a salable name for the project when we take it forward. 'Big Baby' just doesn't cut it."

Jenkins said, "I agree. It doesn't matter what we call them in-house, but somehow Big Baby doesn't work for me, either. How about calling it something straightforward, like 'Hypersonic Cruiser'? That's sort of how we see it, don't we, something analogous to a Navy cruiser, fast, long range, lots of firepower?"

Rodriquez, embarrassed, shrugged and said, "OK. From now on it's the Hypersonic Cruiser. Not a bad name, if it's OK with you, Steve?"

Steve nodded brusquely, saying, "We've got the name, but before we cut any more metal, we should be sure that we all understand just how risky this enterprise is. We are trying to do for millions what the government has failed to do with billions. We can wind up bankrupting ourselves and in debt, if any one of a thousand things goes wrong."

"We knew that from the start, Steve; we knew that when we privatized the firm. What's new?"

"I'll tell you what. I've been poor and I've been rich, and rich is better than poor. And even if I didn't know this, Sally reminds me about twenty times a day."

Rodriquez stood up, suddenly realizing that O'Malley was dead serious.

"Do you want us to stop? We could shut down all our hypersonic work, keep the UAV work going, send everybody back where they came from, and not get hurt too bad. In fact, I think we've already got enough possibilities from the spin-offs to recover our costs."

O'Malley shook his head. "No, we're in this for keeps, I know that. I just want to be sure you know it, so there's no bitching if we go belly up."

Jenkins said, "Let's get to work. No bitching allowed."

Rodriquez said, "Before we start going through the folders, let me tell you my starting point, and what the basic idea is. It seems so good and so logical to me that there must be something wrong with it, and if you think so, I want you to speak up. Not that any of you are ever very reticent."

The three men nodded at him. Rodriquez was always intense, but when he was passionately involved in an idea he seemed to grow in size. He leaned forward, face darkening with color, and talked more and more rapidly. Normally they'd signaled him to slow down, and he would, but moments later would be back, speeding on, the words flying out, his hands racing over the blackboard, charting numbers and formula.

"I think I've found the route for us to follow. It's hard to believe, for it goes all the way back to 1948 and the Republic XF-103. Any of you remember it?"

Only Jenkins spoke. "Sure, it was an advanced Mach 3.0 interceptor. And it was canceled—just too advanced to even try to build."

"That's right. It was way ahead of its time and it led to some other projects. It had a phenomenal projected performance because it used a dual-cycle propulsion system. The main engine was the Wright XJ67-W-3 turbojet that put out about twenty-two thousand pounds of thrust with afterburning. At high speed, it used a ramjet that put out another eighteen thousand pounds of thrust. But here is the kicker: at high speed, they had the air bypass the engine compressor and turbine, and used the afterburner as a ramjet combustion chamber. Then Republic went on, using this same kind of thinking, to develop an even more advanced proposal in 1962, the so-called Aerospace plane. It had ideas that we can adapt directly to the Hypersonic Cruiser." It was the first time he had used the term and he liked the way it rolled off his tongue. He looked around at expressions that were friendly but skeptical.

O'Malley said, "What's the application here, Bob?"

"Look, we've been looking at wave-rider technology, using the bottom of the fuselage as engine component. We can stick to that, but let's locate the fan-jet engine in the rear of the vehicle behind the nozzle for the scramjet. Let me show you my sketches—it will be easier to visualize than just my talking. Open up your folder to page six."

They did as he asked, and O'Malley whistled at the sheer audacity of the concept.

"You can see that we've retained the traditional wave-rider shape—pilot in an escape capsule well forward, dual nose gear aft of the capsule, and the two fan-jets arranged on either side of the fuselage. But what is different is our enclosing the area aft of the scramjet by a cowling. In effect, we are hooking up an afterburner concept to the scramjet. If my computations are correct, and you'll find them over the next fourteen pages, we will get roughly 50 percent more power and 50 percent better fuel economy."

Jenkins slapped himself on the forehead.

"You are trying to do with a scramjet what they did with the fan jet."

"No, I think I'm reversing that. The fan jet bypassed air, adding to the mass flow and getting a free ride. In this one we are introducing more fuel, just like an afterburner, but the numbers show you are getting a far greater return. It sounds impossible, but the numbers are there."

O'Malley's voice was somber.

"This thing is huge; the fuselage is almost one hundred feet long."

"We can make an itty-bitty one like Boeing's X-43A. It doesn't carry anybody, and it malfunctioned on its first flight. We have no chance to make a conventional development program like the Air Force would demand. We can go for broke, or we ought to get out of the business. You know exactly what we are doing. We are depending upon computers for research that used to be done in wind tunnels and in test flights. We'll never get where we want to go with conventional processes. Either we are right in what we glean from the computers, or we will fail in a spectacular manner."

Rodriquez's tone was calm, but he was obviously sincere. They had charted a live-or-die course so far, abandoning all the traditional rules of experimentation that NASA and the military services lived by, and going on experience and gut instinct. It was the biggest gamble of their lives, for the future of all the companies—RoboPlanes, Vance Shannon, Incorporated, and all the rest rode on being correct. There would be no second prize for failure. And failure would inevitably also cost the life of the test pilot. At the moment, this was the most important factor in Rodriquez's thinking.

"Look, let's stop mincing words. We all know that V. R. Shannon is going to be the test pilot for us, no matter which vehicle we create. He's planning on retiring in 2005, and we will be rolling the Hypersonic Cruiser out the door by 2006 if possible, maybe mid-2007 if things don't go as well as I'd like."

He paused for effect and went on. "I want you to think about what we are doing, and realize this: if we fail, we will have sacrificed our businesses, our wealth, and worst of all, one of the great pilots of our time, V. R. Shannon. If we succeed, we will hand the United States a military capability that is suited to fight the war on terror like nothing else."

O'Malley rose out of the chair to stand in a brooding, hunched-over position, looking as he did when he wrestled for the Air Force Academy. He leaned forward, arms spread, his legs positioned to leap, and said, "We've got a psychological problem here. You know that both V. R. and I are obsessed with the Muslim threat. We both vote to go ahead with this project. That puts the onus on the rest of you—Bob, Dennis, and Harry—to come to a measured decision. Right now there are two sure votes to proceed—mine and V. R.'s. We know the risks, all of them, and accept it, for the country needs a manned hypersonic vehicle, and it doesn't look like any other manufacturer will be able to create one in the next ten or even twenty years. But like I say, we are obsessed, and might not be thinking clearly. It is up to you to call Harry, lay the cards on the table with him, and decide. As much as we like and love V. R., he is Harry's nephew, his twin brother's son. He may have strong feelings about this, and we have to listen to them. And I don't want any split decisions. Either it is five to zero in favor, or let's cancel the whole goddamn hypersonic program and concentrate on UAVs."

There was silence in the room.

Rodriquez said, "These brochures I gave you are top secret in the company. The government would classify them immediately if it knew they existed, for we are no doubt treading on black projects that we don't even know about. Make sure you don't lose them. And if you have any questions, call me and I'll come over. I only want to discuss this face-to-face, because I want to see your expressions as well as hear your ideas. We are not just risking V. R.'s life, we are fooling with a lot of lives here—no matter which way we decide."

O'Malley said, "Bob, when are you going to talk to Harry?"

"Dennis and I will go over to Palos Verdes tonight. If he's up to it, we'll talk to him then. If not, we'll wait there until he feels like discussing it. I don't want to make him the first casualty of the program."

CHAPTER EIGHTEEN

THE PASSING PARADE: Jury convicts Libyan of Flight 103 bombing; huge spy scandal as FBI agent Robert Hanssen pleads guilty;
ethnic Albanians rise in Macedonia; scientist, entrepreneur
Dennis Tito pays $20 million to become "first space tourist" on
International Space Station; U.S. economy boosted by huge
Bush tax cut; peace agreement signed between Macedonian
government and rebels; Muslim terrorists, most from Saudi Arabia ram jet liners into New York's Twin Towers, the Pentagon,
fourth attempt aborted by heroic passengers; al Qaeda Muslim
terrorist network held responsible; United States and Great
Britain initiate campaign against terrorist training camps in Afghanistan; Enron Corporation folds due to corporate corruption;
U.S. campaign, combining special forces, airpower, and Northern
Alliance ground forces, succeeds in toppling oppressive Taliban
regime in Afghanistan; Hamid Karzai selected as new leader.

April 29, 2001
Mojave, California

*J*ust as it had been almost every week for the past six months, it was
crisis time at RoboPlanes. Most of the problems stemmed from the
quickly reached agreement to proceed with the Hypersonic Cruiser.
Harry had demurred at first, but yielded to V. R.'s quiet, persuasive
pitch that the company's founder, Vance Shannon, would have gone
ahead. They both knew this was the case, and V. R. added that Tom
Shannon would have cast his vote to proceed as well. It cost Harry a

great deal of his fast diminishing reserves of strength, for V. R. was the youngest surviving Shannon and the only one who might have children and carry on the family name. Still, the final company vote had been five to zero to proceed, just as O'Malley had demanded.

For once, today's crisis didn't stem from the Hypersonic Cruiser. Instead, Rodriquez had insisted on a meeting of the firm's officers to discuss some expected but still unwelcome developments in the UAV end of the business. Harry had again begged off, giving his proxy to Bob as was his wont lately. Only the "usual suspects," Jenkins and O'Malley, would be there.

V. R. couldn't attend and wouldn't have if he had been available. He studiously stayed away from ordinary company business to avoid any possible charge of conflict of interest. Now a four-star general, he was deputy commander of Central Command, and spent almost every waking hour touring American facilities in the Middle East. For V. R. it was a waiting game. He knew that the radical Muslims were going to attack, and he believed that the attack would come on the United States in some spectacular fashion. He combed intelligence reports and closely cross-questioned every one he dealt with. The State Department regarded him as an utter liability in the Middle East, a catastrophe waiting to happen, and had filed numerous complaints with the Department of Defense. None of them held water, for Shannon's job performance was spectacular, and he never quite crossed the line so far that the foreign-service types could nail him.

Rodriquez wanted to get right down to business, but knew he'd have to wait when Jenkins, virtually frothing at the mouth, said, "Did you read about this Dennis Tito? He paid twenty million dollars to the Russians for a ride up to the International Space Station! It's deplorable."

O'Malley always liked to egg him on. "Come on, Dennis, you're just jealous that you've stuffed all your money into this turkey of a Hypersonic Cruiser, and Tito is up there floating around weightless like you'd like to do."

Jenkins took the bait. "I'd never waste twenty million on a stupid, self-indulgent joyride. If he wanted to make a splash, he could have spent twenty million feeding starving kids in Africa, or right here in the States. That's where he earned his money; he should spend it here."

Rodriquez said, "Well, he's no friend of ours, that's for sure. His investment company dropped us a long time before we went private—somehow he got word of what we were doing with UAVs and the hypersonic stuff. Actually, it was pretty shrewd of him."

Jenkins began to settle down, and Rodriquez went on. "Here's the deal, gents. We've been outhustled on two important contracts. You know that we were bidding a whole mixture of subcontracts on General Atomic's RQ-1B Predator, and another bunch of them on the Global Hawk."

The RQ-1B Predator was a new, turboprop-powered version that had flown on February 2. The Global Hawk had just made news with an incredible seventy-five-hundred-mile nonstop flight across the Pacific to Australia.

"Well, we went wrong somewhere, because we got skunked on both programs. It really hurts, because we've been with both from the start."

O'Malley asked, "What was the reason they gave for cutting us out?"

"Cost, pure and simple, was the reason. But I got a signal from Al Bonadies, one of the top engineers at Northrop Grumman. He had me over to his house for a beer last week, and they told me that part of it was the cost, and part of it was losing confidence in RoboPlanes because of what we were spending on the hypersonic projects. In simplest terms, they think we are nuts trying to do something that is a decade beyond anyone else."

There was a stunned silence. Jenkins said, "Well, we shouldn't be surprised. You know how this industry is, there are virtually no secrets, and word has to get out on how ambitious our project is."

O'Malley said, "And how risky. They probably expect us to lose our shirts. Worse, they probably figure that we are using a pencil on their costs to cover some of the costs on the hypersonic program."

He looked into Rodriquez's eyes and asked, "Are we, Bob? Is there some crossover on the program that's hurting us? We'll be a cooked goose for sure if we lose our edge on the UAVs."

Rodriquez shrugged. "There is no fraudulent bookkeeping going on, and I know you know that. But there's bound to be some costs that are melded into the overhead that affect both programs. There's no way to avoid it in practical terms. We can take some artificial measures, run some estimates on what it might be, and then factor it into the proposals. I guess we should have been doing that all along. But I don't think costs are the problem. Credibility is. The problem is there is no way we can accelerate what we are doing. If we move like a sleepwalker for the next six years, never making a mistake, there is still no way we can fly the Hypersonic Cruiser much before 2008. We all know that."

Jenkins spoke up. "I've seen your financial forecasts, Bob. I guess it's just a coincidence that December 2008 is when we run out of funds as well?"

"Oddly enough, Dennis, it is just a coincidence. There's no fudge factor on either side. If everything goes as we want it to go, if all of the decisions we make are correct, we'll have a flight-worthy Hypersonic Cruiser ready for test in the fall of 2008. And if everything goes like we want financially, if the RoboPlanes UAV cash cow keeps on giving milk, we'll have enough money to last until then. After that, all bets are off."

O'Malley broke in. "I'm usually the Cassandra of this bunch, always seeing pitfalls, but I'm more optimistic about the UAVs than ever. Maybe we should just back off from trying to swim with the big guys and doing their subcontracting. You know how their accountants are, going over every penny spent, and their value engineer guys, always poking their noses in. I think we are better off sticking to our own clientele, the small user, foreign governments, and the like. It makes it a lot easier for security purposes, too—we only have to deal with our own internal security and don't have a raft of other people checking us out."

Jenkins said, "Looks like our roles are reversed, Steve; I'm usually the too-optimistic guy around here. But I wonder if we haven't pretty well pushed the UAV market to the limit? The problem is we are making too good a product. Some of the UAVs being used by local police have several hundred missions on them. And the latest wrinkle, the mini-ballistic parachute, has saved half a dozen more. I guess what we need are some self-destruct units that go off after twenty missions or so. Just kidding, of course."

"Well, look what the software people have done, bring out new things that the user 'has to have.' That's what we have to do with the UAVs. The vehicle is the least of it. We need to concentrate more on products, really far-out stuff, that we can put inside the UAVs. Look at the airline security problem—if we could have UAVs flying the perimeter of airports, low altitude, not messing with traffic, with some sort of an explosive sniffer on them, we'd have a gold mine. Or look at the border patrol. We need to get an infrared device that will reach out maybe forty miles in the desert to pick up illegal immigrants making their way north. Our problem is we are all airplane guys, we want to push buttons and go vrroooom. We've got to do like Paul MacCready does, get specialists in arcane fields and let them riff on the problems."

Rodriquez spoke. "Steve's right. We've been doing that all along with the airframe, looking for ways to save weight, just letting the mission come find the airplane. Now we've got to start creating the missions. The environment's the key. We cannot lose if can figure some inroads into saving the environment some way. But we've got to break out of the airplane builder's mode and get some fresh talent in, people who don't give a damn about airplanes, but want to see how glaciers move, or what's happening in the rain forest. We've got UAVs of all sorts now on the books—let's give some to some colleges and let them figure out how to use them."

He shook his head. "Here I am worrying about every dime we spend on the Hypersonic Cruiser, and now I want to give money away to colleges. But still, I think we should. We've got money for six more years for sure; if we use our heads. We could view the gifts to colleges as seed money, maybe we'll be getting a return by 2007, and it will keep us going."

Jenkins put up his hand. "This is the sort of thing I like to do. Let me have a crack at this, and I'll get back to you. I've got some ideas about where a few UAV systems could go to really be helpful. What would you say for a budget, half a million?"

"Let's start with a quarter million and see how it goes."

They broke up in general agreement but with Bob Rodriquez saying, "For Christ's sake, what is the matter with me? I'm seventy-three years old. I'll be damn near eighty by the time the Hypersonic Cruiser flies, if I'm lucky and I live that long. I should start thinking about slowing down."

O'Malley, normally gruff and no-nonsense, slipped his arm around Rodriquez's shoulders and said, "Bob, even if you died, you'd have a laptop in your coffin and be working on something. You'll never slow down. That's why we call you 'Hypersonic Bob' behind your back."

September 11, 2001
Washington, D.C.

By NINE O'CLOCK V. R. was ready for his second cup of coffee, and Julie, his incomparable assistant, had just left the room to get it. Steve O'Malley was sitting bolt upright in his chair opposite the desk, about to shove some figures across the table on the Joint Strike Fighter program when Shannon's red phone rang. It was Snake Clark, who said simply, "Turn your television to CNN."

The indispensable Clark was normally unflappable, but the tone in his voice compelled Shannon to comply immediately, and CNN opened with a view of the North Tower of the World Trade Center wreathed in smoke.

O'Malley said, "It's got to be terrorists, they said they'd be back."

Shannon picked up the other line and asked Julie to get Bob Rodriquez and Dennis Jenkins on the line in a conference call.

"I know it's three hours earlier out there—just get them on the line."

CNN's Carol Lin's familiar voice came through, her professionalism smoothing over the confusion, saying, "This just in. You are looking at a very disturbing live shot. That is the World Trade Center, and we have unconfirmed reports that a plane has crashed into one of the towers . . ."

Julie came to the door, saying, "I've got Mr. Rodriquez and Mr. Jenkins on the line, but you've got a call from the deputy administrator at the FAA, Mr. Greener."

"I'll talk to Greener first, keep the other two on the line, tell them to turn on CNN."

Shannon said, "Hello Bill, what in God's name is happening?"

"V. R., we've got four, maybe five airliners hijacked. One of them just hit the World Trade Center. Can you scramble fighters and maybe locate the others and stop them?"

Shannon whirled to face O'Malley. "Steve, tell my guys to get any fighters they can on the East Coast into the air, armed, authorized to fire on airliner targets only when we give the word."

O'Malley bounded to the next room to ask a pale-faced Lieutenant Colonel Jim Mueller to call NORAD first, then Air Combat Command, then the Air National Guard unit at Andrews. He knew Shannon was exceeding his authority. No one but the President could actually authorize firing on an American passenger aircraft, but there was no time to go to the White House. He had no business giving orders, but they knew he was acting on Shannon's behalf. He went back to V. R.'s office to hear him say, "Bill, we need locations and positive identification of these hijacked aircraft. What can you tell me?"

"We think it was American Flight 11 which—Oh, my God!"

Shannon whirled in time to see another airliner slicing into the South Tower, leaving a clear imprint of its shape before the flames erupted.

"That's probably United 175, out of Boston. It may be too late for the fighters."

"What else have you got? Where should my guys be looking? For Christ's sake, Bill, what's going on?"

"It's terrorism, well coordinated; you and Steve were right all along. Right now we're tracking American Airlines Flight 77 heading your way; United Flight 93 is headed off somewhere, probably toward Washington, too. We are closing all the airports around New York, we're probably going to ground all aircraft. Leave this line open, I'll feed you anything I find out."

O'Malley picked up the other line, saying to Rodriquez and Jenkins, "This is it. The terrorists have struck, and there are two, maybe three more out there. Get the factory on alert; I doubt if they'll try anything in an unpopulated area, but go ahead and warn them anyway."

Shannon's office erupted into a whirlwind of staffers, bringing in or carrying out information and instructions, each one pausing momentarily to watch the unfolding horror.

Colonel Miller came in, saying, "We've got F-15s off at Otis. They are going to orbit till they get a vector to the target. No F-16s off from Andrews yet."

Shannon was on the phone with the Air National Guard at Andrews when Flight 77 crashed into the western side of the Pentagon.

O'Malley leaped up at the thunderous roar, saying, "The White House will be next!"

September 11, 2001
Mojave, California

THEY WERE AS stunned as the rest of the nation, horrified by the incredible turn of events that saw three hijacked aircraft successfully attack their targets, and one, thanks to the heroism of its passengers, fail.

The Rodriquez family was there. Dennis Jenkins had brought Sally O'Malley out, along with Nancy and Anna Shannon.

"When did you last hear from Steve or V. R.?"

"Not since about eight our time. O'Malley phoned to let us know they were not injured in the Pentagon attack. They've both been too busy since."

Anna asked, "Do you think it's over?"

Bob Sr. answered, "If you mean are attacks by airliners over, they are for today; everything is grounded. But if you mean terrorism, it's just getting started. After all the times we've made fun of Steve and V. R. about their phobias, they turn out to be right after all."

Jenkins asked, "What do you think this will mean for Robo-Planes?"

Rodriquez said, "Lots more orders for UAVs; probably a slow-down on the hypersonic work."

Rod spoke up. "I don't think so, Dad. I think the anti-hypersonic cruise missile is going to be more important than ever. I think you are right about more orders for UAVs, but we might get some development money for the cruise missile work."

His father shook his head, saying, "I hope so. We can use it. But I've got the feeling that even this isn't going to be enough to wake America up. I don't like the tenor of the commentary, people are indignant, but they are not as angry as they should be. When the Japanese attacked Pearl Harbor, there was an immediate, universal reaction against the Japanese. I'm already hearing cries for compassion for the peaceful Muslims. What I want to hear is cries for death to the fanatics. I'm not hearing it."

Jenkins agreed with him, but said, "It's early, Bob. People haven't absorbed what's happened yet. There's bound to be a rising tide of anger. This is so outrageous, so cruel. The Japanese attack, however sneaky, was a military event. This is pure terrorism on civilians. I'll never forget those shots of people leaping to their deaths, or the brave first responders going into the burning buildings. We've got to get angry about this."

Anna rarely spoke at their gatherings, but tonight she said, "No. I don't think so, Dennis. We've gotten too soft. I think we will make a big fuss about this for a while, and then go right back to sleep."

No one said anything. Anna's comments were too close to the bone, too apt to be right, and too horrible to contemplate.

December 2, 2001
Lambert Field, St. Louis, Missouri

V. R. SHANNON stepped outside the terminal entrance to soak up a little sun. It was warm for St. Louis in December, and it was good to escape the pall hanging over the airport, a mixture of resentment at the new and still clumsily executed security precautions, and embarrassment that workmen were still replacing the TWA signs with new ones from American. Flight 220, the last ceremonial TWA flight, had landed at Lambert yesterday, to a sorrowful crowd of veteran TWA employees. After many difficult years, the proud old airline, TWA, had given up, purchased by American Airlines. A great airline and a great tradition were no more.

Somehow it seemed exactly appropriate to V. R., for this was his last official trip for the United States Air Force. His retirement ceremonies in Washington were scheduled for December 31. He really didn't have to make this trip, but he felt he owed a great deal to the old McDonnell Douglas team that had created the F-15 fighter. It was the Boeing F-15 now, of course, for just as American had acquired TWA and promptly changed its name, so had Boeing absorbed McDonnell

Douglas in 1996. He could have sent any one of his deputies on this trip, to lay out the costs for extending the F-15E for some possible sales overseas, but with more than fifteen hundred hours in the airplane, he wanted to come and visit with the longtime MacDac people who wore the Boeing logo lightly and somewhat grudgingly.

He waited somewhat impatiently for his car to arrive. This was not like the McDonnell Douglas of years ago—there would have been half a dozen people on hand to meet him at the gate, and they would have had cars waiting outside the terminal doors. It didn't surprise him. Since September 11, 2001, nothing seemed to go right at airports. The Muslim world had not only done the unthinkable, crashing their stolen aircraft into New York's Twin Towers and the Pentagon, they had done the impossible, brought American air traffic to a halt.

Shannon had helped set up Operation Noble Eagle, the combat air patrols instituted on September 14 over major cities, and he had been in on the initial planning for Operation Enduring Freedom in Afghanistan. He had immediately tried to get his retirement deferred—it was no time for him to get out of uniform, not when the fanatical Muslim world had exposed its hand. But even in the heat of planning, his reputation for hating Muslim extremists preceded him, and the State Department let it be known that they did not want V. R. Shannon participating in the war on terror.

Maybe Anna was right. Maybe America was too soft. Well, the State Department was too soft. There was no doubt about that.

So here he was, shut down almost as tight as TWA, and unable to do anything about it. He berated himself for having been so obvious, but knew that there was no way he could have concealed his animosity—it was just too strong. Now he would have to find some other way to express it.

He glanced at his watch and down the curving road to the terminal. No car in view; he signaled to a cab and got in. The Boeing office where the meeting was scheduled was probably less than a mile away, but it would be twenty minutes before the cab could negotiate the departure from the terminal and the entrance to the tight security at the plant.

Shannon looked at his notes. They had invited him out to give a bit of a retrospective on the F-15 program from a pilot's—and a general's—point of view. But he wanted to cover some other things that were important to the future. Shannon always spoke extemporaneously, from a list of bullets, and he quickly jotted down some ideas.

First, the F-16/F-15 programs—their hazards, successes, comparisons. The two programs complemented each other, but both competed for the declining Air Force budget and Shannon wanted to give the Boeing people some idea of how much the Air Force had appreciated concessions that had been made to keep the F-15 program going over the years.

Second, the Chinese launch of two Long March missiles, placing two satellites in orbit. This was a little out of the F-15 plant's normal sphere of interest, and that's why he wanted it included. McDonnell Douglas had once been at the forefront of the space race, and the advances of the Chinese made it seem like Boeing ought to reinvigorate the space effort in St. Louis. The top Boeing guys might not like this sort of suggestion, but he knew the middle management people would soak it up.

Third, Boeing's Sonic Cruiser. He was going to take a little jab at them on this one; no one believed Boeing was serious about their proposed Sonic Cruiser airliner, which was supposed to be their trump card with Airbus. He wanted to test the waters and see what the response was. The Sonic Cruiser looked good—but he thought there might be a Hypersonic Cruiser before there would be a Sonic Cruiser.

Fourth, Paul MacCready's *Helios.* Everybody in the industry loved Paul, who was always coming up with something new and startling. His *Helios,* a huge, unlikely-looking UAV, had recently set a 96,500-foot altitude record. He was going to have to come in with some tie-in on this, as there was no direct Boeing interest in the project. Maybe he could wrap it in with the need for more space activity here in St. Louis.

Fifth, Predator using Hellfire weapons in Afghanistan. He'd have to watch himself on this one. A lot of the material was still classified, but it would certainly generate the most questions. It was incredible, it was just what O'Malley had predicted—a Predator had used a Hellfire missile to take out an enemy in Afghanistan. It opened up whole new worlds for UAVs.

Sixth, Lockheed Martin winning the Joint Strike Fighter competition. This one would have to be soft-pedaled. He couldn't avoid mentioning it, it was too recent and too important. Maybe some nice words on the Boeing approach, but emphasize the lift-fan on the Lockheed Martin F-35.

Seventh, the war on terror. Here's where he would have to be really careful. He knew that many people regarded him as a nutcase on the subject, and he knew that his obsession had ended his career on a slightly sour note. Still, here was the perfect venue to tell important engineers exactly what the dangers were. He'd just have to be measured, and make it sound reasonable.

Shannon read through the notes one more time and put them in his briefcase. He wouldn't need them once he was introduced and started talking. The main thing was not to go on too long. About twenty minutes was all anyone wanted, unless you were a stand-up comedian. The cab pulled to the curb, where Jack Cummings, the Boeing rep, stood, visibly embarrassed at not having been there to pick Shannon up.

CHAPTER NINETEEN

THE PASSING PARADE: Terrorist prisoners taken to Guantanamo Bay; Catholic church cover-up of pedophile problem sparks outrage; Enron scandal spreads, Enron chairman Kenneth L. Lay resigns; in first State of the Union address, President Bush links Iran, Iraq, and North Korea in an "axis of evil" to unprecedented high popularity rating; kidnapped reporter Daniel Pearl killed by terrorists in Pakistan; Muslim/Hindu riots in India claim hundreds of lives; Operation Anaconda launched with mixed success in Afghanistan; despite Saudi proposal for normal relations with Israel, warfare breaks out in Middle East as a result of Palestinian suicide attacks; Hugo Chavez reinstated after ouster in Venezuela, threatens to tighten control, confront United States; Russia and United States agree to major cuts in nuclear forces; United States announces that it will not recognize an independent Palestinian state with Yasir Arafat as its head; another major fraud disclosed when WorldCom files for largest bankruptcy in history; world watches rescue of Pennsylvania miners after three days in flooded shaft; President Bush calls for regime change in Iraq in address to UN; North Korea continues to develop nuclear arms; terrorist rebels take 763 hostages in Moscow theater, many killed in rescue attempt; Washington, D.C., area terrorized by two snipers; UN calls on Iraq to disarm.

September 1, 2002
Palos Verdes, California

*T*alk about blue Mondays! V. R. Shannon had never seen Steve O'Malley so depressed. He was spread out on the ancient leather couch, an untouched bottle of beer on the floor beside him, staring at the ceiling and occasionally giving off the kind of groan you hear in a suicide ward. For the first time that morning, he spoke.

"Look at us. Two retired four-stars, both still young, and almost worn-out trying to keep this Hypersonic Cruiser madness going."

V. R. Shannon knew he had to cheer O'Malley up, no easy task since the week before when the latest experimental scramjet engine blew up in their supersonic tunnel in Mojave.

"I don't know how long we can go, V. R. We've got at least six years to go, and we are hemorrhaging money. Every time I go in the house, Sally is all over me, demanding to know what's going to happen to us, and I cannot tell her a thing. I don't know. I just know we can't quit now."

"That's for damn sure. We'd be idiots to quit now after all we've spent. In for a penny, in for a pound as the Brits say. And we are doing well on the cruise missile and the anti-cruise-missile missile; they're moving right along."

It was true, the two less ambitious projects were going well, and they already had bona-fide proof of it from the government. The proof was not yet in the form of a contract, but in a Department of Defense prohibition of their sale to anyone but a U.S. military service. They had welcomed the "prohibition," for they never intended to sell the missiles anywhere else, and it meant that the government was granting some grudging approval to their efforts.

Shannon went on. "Besides, Bob Rodriquez has never failed yet. Look what he did for GPS, for precision guided munitions, for composite structures. He's a genius, right up there with Rutan and Mac-Cready."

"I know that. Nobody has more regard for Bob than I. But Rutan and MacCready sort of keep their sights on more realistic targets. You don't see Rutan trying to fly into space, or MacCready trying to launch satellites. We're going way beyond anything anybody's even dreamed about. Just the cruise missiles programs are fantastic, but a Hypersonic Cruiser? Look at Boeing, the biggest, maybe the finest, aircraft company in the world, loaded with government contracts, and they don't dare to try what we're trying."

Shannon breathed a little easier. The conversation was taking a direction he could manage: talking about airplanes.

"Yeah, you're right, but of course look at all the other things they are doing that we're not even looking at. They flew their first Airborne Laser aircraft back in July."

He knew O'Malley had been invited to Wichita to see the first flight, because he had been a big backer of the project in the Pentagon. Then he bit his tongue; this might get O'Malley off on one of his anti-Muslim rants. As ferocious as Shannon was about the fanatical Muslim world, he was dead tired of listening to O'Malley's harangues. Sheepishly, he realized that he must bore people as badly as O'Malley bored him on the subject.

"Yeah, it's something else. It's got that big turret—looks like Durante's schnozzle—on the nose. But you got to remember, Boeing's working with Lockheed Martin and Northrop Grumman on this thing—they are not going it alone like we are. Everybody in the industry but us teams up on risky projects."

O'Malley was quiet for a minute and then said, "I was more impressed—and more worried—about Boeing's X-45. They are building a whole family of them, calling them UCAVs—unmanned combat aerial vehicles—and planning to use them for defense suppression."

This time both men were quiet, each lost in his own memory of flying the old Wild Weasel missions, attacking the enemy air defenses, taking out surface-to-air missile sites. It was the toughest job in the world, and if any mission could benefit from being unmanned, that was it. V. R.'s dad, Tom, had told him about the terrible losses the Wild Weasels had incurred in the Vietnam War. Their motto was "First In, Last Out" but all too often they didn't come out at all, victims of the very SAMs they were trying to suppress.

V. R. said, "The X-45 is pretty impressive, and they've got some bigger ones coming along, too. I heard that they even have one that is super-secret, a deep black program that is much farther along than people would believe."

O'Malley immediately switched subjects, convincing V. R. that he had been on target with the deep black X-45 program. If it had been just speculation, O'Malley would have run with the subject, but he clammed up, saying, "All that stuff is great, but I saw something this year, got to fly it, in fact, that is nonmilitary in character, and is just about the most important advance in safety I've ever seen. They let me fly a Gulfstream V with the Enhanced Vision System. It is absolutely incredible."

V. R. had been briefed thoroughly on the EVS at Gulfstream's Savannah headquarters two months before, but didn't say a word. The only way to get O'Malley out of his deep funk would be to get his juices going, talking about airplanes.

"You know, it sounds like the simplest thing in the world. They have an infrared camera, sensing heat and light, a whole bunch of computers and processors and a heads-up display in the cockpit, and it literally turns night into day. I was making an approach into Aspen, late at night, in the soup, and there, on the heads-up display, the HUD, was the whole scene, the valley, the ridge line of the mountains, the runway, the surrounding industrial area, the residences, it was just like it was VFR. But if you looked out the windscreen—nada, nothing. You glance back at the HUD, and it's all clear. Amazing. And scary to realize that most people are flying without it."

"I wish Grandpa Vance could have seen something like that. He used to tell me about flying the radio ranges, doing aural null approaches, and things like that—it must have been terrifying!"

"I know one thing—we're going to have the EVS retrofitted on our Gulfstream—if we still own one after we get through with this Hypersonic Cruiser craziness."

"I agree; it's almost irresponsible to fly an airplane without it. But I tell you something else we are going to get—when we get through with the Cruiser—or it gets through with us. You know Vern Raburn, don't you?"

"Sure, a great guy. Good thinker, straight shooter."

"He had me down to Albuquerque the last week in August for the first flight of his new Eclipse 500. It's one of the new VLJs—Very Light Jets. It is the neatest-looking little business jet you ever saw, six passengers, 370 knots, and he's going to bring it in for way under a million dollars—he hopes!"

"Did you get to fly it?"

"No, I flew in the chase plane with Verne. The number one Eclipse took off, flew forty minutes, and landed, a totally routine flight. The thing I like about it is that it's all metal—no questions about composite construction and pressurization—and they use a special welding process that eliminates most of the rivets. Really a clever design."

"Well, I share your concern about composites and pressurization. We don't have the data on fatigue life of composites yet. It's OK on UAVs, even desirable, because they are expendable. But not in full-size, people-carrying aircraft. I know everybody is going that way, Boeing, Airbus, Cirrus, Rutan, of course. But it's still not like an aluminum structure, not in my mind."

"Well, you've got some company. Everybody's pointing to composites in the crash of Flight 587, you know, the Airbus A300 that went in after departing JFK last year."

The previous November, an A300 crashed after takeoff when its vertical stabilizer and rudder separated from the fuselage. The first investigation reports attributed the accident to the copilot's overuse of the rudder controls after encountering jet wash from a 747 that had departed earlier.

"Yeah—that really chilled me. They are blaming the copilot, but when they look at the attachment, they found that the aluminum and titanium fasteners holding the fin to the fuselage were intact—but the composite lugs were broken. There will never be a straight story on this one."

O'Malley stood up, in a better mood, but obviously still troubled.

"V. R., you know what's worrying Bob, Dennis, and me the most? The fact that you are lined up to test-fly the Hypersonic Cruiser. It's one thing to piss away maybe a billion dollars on a dream. It is another to kill your best friend in it. The pressure on you to fly is going to be tremendous, but I want you to know that we would all understand if you declined the honor."

V. R. was deadly serious as he considered his reply.

"Steve, you remember Jimmy Doolittle, and how we talked about him at the funeral. He was known as the 'master of the calculated risk.' Well, I'm no Doolittle, but I'm going to be doing a lot of calculating. You know that nobody hates the fanatical Muslims more than me, and that nobody thinks they are a bigger threat than me—always excepting you, maybe. I want more than anything to prove the Hypersonic

Cruiser by test-flying it; I want to save the money we've all poured into the project, and I want to put a weapon in the hands of the government that will help it win the war on terror. And I will do it—but only as long as I calculate the risks and believe I have a good chance of success. You can always crash in any airplane, from a Cub to a Concorde, but we know that. What I don't know is what the margin of error is for me in the Hypersonic Cruiser. I've been analyzing it as we've gone along, and right now I think it is slightly in my favor. I think that for the most part, I'll be like the first astronauts, but instead of being locked, controlled by a ballistic trajectory, I'll be locked in, controlled by preprogrammed computer inputs until I get over the target area. But—and I never have said this before, and I should have—if I think it's a suicide mission, I will not go. Call me chicken, call me quitter, whatever, I'm not going unless I think I have a better than even chance of coming back."

"Jesus, V. R., I've chided you for saying some dumb things over the years, but I have to say this is the smartest thing I've ever heard you say. Can I pass this on to Bob and Dennis?"

"No, I should have said this a long time ago. Let me do it. To be honest, I never thought we'd get this far along. I thought that the challenge was worth taking up, but that even Bob couldn't do it. Now that it looks like we might have a shot at it, I've taken a closer look, and I want to tell the other guys myself. We all have our fortunes invested in this, but I know you all well enough to know you don't want a kamikaze test pilot. It's only money, and we all know it's a gamble."

Obviously vastly relieved, O'Malley grabbed his arm.

"You up for some tennis? It's still early, we could play a couple of sets and still get out to the plant before Bob finishes his rounds."

December 15, 2002
Mojave, California

BOB RODRIQUEZ CURSED under his breath. He had just been examining a very positive report on the hypersonic cruise missile, and now he couldn't find it. This happened more and more often to him. He would get up, march smartly over to a file cabinet, and then forget what he was looking for. Like everyone else he was frightened of growing old, particularly now when so much depended upon his ability to bring the missile projects to fruition. As he searched for the report, he pushed a massive pile of paper off his desk. It cascaded to the floor next to an overflowing wastebasket and he realized that it was time for the monthly office cleanup.

He began, as he always did, with the papers stacked under the phone. He would work methodically across his desk, across the credenza, then move to the three folding tables that formed a U around his desk, then to the tops of the file cabinets. In the center of the U was a fifty-five-gallon trash barrel, a plastic bag in place. In another world, another time, there would have been a secretary to help him, but only he knew where things should go and what to throw out, and even though it cost him at least one day and sometimes two days' work, only he could do it.

There was a benefit to it. Doing the filing, creating order out of chaos, always had a soothing effect on him, permitting him to think randomly, instead of following the usual hard, prescribed, mathematical protocols that he used for his work. For the most part he thought about the war that now seemed inevitable. Bush was calling for a regime change in Iraq. It was an ultimatum, one that Saddam Hussein would refuse. So there it was, war in the Middle East again, probably within a few months.

Rodriquez had spent years undercover, several of them in Iraq, and knew how difficult it would be. On the one hand the creation of a democracy in Iraq would be the most fantastic diplomatic coup of all time, far eclipsing anything that Metternich, Talleyrand, or any other great intriguer had ever accomplished. As such, it was certainly worth trying, particularly given the fact that Saddam had already used weapons of mass destruction, and would use them again, if he had them, and everyone said he did. But democracy in Iraq was an oxymoron. The only possible solution was the forced domination of two factions by one—Sunnis over Shiites and Kurds, as at present, or some other, less likely but no less disagreeable combination. And then there was the American military budget, always huge and never enough. To make matters worse there were "managers" such as the Secretary of Defense Donald Rumsfeld in charge. They were determined to somehow transform the existing forces into something leaner and more efficient, and most of all, less expensive—even as they were going into a war. It was sheer madness, utter nonsense, obvious to anyone who had ever managed a company or fought a war, but it was so salable politically that it was inevitable.

He laughed to himself. It was no more mad or nonsensical than RoboPlanes trying to create a world of hypersonic vehicles on its own. But if RoboPlanes failed it meant only that there were some enormous personal fortunes lost. If Bush and Rumsfeld failed, the United States, the world, was in mortal danger. A defeat in Iraq would ratify all that the terrorists had done for the past thirty years, and would clearly chart Muslim course to ultimate victory.

His thoughts turned to V. R. Shannon, and his unexpected decision on not flying the Hypersonic Cruiser if he did not feel the odds were right. "Calculated risk!" he spat the words out. "What the hell does that mean? Life is a calculated risk, every day is a risk, combat is a risk, and you cannot calculate if some goddamn gook MiG pilot is a beginner or a honcho any more than you can tell if a Muslim is a good joe carrying nothing but a handful of dates or if he's a fanatic ready to blow himself up."

Reining himself in, Rodriquez realized this was unfair. When Shannon had given him the message, he had immediately protested that he understood and approved. But he had not. It seemed to him that Shannon was waffling, after they were half a billion dollars into the project, with another half billion sure to be committed. It put Rodriquez in an impossible situation. He could not urge Shannon to fly, nor could he turn to find another test pilot, not before Shannon made up his own mind. And if Shannon declined to fly the Hypersonic Cruiser, who on earth could then be persuaded to try it? It was particularly vexing that they had already created the simulator and software to simulate flying the Cruiser under all conditions. It wouldn't be like stepping into a completely unfamiliar aircraft.

There was always the possibility of testing it in an unmanned configuration, and they could do that even now, if they made the right decision, and diverted even more funds to the program. It would take some redesign, of course, but there would be some trade-offs for that. An unmanned Hypersonic Cruiser would have utility, but it wouldn't be what they had planned from the start. He would have to raise the issue soon, perhaps on New Year's Eve, at the traditional party in Palos Verdes.

His desk was clear. He pulled the bottle of compressed air from the desk drawer and carefully cleaned his keyboard, the printer, the scanner, and the telephone. Then he pulled out a bottle of Pledge and a rag and polished his desk. He stepped back and admired it. Ready for another month's work. He turned to the credenza and started the process over, filing, shredding, and thinking. Maybe he could fly the Hypersonic Cruiser. He was old, his reflexes were not what they were when he was shooting down MiGs in Korea, but the thing would be programmed . . . no, it was a joke. Even thinking about it was another warning sign of senility creep. V. R. should have declared himself earlier. All this talk about killing Muslims, and now he was backing down. He shrugged, knowing in his heart he was being unfair.

He looked down at a box of memorabilia that he had been shifting from one office to another for years. It had his military records, his decorations, all in their leather presentation cases, the citations beautifully done. He had never worn them, not even the ribbons. There was the Form Five that recorded every hour of his flying time from flight school on, and some completely nondescript items—a key chain, a cigar wrapper—that had meaning only for him, souvenirs from his days undercover. There was no room in the office for another file cabinet. With another shrug he tossed the memorabilia into the fifty-five-gallon drum. If the Hypersonic Cruiser was a success, he'd never need them. If it wasn't, he'd never want them.

December 31, 2002
Palos Verdes, California

"WELL, DENNIS, I guess you're happy? The *Endeavor* mission went off without a flaw."

Steve was baiting him, as usual; the Space Shuttle had experienced the usual spate of difficulties prior to launch, on the mission and prior to landing, but they were all inconsequential, and O'Malley knew it.

"Yeah, it went pretty well. The weather delayed the landing for a couple of days, but nobody's complaining. The Space Shuttle's just like an airplane—any landing you can walk away from is a good one."

The group kept up the long tradition of New Year's Eve gatherings in the house Vance Shannon built, even though there were as many bad evenings as good to remember. Just getting it done had become a problem. Harry's wife, Anna, was no homemaker. Mae Rodriquez was always conscious about not presuming, and so didn't take the initiative, and all the warmth had gone out of Nancy Shannon's hospitality. As a result, it fell to the O'Malleys to do the buffet, and Sally's heart was not in it. She saw the Shannons as the architect of their fortunes, and Rodriquez as a time bomb threatening to destroy it. It was difficult for her to play the role of happy hostess. Steve gave up on her making much of an effort and so paid a caterer to come in and put out the standard canapés and buffet that you might expect at a gallery opening. The food was fine, but it had no soul, and of course the alcohol was always backpedaled, out of deference to Anna. There was plenty to drink if you wanted it, but few people bothered, and the evening now broke up on the stroke of midnight, where in the early years it might have gone on all night.

Jenkins went out of the room, searching for Harry to pay his respects and see how he was doing. At eighty-four, Harry was not in the best of health. Amazingly, Anna now seemed to be thriving, although Dennis understood that she still occasionally fell off the wagon.

Harry was back in the library, leaning back in a recliner, a well-watered Jack Daniel's in his hand. It surprised Dennis, and his look must have shown it.

"No problem, Dennis. Anna's dressing, won't be out for a half hour or more, and I thought I needed a drink before we start listening to O'Malley and V. R. go on about the coming war. Join me—the bottle's over there on the bar."

Jenkins went behind the bar and pulled out the same bottle of Johnnie Walker that was there the year before. It looked curiously light in color and he poured a sip into his glass and tasted it.

"Watered?" Harry asked. "She does that pretty much to all the bottles. Usually I empty them out once they are opened, but if I forget she takes a few drinks and waters them down a bit. She seems to be handling it pretty well. I actually think it's a pretty good method of controlling her drinking. We don't spend much time here, anyway, and when we do, she never has a chance to have more than one or two snifters. I think she enjoys the illicit nature of the drinking as much as the whiskey."

Bemused, Dennis opened a new bottle, poured a shot of unwatered Jack Daniel's, and sat down next to Harry.

"At our age it doesn't make much difference, Dennis. We've just about reached the point where nothing matters. I'm just hoping that we live to see the results of this hypersonic folly we're engaged in. It seems pretty improbable right now."

They clinked glasses and Harry went on. "You know Bob's upset about V. R.'s decision on taking only a well-calculated risk."

"I know something's wrong, and guessed that was it, but he hasn't said anything. He is so close to the program that he cannot see the wisdom in V. R.'s decision. It wouldn't make sense to make a sacrificial flight; this isn't the movies where everything is going to turn out right in the last scene."

The door swung open and O'Malley and V. R. came in, talking earnestly. Harry looked at Dennis and winced. They were trapped. It was the kill-the-Muslims hour.

O'Malley started it, saying, "I tell you, Harry, when this war starts, it's going to make the last war in the Gulf look like a Christmas party. I wish Tom were alive to see it; they're using the term 'shock and awe' to describe what the Iraqis will feel. They'll feel a hell of a lot more than that."

V. R. waved his arms. "What a miserable time to be out of the Air Force! All those young guys are going to have the time of their lives, going in with the F-117s, the B-1s, the B-2s, even the B-52s. They are going to level Baghdad in the first twenty-four hours."

Harry said, "Do you think it will go that far? Surely Saddam Hussein won't try to fight."

"Damn straight it's going to go that far. I think Saddam thinks Russia and France are going to save his ass somehow, and I think he thinks he can fight a war of attrition in the desert. They are already talking about America finding 'another Vietnam.' They don't think we have the staying power to fight a long war. They are probably right, but this is going to be the shortest war on record. I see them taking out all the air defenses on day one, then going on to take out the cities, one after the other. The war will be over in a week, and the ground troops can just drive in and take over."

V. R. nodded agreement but Dennis said, "I can't believe the Army, the Navy, and the Marines will agree to this being an Air Force show only. Sure, the Air Force will soften them up, but there will still have to be one hell of a land battle, just to make sure the Army keeps its share of the appropriations. And the Navy's got to use its fighter bombers and missiles, or it will get cut, too."

O'Malley shook his head. "No, listen to me. The term is shock and awe, and that's what you are going to see. We'll probably kill Saddam in the first couple of nights, and the vice president, what's his name, the oily guy?"

Jenkins said, "Tarik."

"Yeah, Tarik will be quick to surrender. He's no fighter like Saddam."

The door opened again, and Rodriquez walked in with Mae.

"Come on, let's break up the warmongering and come on back to the kitchen. Sally told me to get you, everything's ready to serve."

Harry got up slowly, whispering to Dennis, "We got off easy. If Rodriquez hadn't come in, the two of them would have gone on for an hour. What do you think is going to happen?"

"I think Saddam will cave at the last minute. He can go to any Arab country in the world as a hero, and he's already a multibillionaire. He doesn't need any more money, he's supposed to have it squirreled away in bank accounts all over the world."

"Do you think we could get him to invest in the Hypersonic Cruiser?"

Dennis laughed, pleased that Harry still had the Shannon sense of humor.

The rest of the evening passed uneasily, for it was evident that Rodriquez had something on his mind. The women thought he was just preoccupied, as always. The men knew it had to do with V. R. and his reluctance to commit to flying the Hypersonic Cruiser until much later in the program.

About 11:30 the women left them to talk, and Rodriquez got down to business.

"Look, we all agree that V. R. has every right to reserve his decision about flying the hypersonic plane until he feels he is comfortable with it. But it does put a burden on me and the program. There are a couple of ways to finesse it. One is to seek out an alternative test pilot, some professional we could bring in now and get him started on the simulator training, and working with us in the shop as the Cruiser comes together. Another is to decide now to make it an unmanned vehicle. Doing that would set us back maybe six months and another few hundred thousand dollars."

V. R., obviously troubled, spoke up. "Bob, just suggesting this puts me on the spot. Worse, it confirms my fears that you all think I got us into this thing by not being upfront at the beginning. The problem was that I didn't know what the hazards were then, and I was somehow sure we'd solve them. Now even you have some doubts about the success of the program. How is that supposed to make me feel?"

Rodriquez snapped, "I don't doubt the success of the program, not one bit. I'm convinced that we are on the right path, and all the data proves it. And I would never consider letting anyone fly it, much less you, if I didn't believe that the first flight would be completely successful. Surely you believe that. I've done a lot of things in my life, but cold-blooded murder is not one of them."

Rodriquez's face flushed, realizing that this was a blatant lie and that there was no way to backpedal from it. He had assassinated several men in his undercover role. They were all enemies of the state. He had killed them all in the line of duty. But he had killed them, nonetheless.

O'Malley asked, "You've covered what the cost and schedule delay would be if we converted to an unmanned vehicle. What effect would it have on the utility, the salability of the Hypersonic Cruiser?"

Rodriquez shook his head. "I don't know. I don't know if we can sell the thing to the government at all, manned or unmanned. There's going to be a world of resentment if we succeed, you know that. Talk about the 'not invented here' syndrome—this will epitomize it. But a piloted hypersonic vehicle has a tremendous appeal, and I think would have ten times the sales potential as an unmanned one. Who can say? There's no focus group approach on a program like this. We've got to operate from gut feel, start to finish."

V. R. asked, "When is the latest possible date when you can decide to convert to an unmanned vehicle?"

Rodriquez knew this was coming.

"Last month. A year ago. I'm not joking, that's when we should have decided to go this route, if we go this way. But to answer your question, we could shift some priorities, do some testing in a different order, and maybe put it off until 2004."

Dennis said, "Then let's do that."

Rodriquez spoke up. "If we do that, I reserve the right to bring another potential test pilot on board. I don't want to wait until 2004, decide to go ahead with a manned vehicle, and then have V. R. decide to opt out. We should have a backup anyway. V. R. could always have a car accident or something and not be able to go, even if he decided to. Any objections?"

O'Malley said, "No objections. Let me make a suggestion. There's going to be a war, and soon. There will be some pretty hot pilots who'll distinguish themselves. Maybe we can pick out a backup for V. R. when the shooting's over."

They shook hands, V. R. and Rodriquez obviously uncomfortable, the others glad that things had gone off as well as they had.

CHAPTER TWENTY

THE PASSING PARADE: The eastern end of the "axis of evil," North Korea, withdraws from Nuclear Nonproliferation Treaty; President Bush announces readiness of United States to attack Iraq with or without UN mandate; Israel elects grand old warrior Ariel Sharon as Prime Minister; almost seventeen years to the day after Space Shuttle *Challenger* disaster, Space Shuttle *Columbia* burns up on reentry, killing seven astronauts; France, Germany, and Russia, all "customers of Saddam Hussein," insist that military option should be used against Iraq only as a last option; new Chinese President, Hu Jintao, elected; U.S.-led coalition unleashes Operation Iraqi Freedom on March 19; Baghdad captured in three weeks; official combat operations ended on May 1; President Bush signs largest tax cut in U.S. history; Iran's nuclear programs discovered by International Atomic Energy Agency; soldier-turned-president Charles Taylor forced to leave Liberia; in Afghanistan, peacekeeping responsibility assumed by NATO; Lockerbie bombing of Pan Am 747 admitted by Libya; suicide bombings continue around world; UN headquarters attacked in Baghdad; action film star Arnold Schwarzenegger elected governor of California after recall of Governor Gray Davis; huge appropriations made for post-Iraq war reconstruction efforts; gay marriage approved by Massachusetts Supreme Court; former stalwart of Soviet Union, Eduard Shevardnadze, resigns as President of Georgia; D.C. sniper John A. Muhammad receives death sentence; American troops capture Saddam Hussein, hiding in a hole.

February 5, 2003
Mojave Airport, California

*T*he meeting had been set for 9:00 A.M. It was now half past ten, and Dennis was still on the telephone in a private office, talking to friends at Kennedy Space Center.

Rodriquez pulled O'Malley aside, saying, "Look, Harry's just about faded already. Unless Dennis gets off the phone and comes in, let's go ahead and start the meeting without him. I'll fill him in later. He won't care."

"He doesn't care much about anything. He's been so distressed since the *Columbia* disaster that I'm worried more about his health than about Harry's."

The Space Shuttle *Columbia*, after flying an almost perfect mission, had burned up on February 1, during reentry to the atmosphere. Eerily, it was seventeen years almost to the day after the *Challenger* had exploded just over a minute after its launch on January 28, 1986.

"He's deeply affected. He knew most of the crew on the *Challenger*, and everyone on the *Columbia*. It is like losing your entire family in a single stroke."

The door opened and Jenkins, white-faced and obviously shaken, came out. "It was the foam."

The others quickly glanced around, recalling how excited Jenkins was reviewing the television clips of the *Columbia*'s liftoff. Just eighty-one seconds after launch on January 16, a suitcase-sized piece of insulating foam had broken away from the orbiter's huge fuel tank, striking the leading edge of the orbiter's left wing. Jenkins had immediately said, "That's it, that's what caused the accident."

The first official comments on the accident had discounted the possibility of the foam damaging the tile, and no steps had been taken to ask the crew to try to verify the extent of the damage.

Jenkins said, "The irony of this is just so great. You can spend millions of dollars, billions, really, and some cheap nothing will destroy all your plans and dreams. The *Challenger* was destroyed by a two-dollar frozen rubber O ring, about seventy-one seconds into its mission. The *Columbia* was effectively destroyed by maybe two dollars' worth of foam, eighty-one seconds into its mission. This time, though, the damage just didn't come in to play until fifteen days, twenty-two hours, twenty minutes, twenty-two seconds later. The heat of reentry broke through the damage caused by the insulation hitting the wing. Then the heat bored on through, heating up the wing so that the tiles came off, and going on to sear through the metal, aluminum, stainless steel, whatever, until the Orbiter broke up."

They were silent, full of questions, but unwilling to ask, given Jenkins's emotional state. Then he went on. "There probably was not much that could have been done, but they could have made some efforts, done something if someone on the ground had taken the foam hitting the wing more seriously."

He was silent again, and Rodriquez asked quietly, "What does this do to the Space Shuttle program, Dennis?"

Jenkins shook his head. "I don't know. They'll have the usual standdown, the usual committees, but they'll fly them again. They have to, we've got the International Space Station to support, and there are military missions that have to be done. But it will be a while, six months, maybe a year."

He stopped, visibly pulled himself together, and said, "I'm sorry about the delay. You know how important the Shuttle program is to me. But let's get on with today's business. I need to get thinking about something else."

Rodriquez stepped to the podium and said, "As you know, V. R. could not be here today; the Air Force asked him to come down to Central Command—looks like things are getting serious."

O'Malley chortled. "You're damn right it's going to be serious! Shock and awe, shock and awe; I'm just sorry I'm so far out of the loop, persona non grata, that's me. I'm surprised they called V. R., he's as outspoken as I am."

No one spoke. O'Malley was out of the loop because he had become so outspoken about his perception of the Muslim threat since the attack on the Twin Towers and the Pentagon. He had offered his services repeatedly, but the Air Force, trying to keep the State Department happy, had declined. V. R., while outspoken, had not gained the audience O'Malley had, and consequently the Air Force made more calls on his expertise.

Rodriquez picked up his laser pointer and started his PowerPoint presentation, which promptly went blank. He grumbled, "If Orville and Wilbur had to use PowerPoint, we'd never have gotten off the ground."

After a few minutes fumbling, the right symbols came up and the first image came on, two profiles of the Hypersonic Cruiser, one over the other. Although they had all seen drawings of the aircraft many times, it still drew an involuntary whistle of admiration from O'Malley.

"The top drawing is the last version, Model 188 C. Below it is Model 188 D, and you can see that the provision for the cockpit and canopy is gone. This would be an unmanned vehicle, from start to finish, and of course it means we gain a little bit in performance—less weight, less drag."

He right-clicked the mouse, cursed, and bent over the keyboard and pressed the down-arrow button and the slide changed.

"Here is what it costs us: you make a choice. And I already have V. R.'s proxy. I'll tell you what it is after you decide for yourself."

The slide read:

A: Stay with manned program. No change in cost or schedule.
B: Switch to unmanned vehicle only. Add $700,000 and eight months to the existing program.
C: Dual track: build components to convert manned program to unmanned program if required in 2006. Add $1.2 million and one year to the existing program.

O'Malley asked, "Why is it so much more expensive and take so much longer to go the dual track route? I can see why you've got the numbers you have in B, but C seems high."

"It is higher and riskier because we'll have to farm it out to another contractor. We are stretched to the limits now, and I don't see how we could do it in-house."

"Who would bid on this? It seems like we are asking someone to come to the party way late in the game."

"That's the problem, Dennis. If we'd brought people on board early on, this wouldn't cost us so much. But to bring someone in now, we've got to do a lot of back-filling and educating, and they will have a flat learning curve during the time that our learning curve is at last beginning to pay off a little. There are a few companies that could do the work, but none that could come on and operate at our speed and with our level of confidence."

"Then it looks to me like C is really not an option at all. We don't have the money, and without the money, we don't have the time. Am I wrong about this?"

"No, Steve, you are right on, but it is an option. We could do some borrowing, there are ways to get some money, maybe even go public with it—all things we've never wanted to do. But we've got to decide now, because every day we wait is going to send the cost up even more. The same with the schedule; every day we waste now will cost us double at the end of the schedule."

"Bob, I know you have backup on these numbers. Can you run through the rest of the program, just so we see what's involved?"

Rodriquez nodded, and began going through the slides, the Power-Point working perfectly now. He began with the start of the program and walked them through each year, showing the progress, the costs, and at the end of each year, the projections for the future. The slides were remarkably consistent. Rodriquez and his relatively small team had, to date, hit every milestone and had kept slightly under budget.

With the last slide, Rodriquez said, "Before we vote, let's go out and take a look at what has been built so far. You've all seen it before, but we've come a long way in the last six months."

Harry spoke up. "Folks, you go on. I don't feel like suiting up, putting on the rubber gloves and so on. I'll just sit here and do some thinking and you can brief me when you get back."

Rodriquez took O'Malley and Jenkins into the dressing area next to the manufacturing clean room where the Hypersonic Cruiser was slowly taking shape. They donned the usual hospital-like green robes, hat, booties, and clear vinyl gloves, went into the adjacent chamber where a vacuum sucked all the dust from their clothes, and then into the manufacturing area.

The one-hundred-foot-long fuselage of the Hypersonic Cruiser was mounted on a huge jig that could be rotated through 360 degrees. At the moment it was resting with its underside facing the group.

Rodriquez said, "Just as I briefed you, you can see how the shape of the nozzle has been changed. We've probably changed it ten times, now, but I think this is it. Now let me show you the most important thing we've done the last few weeks. This is really the key as to whether we'll get a Hypersonic Cruiser, or just the world's biggest scramjet test vehicle. We all have to remember that a hypersonic air-breathing aircraft requires much better matching between the engine and airframe, because the forebody is really part of the engine inlet."

He signaled to the assembly operator behind the mammoth computer console, who moved a short lever forward.

Rodriquez pointed to the lever and said, "We took that off an F-111 in the boneyard at Davis Monthan."

As the lever moved, the mock-up of the turbofan engine centered in the aft of the long slender fuselage moved down. Simultaneously, the cowling that had been tightly tailored to the shape of the engine rose up, changing its shape from almost perfectly circular to ovoid, and then locking in position where it could channel the scramjet's torrent of power.

"Guys, we live or die with this. If it works as my computer tells me it works, we get a huge boost in power and in range. If I'm wrong, we'll have the world's biggest scramjet test vehicle—and not a lot more."

No one said anything. They went back into the dressing area, pulled off the protective gear, and walked back into the briefing room.

Harry Shannon lay slumped forward in his chair. Rodriquez rushed to him, yelling, "Call 911!"

He put his fingers on Harry's neck. There was no pulse.

April 8, 2003
Palos Verdes, California

STEVE AND SALLY O'Malley moved around the house, at a loss as to where to begin. Harry's death at age eighty-four had been too much for Anna. Traumatized, frightened by life without Harry, she went into an abrupt decline, dying of a stroke less than a month later. With V. R. called back to active duty in Iraq, it fell to the O'Malleys to go through the process of preparing the house for its new role in life. V. R. had not wanted the house sold, but felt that it needed renovation if it was to continue to serve as a sort of guest house for company executives visiting either RoboPlanes or Vance Shannon, Incorporated.

"V. R. wants some kind of little museum set up in the main plant to honor Vance, Harry, and Tom. I've asked Warren Bowers to come over and sort of guide us through the models and the books to see which ones should go in the museum. Bob Rodriquez is coming, too, to look at the drawings and the technical manuals."

"Steve, Warren is the right man for the job, but you've got to promise me that you are not going to unload on him and Bob about the Iraq War, and shock and awe and all that stuff you are always yelling about. I'm fed up with it and so is everyone else. They are not running the war the way you want it run and that's it. Get over it."

Steve's four stars had never cut much ice with Sally when he was on active duty; now, retired, they cut even less. O'Malley wisely choked back a smart reply. He always came off second best in any exchange with her, and he also knew she was right. He'd become what he always swore he would not be, a retired bore, a backseat driver, a Monday-morning quarterback, angry with the way the war had gone. Worse, he made his feelings known on Bill O'Reilly's television program, and gotten a rocket from the Chief's office about keeping his mouth shut.

Still, he fumed as he moved around, picking up one dust-laden model after another, talking to himself as he had been since the opening night's action on March 19, when Operation Iraqi Freedom officially began.

"Shock and awe, shock and awe! More like wimp and scrimp than shock and awe." The doorbell rang, and he moved to it, admitting both Bowers and Rodriquez. Bowers was sporting his latest digital camera—he had a new one about every six months, and moved immediately to the library to take pictures, while Rodriquez made the fatal mistake of asking, "Well, Steve, what do you think of the war so far?"

"We are blowing it, Bob, and nobody should know it better than you. All this concern about collateral damage and minimizing enemy casualties is going to be interpreted as a sign of weakness by the Muslim world. We should have hit them with a massive attack, one that would put fear in their hearts. Anything else is nonsense. You watch, we'll be in there for at least five years now, getting our guys killed, and they will grow a guerrilla movement we won't be able to contain. We had one chance at this, and we blew it."

Sally walked in and in a low voice that sounded as if it had been dipped in liquid oxygen hissed one word, "Steve."

O'Malley caught himself, turned bright red, and asked Rodriquez, "Anything new at the plant?"

Rodriquez got Sally's message as well.

"We're still doing fantastically well on the small UAVs. We've had to open a second production line for the ones the sheriff's departments are buying. And you know the school we set up to train them after they buy the aircraft? It's making so much profit we are going to set up two more, one in Wichita and one in Martinsburg, West Virginia. The demand is skyrocketing."

Rodriquez moved out the French doors to the patio and motioned for O'Malley to follow him.

"I take it Sally's had a bellyful of shock and awe, eh? But I've got a little advance notice on a mission they flew last night. It'll be in the papers tomorrow probably, but I thought this might give you a little peace of mind. It did me."

Rodriquez pulled a sheaf of e-mail messages from a folder and selected one.

"Listen to this. It's copy from John Tegler, a *Washington Times* reporter. It'll be in print tomorrow if they pass it on. Listen."

He began reading in a low hushed tone, with Steve leaning forward eagerly.

"'One of the eleven Boeing B-1Bs deployed to take part in Operation Iraqi Freedom made a sensational attack yesterday evening. Bearing the name 'Seek and Destroy,' the aircraft is one of the much maligned B-1B bombers, and is part of the 405th Air Expeditionary Wing.'"

O'Malley nodded his head vigorously—he had been a leading proponent of the expeditionary wing concept, and here it was, proving its worth. Rodriquez continued reading:

"'The aircraft and its crew of four are part of the 34th Bomb Squadron, 28th Bomb Wing. They are normally stationed at Ellsworth Air Force Base, South Dakota, where the 28th is commanded by Colonel James Kowalski. It is a small world: Kowalski is serving in Operation Iraqi Freedom as commander of the 405th AEW.

"'Late yesterday evening, the crew of 'Seek and Destroy' was advised by the Airborne Warning and Control System (AWACS) controller that Saddam Hussein had been detected at a particular restaurant. The report was credible, and probably from special forces personnel on the ground in Baghdad.'"

Rodriquez stopped and said, "Those special forces guys are terrific. Did you see the pictures of them in Afghanistan, operating on camels, but using a laptop for communications?"

O'Malley nodded impatiently, eager to get to some shock and awe.

Rodriquez resumed. "'The AWACS provided the crew with full information and confirmed the order to attack. The four men, all seasoned professionals, were ready and began a series of closely coordinated tasks. The crew consisted of the aircraft commander Captain Chris Wachter; pilot Captain Sloan Hollis; Lieutenant Colonel Fred Swan, Weapon Systems Officer (Offensive); and Lieutenant Joe Runci, Weapon Systems Officer (Defensive). They were ready. Each man knew that they had twelve minutes to complete all of their tasks and drop the four bombs they were directed to use.

"'Among their tasks was locating the exact target, the al-Saa restaurant, probing enemy air defenses, confirming all decisions with the AWACS controllers, arming the specified weapons (two different types of JDAMs), and finally placing the exact coordinates of the target in the bombs' guidance mechanisms.'"

O'Malley, virtually overcome with anticipation, nodded again. He knew that while still in the bomb bay, the JDAM received constant updating from the aircraft's avionics system. And that once released, the inertial guidance system takes over, and, with periodic GPS updates, guides the bomb to its target.

Rodriquez went on. "'The B-1B was backed up by the AWACS and by Lockheed Martin F-16CJs. The F-16s were there to suppress any enemy missile sites. A Northrop Grumman EA-6B Prowler provided electronic countermeasures. Fortunately, the crew had the benefit of the enormous computer capacity of the B-1B, which stored the electronically captured images of virtually the whole of Iraq. They compared the coordinates given by the AWACS with the high-definition images to make sure they had the exact target.'"

The coordinates themselves were received over the radio, and written down, then transmitted back to the AWACS's controller for verification. There was always the possibility of what the crews called "fat finger error"—the equivalent of a typo. Once double-checked, the numbers are entered into the weapons system, and rechecked again to be sure they correspond exactly to those originally given.

The AWACS gave the crew of "Seek and Destroy" two specific targets, with specific coordinates for each one. The distance between the two targets was only about seventy-five yards.

The crew knew the stakes were high, but so was the risk of collateral damage, and precision was the byword. The twelve minutes passed swiftly, filled with one procedure after another, and "Seek and Destroy" was flying at thirty thousand feet and five hundred knots when the first two GBU-31 version three hard target penetrator JDAMs were released by the automatic mode of the bombing system.

"'These were special two-thousand-pound BLU-109 bombs equipped with the JDAM kits, designed to blast through the restaurant and reach the bunkers beneath where the meeting was to take place. Three seconds later, two of the standard GBU-31 version one JDAMs were released. Because of the difference in their case design, the standard JDAMs have more explosive power than the penetrators. All four bombs followed direct paths to the targets, destroying them.'"

O'Malley snorted, clearly dismayed.

"Four bombs? That's it? What the hell are they worried about?"

Rodriquez read the final paragraph, "'Unofficial reports indicate that more than a dozen bodies were removed from the wreckage by Iraqi personnel. At this writing, the debris is being carefully analyzed to determine if Saddam Hussein was killed in the attack.'"

O'Malley was fuming. "It doesn't make sense! Are we fighting a war or conducting a picnic? They should have put a flight of B-52s in to carpet bomb the entire district. I'll bet Saddam got away. You cannot hit an elusive target like that, not even with smart bombs. We are giving the war away by trying to win the hearts and minds. Goddammit, doesn't anybody understand, we lost their hearts and their minds in the Crusades. We're fighting the war just like Vietnam, with no understanding of the enemy's mentality. They are laughing at us!"

Rodriquez was nonplussed. He'd hoped to cheer O'Malley up, to show him that some of his favorite weapons—the B-1B, the GPS system, the JDAMs—were all working well. Instead he saw only a failure to apply power massively. O'Malley was more concerned about creating an enduring impression on the collective Muslim mind than he was on killing an individual, even one as important as Saddam Hussein.

And maybe he was right. Everything seemed to be going well on the ground, but who knew what the future held. Rodriquez thought about his years of experience in the Arab world. The poverty, the hopelessness, of the young Muslim was the real problem. The complete bankruptcy of their system had created a generation of young people to whom death was a good career move. Precision bombing could not possibly change that. Maybe O'Malley was right. Maybe to win the war on terror, the United States had to conduct warfare on a massive scale, without regard to civilian populations.

Rodriquez shook his head. If that was the case, his nation had already lost. The United States would never conduct a war of massive casualties. The reaction to 9/11 had been relatively mild; the national anger had quickly been supplemented by a sense of national pride in being able to suffer and endure. That was not a winning combination, not when fighting an opponent whose goal is exactly to make you suffer until you acquiesce.

Well, he thought, sometimes it is not bad to be old. The future does not look good. Unless maybe, somehow, we can pull off this crazy Hypersonic Cruiser, and use it to snuff out terrorism at its roots, one crazy terrorist at a time.

December 17, 2003
Palos Verdes, California

STEVE O'MALLEY, THIRTY pounds heavier than when he retired, flopped down on the ancient leather sofa and slipped his arm around young Bob Rodriquez's shoulders, saying, "Let me tell you how a husband should work. I just made the greatest finesse of any married man in history, and since you are thinking about getting married again, and since you don't seem to have a clue about women, I feel I should let you in on how I did it."

Young Bob looked apprehensive. He regarded O'Malley, the retired four-star general, as completely whipped, totally henpecked, and he didn't look to him for advice on women. The problem was that young Bob's marital track record was terrible, far worse than his father's. The senior Rodriquez had married Mae, the love of his life, only to lose her to a blind workaholic addiction to aviation. After years of angst and separation, however, they had come back together and were now truly, happily, and permanently married. Young Bob had been married three times already, each time to a gorgeous young woman who quickly tired of his work obsession and moved on to greener pastures, each one carrying a sizable portion of Rodriquez's fortune. Now he was in the process of marrying a fourth time, once again to a young starlet type, and was being ribbed mercilessly by both the men and the women of the "Shannon gang."

Resigned, Rodriquez said, "Go ahead, it's a cinch I need to learn something."

"Well, Sally had always wanted to fly on the Concorde, and somehow we never got around to it. I tried my best to get on before they stopped service in November, but somehow I just couldn't make it work. When I could get tickets, she couldn't get away, and when she could get away, they were sold out. She kept saying it was because I was too cheap, and there might be something in that, God knows this Hypersonic Cruiser is making paupers of all of us. But I did try."

Rodriquez looked at him blankly, hoping the story was going somewhere.

"Well, needless to say when she saw in the paper that service had ended, she was ticked off. She began the usual treatment, you know, how could you do this to me, all that, and it looked like I was in for a bad night. Then she starts up 'and I guess I'll have to have the annual New Year's Eve party again, just like last year.'"

O'Malley paused, relishing his coming coup.

"As if she'd done anything last year! I did all the work myself, you know I did. But I let her go on, and came in with the winning idea. I told her, 'Let's forget the New Year's Eve party. This whole bunch owes everything to Wilbur and Orville Wright. Let's throw the party on December 17, the hundredth anniversary of the first flight, and let me handle all the details.'"

He sat back, smiling, and Rodriquez said, "So?"

"She went for it. It's the old shell game. I turned the Concorde argument around by taking away the New Year's Eve argument, and here we are. She's happy, forgotten all about the Concorde, and we can sit around and rehash all the stuff going on to celebrate the hundredth anniversary."

Rodriquez said, "Well, it's pretty amazing how no one has been able to do what the Wrights did. I can hardly wait to see the replay on television." With that Rodriquez moved away to get a much needed drink, a feeling that O'Malley often instilled in him.

O'Malley sat back, waiting for someone else to come along to tell his story to. As he did, his thoughts turned to the events of the past year. The war in Iraq, which had been executed so brilliantly by the American armed forces, seemed to have spun into the worst of all worlds, a series of tribal wars where one faction was bent on killing another, and all bent on killing Americans. He could already sniff the tide changing from pride in the swift accomplishment of the military objectives into a Vietnam War-tainted era of criticism.

V. R. Shannon sat down next to him and O'Malley said, "They'll be stuffing flowers in rifle barrels soon. We'll be seeing a whole second generation of peaceniks out there demanding that we get out of Iraq."

Shannon surprised him. "And a damn good thing, too, Steve. You were right. We should have used shock and awe to subdue them, to make the entire Muslim world shiver with fear at what we might do next. Instead we have dozens of factions at war with each other, Syria and Iran helping out, al Qaeda gaining strength. We've made a colossal mistake, and we should get out and let them run themselves into the ground."

"You serious, V. R.? I've never heard you talk like this before."

"I can't help it. The United States is willing to let one percent of the population fight its war, while we are going on the biggest prosperity binge in history. We are not going to get serious until the terrorists set off some nukes here, or London or Paris maybe, and even then, I don't know if we have the will to fight the entire Muslim world. Because that is what it is going to take: fighting the entire Muslim world, way more than a billion people."

O'Malley was distressed. "Jesus, V. R., you sound nuttier than I do! Don't you think we can hound the terrorists out, deal with them in particular, cut them out of the body of Muslims just like you cut a cancer out of a human?"

"I wish I could think like that, Steve. But there's no sign that the so-called nonviolent Muslim world has taken any steps to stop the fanatics.

They are passive about them, just like the majority of the Germans were passive about the Nazis."

O'Malley interrupted him. "I know, when we fought World War II, we didn't just concentrate on the Nazis, we had to fight the whole German people. But, my God, that meant fighting maybe eighty million people in one country. Here you are talking about fighting a billion and a half people, all over the world, lots of them citizens in the United States."

"I know. But that is what it will take."

O'Malley found himself in the unusual position of trying to get someone else to stop talking about the Muslim threat; usually people were trying to stop him. He turned to their mutual favorite, airplanes.

"Did you see where your buddy, Skip Holm, set a new closed-course record in his Mustang 'Dago Red'? He turned 507 mph at Reno!"

V. R. said, "Yeah, that is really pushing it. He won the Unlimited Gold class, too. I don't know how much more they can get out of a P-51. Looks like some time they will have to turn to scratch-built racers to set any new records."

O'Malley glanced at his watch.

"Let's get the news on and see how they did with the Wright Flyer reproduction."

Shannon said, "Tell me about it, I haven't been following it at all. I'm ashamed of myself."

"Well, you know Ken Hyde, out in Virginia. Ken's masterminded an exact reproduction of the original 1903 Wright Flyer, using original documents and reverse engineering to make it as accurate as possible. He even brought in our old buddy Scott Crossfield to supervise training pilots to fly it."

Crossfield was a hero to Shannon and all his colleagues, for he was both a true gentleman and a brilliant pilot. The first man to break Mach 2, he was also a pioneer in hypersonic flight, spearheading the engineering and making the first flights of the North American X-15.

"That will give them a big advantage. They've been running a simulator to teach them how to use the Wright Flyer's controls, and what to expect on the launch. The Wrights are probably looking down with amazement—they could have used some training themselves before the first flight."

"Have they modified the reproduction in any way?"

"No, it is as original as they can make it. They were supposed to fly it at the exact same moment that Orville made the first flight, but the weather was too bad. I think their only concession is to let the test pilot wear a crash helmet."

The CNN station came on the big television set that Bob Rodriquez, Sr., had made personally for Vance Shannon many years before. It was obviously rotten weather, far different than the cold day in 1903, when the Wrights found exactly the wind they wanted and needed.

It was anticlimactic. The reproduction Wright Flyer, estimated to have cost $1.2 million, moved down the track and lifted off about six inches from the ground, then dipped its left wing in a puddle of water and came to a stop.

"Those poor guys! All that effort and then the wind doesn't cooperate."

V. R. Shannon abruptly got up and left the room. The Wrights had ushered in the age of manned flight one hundred years before. In just a couple of years, he would have the opportunity to usher in the age of extended manned hypersonic flight, testing the Hypersonic Cruiser, and he still did not know if he would elect to try to do it.

CHAPTER TWENTY-ONE

THE PASSING PARADE: Ambitious space program proposed by President Bush to return to moon, go on to explore Mars, no funds attached to proposal; evidence begins to accumulate that Saddam Hussein did not have weapons of mass destruction; mass sale of nuclear weapons information to North Korea, Iran, and Libya admitted by A. Q. Khan, who was founder of Pakistan's nuclear program; President Aristide forced to resign and flee Haiti; Spain capitulates to al Qaeda terrorist attacks that killed about 200; NATO expands by admitting seven new countries, many former Soviet satellites, Bulgaria, Estonia, Latvia, Lithuania, Romania, Slovakia, and Slovenia; Sharon becomes peacemaker, announces plan for unilateral withdrawal from Gaza Strip; Abu Ghraib prison scandal erupts; twenty-one-year civil war in Sudan purportedly ends, but war and genocide continue in Darfur; Iyad Allawai first interim Iraqi government leader; dispute erupts over rights of "enemy combatants" held at Guantanamo Bay; John Kerry "reports for duty" as Democratic candidate for presidency; hurricanes ravage Florida; Bush renominated at Republican convention; over 300 killed when Chechan terrorists take 1,200 hostage in Beslan, Russia; no weapons of mass destruction found according to final U.S. report on Iraq; Bush reelected President; Arab leader Yasir Arafat dies; Hamid Karzai inaugurated as first democratically elected President in Afghanistan; massive tsunami kills more than 200,000 in Asia; the United States leads way in immediate compassionate relief efforts.

June 21, 2004
Mojave Airport, California

I still can't believe it. Those guys in Rutan's shop are fantastic. They pulled it off. Imagine, a civilian spacecraft actually going into space and coming back safely. I sort of wish we'd tried for that instead of screwing around with the always-evanescent Hypersonic Cruiser."

Bob Rodriquez looked up with sad eyes.

"That's a hell of a thing to say, Steve. Mike Melvill's flight in *Space-ShipOne* is a tremendous achievement, but it has none of the complexity and none of the problems of manned hypersonic flight. You know that."

At 6:45 A.M. that morning, *SpaceShipOne* had lifted off the Mojave runway, nestled under the *White Knight* carrier aircraft. The *White Knight* had a totally different configuration than the *Proteus* aircraft, but was unmistakably a Burt Rutan product. About an hour later, *SpaceShipOne* was dropped. After a short glide to about forty-seven thousand feet, Melvill ignited the hybrid rocket motor and the gleaming white plane, almost toylike in appearance, streaked straight up. It reached the desired hundred-kilometer, sixty-two-mile altitude that qualified it as a flight into outer space, and then began its descent, with Rutan's brilliant device, a movable tail section, positioned to slow it down. Once back in the atmosphere, the tail was moved back into place and Melvill made a smooth descent and landing at about 8:15 A.M. to the delight of an awestruck crowd.

"I know but, just think, if we'd set our sights on the X Prize and beaten Rutan to the punch, we'd be ahead of the game right now, instead of slipping farther behind."

The X Prize was a ten-million-dollar prize modeled on the twenty-five-thousand-dollar Orteig Prize of 1919, which Charles Lindbergh won with his nonstop solo flight to Paris from New York. Backed by the well-endowed Ansari family, the X Prize was intended to award teams who reach specific goals with the potential to benefit humanity. For this contest, the winning contestant must fly to space in a civilian-built spacecraft, return safely, and repeat the process within two weeks. The hope was that the X Prize would change the space industry just as the Orteig Prize had galvanized the aviation industry. There were other competitors, but none with the genius and the financial backing of Rutan's group.

O'Malley was nothing if not insensitive. No one knew better than Rodriquez that the schedule had slipped on the Hypersonic Cruiser, and he didn't want to be reminded of it, not now and not by someone who wasn't contributing much more than money to the effort. In his heart he was glad for Rutan and his team, and especially glad that Melvill had made the hazardous trip into space safely.

Safety was the heart of Rodriquez's problem. He was building the Hypersonic Cruiser, and the chances were that his close friend, V. R. Shannon, would fly it. Unfortunately, the chances were also very good that something could go wrong, and V. R. would not survive. There would be no ejection at hypersonic speeds, and the craft was too small to have the luxury of an escape capsule.

Rodriquez was not sure he could take the triple disappointment of the failure of his great project, the culmination of his engineering career, and, most important of all, the death of his friend. Thinking about it robbed him of his usual normal composure even though he was absorbed in his work as before. He was just too conscious that every bit of progress moved him toward a life-defining moment that might be laden with tragedy.

"Steve, I've about decided to give up on the idea of manned hypersonic flight, at least for the first time. It will cost us some money, but I think I can make up the time we'd lose on the schedule."

"That's a change of tune, Bob. You've been adamant about manned flight being the way to go. What's changing your mind? Boeing's success with the X-43A?"

After an earlier failure, the Boeing X-43A had flown at 4,780 mph, about seven times the speed of sound.

"No, listen, that doesn't bother me at all. Look at the complexity of what they are doing—they have a B-52 chase plane to carry it to altitude, and then a Pegasus rocket to accelerate it to scramjet speeds. Worse than that, they have a half-dozen bureaucracies overseeing what they are doing. I feel sorry for them."

"Mach 7, that's pretty good."

"It's a small, single-use vehicle! It gets to Mach 7 and then crashes into the ocean. What the hell good is that? What would Kelly Johnson have said about a program like that?"

314 WALTER J. BOYNE

"They are not shooting for a mission capable aircraft—"

"Well, we are, dammit." Rodriquez rarely interrupted O'Malley—few people besides his wife Sally did—but this was too much. "I've got to tell you, Steve, you've got to find something to do. You're getting fat, you come around and bitch, and you are not contributing much but your money to this program. It's about time you got out and drummed us up some business like you did in the old days, when we were chasing F-16 subcontracts in Europe."

O'Malley was stunned. His wife had said virtually the same thing to him that very morning. He stood up and walked into the tiny bathroom to gaze into the mirror over the sink.

"Good Lord. You are both right."

He walked briskly past Rodriquez on his way out the door, saying only, "Thanks, Bob. I'll be back, in shape and with some contracts. And something else. You tell V. R. Shannon that he's got some competition now. I'm going to fly the Hypersonic Cruiser if he doesn't want to. Or maybe even if he does."

Rodriquez went back to his work, still angry with O'Malley for his chafing remarks. He meant no harm, but he should know better. And if anyone should be worried about delays in development, it was O'Malley. He had helped father the F-16 program that took perhaps six years to go from a proposal to entering service. And he had been a big backer of the F-22, which was proposed in 1986 and still hadn't entered service. He had a lot of nerve to complain about "slow progress" on the Hypersonic Cruiser. But O'Malley never had been short on nerve.

September 14, 2004
Maxwell Air Force Base, Alabama

V. R. SHANNON strolled the familiar Maxwell campus in the near-mandatory civilian blue blazer and gray flannel pants, remembering the happy days he'd spent there so long ago as a lieutenant in the Squadron Officers School, and later as a major in the Command and Staff College. It had not been easy at first in either school because he was both younger than his peers and had been promoted more swiftly, neither fact designed to make him popular. Yet he had worked and played hard, and in both schools wound up at the top of his class.

Nominally he was there on an unofficial mission, helping prepare for the next Gathering of Eagles event. The program had started in 1982 when fifteen distinguished aviators related their experiences to students. The Eagles were selected from all nations and all eras, and included such giants as Jimmy Doolittle, Curtis E. LeMay, Joe Foss, Adolf Galland, Gabby Gabreski, and Paul Tibbetts. The program was held every year, and many of the Eagles returned time and again, enjoying the company of the young officers with whom they talked.

The group sponsoring this year's event had invited V. R. down, ostensibly to discuss the possibility of including his grandfather, Vance Shannon, as an honorary Eagle. Shannon knew that this was just a cover, and that their real goal was to get his views—heretical from the Air Force's standpoint—on the war in Iraq.

Colonel Joe Carr was waiting for him on the steps of Austin Hall, the historic building where so many great Air Force officers had studied. Carr was project officer for the next year's Gathering of Eagles, and led him into his small, crowded office.

"General Shannon, it is good of you to come down. I would have been glad to pick you up this morning."

V. R. waved his hand. "No, I wanted to walk and soak up the old Maxwell aura. What a great place this is."

Carr went immediately to the point. "General Shannon—"

"Just call me V. R., that's what everyone does. I'm retired now, and there's no point in standing on ceremony."

Clearly uncomfortable with the idea, Carr went on. "Well, then, V. R., I want to level with you. You know your views on the conduct of the war in Iraq are not very popular in the Air Force. We get a good cross section of opinion through here, but we haven't invited anyone like you or General O'Malley to come in. The brass would frown on it. We know you have what headquarters considers to be really radical ideas, and we'd like to learn what they are. There are about fifteen of us. Would you be comfortable in just talking off the cuff about the war?"

Shannon nodded his head. "Yes, but you know you have to look at the war in context. I'll ramble on, taking in lots of different things— the economy, the media. You can sort it out among yourselves."

"I see you didn't bring any briefcase, so I guess you don't need a PowerPoint setup or anything?"

"No—all I'll need is a bottle of water, an attentive audience, and when I'm done, lots of good questions."

Carr led him down the hall to a small conference room where fifteen officers, mostly lieutenant colonels, but with some majors and colonels as well, were gathered. As they went in, Carr flicked on a sign that said "Top Secret" and closed the door.

After the introductions, Carr said, "General Shannon, this room is secure. No one is taking notes, there aren't any recording devices, and you can be as frank as you wish to be. There will be no attribution in articles, no quotes that might embarrass you. We just want to know what you and, as far as you feel comfortable in telling, General O'Malley think about the war in Iraq."

Shannon hesitated for a moment, then decided to be utterly frank.

"Let me tell you first that whatever I say has to be taken with a grain of salt, because, frankly, I think both General O'Malley—Steve—and I are probably nuts. I *hope* we are nuts and that we are dead wrong, because if we are not nuts, if we are right, the United States is not just in desperate trouble, it has already lost the fight. And not just the United States, the Western world, too.

"And there is a basis for me thinking I am nuts. I have an irreconcilable hatred of Muslim fanatics because my wife was on Pan Am Flight 103—the 747 that was blown up over Lockerbie, Scotland."

There was a shocked silence. A few of the men had known of this, most had not. It put things in perspective.

"Since then, the more I've learned about Muslim fanaticism, the more my hatred has increased. Steve's case is different. His hatred is based on his absolute certainty that Muslim fanatics are going to do exactly what they've said they are going to do: disrupt the Western economy and eventually establish Muslim control of the world.

"Now, with this in mind, let me talk first about the Iraq war. We went in for all the right reasons, but we went in with the wrong intelligence and the wrong methods. We made exactly the same mistake that McNamara and his Whiz Kids made in the Vietnam War. We had no idea of the psychology of the enemy, and worse, far worse, we imputed to the enemy a psychology and values similar to our own.

"It was wrong in Vietnam, but there was an escape clause there.

When the Vietnamese defeated us, we could leave and not worry about them following us. Sure, they would expand into Laos and Cambodia, and they would overrun South Vietnam, and they would even duke it up with China. But there was no clear and present danger to the United States. There is no escape clause in the war in Iraq, or for that matter in the war on terror.

"Our knowledge of the enemy psychology was so faulty that there were idiots who spoke of 'winning the hearts and minds' of the Iraqis, just as others had spoken in the same stupid fashion about the Vietnamese.

"But it was worse, far worse, with the Iraqis, whom we made our substitute enemy in the war on terror. I believe that Saddam Hussein was helping terrorists, but that was not his main goal. His main goal was maintaining his image as the man who had defied the United States and lived to tell about it. With immense oil wealth at his disposal, he felt comfortable that he had bribed enough people in France, Germany, and Russia so that the UN would never allow the United States to take action. And he devalued the United States as well; he believed firmly that the American public, instructed by the media, could not take the casualties he thought he could inflict upon us.

"The problem was that in attacking Iraq we had one chance at victory, and that chance was in making an initial attack so devastating that it would terrify the entire Muslim world, and force the passive Muslim population, through sheer fear, to take control of the terrorists and free us of the problem. Steve used to call it 'shock and awe' and you no doubt have heard the term.

"Such a devastating attack would have killed tens of thousands of Iraqis, maybe more, and would have brought us censure from around the world. You can imagine what the French and the German governments would have said, not all of it just because many of their officials were on Saddam's payroll.

"Further, we would have had to give the impression that we were perhaps irrational, and ready to unleash a similar, perhaps even more ferocious attack on any Muslim nation that opposed us. And we would have had to sustain this impression for years."

Shannon paused to assess how his words were going over. Not well, apparently; some looked interested, but most looked appalled. He decided to press on.

"I've said before that O'Malley and I are probably nuts. And others have said that it would be salutary for a superpower to occasionally appear irrational, so that lesser powers would not be inclined to tweak its nose on all occasions, for fear of an irrational reaction.

"Here is what O'Malley and I believe was our only hope. We could have avoided the war in Iraq entirely if we had reacted properly and angrily after the terrible attacks on the United States on September 11, 2001. Within a week of that date we should have detonated nonnuclear weapons over the capital of every Muslim nation, and over every Muslim holy site—Mecca, Medina, all of them. And we should have issued an edict to the Muslim world: 'Stop terrorism in the next thirty days, or the next series of explosions will not be over your cities, but on them. The explosions will not be nonnuclear: they will be nuclear. It is for you to decide your fate.'"

Most of the expressions around the room registered horror; a few showed agreement.

Shannon went on. "Then we should have added this proviso to the Arab governments: 'If you stop the terrorists, the United States will begin the biggest economic development program in history for Muslim nations, and will bring them from their abject poverty into the family of nations.'

"If we had the brains and the balls to have done this, the Muslim world would have collapsed into a jelly of acquiescence. Muslim leaders would have cut off funds to the terrorists, and would have rounded them up and killed them for us. The whole global war on terror would have been over. And you wouldn't have to be listening to an old bore like me.

"And instead of reacting with anger and an obvious desire for revenge, what did we do? We went through a maudlin period of self-congratulations over our ability to endure tragedy, and through a tedious effort to prove our humanity by insisting we would punish only the guilty, by insisting that there be no racial profiling, and in general by demonstrating all the good traits of a democracy which the enemy—and the fanatical Muslims are our enemy—intends to destroy."

Obviously concerned that the discussion was getting more radical than he intended, Carr spoke up. "But we are in Iraq now, General Shannon. How are we going to get out?"

"Sadly, we are going to get out as we got out of Vietnam—dishonorably, shabbily, and at great cost to the people we were honestly trying to help. We'll have political reasons to find some palpably unbelievable way to leave the country with a counterfeit semblance of what the perpetrators will call 'honor,' and I use quotation marks. Iraq will be submerged in violence, subverted by Iran and Syria, and a clerical state will emerge, one that will foster terrorism again to an unimaginable degree. And we will do this in the name of politics. In effect we will have congressmen selling the soul of the United States in order to win their next election."

Carr asked, "Do you see any way out for us that is not a humiliating defeat?"

Shannon shook his head. "Sadly, no. Despite the bravery and the brilliance of our fighting personnel, Congress will cut the legs out from under them and either cut off funding or demand a prescribed withdrawal date, or both. The question now is not what do we do after Iraq. The question is what do we do after the Muslims carry out their announced intentions and detonate nuclear weapons in our cities."

"Do you believe it will come to that?"

"Absolutely, the minute they are capable of setting off nuclear weapons they will do it. This seems self-evident, even discounting the fact that I may be a nut. They have been far more forthcoming in their pronouncements than Hitler ever was in *Mein Kampf*. We didn't believe him because almost no one read his book, and he was regarded as a passing irritant on the international scene. Even those who saw Hitler as a threat thought he could be bought off—given little countries, some colonies, let him terrorize the Jews, and everything would be OK. But the Muslims have been much more straightforward, much more consistent. Their goal is to convert or kill all of us, and establish a worldwide Muslim caliphate with all the misery and poverty that entails.

"So far they have tried to do everything they have promised us, from the World Trade Center on. And we can expect smaller actions, bombs in schools, in malls, all the things going on every day in Israel.

"The question is: what will we do when this happens. Will we have the guts then to take what the world would call irrational actions, and use nuclear weapons against Muslim states? Or will we slowly trade our civilization for theirs, just as they promise and predict?"

There was a general silence. One major said, "General Shannon, I hope you are nuts. If you are not, life is not going to be worth living for my kids."

Realizing he had to change the thrust of the discussion, Carr said, "General Shannon, you don't have to tell us anything you think is secret or proprietary, but it is generally known that your company is concentrating on building a manned hypersonic aircraft that you believe might be an effective tool to quell terrorism at its source. What can you tell us about it?"

Shannon flushed. He knew this was coming. There was no way to avoid it, *Aviation Week* had been monitoring RoboPlanes for years, and it was rare when the government could keep a secret, much less a private company that had to purchase materials and supplies from vendors who were under no obligation to keep what they were selling secret. It was easy enough to infer what RoboPlanes's goals were, just from the amount of titanium purchased and the kind of software suppliers it was using.

"I'll tell you what I can. But let me put it in context. As you know as well as anyone, hypersonic flight has been around for years, and manned hypersonic aircraft were planned as long ago as the 1930s, with the Sänger experiments. The Air Force's own late, lamented Dyna-Soar project was designed to maneuver in orbit, and would still be in use today if we had not been so stupid as to cancel it. But hypersonic projects are like all air and space projects today, caught up in a welter of budgetary, programming, and media hurdles that attenuate the programs endlessly.

"And let's not forget the hobby-shop factor. Programs become careers for officers and civilian engineers alike, and they want constantly to improve them, so that the original idea gets enhanced and more capabilities get added—but the program gets more expensive and more stretched out. I won't mention any programs by name, but you could pick any program from any service, throw in the Coast Guard if you want to, and you'll find the same factors.

"That's why people like Burt Rutan and Paul MacCready and RoboPlanes's own Bob Rodriquez are so valuable today. It would insult them to use a cliché like 'thinking outside the box.' They are thinking outside the universe to get where they are going. They've managed to break free from the congressional staffer who wants jobs in his boss's home district, and the media mogul who wants a sensational story filled with bad news, and the bureaucrat who wants to be in on everything but doesn't want to be responsible for anything. They make things happen.

"Then there is the sheer factor of size. Once a company gets to a certain size, it is inevitably bound up with its own procedures, mores, politics.

"All of the above is just a prelude to tell you why we are risking all of our collective fortunes on an exceedingly long shot—a successful Hypersonic Cruiser. And I'll tell you where we are today, confident that you will keep it to yourself. I got an update from Bob Rodriquez, our genius in residence, just before I came up here. Incidentally, for you who don't know him, Bob had a tremendously important effect on the development of precision guided munitions, on the adoption of GPS, on the AWACS, on UAVs, and on a dozen other projects.

"Here's what Rodriquez told me, and you can take it to the bank. The construction of the air vehicle is complete. We could have one of the big rollout ceremonies if we wanted to, or do it like the Navy does when it launches a ship, bring in the bigwigs, crack a bottle of champagne over it, all the rest. But we aren't going to do that. Not our style.

"Bob has vacillated on the next point, mostly due to my own uncertainty. I was slated to fly the Hypersonic Cruiser from the start, but for a while, I chickened out, wondering if it was a calculated risk or a certain suicide. Bob was forced to have a fallback position, and built in an autonomous flight capability, making it a UHV, an unmanned hypersonic vehicle. But I've changed my mind, I'm going to fly the aircraft, come what may, and Steve O'Malley is going to be my backup. We've got a complete simulator set up for training, of course. So Bob is pressing ahead with a manned design.

"In terms of our chances for success, Bob is rating it at ninety–ten that we'll have a flight that the pilot will survive. I'm rating it a hundred to zero or I wouldn't go. And Bob is rating it seventy–thirty that we'll achieve our Mach 8.0 design goal."

Shannon let a little rumble of conversation roll through the room, and went on. "We are pinning everything on a radical engine innovation that I am not going to reveal to you, but which will make or break

the project. If it works as Rodriquez thinks it will, and as his computers and wind tunnels tell him it will, we'll have a genuine Hypersonic
Cruiser. If it doesn't, we'll just have a long needle-nose aircraft with
the longest takeoff run and highest landing speed in history. I hope to
walk away from either situation."

The talk concluded with a series of questions, fewer than Shannon had hoped. Some of the men were obviously traumatized; some
were looking at him with either pity or contempt, he couldn't tell
which. A few asked questions that Shannon had difficulty fielding and
had to promise to get back with answers. He signed some autographs,
and then declining Carr's offer to walk back with him, resumed his
stroll back through the Maxwell campus, pondering the mixed impression he had made and wondering what the young officers were
thinking.

Talking in a whisper to himself, as he found himself doing more
and more, he said, "They almost certainly think I'm crazy, about the
Muslims and how we should have stopped them. They must think our
approach to the Hypersonic Cruiser is as crazy as our political views.
And they are probably right. I may very well be crazy, and maybe it is
a good thing. It is a cinch that the fanatical Muslims are crazy, by our
standards. Maybe we need craziness to stop them. Maybe it's guys like
O'Malley and me who will finally be the answer."

He paused to watch an aircraft pass near the campus, its engine
noise noticeably breaking the quiet. When he was attending school,
the air was so filled with the noise of aircraft and landing and taking
off that no one looked up. Now it was quiet and seeing an airplane was
a treat. He went on, saying to himself, "Well, that does it. I'd really
not made my mind up about flying until I saw the face of that major
worrying about his kids. It's time to step up to the plate."

He felt strangely comfortable with his decision. At first he could
not understand why, but came to a rapid conclusion. Taking the risk of
the flight was the one sure weapon he could use to revenge Ginny's
death. It was as simple as that. He wasn't going to be in any hand-to-
hand fights, not unless some Muslim fanatic listened to his talks. He
wasn't going to drop any more bombs. But he could deliver the single
most important weapon ever created in the fight against terrorism.
And now, firmly committed to flying the cruiser, he felt whole for the
first time in years.

November 17, 2004
Mojave Airport, California

THE AIRPORT AT Mojave was never noted for neatness. It couldn't be with acres of stored airliners lining its borders baking in the sun and dozens of start-up businesses that blossomed and withered over the years. But today it was an absolute mess, the detritus of the fantastic celebration for winning the X Prize. Rutan's group, financed by Microsoft cofounder Paul Allen, had done exactly what it set out to do: create a civilian presence in space.

The day before, Brian Binnie took the almost Disney-like *Space-ShipOne* to a very real altitude of 367,442 feet—sixty-nine point six miles—and a speed of Mach 3. On September 29, Mike Melvill had flown *SpaceShipOne* to 337,569 feet, despite having to shut down the new and more powerful engine eleven seconds early because the aircraft was making a series of unintended corkscrew rolls.

The two flights firmly established Rutan's Scaled Composite group as the premier civilian space company, and won the ten-million-dollar X Prize in a convincing way, for *SpaceShipOne* could have flown again, if required.

Richard Branson, the iconic iconoclast of Virgin Atlantic Airways, promptly announced that he would invest twenty-five million in a new space tourism venture called Virgin Galactic. His goal was to sell suborbital flights to tourists for about $200,000 a trip. It was insane, but it was also Richard Branson, whose track record for successful insane ventures was admirable.

Bob Rodriquez was immensely happy for the whole crew, and happier still that they had pulled off the daring venture safely with no loss of life and no injuries. Given the scope of their achievement—*SpaceShipOne* had broken the X-15's altitude record of 354,200 feet—it was little short of miraculous that it had been done safely.

He knew that Burt Rutan would have disagreed with him about its being "miraculous." Burt, his engineers, and his pilots had carefully calculated all the risks, and taken engineering steps of such sheer brilliance that the National Aeronautics and Space Administration paid unabashed homage to them. Rodriquez hoped he would be able to do as well with the Hypersonic Cruiser.

If only the cruiser could go as well as the UAVs and the cruise missiles of RoboPlanes, Bob mused. The company now had a full line of UAVs that ranged from dragonfly-sized miniatures to stealthy, long-range aircraft that approached the Global Hawk in size and capability. They were in use all over the world, and had become so versatile that they had an on-line catalog where prospective customers could pick and choose their own UAV just as they might pick an automobile and its options.

The cruise missile and anti-cruise missile had evolved almost painlessly, with a half-dozen successful test flights and the prospects of contracts for both of them almost certain with the U.S. Navy. As pleased as he was by these results, Rodriquez took special pleasure in the fact that the Hypersonic Cruiser used many of the design features that had proved themselves in the missiles. They were, in fact, miniature test vehicles, and he had designed them to be so.

Since both V. R. and Steve had committed themselves to flying the aircraft, Rodriquez had been able to make up time on the schedule. The Hypersonic Cruiser could roll out anytime, but the internal installations, the guidance and control systems, would not be proven until early 2007. First flight, at best, would be the fall of that year, within three months of the original schedule.

It didn't bother Rodriquez at all that Boeing had successfully flown a larger X-43A for NASA at a speed of Mach 9.6. A flood of glowing press releases showed how the X-43A had been released from the venerable Boeing B-52 carrier plane, on its last scientific mission, and was then powered by a Pegasus rocket to a speed of Mach 10. At that point, the X-43A's fuel system was activated and a ten-second flight followed after which the X-43A then glided down to a crash in the Pacific test range.

What pleased him most was a comment from a NASA official saying that "the next step is to take a turbine engine and a ramjet or scramjet engine and combine those propulsion cycles and put some hardware together and start testing it. Maybe in a couple of years we could put an airplane around that technology. There are a lot of paths you can take from this point, and they all lead forward."

Rodriquez came as close as he ever did to chortling, thinking, *RoboPlanes is doing exactly what NASA was proposing for some years in the future. RoboPlanes is doing for hypersonics exactly what Rutan had done for spaceflight. God grant that they have the same success.*

Steve O'Malley blew into the room, sweating from his jog up and down the tarmac, heading for the shower. Over his shoulder, he said, "Big news for you today, Bobby boy! I've got an offer I hope you can refuse."

Twenty minutes later he was back, polished and relaxed, thirty pounds lighter than he had been six months ago, and ready for another two-hour session in the cruiser simulator.

"What's your big offer?"

"It's our big offer. I got a call from Whit Robinson this morning, very mysterious. He has a foreign buyer willing to offer a billion cold cash for the work we've done on the Hypersonic Cruiser. Not the UAVS, not the cruise missiles, just the Hypersonic Cruiser."

"Who the hell is it? Is he serious?"

"Whit is always serious when it comes to money, and he would stand to make millions if he brokered this deal."

"But who would offer that kind of money without knowing where we are, or what our prospects of success are? It doesn't make sense."

"Nothing makes sense, nowadays, Bob. Who would ever have believed that Airbus would sell more planes than Boeing, but they did it in 2003 and again in 2004. And who would believe that Airbus would come up with something like its A380 while Boeing is putzing around with the Sonic Cruiser? And who would believe that we would be bogged down in Iraq, winning the war there but losing it in Congress and in the media? None of it makes any sense—but there it is."

"When are we going to know more about it?"

"Whit is going to call me this afternoon and tell me who the buyer is. But I told him the chances ran from slim to none that we'd even consider it."

"God, Steve, what a relief it would be to walk away from it with a billion in our pockets and all the experience, and no worry about killing you or V. R. It would add five years to my life and maybe twenty or more to yours and V. R.'s."

"You serious?"

"Of course not. The only people who could come up with money like that are either a European consortium or some Muslim consortium. I wouldn't dream of selling to either one."

"What if it is an American company, Boeing, say, or General Dynamics, Northrop Grumman, even?"

"Then we'd have to take a look at it, not for the money, but for their resources, and the probability of their being able to do what's necessary to get it sold after the first test flight. Or maybe even letting them test-fly it and getting the monkey off my back about killing you or V. R."

Whit Robinson called that afternoon, revealing only that it was a European consortium, probably backed by Muslim money. O'Malley turned him down politely, saying, "That's out of the question. But you might nose around some domestic firms and let them know there is foreign interest. Maybe we can get one of the big guys on our team to buy in."

They chatted for a while until a very disappointed, very dubious Whit Robinson hung up.

O'Malley told Rodriquez about the call.

"A European consortium, backed by Muslim money. That's encouraging. It means they have faith in us delivering a usable product. More faith than our government has shown."

"That's not fair, Steve. We haven't allowed our government to know what we are doing, and we haven't solicited their interest. But it's more than encouraging—it's terrifying. It means we've got a leak somewhere in the company. Somebody, at some level, knows enough about the project to sell it to the consortium. And that is a problem. We are going to have to really sit down and analyze who might be the culprit, and see what we can do about it. We have at least a half-dozen proprietary ideas invested in the cruiser that have value of their own, even if it never flies. I don't want them siphoned off by some spy."

O'Malley was nonplussed.

"We know all our guys personally, Bob, you handpicked them. I can't believe we've got a spy in our midst."

"A spy or a damn good hacker. Something is going on, and we'll have to be alert. Let's see if we can set up some bogus information and see where it appears, then find out who had access to it. It will be a start."

CHAPTER TWENTY-TWO

THE PASSING PARADE: Aid continues to pour in for tsunami victims in Asia; George W. Bush enters second term as President; elections in Iraq successful, 275-member National Assembly in place, 58 percent of eligible population voting; Pope John Paul II dies; Benedict XVI new pope; Lebanon free of Syrian military after almost thirty-year occupation; Tony Blair wins third term; France and Netherlands vote against ratification of proposed European constitution; new Iranian president is Mahmoud Ahmadinejad, advocate of Iranian nuclear arms; first woman Supreme Court Justice, Sandra Day O'Connor, to retire; comet Tempel 1 struck by NASA Deep Impact spacecraft; Islamic terrorists kill 52, wound 700 in London bombing; United States plans to withdraw from Iraq based on ability of Iraqi police force to maintain security; IRA, long bane of Great Britain, announces end to campaigns of violence; much debated Central American Free Trade Agreement signed by President Bush; Israeli settlers numbering about 9,000 evacuated from Gaza Strip; devastating Hurricane Katrina inflicts widespread damage on Gulf Coast, killing more than 1,800 and destroying New Orleans; William H. Rehnquist, Chief Justice, dies; replaced by John Roberts, Jr.; Texan Tom DeLay, House majority leader, steps down after accusation of violation of Texas's election laws; 80,000 killed in Pakistani area of Kashmir by devastating earthquake; Germany elects first female chancellor, Angela Merkel; Saddam Hussein on trial for murder of 148; 2,000th American combat serviceman killed in Iraq; Vietnam War ace Randy "Duke" Cunningham resigns as congressman after pleading guilty to taking bribes.

May 13, 2005
Mojave Airport, California

*F*riday the thirteenth was an appropriate date. After six weeks of gentle nagging, Mae Rodriquez had maneuvered her husband into speaking to the Mojave Rotary Club. Filled with the up and coming young businessmen and women of Mojave, the club asked her to have Bob fill them in on what RoboPlanes was doing in UAVs and, surprisingly, in hypersonic flight. The request for information on hypersonic flight really was innocuous. RoboPlanes was always explaining the horrendous noise its engine cells caused. But to Bob, chronically suspicious since Whit Robinson had inquired about purchasing the company, it smacked of snooping.

He compromised with her by agreeing to speak on the topic of "What's New in Aviation," with the specific understanding he would not talk about anything RoboPlanes was doing, even information already in the public domain. He also specified that he wasn't going to talk about the war in Iraq. Steve had already colored RoboPlanes's reputation with his outspoken comments on the war and on the threat of Muslim fanaticism. Bob didn't want to stir the pot any more.

Worst of all, he did not want to venture anywhere near RoboPlanes's financial status. A recent spate of contract cancellations and some bad investment advice had moved the firm perilously close to bankruptcy. All the principals were aware of the problem, all of them were working on it, but at the present it seemed doubtful if they could carry on past June 2006 unless they found some significant investment assistance. The government was at last being a little helpful. There had been some overtures from NASA, and Porter Chase, a smiling, silver-tongued representative from the Defense Advanced Research Projects Agency, had come by to spend almost a week with them. They had given Chase greater access than they had ever done for anyone else, but still kept secret what Rodriquez called the "nuggets," the essential design elements that would make or break the Hypersonic Cruiser. And there had been no further word from Whit Robinson. Apparently RoboPlanes's approach had offended—or alarmed—the major players in the industry.

Rodriquez had not made a public speech since high school. He hated the thought and the waste of time spent working up the material, most of which would go soaring over the heads of the audience. But Mae had done so much to make life livable in Mojave, where the average annual income was one-half of that for the average United States citizen, that he felt obliged to her. And as the talk began to take shape, he found himself enjoying it.

He planned to give a brief, positive overview of aviation, then contrast two important events in 2005 to illustrate how complex and how important aviation remained. Rodriquez felt that too many people discounted aviation even in Mojave, where it was the city's lifeblood. Almost everyone had flown, and the security arrangements made modern air travel a pain rather than a pleasure. And they were jaded. On any day at the Mojave Airport they could see anything take off from a World War II fighter to the latest exotic product from Rutan's Scaled Composites. Mae had given him a list of probable attendees. To his amusement, virtually no one from the many different enterprises on the Mojave Airport was going to attend. Instead the audience was going to be the ordinary businessmen of the city, doing as they were supposed to do at Rotary Club meetings, advancing their businesses by mutual concern and ethical means. Well, RoboPlanes had advanced their businesses tremendously over the last few years, and done so ethically as well. Now maybe he could lift their eyes from their balance sheets to the skies for a change.

Mae had arranged for the meeting to be held in the largest of the RoboPlanes conference rooms. The sixty seats soon filled up, and fifteen minutes before his talk, the room was standing room only, crowded with people and straining the groaning air-conditioning system. The people lined up around the walls included a lot of smiling sharpshooters from the various businesses on the field. He could tell from their conspiratorial grins that they would have some dandy questions for him.

Mae started the proceedings with some introductions, and the current Rotary Club president Mel Sanchez went through some of the inevitable routine of the meetings—thanking people, pointing out coming events, and at last turning to introduce Bob.

"It gives me great pleasure to introduce a great American hero, and especially so because he is a fellow Hispanic American. Bob Rodriquez has served our country in many ways, not least of which was shooting down twelve MiGs during the Korean War. And in my humble opinion, if his last name had been Richards instead of Rodriquez, the USAF would have left him in Korea to become the leading ace of the war."

Rodriquez's face flushed darkly. Who the hell had given Sanchez this story? It was true, but he had tried to forget about it. It couldn't have been Mae; Harry was dead . . . it had to be that damned Steve, never content to be quiet.

Sanchez went on. "Bob returned to this country and was a leading figure in establishing some of our most important weapons systems. Many people call him the 'father of precision guided munitions.' He also was a leading light in getting the invaluable Global Positioning System started. I could go on and on—but let me leap on to what he's done here in Mojave. With his vision he has created a new industry here, the remotely controlled aircraft we see flying almost every day, UAVs they call them. And he's also created the greatest urban blight in modern history, the screeching sounds of his engine test beds that seem to work night and day."

Sanchez was grinning.

"But that's an urban blight we welcome, for we know it will bring prosperity to Mojave, just like the UAVs have done."

He waited for the mild round of nervous laughter and applause to subside and said, "Bob is not going to talk to us about what he has done here, but about aviation in general, and he'll probably point the way for all of us to get in on the next aviation boom. May I present a Hispanic American hero, Bob Rodriquez."

Rodriquez saw Mae looking at him anxiously, certain he was going to walk out or say something cutting in response. His anger melted, he thanked Sanchez profusely and turned on his first slide, the famous December 17, 1903, scene of Orville Wright lifting off at Kitty Hawk, Wilbur standing amazed at the right.

He had assembled one hundred photos on the PowerPoint, far too many, and sped to a photo of a tiny Bleriot XI, from which an Italian pilot dropped the first aerial bomb in the history of warfare. Next was a photo of the Northrop Grumman B-2 stealth bomber, and Rodriquez said, "Incredibly, between the first flight of the Bleriot, a cranky fifty miles per hour airplane and the first flight of the super-secret B-2 stealth bomber, only eighty years elapsed. That's less than the age of many of your parents. In just eighty years aviation went from a handheld, six-kilogram bomb dropped haphazardly on the desert sands to delivering as many as sixteen precision guided munitions directly on target at almost supersonic speeds.

"That was the story of aviation—incredibly rapid advances, year after year."

Rodriquez watched the clock closely as he cycled through his PowerPoint presentation relentlessly. He was trying to do three aircraft a minute, speaking off the cuff, displaying one iconic aircraft after another, SPAD, Spitfire, Mustang, Messerschmitt Me 262, F-86, F-104, giving a machine-gun burst description of each, telling why they were good and the year they debuted.

Then he said, "And then aviation began to slow down, even as it reached into space with first intercontinental missiles, exploratory spacecraft like the Apollo, and the fantastic satellite networks we all take for granted. It was extraordinary, for as the jet engine allowed us to speed up in terms of miles per hour, it forced us to slow down our development because so many new problems were encountered, not least of which was soaring costs.

"As we pushed for performance, we were aided by the introduction of computers and new materials, but nonetheless the rate of progress still slowed. Instead of seeing a new fighter every two years, we now see them once in two decades. Instead of new bombers every five or six years, we fly them like the poor old B-52, forever, with no replacements in sight. And with airliners, instead of seeing the steady march from DC-1 to DC-8 , within a twenty-five-year period, we've seen a slowdown that forced some of the great manufacturers out of the airliner business—Douglas first, then McDonnell Douglas and Lockheed. Even Boeing rested on its laurels after its great gamble with the 747, and is taking a shellacking from Airbus Industries because of it.

"The reason: it is simply not economical any longer to churn out new designs. The risks are so great that companies have to partner together to share them. That's why we should all welcome this airplane, even if it is built abroad."

He flashed a series of slides of the gigantic new Airbus A380, almost all of which were new to most of the audience. There was a collective appreciative gasp of awe at the size and luxury of the interior.

He rattled off the basic specifications: "Wingspan 261 feet; maximum gross takeoff weight, 1,300,000 pounds; carries up to 853 passengers; great use of composite materials, and cruise speed of Mach .85. It has four engines in the 70,000 pounds of thrust range."

Rodriquez switched to a blank screen and said reflectively, "Mach .85—but they will cruise at about 630 mph, they say, but for fuel reasons they'll probably slow down to about 580. And the Boeing 707 used to cruise at 550 mph. It's harder to go faster as you get bigger. There *is* a supersonic barrier, but it's dollars, not the speed of sound."

He went on. "Airbus was able to pull this engineering masterpiece off because of computers. And incidentally, also in spite of computers, for they are experiencing difficulties. The aircraft is being built in components at French and German factories—and the two factories use different computer-aided design systems, one two-dimensional, one three-dimensional. There are already problems."

He switched the screen, and then superimposed on a three view of the gigantic A380 was the Virgin Atlantic Global Flyer. Not a small aircraft itself, it seemed diminutive next to the A380.

"Now I've probably bored the hell out of you so far, so I'll ask you to wake up and pay attention now, as I'm trying to make my point about why today is the best time to be in aviation. We have gigantic aircraft like the A380, modern in every respect, but following an orthodox formula: the swept wings and podded four engines have been around since Boeing's dash-80, the 707 prototype. But we also are in an era that you probably know better than the rest of the world, one that uses computers and composite materials to make totally unorthodox designs."

The next slide showed a smiling Steve Fossett, just climbing out of the cockpit of the Global Flyer after its record-shattering nonstop, non-refueled flight around the world.

"A lot of you probably know Steve. He has broken more sailing records than anyone and now has extended himself to the sky. In 2002, he was the first to fly around the world nonstop in a balloon. Now, just this March 3, he completed a sixty-seven-hour solo nonstop, non-refueled flight around the world, in an airplane designed right here in Mojave."

He clicked through the next slides, a montage of shots of the Global Flyer, showing its twin booms, central nacelle, center-mounted engine, and cramped interior.

"And here are its specs: 114-foot span—the longest of any Scaled Composite aircraft yet, 22,000-pound maximum takeoff weight, one pilot, no passengers, and a single 2,300-pound thrust engine."

He pressed a button and a slide showed three views and the comparative specifications of the two aircraft.

"My penultimate point is this. Burt Rutan, through his genius and his design team, got to the Global Flyer with exactly the same sort of tools and materials that the A380 has used. The airplanes could not be more different in appearance, in mission, and in cost, but at their roots are similar knowledge, systems, and materials. The greatest difference is in approach: the Scaled Composite design is totally unorthodox by Airbus standards (but not by Scaled Composite's!) but it worked equally well, and perhaps even better, we'll have to see, in achieving its design goal.

"Now here is my final point. The gap in size, weight, speed, and mission between the Global Flyer and the A380 could not be greater, but the tools used on each are common. By that I mean that the two firms started with different goals, vision, and most of all imagination, but used the same body of knowledge of aerodynamics, computers, and materials to achieve their desired results. This has happened continually throughout the jet age, from Frank Whittle and Hans von Ohain's first efforts, right down until today. And this means that we all have at our disposal the same modern techniques that can be applied to any industry, from automobiles to solving global warming, to achieve results on the order of both the A380 and the Global Flyer. We just have to have the courage to reach out and take the risks associated with their use to achieve new heights in whatever we do."

He drew a breath and repeated, "Take the risks, take the risks, take the risks."

He shut the PowerPoint down amid a silence that suddenly turned into wild applause and a standing ovation. Embarrassed, he waved his hands, but Sanchez came up, embraced him, then turned to stand waving their two hands in the air as if he were a referee and Rodriquez were a winning boxer. Bob glanced at Mae. She was smiling, proud, knowing what this had cost him psychologically, and pleased that he had done so well—for her.

As his friends from around the field pressed forward with questions,

Rodriquez thought to himself how much better it was with Mae since he had returned from his crazy covert life. He had come in out of the cold indeed.

December 16, 2005
Langley Air Force Base, Virginia

STEVE O'MALLEY AND V. R. Shannon sniffed the air eagerly, savoring the familiar mix of southern humidity and jet fuel. The flight line at Langley was not as busy as it was in the old days, but the sight of a squadron of Lockheed Martin F-22s was impressive. The early-morning drizzle left the Raptors glistening, reflecting the sun that was now breaking through the overcast.

Lieutenant Colonel James Heller was escorting them, pride written all over his face. He commanded the 27th Fighter Squadron, the oldest in the United States Air Force.

"I know you know these airplanes as well or better than I do, General O'Malley, but I want you to meet some of the pros who are flying and maintaining the Raptor."

The Raptor had reached its IOC—initial operating capability— the day before, and Heller was understandably pleased that the 27th was maintaining its legendary reputation for leading the way. It had done so since its origin in 1917. In the interval the 27th had flown all the first-line aircraft, from the SPAD XIII in which the legendary Medal of Honor recipient Lieutenant Frank Luke busted balloons in World War I through the Lockheed P-38 Lightning, Convair F-106, McDonnell F-4 Phantom, and Boeing F-15E Strike Eagle. It had earned top honors in the Middle East, and was now the vanguard of a new era of total air dominance.

Heller went on, saying, "Normally we give our VIPs an hour in the simulator, but I know you both have done that. I thought you'd prefer just going into the ops area and meeting the troops. I know you have another meeting in a couple of hours."

An hour later, on their way to their meeting in an aging Holiday Inn outside of Norfolk, O'Malley said, "That added ten years to my life. What a bunch of winners. The pilots and the ground people are as good as the airplane."

V. R. nodded. "It was a long twenty-five-year wait—the initial competition started back in 1981."

"Yeah, but you have to look forward, not back, V. R. With its super-cruise and stealth capabilities, it will be the world's premier fighter for the next thirty, maybe fifty years. Teddy Roosevelt used to send his Great White Fleet around the world to project power—it took him months. Right now, today, we could put a squadron of F-22s anywhere in the world in a few hours. It's expensive, sure, but it's worth it."

"I wonder how long it will be till we get the next fighter."

O'Malley said, "If we've done it right on the Hypersonic Cruiser, there won't have to be a next fighter, and it won't show the flag in a few hours, it will be in a few minutes. That is, of course, if we get the money to finish the airplane, and that's why I've set today's meeting up."

"Why are we meeting here in Norfolk? I'd think that anyone wanting to invest in the project would want to meet us back at Mojave."

"No. These troops have been conducting hypersonic research in Australia, and I think they are moving away from government backing to private backing. They have to be very careful what they do, and couldn't afford to be seen at Mojave, or in our plant. They have official business here on the F-22, so it's logical for them to be in Norfolk. Most people won't connect the dots between our visit and theirs. I picked the Holiday Inn because it's one that Bob Rodriquez used to stay in when he was on the road for our company, years ago. He didn't want to come at all, but I persuaded him that this might be the salvation of everything—money, time, even some technology."

"Well, I'm glad we'll be there, but let's be sure that neither one of us goes off on our anti-Muslim sentiments. You are too damn talkative, and I'm too intense, and it puts people off."

V. R. was speaking from experience. He'd received an unofficial rocket from the Chief of Staff on the subject and was noticing how people shied away from him when he got on his political hobbyhorse.

O'Malley pointed to the bearded, dark-skinned taxi driver and said, "Once again, V. R., you really know when to shoot off your mouth."

December 16, 2005
Norfolk, Virginia

THE HOLIDAY INN was like a time capsule. Signing in the night before, Bob Rodriquez felt as if twenty years had evaporated. Apparently nothing—wall paintings, rugs, furniture, smell—had changed, and even the dour clerk seemed identical to the man who had been behind the counter two decades before. Then he had always tried to get the cheapest room, but this time O'Malley had arranged for a suite, with two interconnecting bedrooms and a sitting room for the meeting.

Rodriquez asked, "Did you call down for coffee, juice, water? They should be here in the next five minutes."

"Take it easy, Bob, no need to be nervous, these are prototypical Australians, good people. You are going to like them. John Honey is a retired Royal Australian Air Force pilot, flew everything from Wirraways to F-111s, and has a doctorate in aeronautical engineering. He teaches at Queensland University. His sidekick is Barry Martin, another Ph.D., a specialist in thermodynamics. I've gotten to know Honey pretty well, and I'll vouch for him."

There was a knock at the door, and Honey and Martin came in, cheerful, poised, and obviously ready to talk business. After a few preliminary comments, Rodriquez turned to the Australians and said, "Steve told you that we are in a bind, financially, and he has vouched for you personally. Still, I understand you are asking me to give you insight into almost a decade of work and nearly a billion-dollar investment."

Honey smiled. "It's not a one-way street, Mr. Rodriquez. We are not just offering you money for ideas. We are offering money and ideas, and I think it may be that the latter is more important than the former. You'll have to decide that yourself. But before we go much farther, I have to know where you are in your approach."

Rodriquez shook his head. "This is no way to do business. I don't have any of my materials here, I cannot give you any of the mathematical backup, I don't even have copies of some of the analyses we'd done from wind-tunnel data. I only agreed to meet you here, all the way across the country, because you insisted."

Honey nodded. "There was no way we could be seen going to Mojave, much less RoboPlanes. And we are not asking for proof, we are just asking to listen to your story. Barry and I know enough from our own experiments to be able to determine whether it makes any sense to proceed with a discussion. We are not trying to gain information from you, then cut and run."

Honey's manner was ingratiating—concerned, polite, and friendly. He was obviously the sort of man you'd want to have a pint with after the meeting. Still, Rodriquez stalled, considering his limited options. He could just say no, now, and forgo the possibility that the Australian's interest was legitimate and possibly a way out. He could stall and risk the Australian being turned off. Or he could go ahead and give a carefully filtered description of the Hypersonic Cruiser and then try to determine from Honey's questions what to do next. If Honey kept pressing, and was obviously just looking for free information, he could end the discussion. The risk would be significant, especially if the Australian was as astute as he seemed to be, and if his motives were wrong. But Steve had worked with him when Australia bought General Dynamics F-111s, and then later helped advise on the Aussie purchase of the Boeing F/A 18E Super Hornets. It wasn't as if he were an unknown quantity. Martin was—but he doubted if Honey would have brought a ringer with him.

"Steve, did you have this place checked for bugs?"

O'Malley laughed. "No, I'm sorry, it didn't occur to me. I only made the reservations for here yesterday—I doubt if the sharpest industrial spy would have had time to bug the room."

Feeling faintly ridiculous, Rodriquez turned back to Honey, saying, "OK. I'll give it to you in abbreviated form. You know that heat dissipation is one of the biggest headaches in hypersonic flight, and that remains our biggest problem. Fortunately we've made the airplane big enough, almost one hundred feet long, and the fuel load large enough so that we can use fuel as a heat sink. We turned the nose of the airplane into a radiator using two techniques. One is passing fuel lines through it to soak up the heat, much more efficiently than the SR-71, I'm glad to say. The other is brand-new. We've a heat pipe, same composite material as the aircraft itself, containing lithium. The lithium vaporizes as the wing heats up, distributing the heat evenly throughout the leading edge. When the aircraft slows for descent and landing, the lithium condenses back into a liquid."

He paused, watching Honey for a reaction, then went on.

"We had to have a big airplane to hold the fuel to get the range we need, so there is ample tankage to dissipate the heat. We also needed a big airplane because of the real secret—I hope—of what we are doing."

Rodriquez pulled a yellow legal pad from his briefcase and sketched the hypersonic liner's long, narrow profile.

"You can see that we've stayed with the wave-rider design—I don't know any way around it—but that we've extended the scramjet over a much longer, narrower portion of the undersurface of the fuselage. The entire structure is composite, and actively fuel-cooled, for we've established Mach 8.0 as the goal."

Rodriquez kept looking up and staring at Honey the way boxers do as the referee gives them instructions at the start of a fight. Honey appeared not to notice.

"We've spent five years making some key discoveries in how to lay out the nozzles that turn the bottom of the fuselage into an engine. At the rear of the fuselage, we have a modified Pratt & Whitney F119 with about forty thousand pounds of thrust the way we have it tuned. It is mounted behind and below the main fuel tank."

Rodriquez hesitated. The new element that had changed all the equations was radical—and at first glance, so apparently ill-advised—that he was sure Honey would laugh. If he did, the session might end right there.

"I've never shown this to anyone besides the major partners and to some key engineers and machinists. Don't leap to any conclusions. Let me explain it."

Honey concealed his impatience, nodding affirmatively.

Rodriquez took the yellow pad and made another drawing.

"Here's what happens, believe it or not. The engine is moved up and forward into a flexible tunnel that is built into the bottom of the fuel cell. The cowling remains below and acts as a channel for the scramjet efflux. As the engine moves, the cowling is extended and re-configured to maximize thrust. At the present time we are not introducing fuel into it to make it a genuine afterburner, but it still has the effect of increasing the thrust of the scramjet by about 50 percent—at no increase in fuel consumption. More important, it helps maintain a constant pressure, avoiding the 'choke' that has been the bane of most scramjets so far."

Rodriquez stopped again, looking closely at Honey, ready to fly off the handle if the Australian smiled or joked. This was too serious, it was his life. The man could choose not to believe it if he wished, but he'd better not laugh at it.

Honey said nothing. He reminded Rodriquez of Paul MacCready, silently running figures through his head, checking ideas, balancing out the pros and the cons.

At last he said, "You say that you've checked this out in wind tunnels? Your computer analysis confirms this?"

Rodriquez could not tell if his tone was friendly or derisive.

"You're damn right I did. I can't tell you how many times I went over the numbers before I committed to the design."

"You can stand the shift in the c.g., the center of gravity, when the engine moves?"

"It's automatically offset by fuel transfer from the tunnel area. In the few seconds it takes to move the engine up and forward, fuel is transferred at high pressure from the bladder in the fuel tank out to the wings. It's a zero sum transfer, the airplane never knows the c.g. is changing. When the engine moves back, it moves much more slowly, and the pilot can trim out the change in c.g. as it happens."

"What about the engine's heat? It's like moving a flaming torch into the fuel cell."

"The whole thing is purged with nitrogen. The tunnel is actually a bladder placed next to the main fuel cell. It contracts as the fuel is pumped out, so there is no fuel or fumes in contact with the engine during or after the move. There is some danger that the nitrogen will have some effect on the hot engine metal, but we've been experimenting with ceramic coatings on the most critical areas, and I think we have that beaten. Later, after reentry, the engine is moved back into place to start up for a powered landing."

Honey was quiet again, a long, tapered finger going over the outline of the drawings, back and forth.

"I see you've elected not to have a conventional cockpit canopy, no doubt to avoid the heating—"

Rodriquez interrupted him, saying, "Exactly. We are using our own specially developed composite material creating a bonded pi-joint structure. We'll rely entirely on electro-optical means to create a virtual cockpit for the pilot. To Shannon, here, who will be flying, it will appear just like the simulator, a big beautiful blown canopy but with 360-degree visibility. And we did it for safety reasons as well. The entire cockpit serves as an ejection capsule, if it were ever necessary."

The ejection capsule had been a late addition, a sop to Rodriquez's concern over V. R.'s safety.

There was again a long silence as Honey and Martin examined the sketches again. Neither man spoke until Martin suddenly nodded to Honey, who said, "Mr. Rodriquez, you've asked me to take a lot on faith. I've got to believe that you can get the aircraft to scramjet speed on fan-jet power, not using a rocket. I've got to believe that you can move an engine a full four feet up and ten feet forward and nestle it in a fuel cell, for God's sake! And toughest of all, I've got to believe that the engine's cowling, extended and shaped, is going to add thrust to the scramjet. That's a lot to take on faith."

Rodriquez's temper flared, "Goddammit, I never asked you to take anything, you asked me, and I told you. And furthermore—"

Martin, Shannon, and O'Malley looked apprehensive, but Honey smiled, shook his head, and said, "Let me finish. You are asking me to take this on faith, and I do, for I believe what you've told me is true. I have the greatest respect for you and what you've done for aviation. Now, please, you are going to have to listen to me, and take on faith what I am telling you. These ideas are as radical as yours, and as proprietary. I am taking exactly the same risk with you that you are taking with me—but frankly I don't think either of us believes there is any security risk involved. We wouldn't be talking if we did."

Rodriquez's anger fizzled out in a wave of embarrassment. This man was being a gentleman—and, as usual, he was not. He was glad Mae wasn't there.

"May I call you Bob? Bob, I'm going to do some sketching on the yellow pad, if I may, and I'll show you what I'm proposing to offer you as an idea, in addition to some funds. A lot of funds."

Honey sketched quickly and expertly, his drawing much more precise than Rodriquez's. He deftly replicated the outline of the Hypersonic Cruiser in his own drawing, but changed the nose. Instead of the stilettolike needle of Rodriquez's creation, there was now a wide, lip-like disk shape that extended out perhaps four feet before being streamlined back to the fuselage, serving as a chine where it merged into the meld of the wing and fuselage.

Honey handed him the sketch, laughing. "Makes it look like a bit of a platypus, eh, very appropriate for an idea from Australia."

Rodriquez looked blank for a moment, then asked, "For cooling?"

"Yes, but even more important, drag reduction. Your needle nose is a physical air spike; this is a virtual air spike. We've done studies for years on saucer-shaped vehicles—it does the hearts of the UFO people good—and finally come down to this. As small as this extension is, it is almost a 'virtual saucer' and its effectiveness is boosted by high velocity air being pumped out at explosive speeds in incredibly small quantities all over the lip. You might think that this would be 'reverse thrust' and cost you but it does not. If you wanted to look for a primitive example, it is the super Russian torpedo, the VA-111 *Shkval*, that hits high speed by releasing bubbles. Except in this we are ejecting superheated air from the scramjet in ultra-microscopic jets. The effect is almost miraculous. It reduces your cooling problem by a major factor, and cuts your drag by perhaps 50 percent."

"You've tested this?"

"Just as you've tested your ideas—on the computer and in the wind tunnel. We could never get enough money from the government to fly a vehicle. Besides, it is too radical an idea for the establishment to accept without twenty-five years of testing."

Rodriquez sat down, weak at the knees. His heart was pounding and he worried, as he did so often lately, whether he was going to have a stroke. His father had died of one at seventy-seven, his age. He was suddenly flooded with remorse. What in hell had he gotten into? Had he given away his fundamental secrets for nothing? Did Honey have a crack-brained idea, or was it the solution of a lifetime?

Honey reached for the telephone saying, "Shall I call 911? Are you all right?"

Rodriquez shook his head.

"Get me some water, please. Give me a few minutes. I'll be OK."

He sipped the water slowly, gazing at Honey's drawing, his mind racing, a thousand ideas flowing through it. As he stared at the drawing he saw how the cruiser would have to be revised. The first flight date would slip, but if Honey was talking serious money, that would not matter.

"I won't ask you how much money is involved now, but tell me, would you offer it whether or not I adopted your virtual air spike, your platypus nose?"

Honey said, "The offer is for half a billion dollars, and it depends solely on your adopting our idea. Frankly, I think your concept might work. But I know it will work if you mate it with our virtual air spike."

Steve O'Malley had been quiet longer than he had been in years, repressing every bad Crocodile Dundee gag he could think of. Now he couldn't stand it anymore.

"Bob, first you've got to decide what it does to the flying characteristics of the Cruiser. V. R. and I have been flying the simulator for two years now, and think we can handle your design. If this is going to alter the handling significantly, I think we have to look at it. But if it won't alter them too much, then I'll tell you how I'm voting, and I can tell from the look on V. R.'s face how he's voting. I'll bet Dennis will go along with us. Bob, you don't have to decide now, but if you tell me the flight characteristics won't change, I say we go ahead with the Australians. You are a hell of a lot smarter than I am, and so is Mr. Honey, I'm sure, but I've got a gut feel about this. It is the way to go."

Honey said, "Look, there's no hurry. If we are right about this, we are ten years ahead of everybody else. If we are wrong about it, delaying will give us a few more days not to worry about going broke. Why don't you take this and go back to California and do your own computations? Then let us know. We'll be in the States for another month, looking into another Super Hornet buy."

He handed Rodriquez a set of computer discs.

"Everything we know is on them. I'm giving them to you on faith. And I'm not worried a bit about it. Don't lose them, though."

CHAPTER TWENTY-THREE

THE PASSING PARADE: Sectarian violence continues undiminished in Iraq; veteran general, politician Ariel Sharon felled by massive stroke; Jacques Chirac announces that France will use nuclear weapons in response to any terrorist attack on French soil; Iran announces plans to restart work on its nuclear energy program, denies warlike intentions; Iraqi government formed with Shiite and Kurd coalition; Sunnis form minority opposition party; evidence of mass fraud in Iraq reconstruction fund distribution; Samuel Alito confirmed as Supreme Court Justice; satellite images confirm extensive underground Chinese nuclear facilities; insurgents bomb Askariya Shrine in Samarra; vicious fight between Shiites and Sunnis, killing more than 1,000; Muslim world erupts in furor after publication of cartoons of Muhammad in a Danish newspaper; Canada has first Conservative Prime Minister in years, Stephen Harper; Slobodan Milosevic suffers heart attack and dies in cell; super-lobbyist Jack Abramoff sentenced to almost six years in prison on fraud charges; widespread fallout among congressmen and staffers expected to follow; Tom DeLay announces his resignation; only 66 percent of U.S. chemical weapons stockpiles will be destroyed by 2007, British police prevent al Qaeda terrorist attack using poison gas; in massive test, North Korea launches series of missiles, including two that have range to reach United States; terrorist plot to blow up airliners between United Kingdom and United States foiled by Scotland Yard; in surprising reversal of form, Marine veteran Congressman John Murtha accuses Marines of killing Iraqis in cold blood; bombs kill Abu Musab al-Zarqawi, a particularly violent terrorist; General George Casey estimates need for a year to 18 months more training for Iraqi security forces before they can take over; Saddam Hussein found guilty of crimes against humanity, sentenced to death; Iraq Study Group report released, recommends reaching out diplomatically to Syria and Iran, states that situation is "grave and deteriorating"; Saddam Hussein hanged; American death toll reaches 3,000.

December 31, 2006
Palos Verdes, California

I'm glad you insisted that we not sell this place. If we had, the money wouldn't have helped much and we managed to scrape by. Now we've got the old Vance Shannon library for our party, just like the old days. And the Australians seem to be having a good time. I thought I'd never get Honey away from Vance's model collection."

Steve O'Malley and V. R. Shannon were, as usual, sitting apart, going over the prospects for the early 2007 mission of the Hypersonic Cruiser, the immense dangers of the first flight weighing on them equally. Shannon was still scheduled to fly, but both were ready. As always, their conversation centered on the mission, rehashing subjects they had discussed a dozen times before, always trying to find a new slant.

"Sometimes I wish we had not been so damn audacious. It is enough to fly this thing, without doing an operational test with a missile. The Air Force spends months flying its prototypes before it ever launches a missile."

"I know. I flip back and forth on this. Remember Delmar Benjamin?"

V. R. looked blank.

"Benjamin built the exact replica of the Gee Bee R-2 racer, the one Doolittle set a speed record in. The airplane had a reputation as a pilot-killer, terribly dangerous to fly. On the first flight, Delmar flew it in knife-edge flight, and then flew it low-level, inverted. Everyone said he was crazy, but Delmar had confidence in what he had built. I have confidence in this, and I know you do, too, or you wouldn't be flying it."

He hesitated a moment and said, "And remember the Boeing 777; they didn't build a prototype, they went right to a production aircraft, and did it all depending on computers."

V. R. winced, saying, "And remember the A380 and the mess they are in now because of computers! Overweight, behind in production, lots of wiring problems."

O'Malley said, "Rodriquez really called that one, didn't he! But we've just used one computer system, and by chance or by the gift of God, it's exactly compatible with the one the Australians are using."

V. R. pulled out the well-worn sheets of the mission profile and they huddled together, going over it item by item as they had done already, dozens of times before.

Dennis Jenkins peered in the room at them, aware of their intense concentration, not wishing to intrude. This flight was life or death for Shannon and for RoboPlanes as well as for the Australian group that joined them and added so much to their engineering and their finances.

Beside him, John Honey spoke quietly, "Dennis, you know, I'd been warned that those two men were mentally unstable, that their obsession with the terrorist threat made them unbalanced. But in all the time I've known them, they've hardly said a word about it. What happened?"

Dennis took him by the arm as they walked toward the kitchen over the now-worn Mexican tiles that had supported so many parties like this.

"They believe that they are creating the perfect weapon to control terrorism. This is just intuitive on my part, but I think their actions are taking the place of their words. I've never seen two men work as hard as they have in the past year, getting the cruiser ready for flight."

It was true. When Honey and Rodriquez had combined their teams to modify the Hypersonic Cruiser and incorporating the Australian concept of a virtual air spike, Shannon and O'Malley had thrown themselves into the program with an intensity that reminded Jenkins of them in the old days, when O'Malley was feverishly getting new business for their company and V. R. was all wrapped up in the F-117 stealth fighter program.

They went into the kitchen where Steve's caterer had done what he thought as an Australian theme, with Foster's beer, Penfold wines, and an array of barbecued shrimp, beef, and ribs. Dennis winced, for Honey often talked longingly of the finer Australian wines, and he knew that the caterer should have stuck to his Mexican food specialties. No matter. The events of the last year and the coming year were so heavy on everyone's minds that not much would be eaten and still less drunk.

Only two women were there, Sally O'Malley ineffectually puttering around the kitchen, the caterer following her and rearranging what
she had done, and Mae Rodriquez, drawn and obviously very worried
about her husband. Their son, Rod, was on the east coast, working out
some further leasing deals, and she wished he were there, for "Bob the
father," as O'Malley called him, could draw strength from him.

Jenkins and Honey wandered out onto the veranda. V. R. had installed an open-pit fireplace and thrown some branches of mesquite
on the brightly burning wood, giving off a taste of the desert.

Bob Rodriquez, a jacket thrown around his shoulders, was talking
with Barry Martin. They were unlikely friends, for both were silent
men of strong convictions, but had somehow found themselves on the
same wavelength on virtually everything, from religion to politics to
the heady state of the aviation industry prospects to, always and eter-
nally, the prospects for the Hypersonic Cruiser's success.

Rodriquez gestured to two empty chairs, and Jenkins and Honey
sat down. Sally O'Malley came out with a tray of drinks and put it on
the small folding table.

The four men were quiet for a while, Jenkins assessing Rodriquez
closely. He was no longer young and the strain of converting the Hypersonic Cruiser to accommodate the Australian's suggestions had further diminished his energy. He tried to cheer him up.

"Well, chaps, every time we think the air and space industry is going
down for a count, we have a year like 2006, where everything was looking up. Incredible stuff happening, all across the country, all around the
world. I just wish I were thirty years younger, starting all over."

He realized it was the wrong thing to say. Rodriquez was already
worried about his age and his health. He tried to recover. "Bob, did
you ever think the Air Force would have a full wing of UAVs? They
are going to set one up at Creech Air Force Base next year, using the
MQ-1 Predator and MQ-9 Reapers."

Rodriquez just nodded, but Honey and Martin caught on immediately and jumped into the conversation.

"I see they are changing the terminology from UAV to UAS—
unmanned aerial systems. I'm surprised the feminists have let them
get away with 'unmanned.' But I wish O'Malley would come out, I'd
like to hear what he has to say about the F-22s getting ready to deploy
to Japan."

Martin added, "I managed to get to the Experimental Aircraft Association fly-in at Oshkosh this year. They had the F-22 there, and the HondaJet, too. It is always an impressive sight to see those acres of airplanes."

Martin's comment seemed to stir Rodriquez, who sat up and said, "The EAA is the best thing that's happened to aviation. Without it there probably would have been no Burt Rutan as we know him, nor any Cirrus or Lancair or HondaJet or a lot of other things. Do you guys know Paul Poberezny?"

Jenkins did but Martin and Honey said no.

"You've got to meet him. He's older now, like me, but he's still impressive, and even now you see the Messianic aspects of his personality that allowed him to create and shape the EAA. There'll never be another like him."

He paused for a moment and went on. "It is a great time. Look what's happening with Air Traffic Control! It's moving into the twenty-first century at last, and beginning to use satellite technology for traffic control and approaches. It's about time. If they had waited much longer, the whole system would have ground to a halt."

Jenkins said, "Bob, what do you think are the three or four biggest advances in the last decade?"

Rodriquez smiled.

"In a few months—maybe less—we are going to make the biggest advance, and don't you forget it. We are going to give the government the capability to reach out virtually anywhere in the world and strike any size target, big or small. But besides us? Stealth has been around a long time and so have precision munitions. I think the biggest advances are in materials and in management. Look how Boeing is building the 787! They are outsourcing most of it. Mitsubishi, who built the Zero during World War II, is building the wings; the rudder is being built in China, along with the fairings for the wing. Boeing's even modified three 747s, made 'pregnant guppies' of them, so they can haul fuselage sections from Japan. Boeing is the integrating assembler, and it's causing a lot of grief, naturally, with the older engineers who think their 'tribal knowledge' is being given away. The unions object, too, it's inevitable. This much outsourcing was unthinkable even ten years ago."

He was wound up, his fists clenched, and they knew he had more to say.

"Worst of all, I think there have been much bigger advances in China than just building things for Boeing. And sad to say, we don't have the slightest idea of what they are. It wouldn't surprise me if they flew a hypersonic aircraft."

"But not before we do." Martin rarely spoke, so when he did, they listened. He went on. "They have brilliant minds and a booming economy, but they are getting big, too, and their bureaucratic tendencies dwarf ours. I suspect that the next thing out of China will be a big boom, all right, but it won't be a bomb, it will be the sound of their economy collapsing from going too fast too far. You can't go from rickshaws to Rolls-Royces in one generation without some turbulence. They will experience the ups and downs of capitalism just like everybody else has, and they've been zooming up so long, they are bound to have a setback, like your great crashes in 1929 or 1981. I see them having a depression that will cripple their economy for decades. Unfortunately, it will cripple everyone else's economy, too. But the real danger there is that they haven't had their nationalist wars yet. Every emerging country, especially one that was treated as shabbily as China by foreign powers, wants to assert itself, it wants revenge. I can see them having a big bust, and some Red Napoleon emerging, ready to take on the world to take the people's minds off the fact that they are no longer getting rich."

It was the longest speech Martin had ever made to them, and the others were impressed into silence.

Rodriquez finally spoke. "Martin, you may be right, and if you are, it is the only bright side of being as old as I am—it won't happen until I've cashed in my chips."

V. R. Shannon had been standing at the door, listening. He turned and walked away. He was probably a lot closer to cashing in his chips than Rodriquez or anyone else. So many things could go wrong on this mission, from the failure of the basic premise to some mechanical hazard to some in-flight incident. Yet he knew that it was the most valuable thing he could do for his country, far more important than his combat experience or his work on the stealth fighter. The Hypersonic Cruiser could be the answer not only to the war on terror, but also to any Red Napoleon that might emerge from China.

NOT AN EPILOGUE . . . A PROLOGUE

THE PASSING PARADE: President George W. Bush announces a surge of troops necessary in Iraq to allow stabilization and ultimate withdrawal; on board International Space Station astronaut Suni Williams participates in Boston Marathon; Estonians nostalgic for Soviet era rebel against removal of monument celebrating "Great Patriotic War"; six Muslim men arrested for planning assault on Fort Dix; scandal grows involving Attorney General Alberto Gonzales and dismissal of U.S. Attorneys; brutal war continues in Somalia; child abduction hits new heights in Sri Lanka; Saddam Hussein's half brother executed by hanging; USAF to train pilots specifically for operating unmanned aerial vehicles; more than 34,000 Iraqi civilians killed during 2006; Lockheed Martin F-22s complete three months overseas deployment; all charges dropped in Duke rape case; estimated 42,499 aircraft, worth $1.253 trillion, to be manufactured between 2007 and 2016; USAF retiring advanced cruise missile, retaining old B-52, B-1, and B-2 bombers in service indefinitely; Nicolas Sarkozy elected President of France; Airbus Industries announces A320 production rate to reach 40 per month; Tony Blair announces plans to retire.

May 20, 2007
Mojave Airport, California

V. R. Shannon sat in the cockpit of the RoboPlanes Hypersonic Cruiser, poised at the end of the twelve-thousand-foot-long Runway 12 at the Mojave Airport, connected only by a single cable to ground equipment 150 feet away. The Federal Aviation Administration had cleared the flight by placing the Hypersonic Cruiser in the same category as Rutan's *SpaceShipOne*, an unusual civilian flight into space.

His many hours in the company simulator made it all familiar to him. So much was the same—the wonderful visibility, the beautiful ergonomics, the solid feel of the controls, the assurance of the quadruple, sometimes quintuple, redundancy of every system. But there was a major difference. Today he was within minutes making the most revolutionary advance in aviation history—or of dying. There was an escape capsule to use, but no one, least of all V. R. Shannon, thought it would survive an ejection at Mach 8.0.

Shannon mentally blessed the Australians for their invaluable work. Their ideas, expertise, and money had enabled him to accelerate the production program and expand the performance parameters.

The flight was supposed to have taken place yesterday when he went through the ritual suiting up and prebreathing exercise. Other factors intervened. He hoped they would not today—the letdown of yesterday's cancellation made strapping in today more difficult than ever.

They were determined to fly a complete mission—Rodriquez called it a "Kelly Johnson-style mission"—from the start. It was evident that the Hypersonic Cruiser would have its greatest use in the vast reaches of the Pacific, so they were simulating a strike mission ranging out from Hawaii on a suspected terrorist missile launching ship stationed eight hundred miles away. The real takeoff would be from Mojave, but their contract ship was placing two targets seven hundred miles off the California coast. The day delay had occurred when the first target had collapsed and sank. Fortunately, they had foreseen this and had a spare on board the ship.

In an attempt to make the mission as realistic as possible, Shannon would not get instructions on which target to strike until the last possible moment. He would launch his missile—a real launch, nothing virtual about the mission—and his sensors would instantly detect the success or failure of the strike even as he streaked back to California at Mach 8.0. The first flight mission was as unprecedented in the world of testing as the Hypersonic Cruiser was in the world of flight. Already called "the lawn dart" by the workers and engineers who labored so hard to create it, the Hypersonic Cruiser was a concatenation of advances in design, propulsion, structures, cooling, and aero-dynamics. The combination flew beautifully on the computers, with little more input from the pilot than advancing the throttles and selecting the target from the right upper glass panel that monitored the weapons systems.

The U.S. government still steadfastly distanced itself from the project, wanting to avoid association with what many believed was certain, inevitable failure. It was easy for the Air Force or NASA to do, because if by some wild chance the Hypersonic Cruiser was a success, they would fall heir to its achievements automatically. There was no feasible commercial application as yet, although there might be hypersonic airliners in the future.

Shannon felt curiously calm. He was committed to the task, determined that he would place an instrument in the hands of the government that could contain any future threat. If he failed, then so be it. It had been a great effort, with his fortune and the fortunes of his closest friends riding on it. And it had a great heritage, reaching back to his grandfather Vance Shannon, and continuing on through his father, Tom, and uncle Harry right down to the present.

Looking at the great screen that surrounded him as a conventional canopy might, he could see Steve O'Malley—suited up and ready to replace him—standing next to Dennis Jenkins. To their left, bent over a computer console, was Bob Rodriquez, who had contributed so much grief and so much good to their collective lives.

Rodriquez's voice came over the intercom.

"Are you ready, V. R.?"

"Yes, let's go."

The engine start system was entirely automated; even the cord connecting the Cruiser to the ground equipment was withdrawn mechanically.

Rodriquez's voice came over the radio, controlled, matter-of-fact.

"You are cleared for takeoff, V. R."

Shannon had prepared his answer in advance. He'd planned to say, "Roger. Cleared for takeoff. To the future."

Instead he said simply, "Roger."

Power came up automatically, and the aircraft began to roll. He was a passenger, just as Alan Shepard, Jr., had been in the first American spaceflight. Acceleration was slow at first, but speed built up and he noted with satisfaction that the Hypersonic Cruiser broke ground at the precise 145 knots he had calculated.

The televised view was amazing; his visibility was far better than any canopy they could have devised and it had none of the distortion that sometimes crept into simulator presentations.

Speed built and the aircraft climbed swiftly; in three minutes he was level at sixty thousand feet, heading out over the Pacific Ocean, his speed stabilized at six hundred knots, just as planned. His hand had never left the side stick controller, but no inputs had been required. He was a passenger, pure and simple, and somehow he didn't mind it.

Rod's voice came over the radio.

"In thirty seconds, you'll begin your hypersonic run. Ready?"

"Roger. I'm just sitting here, the airplane's doing the work."

"V. R., hold tight. You're about to take off into the future."

V. R. thought, *Damn, he stole my line*, as the acceleration pressed him back into the seat and the airspeed, altitude, heat, and his uncertainty built up. But there was no time to dwell on any of that now. V. R. tightened his grip on the side stick controller, watching the speed build as he flew into history.